HEART OF MIST

HEART OF MIST

BOOK I: THE OREMERE CHRONICLES

Helen Scheuerer

Talem Press
SYDNEY, AUSTRALIA

Published by Talem Press, 2017

An imprint of Writer's Edit Press

www.talempress.com

First printing, 2017

Print ISBN 978-0-9941655-4-1

Ebook ISBN 978-0-9941655-5-8

Cover design by Alissa Dinallo

For Kyra and Claire

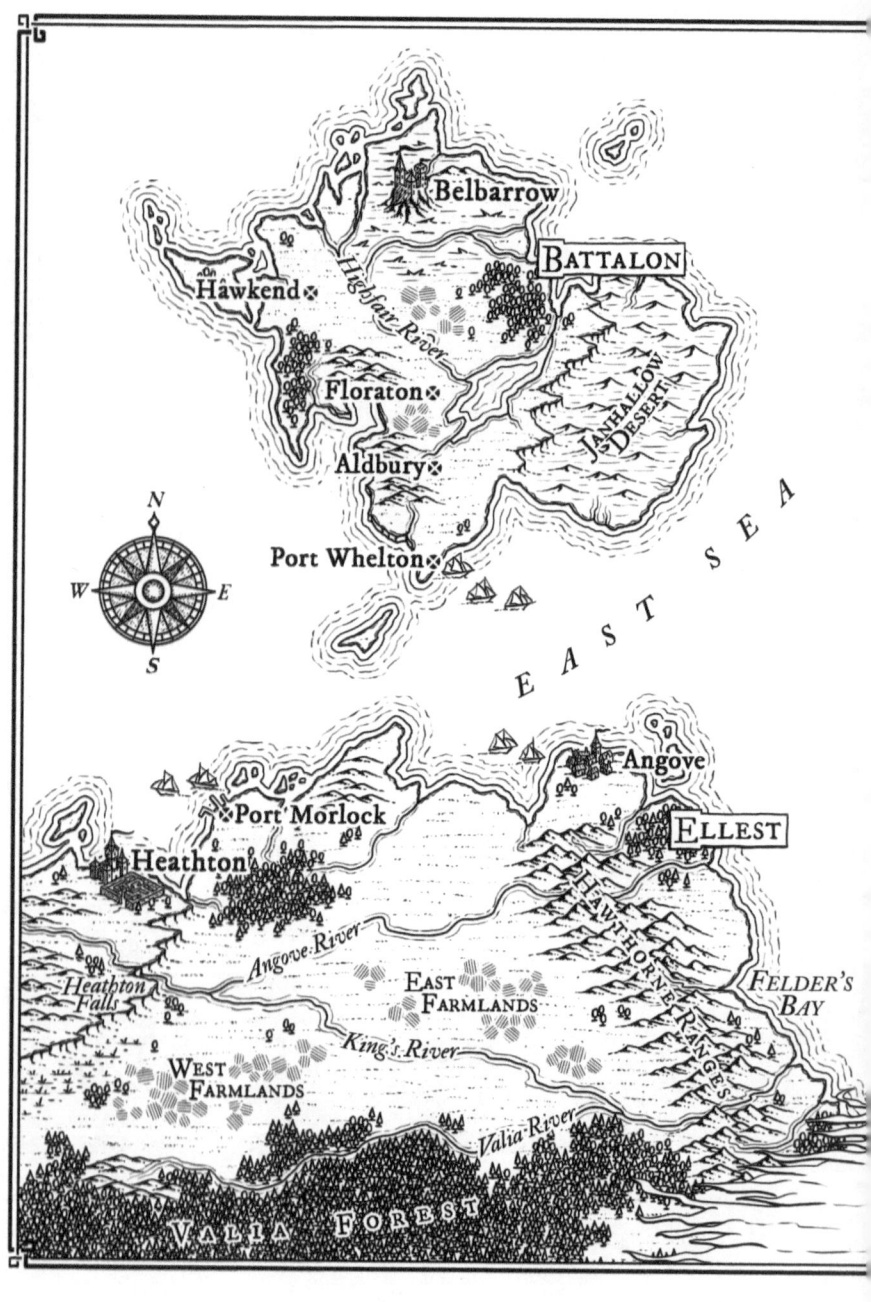

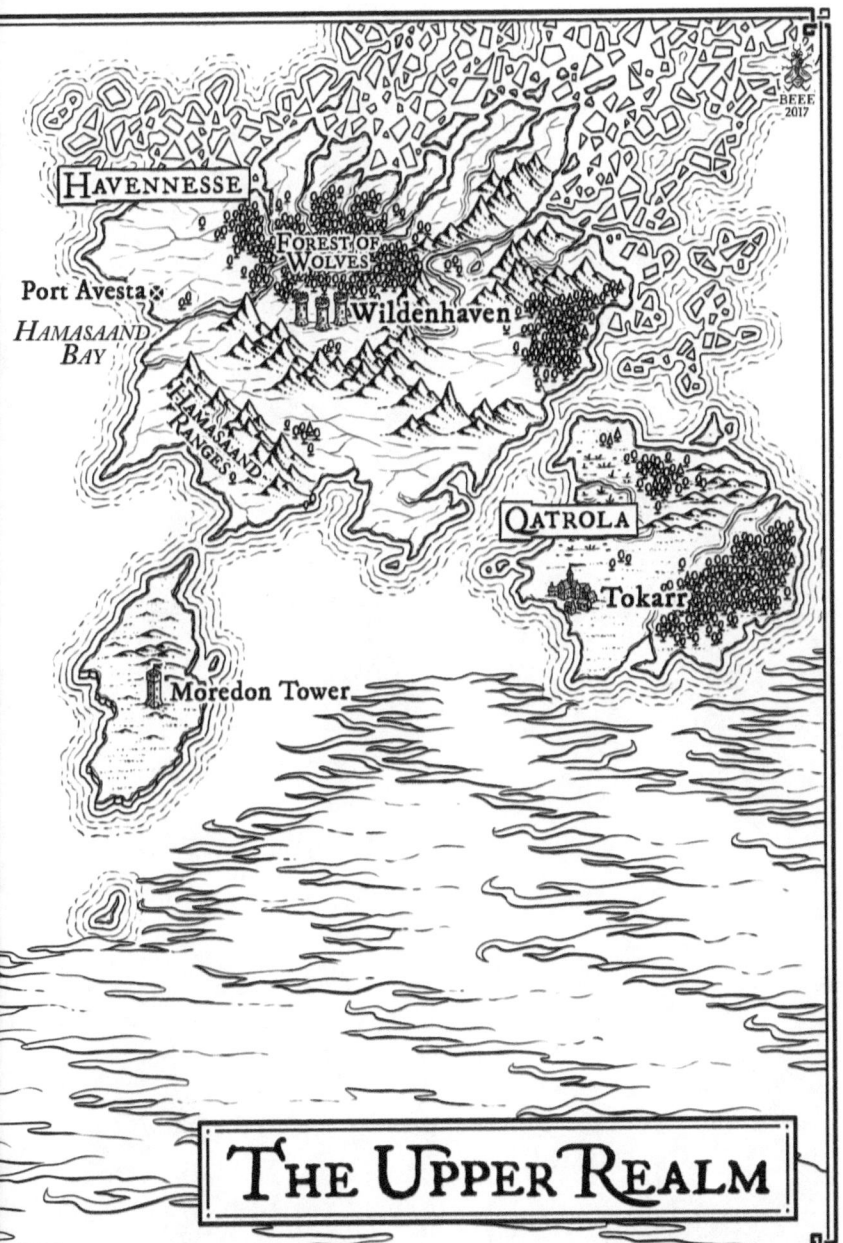

THE UPPER REALM

Prologue

The branches of the canopy were like springs beneath the balls of her feet, making her lighter than air as she leapt from one tree to another, towards her freedom. None of the sentries stirred. She knew how to use the dark cloak of night to her advantage. She was no more than a shadow, flickering with the rest in the dappled moonlight. She wove through the branches like a ghost, leaving the sleeping keep, her family and her future behind. When she got to the outskirts of the forest, she dropped down onto the soft earth and ran. Although she had rigged the guard changes, it wouldn't be long before they realised she was gone. She sprinted. Her feet barely touched the damp ground as she darted between the lean trunks, her breath forming small clouds before her in the cool night, her dark hair sticking to her face. She had the build of her kind: tall, lean and corded with muscle. A body that had been pushed to the limits of endurance, moulded by a strict regime of discipline, forced to fight with blade, arrow, spear and fists. She was meant to be a leader, a warrior, a queen of the Valian people, but she couldn't be. Not when there was another choice.

Each thought pummelled into her, spurring her on, while branches stung her face and the wind tore through her leathers. Too soon, she was at the border. All that marked the end of their territory was the mist. It rolled in slow, thick waves, stopping abruptly at her feet, as though an invisible fence kept it contained. It rose up into the sky, as far as she could see. A seemingly impenetrable wall. Beyond it was more mist.

The young woman tugged off one of her leather gloves, letting it drop to the ground. She stretched out a hand into the shifting mist. It escaped between the gaps of her long fingers, and a cool sensation crept along her skin. Magic. She could feel it pulsing before her. The air in there was different, people said, thinner, unbreathable. Slowly and steadily over the past few decades, the mist had encroached, inch by inch, thirsting for more life, more magic. Those who went beyond it fell off the face of the realm.

She swallowed, her heart hammering as though it would burst from her chest. She looked out. *Magic.* Once widespread, the Ashai folk, whose powers thrummed in all four corners of the realm, had greatly diminished over the years. The mist hungered for that power. Like a tide, it lapped at the lands, engulfing whatever lay in its path. It became a form of execution reserved for specific traitors of the crowns: those who wielded magic against the law. Forced to walk in at swordpoint, criminals would often try to impale themselves rather than endure whatever horrible death awaited them within.

The woman who stood surveying the mist had no magic. Though her bloodline was strong with rare talents, she was unblessed, unremarkable. Most in the realm would call it luck, but for a leader in her lands, it was a failure. Now, her mouth was set in a serious line, and her grey-green eyes stared out into the uncharted distance ahead. Though death awaited her, she did not fear it. What was it but another form of freedom? She tucked her cropped hair behind her ears, and turned back, just once more, to take in the forest-covered mountains of Valia, her home. Her mother, the matriarch who was so sure her daughter could do anything, despite her lack of magic, would have fallen asleep long ago, and her sister ... Her sister, only younger by minutes, would be training. Always training.

The mist stirred at her feet, wrapping around her ankles, and she could have sworn she felt a gentle pull, an invitation: the roiling clouds before her luring her into their deathtrap. She needed no enticing. Although guilt tugged at her as she thought of her family, she knew this was the right way. The only way. The Valian Way. Her people deserved the best, and this was how she could give that to them. She turned to face the mist, and after a deep breath, walked in.

Chapter One

Bleak's gut clenched as she vomited onto the dirt that spun before her. And again. And again. She lay there on the ground, a line of sick and phlegm still dangling from the corner of her mouth. Her body heaved several more times and bile burned the back of her throat. Gods, she felt like rubbish, and the sound of people clanging about their daily business was doing nothing for her pounding head.

She had returned the night before from yet another failed quest to find herself a healer in Heathton. It had been her fourth journey to the capital in a month, and the seas had been savage. Her small sailing boat had been thrown about as though it were a child's toy. She had only just managed to moor in the docks before the storm fully hit, and she'd promptly made her way to the local tavern. It had only taken her a quick four pints of their watered-down ale and the last of her silver to remember that their brews did nothing to cure her problems. With no coin left to spend, and her condition still pulsing wildly, it had been back to the warehouse, where her home-brewed mead had burned its way through her body, drowning out the voices and her most recent shortcomings.

With no idea how she'd ended up in the town square, she crinkled her face in a grimace, realising that the skin across her forehead and nose was tight with burn. How long had she been subjecting herself to the blazing morning sun? Too long, from what it felt like. The right side of her face was already tender. She peeled her torso off the ground and leaned back against the water trough behind her. Using the shoulder of her dirty tunic, she wiped her mouth, feeling her dry, cracked lips snag on the rough fabric. Looking out, she squinted against the harsh daylight and rubbed her aching temples.

What time is it? How in the realm did I get here?

The coastal village of Angove was bustling. The town square was brimming with locals and tourists alike, and it already reeked of sickly sweet foreign perfumes. The wealthier women waved their delicate lace fans before their faces, while the more common folk dabbed at their sweating necks with aprons and sleeves. The dirt streets were packed with overflowing market stalls. Colourful spices imported from Battalon spilled out onto the walkway in giant wooden barrels, heavy rolls of intricately patterned fabric jutted out from a countertop, while wine-infused strips of dried meat hung from hooks at the front of one stall. Shopkeepers and opportunists flogged their wares from crates hanging off their chests: vibrant toffee-coated apples, thick skin creams in carefully labelled jars and dark bottles of Angovian cider.

And then the thoughts of those around Bleak barraged

into her mind in a crashing wave.

Will Mihael have a stall again? I swear that tart was laced with wildflower.

So that's two jars of flour and seven —

If Lucinda gets there early —

Bleak sniggered. *Such easy marks, all of them,* she thought, as she hauled herself upright, eyeing the unattended pocket watch of the candlemaker as he ogled the baker's daughter. And the sailor whose full coin bag was visible through his vest pocket. Despite her raging hangover, the day was looking up. Loose sand stung her face as the seaside breeze took hold, and a shadow cast over her shoulder.

'Hit the tavern again, did ya, Bleak?' said a gruff voice from behind her.

'No,' she muttered, without looking up.

'S'not what it looks like?' Her friend Bren, one of the young local fishermen, came into her line of sight and stared pointedly at her dishevelled state.

'None of your business what it looks like,' she said.

Bren shrugged, scraping his sun-streaked hair back off his brow. They'd known each other since they were children, so he was rarely ever bothered by her direct nature. *Bren. Bloody Bren.* One of the many reasons she sought a healer to cure her 'condition'. So far, the best cure she'd found was the drink. In fact, despite her raw throat and churning stomach, she thought it was about time for a refill.

'Saw yer boat all tangled this morning – ya must have

been in a state.'

'She's still afloat, isn't she?'

'Barely.'

'That's a yes.'

'I fixed up them ropes you knotted wrong.'

'I don't get knots wrong.'

'Do so.'

Bleak sighed. 'Well, I didn't ask you to fix them.'

'Ya never do.'

Bleak only stopped herself from rolling her eyes because they felt as though they'd fall out of their sockets.

'Ya know,' called Bren as he made to move on. 'Ma'd be happy to mix something up for ya.'

'I said, it's none of your business.'

With his back to her, Bren put his hands up in surrender, and walked away.

She inhaled the salty ocean air, mixed with the scent of herbs and spices and freshly baked bread. The bakery on the corner called to her, where golden loaves covered in flour were piled high behind the window. *I'll need some coin*, she thought, as she walked into the crowded square. Crowds were the best for this kind of work, and peak market time was the most lucrative by a long shot. People were distracted, flustered and irritated. With their attention divided and their bodies already pressed up against others, what was one less coin in their pocket? What was a trip of the feet and the loss of a bracelet?

Bleak knew she was a mess, so she'd have to be extra

diligent with any work she carried out this morning. Her shoulder-length, ash-blonde hair was knotted and tangled from yesterday's plunge into the ocean; it hung loose around her grimy face. Her tunic and pants were spattered with sick and, feeling the sharp, intrusive pain at the soles of her feet, she realised she wasn't wearing shoes.

Damn, she cursed silently, *where did they end up?* She looked back to where she'd woken at the water trough – there was nothing there but the pink patch of vomit she'd left in the dust. She wanted to kick herself. As if she could afford *another* pair of shoes. She'd have to raid Bren's mudroom for his brothers' smallest and least offensive pair.

People tried not to look at her as she passed; the skinny, odd-eyed orphan girl, the town drunkard, returned from yet another of her deranged solo sea trips. They tried not to look but failed, as always. She could hear them, too, their thoughts barrelling into her.

Only evil could have eyes like that, referring to her odd-coloured irises (one hazel, one blue). *Look at the filth on her, she's been lying in the sty again – or the whorehouse. She had that poor old fisherman under a spell, he's better off dead than with her. Where does she go? What's she done to herself now? Who in the realm is she looking for?* It was always the same. But it worked to her advantage, mostly.

Bleak could hardly walk straight, which didn't help with the staring, or the job at hand. As she glared at another passer-by, she wondered if she was still drunk. It was possible. It wasn't as though it hadn't happened before. Or perhaps she *was* as crazy as they all thought. They looked at her as though she had the plague. Trying to ignore how hot the cobblestones had grown beneath her feet, she pushed the intrusive thoughts from her mind as she selected a target. A tourist. Definitely not from around here, swishing about in vibrant, impractical skirts, with a glimmering beaded bag dangling from a delicate, pale shoulder, already turning pink with burn.

Yes, that will do nicely, Bleak thought as she began to weave through the crowd. Someone barged into her, hard. She fell, landing on her backside.

'Going somewhere, little Bleak?'

Swearing, she started to get up, but a heavy boot pushed her back down. Maz, the brawny son of the town blacksmith, was staring down at her, lip curled.

'You can't be serious,' she muttered.

'What did you say?'

If people hadn't been watching her before, they certainly were now. But no one stepped in, no one told the brute to remove his boot from her shoulder.

'Get off, Maz.'

His kick was swift and direct to her tender stomach. Once, twice. Her body contracted around the pain, and tensed in anticipation of more.

Stupid bitch, thinks she can turn me down. Like I'd want her now. Dirty, drunk scum. Maz's thoughts came out of nowhere.

A couple of years ago, when her condition had still been manageable, sometimes even dormant, she'd thought differently of Maz. He was the handsomest and brightest son of the talented Angove blacksmith, and had been popular among many of the young village girls, including a much younger, more naive Bleak. Now, she ground her teeth, cursing her former impressionable self. Now, nineteen-year-old Bleak knew better.

'Gutter rat,' he said, preparing to land another blow.

'Piss off, Maz,' Bren's voice sounded, and Bleak looked past the sun's glare to see his muscular frame move to stand between her and Maz.

'Playing hero again, Clayton? Gonna fight me for her honour?' Maz leered, sizing Bren up against his own well-built body.

'Get outta here, or next time I stop by the forge, I'll be followin' up on a package yer father apparently sent over to Battalon.'

Maz's eyes snapped up to Bren's. 'You wouldn't —'

'Wouldn't I?'

A muscle twitched in Maz's jaw, and he spat at Bleak, who was still clutching her stomach on the ground.

'You'll get what's coming, both of you. Fucking gutter rats,' he snarled, and then disappeared into the throng of people who had crowded around them.

Bleak clasped Bren's offered hand, and he hauled her to her feet.

'I had it under control,' she said, dusting off her clothes.

'Yeah, looked like it.'

'I was fine.'

'Bleak, just say thanks and be done with it.'

Bleak turned to him, stomach dipping. She hated being in his debt, and she *always was*. Frustrated, she opened and closed her mouth, sifting through the words to use. Bren's brows rose. Silently, they began walking through the square.

'What'd he send to Battalon?' she asked after a few moments, tentatively pressing the soft part of her abdomen where Maz had kicked her.

Bren rolled his eyes and nudged her with his elbow. 'A bastard son and a purse full of gold.'

Bleak whirled back to him. 'What? Whose?'

Bren shrugged with a smirk. 'A sailor's true trade is secrets.'

'You're a fisherman.'

'Semantics.'

'Big word for an uneducated oaf.'

'Takes one to know one.'

Bleak felt a smile tug at the corner of her mouth. 'Would you have fought him?' she asked.

Bren smiled grimly. 'Ya know I would've. But for folks like us ... We should play to the strengths we're given, least at first.'

Bren's wintry-blue eyes met hers for a moment, before something glimmering across the crowd stole Bleak's attention. She had spotted her mark again, and the beaded bag sang out to her. She flicked open her pocket knife and slipped from Bren's side, easing her way through the horde of people, their collective body odour clinging to her nostrils. She ignored it as she closed in on her target. The pungent aroma of perfume hit her, and she tried not to gag.

Definitely not from around here, Bleak thought, as she tripped up the man beside the wealthy woman. The man stumbled right into her target, and Bleak sliced clean through the bag's strap. The collision was awkward and filled with stammered apologies, as both parties straightened themselves, faces flushed. Bleak was already back at Bren's side, flattening the beaded bag against the tender skin of her stomach beneath her tunic.

Bren shook his head, his face an undecided mix of disapproval and admiration. Bleak shrugged innocently.

'What?' she said. 'We have to play to the strengths we were given.'

Later, Bleak went down to the wharves to watch the sun set. She sat at the end of an abandoned jetty, chewing half a loaf of freshly baked sourdough and swigging from a flask of wine. Pondering which of the moronic village girls had bedded Maz without using the contraceptive potion, she was momentarily content, dangling her feet over the edge of the jetty, the dark water below licking at her toes. The stolen beaded bag lay beside her, its contents splayed out across the timber planks. She was quietly pleased with the day's plunder. First, a dainty coin purse with Connos, the earth god, embroidered in painstaking detail on the front.

Connos. She'd almost laughed when she'd seen the likeness of their continent's god – what had he ever done for Ellest, for her?

The purse itself held plenty of silver, enough for a few days' worth of mead at least. Then there was the rose-gold pillbox and its contents. Bleak reckoned it would fetch a pretty price at the moon market if she played her cards right. Plus, there were some jewelled hairpins as well. She let her fingers wander to the ratty knots of her own hair, and nearly laughed aloud at the thought of using the accessories herself. Where would a gutter-rat-pickpocket wear jewelled hairpins?

She glanced at her reflection in the water and snorted. She'd always thought her round, odd-coloured eyes made her look as though she could be split into two different people. There was a strangeness there that made people turn away and shift uncomfortably. Freckles speckled the skin across her button nose, and her pointed chin often jutted forward in a show of audacity. But she looked gaunt – the half-starved appearance of a stubborn, orphaned pickpocket.

She held the last item, a trinket of her own – a length of rope. Its ends were frayed and it smelled of the sea. She didn't know how long she'd had it, years – many years. Bleaker Senior had given it to her. He'd made her practise every knot to perfection before he'd agreed to allow her on his ship.

'If I'm gonna be hosting a woman on board, she's gotta at least be better than every man. Nobody can argue with skill,' he'd say. 'Show me a barrel hitch. Show me a bowline.'

She threaded the rope through her fingers, smiling at the memory. Such a simple thing – a length of rope – and yet she swore it had saved her sanity, saved her life on more than one occasion. She began the loops for the double overhand knot, before pausing to guzzle from the flask. Her eyes scanned over the drag of the current before her, the water slapping against the sides of pontoons and pleasure yachts, as she tasted the sharp bite of the cheap wine on her tongue.

A cure was all she'd ever wanted. Something to stop the voices in her mind, the judgements, the bitterness, and the despairs that weren't her own. Something to put an end to her condition. Her life would be simpler, more enjoyable without it, not to mention less dangerous. The use of magic by anyone other than a royal had been illegal for one hundred and fifty years, and the penalty was death by mist. But Bleak was a mind whisperer, a reader of thoughts, and she'd never learned how to control it. At any moment, her mind was flooded with the thoughts of those around her. She was a rebel to the crown without intent. *Ashai folk*, they used to call them, the people who could wield magic. But uttering that word nowadays, even in Angove, was asking for trouble. From the posters she'd seen during her trips to the capital, the crown was still very much on the hunt for people like her, people with 'conditions'. But after years of enduring, and years of searching, she was at her wit's end. She had chased healers all over Ellest, none who had either the skill or desire to help her. And so, as she had drunkenly moored her boat the night before, she'd decided she'd have to venture across the seas, perhaps to Battalon or Havennesse, to find a cure. When she found one, she could quit the drinking, she could start her life.

Bleak looked at the completed overhand knot in her hands, and undid it to start again, a sheepshank knot this time. She didn't have to think, she didn't even have to look; the looping, threading and pulling of each different knot was second nature to her. The knots of a sailor, the knots of a fisherman. She would tie and untie them absentmindedly, letting her thoughts unravel along with the rope ...

Her small fingers wrapped around the damp rope along the dock. She was six years old, gazing out onto the water, with her ma and pa by her side. She was thrilled to be out of the stuffy terrace house. They had taken her down to the wharves, where she loved to watch the fishing ships depart. They had come too early that day, and the fishermen were still packing up their equipment, after having sold their produce to the local marketers, chefs and royal kitchens. Her mother had screwed up her nose at the smell, and winced as the hem of her skirts had dragged through the muck, but she'd said nothing.

The family of three wandered along the wharves for

a time, the little girl giggling at the silly names her pa dubbed the ships. Finally, Ma had abandoned hope for her gown and turned to her daughter, a beaming smile upon her face.

'Let's play hide and seek,' she said.

Here? They were never allowed to play on the docks! In her excitement, the little girl hadn't realised that her mother's grip on her arms was too tight, and that behind her, Pa was throwing his hands about wildly as he spoke to a foot soldier who had appeared from nowhere.

'Quick,' her mother said, her face a mask of enthusiasm. Turning around to face the sea, she began counting. 'One ... Two ...'

The little girl didn't wait another second – she was an amazing hider, her pa said so.

'Three ...'

She ran towards the stacked crates where all the fishermen were washing their hands and faces in great big barrels of water.

'Four ...'

Her mother's voice followed her.

'Five ...'

The little girl weaved between the fishermen, some of them crying out in protest. She ducked under tables and crates, the smell of fish scraps suddenly overpowering. Her ma definitely wouldn't look here.

Beyond the familiar voice counting, there was shouting and the clang of metal.

'Eight ...'

Ma was getting close, but there was no way she'd find her here. She drew her scraped knees up to her chest, feeling the dirty water and fish innards soak into her dress. Ma couldn't be cross – she was hidden *really* well. She was going to win!

'Ni—'

The little girl saw the puddle of water around her change colour. Murky trails of pink seeped into it, and then a deeper, darker red saturated the hem of her pastel-yellow petticoat. From beneath the tables and crates, she saw Ma, and Ma saw her. Ma put a single bloodied finger to her lips, her eyes fighting to stay open.

Shhhh …

Wide-eyed, the little girl nodded.

Bleaker Senior, his men and a much younger Bren were packing up for the day and washing down the streets when, with a bundle of nets in his arms, Bleaker Senior spotted her, her face peering out from behind a stack of empty crates.

'What in the realm —' he started, before looking around and falling silent. He paired the blood on her face with the commotion earlier and scratched his chin.

Is she hurt? Where's all the blood from? By gods, what am I going to do with this? Who is she? The guards want —

She jumped at the man's internal voice, a sudden intrusion into her own mind. He was inside her head.

There was a crash down near the docks. From where she was still crouched, she could see the guards kicking over stalls and rifling through people's trunks and carts.

They went so far as to attempt to lift a woman's many-layered skirts. She shrieked at the indecency and her husband came running, objecting furiously.

'Maybe the girl wasn't with them,' said one guard to his superior as they moved closer to her hiding spot.

'Like hell she wasn't. I want this place searched from top to bottom. I don't give a damn whose skirts you've got to ruffle, and I don't care if it takes all bloody day. Find her.'

Gods. Those bastards. Hunting down a child. Her parents —

Bleaker Senior took a final look at her before striding forward and dumping the pile of nets he was holding on top of her.

'Not a sound,' he murmured, as he scooped her and the nets up in his arms, and dropped them into something else. She landed on her tailbone, pain blooming, but she had sense enough to muffle her cry. Wheels moved beneath her. As she was rolled down the dirt path and onto the timber planks of the wharf, she could hear Bleaker Senior's thoughts. Questioning himself, cursing himself and then —

'Evening, fellas,' his gruff voice sounded.

'Bleaker,' said a guard in greeting. 'Seen anything odd today?'

'What do you mean, odd?'

'Little girl, dressed up little thing. Hanging about the docks?'

'Now that *is* odd ... What would a little one like that

be doing around here?'

'None of your concern. You seen her?'

Senior laughed. 'As usual, gents, I never see nothin'.'

He pushed the trolley onwards, and no one stopped him.

Later, when Bleaker Senior asked her name, she repeated his back to him.

Bleaker. Bleaker. Bleaker.

The sun pulsed red as it lingered on the edge of the realm and Senior's ship set sail for Angove. The rowdy fishermen were soon drunk on ale, with market banter flying between them, as the little girl cowered in the corner. Senior draped a woolly blanket over her small shoulders, and rested his hand on the crown of her head.

'You'll come to find we're not so bad, Half-Pint,' he said.

The sun had dipped below the horizon, and the muted purple dusk brought Bleak back to the present. The gentle salt breeze was cool against her sunburnt skin, soothing her churning thoughts. Lanterns glowed on the decks of the docked yachts, and a lone fiddle sounded in the distance. The timber planks creaked beneath her as someone sat down next to her. Bren's callused hand offered a paper bag.

'Thought you might be hungry,' he said, looking out onto the water, the reflections of the moon, the stars and the lanterns glimmering atop its surface.

Bleak took the warm paper bag from him. How long

had it been since she'd had a hot meal? Her mouth watered as she opened it up and spotted golden pastry.

'Ma's famous palma pie,' he said, not taking his eyes from the flat expanse of sea.

She bit into it and stifled a moan. She remembered Mrs Clayton's palma pie – spiced meat and gravy held together with buttery, crunchy layers. Growing up, she and Senior would often have dinner at the Claytons'. Mrs Clayton was one of the few people Bleak knew who felt happier when she had more mouths to feed.

Bleak offered Bren her flask. Taking it, he gave it a little shake, listening to the contents slosh around inside, before drinking.

'Calm tonight,' he said, nodding to the lazy pull of the sea.

'I noticed.'

'Been a while since we been on the water together.'

'I prefer solo trips.'

'Ya might need another set of hands if yer planning on heading to Battalon or Havennesse.'

'Who said I was?'

'It was only a matter of time, wasn't it? Ya ain't found what yer looking for in Ellest. I could help ya find it if you'd tell me what it is.'

Bleak was quiet.

'This tastes like shit,' Bren said, passing the wine back to her.

'I know.'

She grimaced as Bren's thoughts began to leak into

her mind, his questions, his observations about her, his sadness.

Why won't she ... All I do ... If I could just have a chance ...

She couldn't listen anymore. Getting to her unsteady feet, she bid him goodnight and left him on the jetty. *Home*, she needed to get home.

Right near the base of the cliffs was the marina and Bleaker Senior's old warehouse. It now housed ropes, spare sails and parts for many of the vessels that docked at Angove, but above it was the loft: her quarters. The only place in the whole realm she called her own. Bleaker Senior had lived in the cottage beside it, but that had been seized by the town mayor only days after Senior's passing. It had been torn down not long after. It'd been nothing short of a miracle that she'd been allowed to stay in the loft. Although, they had never allowed her to read Senior's will, which she suspected favoured her.

She tried to remember a time when the people of Angove hadn't reviled her. Perhaps it just hadn't seemed so bad when Senior was around. By now, she'd gathered that he'd shielded her from a lot of ill treatment, he and the Claytons. But she couldn't keep asking that of them, not after Senior passed, not after they'd lost Willem and Tobias. She had to rely on herself, especially if she wanted to sail to Battalon, and Bren ... She'd have to leave him behind.

Bleak clawed her way up the ladder into the loft and drew it up behind her. The loft itself wasn't much. She'd dragged bales of hay around to create some semblance of furniture, but it hardly mattered. She had few possessions, and certainly wasn't one for entertaining. In the corner lay a crumpled pile of clothes, handed down from Bren and his brothers, and a thick, waxed cloak – one of the few things she had as a keepsake from Senior. There were also several flasks and glass bottles she used to store her mead. She reached for one now, the silver one – her favourite. She kept this close to the pile of hay on which she slept.

Alone. She exhaled a shaky breath. *Alone again at last.* She drank from the flask, the liquor burning her insides as she gulped it down. And then she slept. A sleep filled with surreal details: sailing knots and mist, her name on a stranger's lips, and heat, a pulsating heat throbbing in the air around her.

Chapter Two

Bleak's nose itched as the smell of smoke filled her nostrils. Her skin was clammy, her hair wet with sweat, and – she opened her eyes.

The warehouse below her was ablaze.

Flames were devouring the rope, the nets, the wooden planks, everything. Fire licked up the beams of timber, racing towards the bundles of hay, the stash of liquor serving as fuel. She had to get out. *Now*. Bleak scrambled towards the ladder, hauling it up into the stifling heat of the loft and angling it towards the window. It was the only way out. She glanced down at the angry flames below, and pushed the ladder through the window, her heart in her throat.

This was *not* how she wanted to go. Death by fire. *No*, not like this.

Something exploded behind her – the alcohol. She didn't have time to scream. She flung herself out of the entrance with the ladder, and pushed off from the building. Falling took forever, and also no time at all. Bleak tried to twist the ladder around, tried to position herself so she'd land nimbly on her feet, but she plunged towards the earth. She hit the ground with a thud, and the heavy ladder crashed down on top of her. She didn't move. She didn't know if she could. She was afraid to try.

Am I dead? But she could hear her own ragged breathing, taste the smoke she was coughing up from her lungs. Her chest burned as she spluttered. *What happened?*

Someone kicked her side, sharply. Bleak groaned, bringing her knees up to her chest and her hands up to protect her face, but thick, rough fingers closed around her upper arm and dragged her upwards. She staggered, grimacing at the pain in her side from the kick, and the jarring in all her muscles and bones from the fall. How was she alive?

Daylight blinded her.

'Thought your fisherman could blackmail me?' growled a deep voice.

Bleak's eyes flew open. Blinking through the haze, she saw Maz's face only inches from her own.

'What?'

'Don't deny it, it's too late for that.'

'Maz, what ... what happened?'

Suddenly, she became aware of all the people. Maz's friends, and beyond them, some of the villagers who had come down to the water to enjoy the show. She could hear a group of sailors struggling to put out the warehouse's flames.

'What do you want?' she said, trying to twist out of his grip, ignoring the painful protest in her arms, her heart racing.

'To teach you a lesson,' he snarled.

'Consider it taught. You've burned down my home.'

Maz snorted. Bleak searched the faces of those around her. *Nothing.* No pity or empathy; none of these people would step in. She was the town drunk, the town freak, a nuisance, a nobody. What did they care what was done to her, whether she lived or died?

Well, *she* cared. And she wasn't going to let Maz touch her. But Maz's grip was firm, bruising her upper arms with his meaty hands. If only she had a weapon. A thrill went through her as she remembered – *the rope!*

Slowly, she edged her hand to her trouser pocket, disguising the movement with a bigger, bolder struggle. She loosed the length of rope between her fingers at her side. Maz was momentarily distracted, making a vile remark to one of the leering men nearby. She twisted from his grip and flung one end of the rope to her other hand. She pivoted and landed behind him, with the rope now burning a line around his throat. She pulled the two ends tight, and Maz gasped for air, his hands flying up to fight the rope cutting into his windpipe, but Bleak held firm. She looked around wildly, knowing that this moment of advantage wasn't going to last long, and that if they caught her after this, things would be even worse for her. She rammed a knee hard into Maz's kidney, and his legs buckled beneath him. He was rasping for air;

any longer and she'd kill him. Bleak took a deep breath, released the rope and shoved him into the crowd.

She sprinted for her life. Her legs pumped hard beneath her as she tore up the hillside, wincing as her bare feet stumbled over sharp rocks. She left the sea and the docks far behind, and didn't look back; there was no time. She shoved the length of rope back in her pocket as she ran, ignoring the pain from the fall and the burning in her calves from the steep incline back up to the village centre. The coastal sun was hot on her back, and she was panting now, her whole chest heaving. Gods, she was unfit. She raced through the town centre, weaving through the throng of staring people. Their thoughts slammed into her.

What's she done now?

Should we grab her?

Senior should have let her rot —

Faster, she had to move faster. She risked one quick glance behind her, and saw no one, before colliding with the front of a horse.

The stallion reared and sent her flying backwards, sprawling across the dirt. Swearing, she staggered to her feet, her forearms and palms stinging where the rough ground had shredded her skin. The stallion was huge, thick with muscle and well-bred, nothing like the usual shabby Angove mares. In one swift motion, the rider swung down from the saddle and landed deftly with a soft thud. He calmed the horse with a single touch.

'Sorry,' Bleak muttered and made to move past him

and the horse.

He put a firm hand on her shoulder. 'Where do you think you're going?' he said in a low voice.

'Sorry?'

But then she saw – behind him were ten men on horses. She recognised none of them. They were dressed all in black, except for the two crossed axes circled with a crown of fire embroidered on their chests. Her stomach leapt up into her throat. The royal sigil.

She turned to the man before her and squirmed. Although she'd never met him before, she knew who he was. Fierce and unflinching, with dark features and burnt-umber eyes to match. It was Commander Swinton of the King's Army, the celebrated son of Sir Caleb Swinton. He was the leader of the King's Army, and he was all the way out in Angove.

He towered above her, lean and muscular beneath his uniform. His coal-coloured hair hung to his collarbone in waves, his cheekbones sharp above his hollowed-out cheeks. A trimmed black beard made his square jaw even more defined, highlighting a thin white scar running from his right cheek down to his chin. His pale lips were set in a mean line.

What is he doing in Angove? And what —

'You're the one they call "Bleak"?' he said, disgust etched on his face as he surveyed her ragged appearance, dirt-covered skin and odd eyes.

'Why?'

'I'll take that as a yes.'

'What do you want?' she said, glancing behind her, where she could see Maz and his lackeys reaching the edge of the town square.

The jangle of metal sounded, and Bleak turned back to the commander to see him pull a pair of manacles from his belt.

'What're you doing?' she demanded.

'You're under arrest. You've been summoned by the king.'

'For what?'

'For the illegal use of magic,' he said, reaching out to grip her wrists. She stepped back.

'Hold out your hands.'

Ignoring the wild thumping in her chest, and every instinct that told her to run, Bleak lifted her chin in defiance. She was slammed down into the dirt, chest first. Pain bloomed across her breasts. A knee pinned her at the centre of her back. She groaned.

'He said, hold out your hands, *girl*.' One of the guards spat the last word as though it were vermin. 'This is only going to go one way – his. The sooner you learn that, the easier this will be.'

'Lennox,' said Swinton, his voice laced with dark frustration, 'just get her ready.'

She was wrenched to her feet and the cool metal was fastened around her wrists. Her heart sank. She couldn't con her way out of this one. There were too many of them, and the realm's most skilled fighters at that.

'We're going to the capital?' she asked.

The commander nodded as his guard shoved her towards a horse.

'On foot?'

'Enough questions,' the guard called Lennox snarled.

'You can't be serious, it'll take weeks to get to Heathton —'

That comment resulted in a swift knock to the back of her head. She flinched as the blow landed on her matted hair.

'You have to tell me what's going on,' she said to Commander Swinton's back.

'I don't *have* to do anything,' he said.

Bleak felt the panic rising in her chest as the guard lifted her up onto a horse, and tied her manacled hands to the saddle horn.

'Bleak!' a familiar voice called. 'Bleak – hey! Where are you taking her?' A head of fair hair came into view – Bren, with a box of fishing hooks under his arm.

'Who are you?' Swinton demanded.

'Bren. My name's Bren Clayton.'

'Well, Mr Clayton. The girl has been summoned to the capital.'

Bren looked from Swinton to Bleak. 'What? What for? You can't just take her ...'

'Watch me.'

Swinton glanced at Maz, who was now standing at the front of the crowd with a smirk across his face. Swinton took two long steps towards him and Bleak revelled quietly in the glimmer of fear that crossed Maz's face, but Swinton simply flicked a silver coin at him.

'As promised,' he said.

Bleak's blood surged. *That bastard. He sold me out. But how?* No one knew about her magic, not even Bren.

Bren swore, his box of fish hooks clattering to the ground as he threw himself at Maz. One of his brothers lunged and held him back, eyeing the battleaxes strapped to the commander's back and the longsword at his hip.

'You made up some horseshit about her and turned her in?' Bren yelled.

Maz rolled the coin between his fingers, saying nothing.

The commander scratched the scar marring his stubble. There was no amusement on his face; his brow twitched in irritation. He mounted his horse in one smooth, effortless motion.

'Move out,' he told his men.

The guard in front tugged Bleak's horse along, and she twisted in the saddle to look back at the smouldering ruins of the warehouse, and at Bren. His eyes were wide with disbelief. He was still struggling to free himself from his brother's grip. Bleak caught his eye and shook her head.

Let me go, she tried to tell him. He was safer this way. And she couldn't live with herself if he got into trouble with the king because of her. She turned away and focused on the back of the guard ahead of her. She had to use all her strength to stay atop the horse as her new company cantered away from the only place she'd ever called home. Below them, she could still see the waves spilling their foam across the golden sand and the fountain grass waving in the briny wind, as though Angove was saying its own goodbye.

Chapter Three

'If I'd known I'd be trekking across the country, I might have worn some shoes,' Bleak said to Fiore, the man who was pulling her horse along. She'd never seen shoulders so broad and skin so deeply tanned. He ignored her. He had to be from Battalon, the neighbouring realm known for its red, sandy deserts and treacherous terrain. Many of its people had the same smooth, sun-kissed complexion. Unlike her, their skin never burned or freckled beneath the sun's rays. Fiore's hair was shaved short, unlike the others. He *had* to be from Battalon, perhaps even Belbarrow, that continent's capital, if the black flames of the fire goddess tattooed on his forearm were anything to go by.

They hadn't taken long to leave Angove and cross the Bridge of Lamaka. Bleak wondered if she'd ever see the structure again, with its thick greying timber planks and immense wooden sculpture of its voluptuous goddess's namesake. The King's Army had no such appreciation for the landmark. They spouted rubbish about the supposed Angovian beauties they'd missed out on, while their horses' hooves clopped loudly atop its surface. They rode south, towards Felder's Bay. Having only ever visited the capital by sea, Bleak didn't know much about horseback riding or their current journey, except for the fact that it was going to test her. She was itching to know why they weren't travelling by sea, but the thoughts of the guards around her gave nothing away.

Bleak's backside was numb and her wrists ached from being bound to the saddle horn. She had only been riding for a few hours and was already dreading the days to come. No shoes, no coat, nothing for when they passed through the mountains or for when the night air became chilly. Just her, Commander Swinton and ten of the King's Guard for company. Her heart sank – Bleaker Senior's coat had no doubt perished in the fire. It was the only belonging of his she'd been able to keep after his death. It had served her well on countless sea journeys, and she'd always felt comforted; a hint of his scent still clung to it. She felt the hot sting of tears, but blinked them back, steeling herself against the loss. Senior hadn't really been one for keepsakes.

Her head was pounding, throbbing insistently behind her eyes. Her headaches had got to the point where she didn't know if they were caused by the drink or the lack of it. In any case, she hadn't had a drink in what felt like ages, and the hum of voices around her was making her dizzy. She hadn't done it in a while, but to distract herself from her discomfort, she dipped into their thoughts. She couldn't control when she heard other people's thoughts, but when they were out in the open, she could clumsily focus on one mind over others.

I hope he sees I've taken the initiative, the youngest guard, Stefan, was thinking, eyeing the back of Swinton.

Ah – an ambitious foot soldier, Bleak thought. He rode beside Fiore and looked between the Battalonian and the commander, his expression equal parts admiration and envy. Another guard, to her left, was thinking of the yellow-haired beauty he'd left in his bed before they rode out. Bleak continued to sift through their minds.

What's she bloody looking at, scummy bitch.

Did we bring enough wine? An excellent question.

So we left a week and a half ago, but the girl is slow, so we might take longer to get back – gods, what I'd give for another piece of that pie from Willma's.

Commander never tells us squat. What's this piece of trash done to warrant a full escort from Angove to Heathton?

Women, gripes with each other, food and insults directed at her were the main topics of thought, and Bleak paid them about as much heed as she did the dirt beneath her fingernails. For most of her life she'd been spoken about this way, not to mention kicked around. She was nothing and belonged to no one. Stared down or avoided entirely, it was all the same to her. But it *was* intriguing that none of the guards knew why she was being summoned.

She focused on Commander Swinton, noting the signature battleaxes strapped to his back. He, at least, would know why. Awkwardly, she drowned out the voices from the others and zeroed in on his mind and –

nothing. She didn't have much control over her magic. There had never been anyone to teach her *how* to use it, no one to guide her, thus her methods were unchecked, unpractised and unpredictable. But she could still get results, most of the time. Until now.

She frowned. *How is that possible?* She tried again, and still – nothing. She cursed under her breath. The one time she actually wanted to use her 'gift' and it was useless. *Gift* – what a ridiculous notion that was. It had been Senior's word for magic, not hers. Her 'gift' was one that just kept on giving, in the form of overheard insults and pity, constant questioning about her heritage and the permanent feeling of exile in her own home. Gift? Bleak didn't think so.

Still unable to read Swinton, she focused on the wineskin hanging from his saddlebag.

What I wouldn't give for a drink right now, she thought, pressing her cracked lips together.

By the time the company stopped to set up camp, most of the beach was in the shadow of the Hawthorne Ranges. A chill rushed over Bleak's clammy skin as she was untied and pulled from the saddle, her feet sinking into the cool, coarse sand.

'Go clean yourself up if you want,' said Fiore, his voice surprisingly gentle.

Bleak looked to the rest of the men, unsure.

'They'll leave you be.'

'I don't believe that.'

'Then stay covered in filth. Your choice.'

Bleak ground her teeth. She could feel the layers of dirt, soot and sweat caked onto her skin, thick and greasy.

'Fine,' she said, and left the Battalonian standing by her horse.

It was hard to stay upright in the dunes. She couldn't hold out her manacled hands for balance as the sand shifted and slipped beneath her feet. But she managed. The crisp sea breeze tangled the stray strands of her hair and rushed through the thin material of her tunic. She walked towards the sigh of the waves lapping at the shore. As she got closer to the foamy water's edge, she saw that the beach was littered with pieces of dry, dead coral, washed up from the depths of the sea, white as bones, bleached by the sun. They crunched and rattled under her weight, their blunt ends pressing into her tender soles. The turquoise water washed over the tops of her feet, cold and soothing. She hunched over and rolled up the legs of her pants to just above the knee, and moved further into the shallows. It had been a long time since she'd seen water this clear, probably not since she and Bren had ventured this far south over a year ago.

Bleak looked out to the open water, the final rays of the day's sun shimmering across its flat, seemingly infinite surface. She sighed heavily. She wished she could be out there. It was both liberating and crushingly desolate. Gazing at it, the depth of her despair, which she ordinarily fought so hard to suppress, would open up like a raging whirlpool, threatening to suck her in and pull her under. Other times, the solitude was freeing – her relief swelling, rising up within her like a wave. There were no voices out on the water, no one's thoughts pummelling into her own.

The deep laughs from the men back on the shore brought Bleak out of her reverie. She scooped up the water in her palms and splashed her face, rubbing vigorously.

Gods, what I'd do for a bar of soap, she thought, realising she was likely just rubbing the grime further into her skin. Reluctantly, she turned and trudged back to where the men were assembling the commander's tent. They had set up at the foot of the mountains. Before them, Felder's Bay and the East Sea were calm and empty, but for a few clouds drifting on the horizon. The commander's tent was the only one being pitched; the rest of them were to sleep under the stars. From the way he stalked around the camp, Bleak saw the discipline in the commander's every action. He unsaddled and cooled down his stallion, waxing the tack and watering the horse himself in precise and considered motions. His features seemed to soften when he spoke to the beast, but those moments were few and far between. He didn't join in the banter between the guards, and spoke to almost no one except Fiore, the two men standing side by side, conferring in inaudible voices.

As soon as the sun dipped behind the mountains, Bleak began to shiver. But she didn't ask for a cloak. Despite her growling stomach and dry throat, she said nothing and asked for nothing, though she edged as close to the fire as she could.

She watched the men go about feeding the fire, pegging the commander's tent and unravelling their bedrolls. Someone dropped a heavy blanket into her lap – Fiore. By the light of the fire, Bleak saw his face. His brows were raised in amusement, and his broad nose and round golden eyes made him the commander's opposite – warm and kind. He rubbed the nape of his neck as he walked through the camp, chatting with the men, leaving them chuckling while they went about their chores.

Bleak spent the next while scanning the ground for discarded weapons she might be able to steal. Her hands were still manacled, but she wanted something to protect herself. She spotted Fiore, who she now realised was the commander's right-hand man, heading into the woods with Swinton to hunt game. Bleak frowned. They were odd companions to her, like light and shade. And didn't one's choice of companions speak volumes about a person? As soon as the thought entered her head, she pictured Bren. What did it say about him that he was friends with someone like her? She wouldn't think on it now.

After a time, the men emerged from the woods, Fiore with a small deer slung over his shoulder.

'Never fails to amaze me, our commander,' said Fiore with a grin, slinging the carcass onto the ground by the fire and slapping his superior on the back.

Bleak could have sworn she'd seen the ghost of a smile on the commander's face.

'Stefan, you can do the honours,' Fiore called, and handed the foot soldier his hunting knife.

'Has someone given the girl a drink?' the commander asked.

Bleak's head snapped to attention.

'No, Commander,' said Stefan.

Someone threw her the wineskin, but the commander caught it before it reached her.

'Water only.'

Bleak glared at him, yet took the canteen of water handed to her. It was still warm from the day's travel, and it did nothing to quench her real thirst. The liquid sloshed around her empty belly, making her feel queasy. She moved back from the fire as Stefan skinned and carved the meat. Soon, it was roasting over the open flame, the smell making her mouth water. The men gathered around, passing the wineskin between them, telling stories of battle, as though she wasn't there. And that was how she preferred it. Except the commander was watching her. With his dark eyes narrowed, he toyed with something on the end of a chain around his neck. From the movement in his sharp jawline, he was grinding his teeth. Bleak turned away and chewed on the meat she'd been given. He could stare all he liked. She finished eating, and when she finally turned back, he'd gone.

Some of the men went down to wash in the low tide

of the bay, including Fiore. They stripped off with no shame, and scrubbed at their naked bodies. Bleak looked at the dirt still lining her palms. She could only imagine how filthy the rest of her was, but she'd walk through fire before bathing in front of that lot.

Most of the men tugged their pants and shirts back over their wet bodies down by the water, except for one man, who strode back to camp in the nude. Bleak looked away, only it was too late.

'Bet you haven't seen one of these before, have you, gutter rat?' he said, tugging on himself, moving towards her. His wet, mud-brown hair clung to his face, and drops of water glistened in the fuzz that carpeted the rest of his body. 'Bet I could teach you a thing or two.'

'Lennox,' a sharp voice called, 'that's enough.'

'Was only playing,' he growled.

'None of us want to see your arse gleaming in the moonlight, get some clothes on,' said Fiore, stepping in front of Bleak.

Lennox muttered to himself. However, Bleak could hear his thoughts clear enough, and they made her grateful that Fiore had been there.

The night grew late and Bleak was exhausted. Her body was stiff and aching, and she was wary that tomorrow would be a longer, harder day. With the embers of the fire glowing, and the men's speech becoming slurred and sleepy, she curled up in the sand with her blanket. She'd slept in worse places. And despite the thoughts around her becoming clearer as the night itself became quieter, Bleak slept.

She dreamed of Bren. Of having the conversation she's always feared having, where she told him she was an Ashai, a mind whisperer. In the dream, she sat with him on the damp sand in Angove and told him everything, how she could hear his thoughts about her, everyone's thoughts about her. He sighed, ran his fingers through his fair hair and then reached out to her. There was a sound, like a hissing breath, rolling towards them. She turned to see a towering wave rising above them, casting a dark shadow across the whole beach.

'Bren!' she cried out, but the wave crashed down upon them both.

Dawn announced itself all too soon. Muted shades of lilac and blush pink rippled around the hint of sun on the horizon, and a flock of gulls dipped and rose in formation, their reflections dancing on the surface of the sea. Bleak rolled out of her blanket with a moan.

'Get up,' the commander snapped.

She felt pain all over. Her feet were raw and blistered from being bare in the stirrups; her wrists stung where the manacles had rubbed her skin; her tailbone and backside were tender from the saddle. And the rest of her? Her body was just in general agony. She also needed to relieve herself. Around her, the men were packing up their bedrolls and saddling their horses. After a quick glance around, Bleak dropped her blanket and edged towards the woods.

'Going somewhere?'

She whirled around. Fiore was there, picking his teeth.

'I ... Uh ... I need to ...' She was squeezing her knees together.

Fiore sighed. 'Come on, then,' he said. Just before they entered the woods he stopped and eyed her bare feet. 'Wait a moment.'

He left her there and she didn't run. She wasn't an idiot. How far could she possibly get without shoes, water and a cloak in mountains she knew nothing about?

He came back and threw her a pair of tattered boots. 'The men have been pissing and shitting in there all night.'

Wonderful, she thought, tugging on the boots. They were enormous, and she must have looked ridiculous clomping towards the trees in them, but they were better than nothing. And had the commander been with her, she knew she'd have been trudging through all manner of filth, barefoot.

'Can you undo these?' Bleak asked, holding out her bound hands.

He looked at her wrists for a moment before shaking his head. 'The irons stay on.'

Fiore followed her in, but was gentleman enough to turn his back as she squatted among the shrubs. Her face burned with humiliation as she struggled to pull down her pants with her bound hands. And despite feeling as though she was going to burst, it took her several minutes before she could go.

As they made their way back to camp, Bleak swiped a dagger from Fiore's belt in a quick, practised motion. They didn't call her the Angove Fingersmith for nothing. Fiore didn't notice the missing weight, and as he bent down to untangle some vines from his boots, Bleak hid the weapon down the side of her trousers.

When they reached the horses, Lennox shot them a filthy look.

Fucking hypocrite, he glared at Fiore, *not letting the rest of us have any fun, keeping the gutter rat for himself.*

Fiore seemed to know what Lennox was thinking without telepathy. 'Don't you have work to do?' he said.

'I don't answer to you, no matter how damn friendly you are with the commander. Wouldn't surprise me if he came outta there with you. Sharing the gutter rat with him, are ya?'

'Mind your tongue, Lennox, wouldn't want to lose it.'

'Go to hell, Fiore, and take the rat with you. She stinks.'

Bleak felt Fiore give her a push, and she clomped past Lennox, not daring to look him in the eyes. Fiore took her back to Stefan, the young guard from the day before. He helped her up onto the horse and bound her hands to the saddle horn again.

'Is this really necessary?' she asked.

'Orders.'

The guard assembled and waited for the commander's instructions, while Bleak looked ahead. The Hawthorne

Ranges loomed before them, dark, dense and whispering centuries-old secrets. Bleak was used to the open seas and clear skies, not the suffocating vines and tangled thicket that awaited her now. The horses lurched forward, and one by one began disappearing into the trees. Bleak gulped down the lump in her throat as she followed Fiore in, the pale tree trunks and heavy air seeming to swallow them all whole. Inside, everything was tinged with blue – a navy hue pulsed around the foliage. Emerald-green vines strangled branches and linked them together, creating a blanket of darkness across the canopy, leaving only a few narrow beams of light to filter down, producing dappled patterns of gold atop the leaf litter.

'What are you waiting for?' the commander's voice barked. 'Let's move.'

Bleak squeezed her horse's sides with her heels, and the mount trudged further into the forest, giving her a better view of the famous 'King's Trail'. It was a rocky dirt path, only wide enough for them to proceed in single file on horseback. Beneath the horses' hooves, the earth was worn down from centuries' worth of travellers. Bleak's steed stumbled and she winced, gripping the saddle with her sore thighs. This was not going to be easy.

So *this* was the legendary King's Trail. It was the only known passage through to Heathton. The only other access was by the East Sea, and Bleak still wasn't sure why they hadn't come by ship ... The only one who knew the reason was the commander. She still couldn't get inside his head.

As they moved deeper into the forest, the air became thick, and once again, the hum of voices in Bleak's mind became loud. Gods, she needed a drink. She needed a drink so bad.

'Psst, Stefan ...' she whispered.

The youngest guard looked back at her and hissed, 'Don't talk to me.'

She could see enough anxiety in his face that she needn't read his thoughts. He feared falling out of favour with the commander.

'I'll do you a deal,' she said a little louder, feeding his panic. 'Give me some of that wine in your saddlebag there, and I won't say a peep.'

'What? No!'

'Oh, come on!' she said, and the guard in front of Stefan turned as well.

'What's a little wine compared to the wrath of charming old Swinton?'

'Shut it,' he said.

'Where's your team spirit? Just a few sips ...'

'I said, shut it, or I'll hand you over to Lennox.'

That silenced her.

The forest swallowed them, and the incline of the trail increased steeply. Every now and then, Bleak's horse slipped on a loose vine or a patch of leaf litter and she'd hold on for dear life. The manacles around her wrists, which were bound to the saddle horn, were becoming unbearable. Not only did it mean she was constantly hunched over, unable to sit up and stretch her back, but she'd lost layers of skin. Beneath the iron and rope, her flesh was open, pale and sticky, with bits of rope and dirt stuck to it.

'We'll take them off when we stop,' Fiore said from behind her.

She nodded without turning back to him. *How long will that be?*

Bleak had never been in a forest before. She marvelled at the dizzying height of the trees, their sheer density and volume, and the earthen scent of the trail, so unlike the fresh coastal breezes she was so accustomed to. However, despite her lack of experience with forests, she got the distinct feeling that this one was different. The further up the mountain they trekked, the more uneasy the horses became. Bleak noted the way her own mount's ears flicked, aware of sounds her human ears couldn't detect.

'Are we in Valia?' she asked, just loud enough for Fiore to hear her.

He didn't say anything for a time, but Bleak could hear him debating with himself.

Do I tell her? I shouldn't even be talking to her. But she'll just keep asking questions, drawing attention to us. What harm could she —

'Technically, no,' he said, 'the forest and mountains this side of the King's River belong to the king. But the Valia kindred know these parts better than anyone. And whatever the official story, it's likely they still consider this part of their territory.'

The Valia kindred. She'd only ever heard stories about the warrior society that lived among the trees and mountains, whose people bent and broke the rules as they saw fit.

'Did you see any on the way here?' she asked.

'No. Not one, thankfully.'

Bleak looked around. It was rumoured that the leader of the Valia, Henri, had magic, and despite the laws that only royalty could wield it, was some kind of unspoken exception. From the tales Bleak had heard, the leader was a powerful Ashai, an energy shifter, whatever that entailed. Like many others, Bleak had never had access to Ashai histories. Magic had been abolished before she was born, and along with it, any books that divulged the sort of powers the Ashai folk had once wielded. She'd never met another like her. Henri's powers might explain the strange sensation she was experiencing being in the forest. At first, she'd chalked it up to claustrophobia and being in such close quarters with so many of the King's Guard. But as she thought of the stories she'd heard about the kindred and their leader, she realised it might be something else. Her skin was crawling, as though the magic thrumming beneath her flesh was answering something out there ...

They rode for six hours straight, and just as Bleak was about to pass out from exhaustion, the commander led them off the trail and into a little clearing. With surprising gentleness, Fiore untied her from the saddle horn, and she slumped down the side of the horse into his arms, her hand skimming over the tattoo on his forearm.

He tugged his sleeve down.

'You gotta stand,' he hissed, but her knees buckled and she fell into the support of his body several times before she could hold herself steady. He was a wall of solid muscle, big hands and a towering frame. He waited for her to gather herself, and then got to work undoing her manacles and binds. Each movement stung and she inhaled sharply as he peeled away the final piece of rope.

'The second you fall out of line, these are back on. You understand?'

She nodded, testing her wrist joints.

'Good. Come on, then.'

She limped after him, her inner thighs feeling as raw as her wrists. The stolen dagger jabbed at her side beneath her clothes, but she didn't care and she was too wrecked to think of ways to use it to her advantage.

The commander noted her free hands from where he was cooling down his horse, a chain with a bronze medallion on the end peeking out from beneath his shirt.

'She does something stupid,' he said to Fiore, 'that's on you.'

'Understood.'

The rest of the guard eyed her as she shuffled along to the tiny stream that ran past the clearing. Her knees cracked loudly as she knelt down beside it. As she went to cup the water, she realised her hands were shaking. Although her situation was hardly ideal, she wasn't at that moment afraid. She held out her hands, palms down before her and watched them tremble in wonder. Hearing Fiore clear his throat behind her, she plunged them into the water. She stifled a cry of pain as the icy water stung her open wounds, but she held them in there.

Once her wrists were numb, she splashed her face and tried to rub at least some of the dirt away. She could hear Lennox's thoughts nearby; she didn't so much as roll her sleeves up to wash elsewhere. She stank, but perhaps in this case, that wasn't a bad thing.

She sat, legs outstretched on the outskirts of the company, next to Fiore, who handed her a waterskin and a piece of stale bread. Bleak wolfed it down, the hard dough drying out her mouth. She received no more. Gods, she was starving. She sipped the water slowly, letting it soothe her fat, swollen tongue. She had to avoid relieving herself again until nightfall.

She wanted to ask Fiore more about the Valia kindred, but didn't want to get him into any trouble. He'd been kind to her, and if there was indeed over a week left of this journey, she may need to lean on that kindness again. Instead, she thought about what she knew. She knew that the Valia kindred were the oldest society in Ellest, and had perhaps been here even longer than the royal family. They were a warrior clan, who trained their young in combat and survival from the age of five. She had heard that the weak, unconventional and disobedient were exiled to the outskirts of their territory, to work the essential but lesser jobs. That was just gossip, though. People feared the Valians, and fear created all kinds of stories.

When Bleak had still been spending a lot of time at the tavern in Angove, she'd heard drunken tales about how some believed the Valian leaders to be demigods, descendants of Rheyah the Huntress. Or at least they had been in the past. Their magic was passed down through generations, although still outside the laws of the four continents. Some people blamed them for the mist that encroached on the realm, inch by inch, year by year. If Bleak had learned anything through her condition it was that people loved to blame, and that like all negativity, blame festered and rotted the good away.

She turned to Fiore. 'Whereabouts in Battalon are you from?'

Fiore raised his eyebrows. 'I never said I was from Battalon.'

'But you are.'

He considered her for a moment. 'I am.'

'And?'

'And nothing.'

Bleak rolled her eyes. 'Give a pauper a bone, would you.'

'You're a pauper by choice. That's a different poverty.'

'What would you know about poverty?'

'Same as you – not much.'

'You don't know anything about me.'

'I know self-pity when I see it.'

Bleak glared at him. 'Got a lot of experience, then?'

A smile tugged at the corner of his mouth and he shrugged. 'Everyone's allowed a free pass every now and then. Key is not to get stuck. Guests don't stay long at a pity party.'

Bleak scoffed. 'Thanks for the advice, soldier. I'll try to remember that when I'm breaking bread and swapping life stories with the king.'

His thoughts hit her then – so loud that she couldn't hear his actual retort. She saw herself through his eyes, a scrawny teenager, rags hanging from her jutting bones, angry odd eyes and a chip on her shoulder. And she heard his concern for her – none of them knew what the king wanted from her, or what he'd do with her. She plucked a leaf from the forest floor and began shredding it, attempting to force her thoughts back to the Valia kindred rather than the uncertain fate that awaited her in the capital.

'Oi,' Fiore's voice hissed, 'you got a death wish? I said move.'

Around them, the guards were mounting their horses and making their way back to the trail. She almost groaned aloud. Back on the horse already? Her body would be permanently damaged, she was sure.

She stood and the world slowed.

In the distance, she could hear the sad notes of a fiddle, pulling her along like a current. A metallic taste spread over her tongue, and then she was falling ...

'There is no cure for what you have, girl,' the Heathton healer had said, cupping Bleak's hands in hers, studying the lines of her palms as though they held the answer.

'And what is it that I have?' Bleak asked, pulling back from the craggy-faced woman and glancing around the dim, pokey room.

'You're a mind whisperer, an Ashai. The magic in you is potent, passed down from your mother, if I'm not mistaken.'

'You are mistaken. My mother wasn't an Ashai.'

The dozens of candles around them flickered, and Bleak realised she was uncomfortably warm.

'Oh? Is that so.'

'Yes,' Bleak ground out. 'You going to tell me something worth that gold-coin payment?'

'It wasn't your gold.'

'Not my fault when folks are careless. Besides, gold is gold, and it can be yours by the end of this conversation.'

'It's already mine.'

Bleak wiggled the coin at the woman. She'd stolen it back moments after she'd handed it over. 'It's yours when I say it's yours.'

'Be careful who you threaten, girl. Ashai aren't as safe as they used to be, not now that the great Casimir is dead.'

Bleak snorted. 'Casimir? He's been dead over a decade, and even before that he was useless. The plague got him in the same way it got ordinary Ashai. Some saviour he turned out to be.'

'Is that what you're looking for, girl? A saviour?'

'No such thing as saviours.'

'No?'

'No. Only time-wasters.' She made to leave.

'What of my gold?'

'You had no answers for me.'

'Just because it was an answer you didn't like, doesn't mean it wasn't an answer.' The healer glared at her. 'What is it you need to know?'

'How do I stop it?'

'You can't.'

'Control it, then? How can I manage it? So that I don't hear people's thoughts as soon as they think them.'

The woman considered her, leaning back in her cane chair. 'It truly plagues you?'

'Yes.'

'And the drink, it helps?'

'It's the only thing that does.'

The woman nodded. 'I have no experience in managing Ashai affairs. I am a healer of flesh and bone, not of the intangible. Keep your gold, girl. You and your habits will need it more than I.'

When Bleak came to, the saddle was as uncomfortable as ever – worse, in fact. She opened her eyes and discovered why. She was sharing the saddle with Fiore. She was seated in front of him, his tattooed arm holding her across her middle, while he held the reins with his other hand.

'What —?'

'You fell.' His breath was hot in her ear.

'What do you mean?'

'You collapsed, had some sort of fit. You were convulsing on the ground.'

'What?!'

'I don't know what caused it. Only the commander knew what to do. He put you on your side so you didn't choke, held you in place so you didn't smack your head on something. When you stopped shaking he said it was safe to get you back on a horse. So here we are.'

Bleak shifted in the saddle and Fiore hissed.

'Careful,' he said. 'You're not the only one in this thing.'

Despite herself, Bleak laughed.

'Not funny,' Fiore said, and then, more quietly, 'That happened before?'

Bleak gnawed the inside of her cheek. 'I don't know.'

'How can you not know?'

She looked down at the tattooed forearm across her middle, the thick black flames creating the illusion that the fire was enveloping Fiore's skin.

'Did it hurt?' she asked.

He looked over her shoulder and followed her gaze. 'Like you wouldn't believe.'

'How bad?'

'I passed out ten minutes in.'

Bleak snorted.

'Laugh all you want, but where I come from, it's a

rite of passage. The masters put chemicals in the ink so it feels like fire – you can't get a tattoo of the goddess without it. They said ten minutes was the longest anyone's ever lasted.'

'Oh.'

Silence settled between them, until Bleak realised she was easing into the press of his hard chest against her back, and was acutely aware of the broad hand resting on her stomach.

'I'm fine now. I can ride my own horse,' she said.

'Not taking chances. Can't deliver you to the king with a broken neck, can we?'

'I don't know what you can and can't do. It might be that the king wants my neck broken anyway.'

'If that was the case, you'd be dead already.'

'You don't know that.'

'Don't I?'

Bleak shrugged. She could feel his heart beating against her through his leather jerkin. It felt intimate, wrong, given her current situation. She took a deep breath and focused on Stefan's back, their horse following his up the narrow strip of worn path. Behind them, Felder's Bay and its turquoise waters had long since vanished from sight. Now, there was nothing but trees. Thousands upon thousands of them, their limber branches shooting up into the dense canopy, the spots of escaped sunlight growing fewer and far between. As they ascended, the air became thinner and colder, a mere whisper of a breeze sending goosebumps racing across Bleak's skin.

Orders were passed down from the front of the company: *Make haste, we want to reach the summit of the mountain by nightfall. We won't be stopping again.* Bleak heard the collective complaint among the minds around her. She took comfort in the fact that she was not alone in her pain.

After another hour or so, the incline became so great that the muscles in her abdomen were constantly tensed from pulling herself upright in the saddle, trying not to slide both her and Fiore off the back. What few jokes and conversation there had been before among the men ceased altogether. At the front of the company, Swinton hacked away at the encroaching undergrowth. The branches and vines creeping onto the trail didn't stand a chance with his battleaxes swinging. The blades sliced clean through the foliage.

I'd hate to see what they'd do to a person, Bleak mused as they passed the jagged remains of the amputated branches. Her chest felt heavier at the thought of the untouched forest being destroyed, one violent slash at a time. Her tongue was dry and her stomach growled; she really wished Stefan would hide the wineskin from her sight. She thought back to the alcohol that had burst into flames behind her as she had escaped the barn inferno. What she would do for a swig of that good stuff right about now ...

The journey seemed to go on and on. It was punctuated by bursts of hunger and thirst, and clumsily slipping into the guards' minds for amusement. If she was going to do the time, she may as well do the crime.

When it seemed they could go no higher, they did. The mountain was never-ending. Finally, Bleak saw glimpses of pink sky ahead. The trees were thinning out and the land was flattening; they were getting close. Up here, the air was even colder, and she found herself grateful for the warmth of Fiore behind her.

After another half an hour or so, they arrived at the summit. The men rolled off their horses, aching and exhausted, but there was work to do. Fiore jumped down from the horse with surprising agility for someone so large, and he reached up to help Bleak. Ordinarily, she'd be too stubborn to let someone, let alone a member of the King's Guard, help her. But her body felt a hundred years old, and the pain searing across her lower half was almost unbearable. As he lowered her carefully, she realised that the pressure of the dagger against her thigh was missing, and without thinking, she patted herself down, wondering where it had got to.

'Ah, *that*,' Fiore said, 'that belonged to me.'

'How'd you —' Bleak started, horrified.

'When you fell.'

'Right.'

Bleak chastised herself. That had been her only edge against these bastards. She'd have to steal it back.

Not too difficult, she mused, recalling how she'd got the dagger in the first place. From where she sat, she watched as the men unsaddled their horses wearily and led them to drink at the nearby creek. Stefan and two of the other guards dragged themselves back into the forest on foot to collect wood for the fire, while Fiore and another set up the commander's tent. The commander himself was poring over a map he had spread out on the ground, absentmindedly rubbing the scar on his chin. His necklace had escaped the confines of his shirt again, and now hung visibly over his chest. Bleak couldn't see the map from where she sat at the edge of the camp, and so she edged closer. A little further, a little further.

It was a map of the trail they were on. It would bring them down the other side of the mountain and out into the West Farmlands, by Angove River. The tiny trail on the map made the rest of the forest and mountain range look enormous. She had no idea the Hawthornes were that vast. All along the trail were little Xs drawn in red ink ...

A hand came out of nowhere and grabbed a fistful of the front of her tunic. She was slammed into the tree behind her.

'If I catch you snooping again ...' The commander's breath was stale on her face, his umber eyes furious. Up close, he looked haunted – his skin sallow, with circles the colour of lead beneath his eyes. He shoved her away, scowling.

'I —'

'Save it.' His nostrils flared, and he stepped back, tucking his medallion into the front of his shirt. He shook his head, more to himself than her, and turned back to his map, folding it up and stuffing it down the side of a lumpy-looking bag. Despite his obvious anger, he picked up the bag with an odd level of care. It clinked as he put the strap across his shoulder. *How strange.* She opened her mouth to question —

'Don't even think about it,' he snarled, before striding off to his tent, the bag clinking softly at his hip.

She wondered what the Xs on the map were. Gold? Other Ashai? Although she'd received no clear answer from the company of free-flowing thoughts around her, she had gathered that this mission was about more than picking up a stray Ashai from Angove. The Xs on the map proved that – they were why they hadn't come for her by sea. She kept herself busy creating a nest of kindling for the fire, and had it smoking by the time Stefan and the others came back with the wood. They said nothing to her as they fed the first few logs to the flames.

Stefan made stew with leftover meat, and they took turns passing it around in a few odd cups and bowls. By the time it got to Bleak, she was salivating, and it tasted amazing, like the beef broth Bleaker Senior used to make in the winter. She slurped it down without pausing, and Fiore refilled her cup, sneaking her a chunk of hard bread to dunk in it. In a way, he reminded her of Bren – his kindness, the sturdiness about him. She wondered what her friend was doing now. Was he trying to rally his brothers to help find her? They wouldn't come. Although she'd been practically raised alongside them, the rest of the Clayton clan had always kept their distance, understanding that she carried with her an element of self-destruction, a secret that would ultimately be her undoing. And here she was.

For the first time in two days, she wasn't starving. But she was sore all over, and she eyed the wine enviously as it was passed around between the men. Sometimes it was close enough to smell, but she didn't move. Not while the commander was still here. The men got drunker than the night before, complaining about the bite of the cheap wine, but guzzling it down all the same. She managed to steal back Fiore's dagger. It was of Battalonian make – well-balanced and simple, without the embellishments and engravings so many of the Ellest weapons boasted. She tucked it into her boot this time, still wearing the enormous pair she'd been given that morning. Then she sat back and watched, threading her length of rope between her fingers, finding comfort in the methodical patterns in which the knots were created. Knots were all about finding a solution to suit a greater purpose – problem solving – and in this respect she liked to think she was good at it. Looping the rope around her hands, feeling its permanently damp and frayed texture on her skin calmed her. So she tied knot after knot, undid them, and then started again.

Bleak was thrown the same blanket as the night before, and she was grateful. The air at the summit was icy and the earth beneath her was wet. As darkness settled, her teeth were chattering. One by one, the men nodded off, chins resting on their chests, or faces pressed carelessly into the dirt. The commander retired to his tent after shaking his head at his sorry company. Bleak felt restless. She couldn't let the King's Guard drag her all the way to the capital, not knowing what would happen. Despite her haphazard lifestyle, she liked having a plan, a sense of direction – a purpose, if that wasn't too much of a stretch of the word. And that's what she needed now – a plan. A plan to rid herself of Swinton and his men, a way of getting back to Angove, back to Bren and her boat, so she could move on. She would find a healer and be done with all of this. So far, she had her length of rope, Fiore's dagger and a pair of overly large boots. She'd need more than that. She glanced around, eyeing numerous weapons she knew she could barely lift, let alone wield. Then, her attention snagged on something: a discarded wineskin. It called to her from beside the glowing embers of the fire.

Yes. That will do nicely, she thought as she inched her way towards it. She was so focused on what that first delectable sip was going to taste like, that she heard no thoughts around her. Not even those of Lennox, as he clapped his thick, callused hand over her mouth.

'Listen here, girly, we can make this nice and simple. It can hurt a little, or it can make you wish you'd never been born ...'

Panic surged as she felt the tip of a knife at her throat. She dug the heels of her boots into the soft ground, wanting to scream, but the blade pressed against her, stinging her skin. Warm blood trickled from the cut.

She couldn't fight him, she'd kill herself in the process. Terror iced her insides. He dragged her deeper into the woods and grabbed at her roughly, forcing his other hand down the front of her tunic, squeezing her breast.

And then, the air changed.

Chapter Four

Five women, unlike anyone Bleak had ever seen, stood before them. Tall and limber like the trees around them, their every limb was lined with tight muscle. They wore clinging leathers of deep forest green, which covered their skin from the base of their throats to their knee-high laced boots. Each of them had long, thick hair braided down one side, and their eyes were lined with black kohl. A woman with rich, fiery-red hair stood at the front of the group, her chest out and shoulders pushed back. The men must have also sensed the shift in the air, because they began to rouse from their drunken slumbers. Stefan, the youngest guard, stoked the fire back to life. However sluggish and unprepared, the men still outnumbered the women, two to one. Bleak's heart hammered against her sternum. But there was an unnerving calmness in the five.

The flickering light of the campfire illuminated their faces, which were alert and surprisingly young. Their stances, however, were those of experienced warriors – feet apart, hands resting casually on the grips of their weapons: swords, spears, daggers ... Lennox had just set something in motion that could never be undone.

A wave was cresting, and it was about to come crashing down on them all. The women said nothing, only waited for the men to gather themselves.

Lennox's hands were still on Bleak. Fiore wrenched him away from her, causing Bleak to stagger back into the Battalonian. The women watched them coolly, noting the rope burn on Bleak's wrists and the knife in Lennox's hand.

'What's your business here?' Lennox sneered. He was fuming he'd missed his chance to ravage the gutter rat, Bleak understood.

'Do you know where you are?' the redheaded woman at the centre of the group asked, her voice mild.

'We're in the Hawthornes, bitch. This is the king's territory,' said Lennox, his knuckles paling as he clenched his fists.

The woman smiled. 'Only a fool would call any part of these mountains the king's territory.'

'Oh yeah? This is the King's Army, the king's land. What are you going to do about it?'

'I was hoping you'd ask for a demonstration.' She took a step forward, her hand at her sword pommel.

'What's going on?' Commander Swinton emerged from his tent, buckling his sword belt at his waist, his nostrils flaring. He stopped in his tracks at the sight of the kindred.

'We were going to let your company pass through our lands peacefully, until one of your guards sought to insult us by assaulting your prisoner. You know we don't take kindly to that kind of behaviour.'

Swinton flung a repulsed look at Lennox before turning back to the woman. 'I'm well aware. Who are you?'

'First-in-command of the Valia kindred, Athene.'

Swinton examined the women before him, and following his gaze to each of their weapons, Bleak realised these were no ordinary women of Valia.

'I see,' he said. 'In that case, I apologise for my soldier's actions. I'll see to his discipline personally.'

Bleak gaped. The commander had *apologised*? Where was the snarling, brutish bastard who'd manhandled her earlier? His eyes did not leave Athene's.

'We appreciate that,' said Athene. 'Now if you'll hand over the girl —'

Bleak started. *What? What do the Valia kindred want with me? What do* any *of them want from me?* She tried to focus on their minds, but they, like Swinton, were unreadable. She wasn't sure if it was panic that was blunting her abilities or something more sinister. As if in answer, her stomach churned.

'That won't be possible,' Swinton said.

'I assure you, it can be made possible in a number of ways, Commander. I hope you choose the simple option.'

'Take her out, Commander,' jeered Lennox. 'What's a bitch like her —'

'Speak out of turn again, Lennox, and I'll kill you myself,' the commander cut him off.

Athene gave the man an icy glare. 'The girl. Now.'

'She's been summoned by the king.'

'How intriguing. Here I was thinking you just wanted her for sport. What *does* His Majesty want with a commoner?'

'You know I can't tell you that.'

Athene sighed and drew her sword. 'Then you're merely postponing the inevitable, Commander.'

'Where is your leader?' he snapped. 'Why is Henri not here to face us? Hiding out in the Valian keep? Protected by enchantments? Still in mourning —'

Quiet fell.

'You know that's not my style, Swinton,' said a soft voice. The woman at the end of their formation stepped forward, two gleaming katars at her sides. Athene bowed her head and stepped back in line. Bleak inhaled sharply between her teeth. This was Henri Valia? The famous warrior? Like her kindred, she was slender and muscular, her forest-green leathers covering nearly every inch of skin. Lined with heavy black kohl, her eyes were striking, a graphite grey with vibrant flecks of green. Waist-long blue-black hair was braided tightly down the left side of her head, framing her sharp, determined face.

'We'll take the girl and leave you be,' she said.

The commander shook his head and drew his axes. 'As I said, that won't be possible.'

Henri unsheathed her own katars. 'Alright, then.'

In a blaze of anger, Swinton lunged first, his battleaxes whirling through the air. Henri sidestepped and waited for his next attack. Around them, the King's Guard attacked the kindred in an ear-ringing clang of steel upon steel, but Bleak couldn't tear her eyes away from Swinton and Henri. While Swinton's face was contorted with rage, Henri was eerily calm. She hadn't bothered to attack yet, but knocked Swinton's blows aside with her katars, one brow raised in quiet amusement.

'Enough games,' Swinton muttered, before charging again, his well-muscled arms wielding his axes in a way that would have meant death to any other sparring partner.

'Don't tell me you've lost your touch, Commander.' Henri deflected another of his strikes and let Swinton catch his breath.

'Don't make this personal,' he said.

'It's always personal,' Henri replied, dodging another blow. He swung at her, leaving his mid-section open. Henri's sharp kick to his exposed abdomen sent him sprawling. He flipped himself up on his feet once more, but now, Henri was on the attack. Bleak looked on, her heart threatening to punch through her chest as Henri drove herself forward, slicing at Swinton with her katars. He didn't stand a chance, Bleak realised. The Valian warrior advanced in short bursts, her weapons clenched around her gloved knuckles. She was a whirlwind, as fluid as water, moving through a deadly dance only decades of training could have honed. Bleak had never seen anything like her.

The yells and cries around them came only from the

men, whether in pain or frustration Bleak didn't know. She edged away from the centre of the chaos, towards the forest. Not a single blow had yet been landed against the Valia kindred. Bleak looked for Fiore. His sheer size should have been enough to deter any challenger, but Athene, with her nimble steps and shining longsword, kept his hulking mass at bay with ease. She used his height and weight to her advantage, and parried around his strikes, ramming her elbow into his face. Blood trickled down his nose, and Athene gave a predatory grin. She was used to winning, it seemed.

A meaty hand closed around Bleak's arm.

'I'll teach you, I'll teach you and those forest bitches what real men can do ...' Lennox had her by the throat now as he dragged her into the thicker part of the woods. Bleak tried to cry out to them, to anyone, but Lennox's sweaty hand was clamped painfully tight across the lower half of her face. He was gripping so hard that one wrong (or right) twist might snap her neck. She struck out with her legs and flailing arms, clawing at Lennox's grimy face, his skin shredding beneath her jagged, chewed nails. The boots she'd been wearing had flown from her feet in the commotion, taking Fiore's dagger with them.

Think, Bleak, think. She tried to calm herself. She had scraped out of every dire situation in life so far. But panic surged deep in her gut as she smelled the bastard's sour breath on her face and heard the clink of his sword belt being undone. His thoughts were vile, and she gagged as

69

his hands moved on her, readying himself —

A dagger – no, a *katar* – shot through the air and buried itself in his eye, causing blood to spurt and spatter onto Bleak's hair and tunic. The scream that came from him was primal, a strangled noise wrenched from the gut, terror and agony manifesting in a core-shattering screech. His grip fell away from Bleak and she scrambled backwards, his warm blood soaking through her tunic. He kept screaming, an endless shriek, the wail of an animal who knew death was coming for it. He waved his hands blindly, but he didn't touch the weapon embedded in his face. Nearby, the commotion stopped. Henri strode towards them, each step measured and even, her expression unreadable. She rested a leather boot on Lennox's chest and yanked the katar from his eye, blood gushing from the gaping wound. He screamed again; this time the sound cut short. He slumped to the ground, unconscious. Bleak could feel her legs trembling, threatening to give out beneath her. She swallowed the bitter taste of bile.

'Come,' Henri said to Bleak.

A new wave of panic washed over her. She was trading being a prisoner in one camp for another. What did these people want from her? Henri was standing very still, those grey-green eyes boring into Bleak, those dark brows raised and expectant. Henri had just saved her from a horrific fate. She certainly couldn't say the same for the commander and his men. Adrenaline roared in her ears. Bleak met the Valian's eyes and nodded. She followed the matriarch's long and confident strides back to the centre of the camp, picking up her fallen boots and Fiore's dagger along the way. Around them, the Valia kindred had the men at swordpoint. The rasp of cotton tearing sounded as Swinton ripped himself free of Henri's other katar, which had him pinned to a tree. Nobody moved as Henri approached him, and in one sharp pull, freed her blade from the trunk. She eyed his torn shirt but said nothing of it. Instead, she turned her attention to the surrendered King's Guard. The men were panting and bleeding. Fiore was on his knees, a spear tip to his back. The kindred hadn't broken a sweat.

'This,' Henri gestured to the injured men around them with her katar and looked back at Swinton, 'is your doing.'

Although Bleak could hear neither of their thoughts, she sensed a great many unsaid things between the two leaders. The tension was palpable.

Just as Henri made to leave, Swinton called out, 'Lost your magic, Valian? Think we don't know what you are?'

'Wouldn't have been fair on you,' Henri called out, her kindred following.

'Coward,' Swinton muttered.

Bleak's stomach dropped to her feet as Henri turned back to face him. She thrust her hand out before her and with a blank stare, raised it slightly. To Bleak's horror, Swinton was lifted from the ground, kicking helplessly as Henri brought him higher into the air, and then slammed him into the side of a tree. He slid down its trunk, unconscious.

'You're a fool, Dimitri,' she said. She cast a final look of distaste at the broken troop of men before nodding to Athene. The kindred moved out, with Athene pulling Bleak along gently, and Henri in the lead.

Chapter Five

As they made their way into Valian territory, Henrietta Valia pulled herself up into the treetops with ease. She had been doing this all her life, and was more at home in the vibrant canopies of the forest than anywhere else in the realm. She had seen the crystal glaciers and jagged snow-capped cliffs of Havennesse, she'd trudged through the scorching sands and firestorms of Battalon, and she'd strolled through the decadent halls of Heathton Castle, but here ... Here was special. Where the trees in the Hawthornes had been as smooth and pale as pallid flesh, the trunks now became rough and dark, tawny flakes crumbling away at the faintest touch, a soft casing for the formidable strength that lay at their core. Henri's hands brushed over the broad, silken leaves, a green so dark it resembled black ink. Drops of dew rested on their smooth surfaces. She looked out across the treetops, where tall trunks shot out into a fan of branches and leaves; she couldn't tell where one tree ended and another began. The melodic notes of unseen birds sounded, and for a moment, this place, Henri's home, felt like a dream. But above all else, it was the living bridges that sang out to her. A map of paths created by the trees themselves onto which Henri now stepped, waiting for her kindred and the girl to finish their ascent. These bridges were high above the forest floor, away from the prying eyes and lowly laws of the rest of the realm. Here, the branches linked together like lattice, like a sheet of lace connecting all of Valia. The bridges were full of life, full of magic of their own. To Henri, they always seemed to sing, *we are wildness.* The vast drop on either side of the walkway embodied nature's danger and its unpredictability, while the soft emerald moss beneath Henri's boots, which sank in and sprang back with each step, spoke of nurture. Henri sighed with relief as she started the journey across the ranges among the treetops, back to the Valian keep. Behind her, her elite kindred, Athene, Marvel, Tilly and Petra, were quiet, and Henri could hear the girl struggling to keep her footing. Henri turned. The girl was wearing ridiculous men's boots that made her steps like the lumbering gait of a newborn calf.

'Leave the boots,' Henri said.

The girl looked up, panic etched on her face.

Henri crouched down and ran her palm across the spongy moss beneath them. 'This will soothe your feet – the blisters, the aching. The boots are doing more harm than good, and they're slowing us down.'

The girl stared at her for a moment before pushing the boots off by the heel. She sank barefoot into the alleviating coolness of the moss. Her whole body sagged in relief.

'Thank you,' she said.

Henri nodded and stood, drawing her compass from her waist. Although there was the odd watchtower here and there, this far out in the Hawthornes, even a native Valian needed a compass to navigate the sprawling treetop city. The bridges and pathways, knotted together with sturdy branches and vines, grew in every direction – a natural maze amidst the canopy, designed to trap and confuse those who did not belong, and guide those who did.

'Why am I here?'

Henri looked up from her compass to find the girl wringing her hands, still staring at her.

'Would you prefer to be with the king's men?'

'No. I just don't know what's going on. My house burns down, they show up, drag me away from my village, and now you show up and take me away from them ... Why is this happening? What do you want with me?'

Henri let the question hang between them as she felt the girl's energy pulse around her. This was raw, untrained magic, throbbing outwards from the girl's thin frame. The power was entwined with palpable loneliness and grief buried deep below the surface.

'You have magic,' Henri said.

'So?' The girl's chin lifted in defiance.

'That makes you a person of interest to anyone these days, but especially to the king.'

'I haven't done anything wrong. I ... I hate it. I don't

want it.'

'Careful what you say, girl. Despite the laws, there are folk who would kill for a drop of magic.'

'I never asked for this.'

'Nobody asks for anything. You get what you're given in this life,' Henri said.

The girl shuffled her feet in the moss. 'It wasn't always like this.'

'No, it wasn't. You can thank the king, his ancestors, the plague and the death of Casimir for that.'

'Casimir.' The girl shook her head. 'Like he could have saved us. He ran off with some woman, left our people to rot —'

'You're too young to cling to that kind of bitterness. The last plague was over a decade ago. Can you even remember it?'

Quiet anger flashed in the girl's eyes, and for the first time, Henri realised they were oddly coloured, one hazel and one blue.

'Enough talk of a now irrelevant past.'

'The past is never irrelevant,' the girl countered.

Henri ignored that comment. 'What's your name?'

'Bleak.'

'What's your real name?'

'It's Bleak.'

Henri studied the girl. 'With a name like that, no wonder you feel sorry for yourself.'

Before Bleak could reply, Henri turned on her heel and set the pace for their journey back to Valia.

They camped atop the bridges at odd hours, and for two days, they headed south-west, down through the Hawthorne Ranges. No matter how many times Henri did the trek, she still marvelled at it all. The fountains of strappy leaves shooting up from the crevasses in the bridges, the vertical stripes of lemon yellows and salmon pinks, the foliage with jagged, almost zig-zag edges splashed with splotches of mahogany, as though someone had dropped a palette of paint on them. She never tired of the sheer vastness of the forest, the strength of ancient trees, and the spider webs, their finely spun silk glinting in the dappled moonlight. Everything about this place calmed her very bones. The mountain air bit at exposed skin, and Henri noted that Athene had given Bleak her cloak. Henri said nothing. If Athene wanted to sympathise with the girl at the cost of her own comfort, so be it.

Henri tried to savour the quiet of the canopy. Sometimes, she needed to escape the training, the decisions and the thrum of all the different energies around her. Many a day left her feeling drained and heavy – the weight of all the kindred's problems resting on her shoulders. The canopies provided a sanctuary and much-needed solitude.

But in the soft light of the third morning, Henri found herself listening to the new voice among them.

'How did she know I have magic?' Bleak asked Athene.

'She can feel it. You saw her power, she manipulates energy.'

'What do you mean?'

'It's hard to explain, but I guess how I've understood it is … It's like everything living or otherwise has some kind of beat of energy, and Henri uses that to move things without touching them.'

Henri paused. She could only remember explaining how her ability worked to Athene once, many years ago, and yet she'd recited her description nearly word for word.

'Do you have magic?'

'No, only the descendants of the first Valia kindred do now.'

'Is … Is she the only descendant?'

Henri could sense Athene hesitate before saying, 'Yes.'

Henri quickened their pace, lengthening her strides. They were clearly moving too slowly if there was enough time for chitchat. It didn't stop the questions.

'My magic doesn't work here,' Bleak said.

'It does.'

'No, I've tried – I can't get it to work.'

'What's your ability? Are you a seer?'

Bleak hesitated, and Henri realised how intently she'd been listening in, despite her pace.

'It's alright – no need to say if you don't want to. These things take time.'

Henri could have walloped her first-in-command. The more they knew about Bleak the better. At the moment, they didn't know much at all. Henri glanced back at them. The rest of her kindred were doing their best to look disinterested. Bleak ran her hands over the warm palma coat Athene had lent her, and locked eyes with Henri.

'I can hear things,' she said, the words sounding foreign, hesitant on her lips, as though she'd never said them aloud.

Henri's skin crawled.

'What do you mean? What things?' Athene pressed.

The canopies were eerily quiet, and the group had stopped to listen to Bleak. She swallowed, her odd eyes darting around to each of the kindred, clearly wondering if she'd shown her cards too early.

'People,' she said. 'I hear people's thoughts.'

Athene, Tilly, Marvel and Petra all turned to look at Henri. They, more than anyone, knew how rare this was – how much of a game-changer someone like Bleak could be.

'You're a mind whisperer,' Henri said.

Bleak nodded. 'Can you do it, too?'

'No.'

'It doesn't work on you though – my ability. Is there some kind of Valian enchantment?'

Out of the corner of her eye, Henri saw Athene's hands move to the concealed breast pocket of her leathers, reaching for the pouch of herbs Henri made each of her elite kindred carry.

'That's enough, Athene,' Henri said.

Athene's fingers froze where they were, and she

nodded stiffly.

Henri turned back to Bleak. 'And that's enough questions for now. We'll see if you're worthy of answers when we're back at the keep.'

For a time, Henri stayed well ahead of her guard and Bleak. She was growing tired of their chatter, and she needed to mull over the bigger concerns at hand. Like what the king would do once word reached him that she'd stolen a prisoner. The Valians and the Heathton royals already had a complicated and tense relationship. The moment she'd struck Commander Swinton, she'd risked what little peace remained between them.

Henri reached a fork in the path, one bridge veering off to the right and one that continued straight. She looked at the branches around her and raised her arms. A faint smile played on her lips as she twisted and contracted her hands in midair, the nearby branches bending to her will and bowing inwards, blocking off the path that led straight. Athene would know which way to go now. The branches would hold until the kindred passed, and then return to their natural place. Henri continued on, glimpsing over the side of the bridge. The height at which she now walked was dizzying. Heights had never bothered her, though ...

'Come on,' Henri called down to Sahara from the treetops. They were on scout duty, but Sahara refused to climb higher than a few feet.

'How are you supposed to scout anything from down

there?' Henri said.

'You know I hate heights.'

'We don't even have to go that high!' Henri could hear Sahara scratching the tree trunk impatiently – no, not scratching, carving. *She'd taken to doing that lately, despite Henri's protests that it disrespected their home. Sahara continued to do it, the same word dragged into the tree's bark. It was unusual, unheard of – Henri could never remember what it was …*

'You think that's not high?!' Sahara called.

'Well, I can go higher.'

'Don't! What if you fall?'

'I don't fall.'

'Come down from there, you're making me nervous.'

Henri laughed and slid easily down to the forest floor. 'Happy?'

With her back against the tree trunk, Sahara studied her – taking in Henri's identical form, tall and gangly at that age. The only difference between them was that Henri wore her long, midnight-black hair in the traditional side braid, while Sahara had rebelled and cut hers off so that it hung loose, lining up with her chin.

'You should be queen,' Sahara said.

'What?'

'You're what they want, and what the people need …'

'Don't be stupid, Sahara. You're the heir.'

'I can't fight —'

'Won't – you won't *fight.'*

'It's the same thing.'

'No, it's not.'

'It is. You just can't see it yet. Plus, I have no power.'

'You have plenty of power.'

Sahara shook her head. 'We both know that's not true.'

Henri hadn't meant magic. Sahara was a force to be reckoned with all on her own.

It wasn't until Sahara pushed off from the tree trunk that Henri spotted the familiar carving. There, in looped cursive, was one word: OREMERE.

Around them, the mountains were beginning to drop off into sheer cliff faces, and Henri could hear the powerful crashing of the falls nearby. She tucked her compass back into her leathers. She knew the way now. She turned to find Athene behind her, waiting. For as long as Henri could remember, Athene had been by her side. In training, in battle, in disputes with her mother, in friendship ... Although Athene's protective streak sometimes got in the way of her ability to take orders, Henri could think of no one stronger, no one more unflinching to have as her right-hand woman. The fierce redhead was watching her now. Her mouth pulled up at the corner in a small, content smile.

'We're nearly at the crossing,' Henri said.

'I know.' Athene's face regained its neutral expression, and she signalled to the others.

Henri inhaled the clean mountain air. Up here, nearly among the clouds, was where freedom so often teased and tempted her. She would relish it, fight it and relish it again. But she could never stay.

They had reached one of her favourite spots. Water plunged loudly beside the bridge, barrelling hundreds of metres down into the gorge that opened up to the King's River below. The falls were the single most beautiful and terrifying thing Henri had ever seen in all her travels. The sheer force and violence of them demanded awe and made her breathless, no matter how many times she'd seen and crossed them. There was something ancient in that water, some irrevocable sense of history etched into the cliffs. The pathway on which they stood ended, but resumed on the other side of the gorge, along with the forest and mountains, where *official* Valia territory began. Henri looked down. If the kindred took a few more steps forward, they would plummet to their deaths.

'Whoa,' Bleak breathed, looking over the side of the bridge, her mouth agape.

'Welcome to the crossing,' Henri murmured.

'This is ... Whoa,' Bleak said again, before looking to Athene. 'What now?'

It was Marvel who answered. 'What do you think? We cross.'

'We're crossing *this*? Are you insane?'

'It's not called the crossing so we can sit and watch.' Marvel laughed.

Standing on the edge, Henri closed her eyes and stretched out her hand. She felt a tug of energy from the other side of the gorge, as though she had cast a net and caught something. She beckoned that energy to her. There was a loud *swoosh*. A thick, knotted vine came flying from the other side of the gorge, landing in Henri's hand. She savoured the cool, rubbery texture of it against her palm.

'You're kidding?' Bleak said.

Athene smirked. 'I don't know if you've realised this, but our queen doesn't joke much.'

Henri shot her a warning look. Athene bowed her head, unable to suppress a sly smile.

'How's your strength?' Henri asked, turning back to Bleak.

Bleak baulked. 'Uh ...'

Henri eyed her scrawny frame. Surely the girl could support herself – there was barely anything of her.

'Tilly, Petra,' Henri turned to the others, 'you're after me. Athene and Marvel, stay behind and make sure Bleak knows what she's doing.'

The women bowed their heads, and that was all Henri needed to see before she launched herself onto the vine and sailed across the void.

Chapter Six

Blood roared in Bleak's ears and her legs trembled uncontrollably. Were these women crazy? They wanted her to swing across some gorge on nothing but a measly vine? She'd heard often enough about the Valian fearlessness, but this wasn't fearless. This was stupid. Really, *really* stupid. Especially given that most of her arm strength was acquired from lifting a flask to her mouth. With the vine clasped tightly in her hands, Tilly ran towards the edge, her powerful legs like springs beneath her, and leapt from the safety of the bridge. Moments later, the vine swung back towards them. This time Petra caught it. She followed the others, a warrior cry escaping her as she flew across the deathtrap.

'Uh, you realise I'm not doing that, right?' Bleak said to Marvel, who was standing to her left, casually re-braiding her chestnut hair.

Athene smiled. 'It's not as bad as it looks.'

'I know – it's worse.'

'Don't be so dramatic.'

'Dramatic? You're the ones who are opting to jump across a fucking crater rather than rebuild or extend this very lovely, and might I add, safe, bridge.'

'The queen gave us an order.'

'If *the queen* asked you to jump instead of swing, would you?'

'Yes.'

The vine came flying back over to their side and Athene caught it.

'You're up.'

'Told you, I'm not doing this.'

'It's an order.'

'I'm not some soldier you can boss around, and *she's* not my queen.'

All traces of fun vanished from Athene's face. 'Careful.'

Bleak took a step back. Athene was one of the good ones; she thought they'd got along, but now ... The warrior's stare was cold and impatient. Panic rose up in Bleak's throat. She couldn't do this. *Wouldn't.* The terror must have been etched on her face.

'There are plenty of places you can hook your feet into – you need not hold up your whole body with only your arms,' Athene said.

'Gods,' Bleak muttered as the vine was forced into her hands. She needed a drink. A very big drink.

'Best to take a run-up, and don't hesitate when you get to the edge.'

Bleak shook her head; this week had continued to go from bad to worse. Her heart thudded wildly, rattling her ribcage as she shuffled backwards to make her run-up. *All the wine in the world isn't worth this horseshit.*

'If I die,' she said to Athene, 'it's your fault.'

Athene merely shrugged.

'Get on with it,' the other woman, Marvel, said, flicking her braid back over her shoulder and examining her nails.

This is it, Bleak thought, *I'm going to die.* She inhaled deeply through her nose, and with the vine in her hands, she sprinted towards the gorge and leapt.

She was flying, flying so fast it was like she weighed nothing. Water from the falls sprayed across her skin, and cold wind whipped her hair into her face. Henri and the others came into view, waiting at the edge of another tree bridge, ready to catch her. And then Bleak looked down. The sight of the churning white foaming water and jagged rocks below made her head spin. Her feet lost grip. She clambered and struggled and – she fell.

A high-pitched scream of terror escaped as Bleak hurtled towards her death, her stomach in her mouth, her eyes streaming – *this is really it. The end.* It would be quick, when she finally got to the bottom. On and on she fell, the horror of her imminent death settling around her like a cocoon. She closed her eyes.

And then something pulled her upwards. Her fall had not only stopped, it had reversed. She opened her eyes and looked up. As she rose higher and higher back into the air above, she spotted Henri. Hand outstretched, she brought Bleak closer and closer to them, until her feet planted softly on the moss of the bridge. Bleak collapsed. Quick and shallow breaths took over; she couldn't get enough air. On her haunches, she dry-retched as Athene and Marvel swung across and landed silently beside her.

'What happened?' Athene asked, kneeling down next to Bleak, a comforting hand on her back.

'Nothing,' Henri muttered. 'Let's go.'

Athene helped Bleak to her feet without saying anything.

'Gods,' Bleak managed, 'is she trying to kill me?'

'Looked to us like she saved you,' said Tilly, hooking the vine into a nearby tree.

'By forcing me to jump off a cliff?'

'Details,' Tilly said, before jogging after Henri and the others.

Bleak turned to Athene. 'No more cliffs?'

'No more cliffs.'

Once Bleak had her heart rate back to a steady beat, and she could suppress the urge to heave, she realised that whatever magic she had felt upon entering the mountains with the King's Guard was at least ten times stronger here. The breeze tickled her skin, and the sound of a thousand soothing whispers danced around her. The anxiety that had been building up in her quietened.

'Even people without magic can feel it,' said Marvel, watching Bleak search the trees.

'Feel it?'

'Our history, the magic embedded in these bridges. It radiates from the trees into the air here.'

'Can everyone hear it, too?'

'Hear what?'

'The —' Bleak stopped herself. 'Nothing.'

'There's never been a mind whisperer in Valia,' Henri said, turning back to face Bleak. 'I imagine you can hear our ancestors. Their essence lives on in this part of Valia. Do they frighten you?'

Bleak shook her head.

'Do they speak to you directly?'

'No. They're just ... whispers. Remnants, perhaps, of what was here before.'

'I doubt they'd speak to a non-Valian anyway.'

Bleak shrugged. 'They're calming, reassuring me. Maybe it's a trick, I don't know. But I trust them.'

The magic seemed to flow freely around Bleak, making her feel lighter, soothing her entire being. It spoke to whatever magic lay beneath her own skin. Henri's brow furrowed, and then she whirled back around to press on and continue the trek.

'Come on,' Athene said, nodding to Marvel to pick up the pace.

'Has it always been like this?' Bleak asked.

'Ever since the Valian line came to be.'

'They're that powerful?'

'So I hear.'

'And Henri is that powerful?'

Athene shrugged. 'She's the last descendant of the Valian line. She's incredibly powerful.'

The sky darkened for the third night and the blanket of stars swept across it. It looked like rich, black velvet, with thousands upon thousands of gleaming specks of light. In that moment, the realm could have been upside down, its sky as vast and awe-inspiring as the ocean. Its immensity was overwhelming, forcing Bleak to realise how small a piece she was in this giant game.

Against the offers and protests of the kindred, Henri took the first watch and disappeared down just below the canopy. The kindred didn't light a fire. The bridge of branches and foliage was too damp, and Bleak understood that it was also a matter of showing respect to the trees that held them. Tilly passed her a generous slice of fruit bread and a flask of water. Bleak wolfed down the food. Its soft dough was spiced with bursting flavours she'd never tasted before. She could get used to Valian meals, she decided. She swirled the bland water around in her mouth. Though it was cold and fresh from the falls, the best water in all of Ellest, said Athene, it couldn't take the edge off her real thirst. Bleak settled into a nook on the bridge where they were bedding down for the night, and fantasised about wine, about its warm, woody aroma, about its mouth-watering taste. And mead, that crisp, effervescent first sip ...

'Are you warm enough?' Athene interrupted her thoughts.

The black cloak Athene had given her insulated her body heat magnificently. Even with only her thin tunic beneath she was toasty. She nodded, curling up on her side, and tucking her feet under her. Athene was sitting up against a tree, her long arms exposed to the icy night air.

'Aren't you cold?' Bleak asked.

Athene smiled. 'We're trained to withstand much colder climates than this.'

'Well, thank you for this.' Bleak tugged at the cloak.

'It's made of palma furs,' Athene said. 'You could be in a blizzard and be warm as summer in that. You should sleep. Henri is eager to get back by nightfall tomorrow.'

Bleak closed her eyes, and tried desperately to quieten her thoughts. But her anxiety, although somewhat muted, tugged at her. She had no idea what she would be walking into tomorrow. *What does Henri want from me? Why did she bother saving me from Lennox and the King's Guard?* Her thoughts whirred around in her head, dizzying. They took her back to Bren and the dream she'd had in Felder's Bay. What was he doing now?

Bleak pulled the cloak tighter around her. She may not have known where she was going, but it couldn't be worse than the places the King's Guard had planned on taking her, or worse than the places she'd already been.

Chapter Seven

Ten-year-old Dash felt like he was flying through the castle – the tapestries and oil canvases of the royal families were but a mere blur. With the warm biscuits he'd stolen from the kitchens sweating in his hand, the grey stone halls were obscured as he ducked between guards and courtiers, ignoring the yells of the cook he'd left far behind. He was *fast*. The fastest boy Heathton had ever seen. And when he was a grown man, he'd be the fastest knight in all of Ellest. Maybe even all four continents. King Arden would give him his own estate, and his own troops and – he was daydreaming. He knew the castle cook well enough now to not lose focus midway through an escape.

He considered cutting through the music room, but the melodic notes of a harp from within meant that it would be crowded – a private performance was in progress. He wouldn't be making *that* mistake again. He sprinted down the gallery of the east tower, twisting his small frame and leaping from paths of near-collisions with the sculpted busts of famous kings and knights, their marble heads left wobbling in his wake. He turned a sharp corner, shoving his dark hair from his eyes, and nearly barrelled straight into Prince Jaxon.

'Sorry, Your Highness!' Dash shouted, and kept running, barely even out of breath.

The young prince shook his head and called after him. 'You know if you want food, Dash, you need only ask!'

Dash waved his biscuit-free hand in acknowledgement, then leapt down the steps to the grand entrance hall. He nearly skidded to a stop – it was mighty crowded, packed with layers of swollen, colourful skirts, and swords in scabbards jutting out from noblemen's belts every which way. Dash grinned – *a challenge!* He darted in and out of the courtiers, ignoring their cries of surprise and annoyance. He burst out into the courtyard, laughing. Looking back at the grand castle, he couldn't see the cook anywhere; he'd bested her yet again. Dash took a bite. Nothing tasted as sweet as stolen sugar-oat biscuits. He pocketed the second one for Olena.

'You better not be harassing the cooks again.' His father, the stable master, was leading one of the nobleman's horses out across the cobblestones into the mid-morning sun.

Dash wiped the crumbs from his chin.

His father shook his head. 'You're going to get yourself in a lot of trouble one of these days, Dash.'

'Have you seen Olena?' Dash asked.

'*Princess* Olena, Dash. How many times must I tell you?'

'She doesn't like being called that.'

'Well, that's what she is, and it's what you should call her. At least to others, to show your respect.'

Dash sighed. 'Have you seen *Princess* Olena?'

His father turned back to the horse, adjusting the stirrups. 'In the gardens.'

Without another word, Dash was off again. The sound of the wind roaring in his ears and the sense that he actually would lift off from the ground if he ran just that little bit faster was all the fun in the world. He tore across the courtyard and straight through the open embellished iron gates to the royal gardens.

A sea of blooms greeted him, tulips and roses, their smooth petals gleaming like silk in the bright morning sun. Their scent was light and sweet, tickling his nose as he slowed to a jog to navigate the narrow garden paths lined with loose, crunchy gravel. He did his best not to snap any overhanging flowers, but it wasn't *his* fault that the gardeners were behind on their maintenance. Dash didn't like flowers; he wasn't a *girl*, after all. But he did like the gardens. And the maze. The maze called to Dash like nothing else. Its towering, vibrant green walls and its confining pathways bewitched the explorer within. The royal squires would take turns at trying to make it to the heart of the maze. The rumours were that only one boy had ever made it. He'd returned clutching red flowers with black centres that grew nowhere else. These particular blooms were proof that the squire had conquered the maze. The boy had long since finished his training, and the legend was passed down to the next generation of noble soldiers. Dash was sure that one day soon, he'd find his way in – that is, if the guards stopped telling him off every time he got near.

The hedges cast long, looming shadows across the opulent flower beds and ladies' tables and chairs, and whenever the wind blew, it would cause a ripple through the leaves along the wall, as though the maze itself was shivering. Dash knew there was adventure to be had in there. He'd often pretend he was a knight travelling through the Valia Forest, slaying dangerous beasts and protecting the prince and princess. Sometimes, he would tell Olena these stories and she would laugh. He liked making her laugh, though he didn't think knighthood was a particularly funny matter.

'Is that you, Dash?' the princess's voice called. 'It *has* to be you – I can smell sugar-oat biscuits.' She smiled warmly as he approached, her clouded blue eyes flitting constantly.

'Hello,' Dash said, sitting beside the princess. Her guards took no notice of him.

She tucked a loose strand of golden hair behind her ear and gripped his hand. 'I'm glad you're here,' she said. 'I need you to tell me what colour the sky is today.'

One of the guards looked at her. 'We already told you, Your Highness. The sky is blue, same as every other day.'

Olena shook her head and turned back to Dash. 'Well?'

Dash looked up and took in the sky for the both of them. 'Today most of it above us is bright and happy, but,' Dash stood up and looked across the garden for a moment, 'yep, there's definitely some doom and gloom coming in from the south.'

'Doom and gloom? Really? I thought I could smell rain. I do love thunderstorms.'

'Ugh, I know. But then we can't come outside. And I hate helping you with your embroidery.'

Olena shrugged. 'Did you bring one of those biscuits for me?'

Dash pressed the sugar-oat into her palm. 'Cook nearly killed me during the biscuit siege.'

'She did not.'

'Did so, came at me with a meat cleaver and everything.'

'Did you use your knight's axes on her?'

Dash gasped in mock-horror. 'She may be a nasty cook, but she's still a lady – can't be using axes on them. It's not very knightly.'

'I suppose you're right.' Olena bit into her biscuit, the dough crumbling down her front. She paid the mess no heed.

'So why don't we have lessons today?' Dash asked.

Olena nibbled on her biscuit for a moment before replying. 'Jaxon's governess was ill today, so Mrs Milner is teaching him.'

'Why don't we just do lessons all together?'

'A prince learns different things.'

'We learn the same things! He said so himself – histories, sigils, territories ...'

'You're lucky to be learning at all, boy,' said the younger of the princess's guards. 'Let alone sharing royal lessons with Her Highness.'

'I know.' Dash rolled his eyes. He was tired of learning about the four continents. He always got the capitals wrong and Mrs Milner would make him recite them over and over, until they were even more muddled in his head.

'I'm lucky to have Dash in my lessons, Thomas,' Olena said, her eyes staring ahead.

'Of course, Highness.'

Dash saw Thomas' jaw clench, as it always did when the princess shared her views. The guard's frustration was obvious to those around who had the gift of sight. Beside Dash, Olena shook her head, ever so slightly. Olena didn't need her sight to know that Thomas was a disrespectful fool.

'Education should be afforded to everyone,' she continued, 'no matter what their social standing.'

'That's a nice sentiment, Princess, I meant no offence. Only that a stable master's son is privileged to have access to the royal tutors.'

'As you are lucky to be in the royal guard,' Olena said simply.

Thomas opened and closed his mouth, before opting to remain silent. It was rare that Olena used her sharp tongue, but when she did, her opponent was usually left nursing wounded pride. Dash knew she'd have made a fine queen someday had Jaxon not been first in line.

Olena turned back to him.

'Did you like yesterday's lessons?' she asked.

Dash nodded. 'Do you think the East Sea really turned red with blood?'

'Maybe, if there was as much death as Mrs Milner said.'

'Learning about the treaty of Moredon Tower, are you?' asked Jonathan, the older guard.

Dash nodded. 'Do you know it?'

'Everyone knows it. The war to end all wars. Her Highness's ancestors were the ones that put a stop to it all and built that tower to unite the four continents. It's a symbol of peace,' the guard said.

'I don't need the same lesson again today,' Olena said, but she smiled in Jonathan's direction.

'What do you want to do, then?' asked Dash.

Although Dash knew she couldn't see it, Olena turned towards the maze.

'I'd like to go in there.'

The maze, it seemed, called to everyone. Dash had described it to Olena countless times. They'd even had hushed conversations about sneaking off and attempting it together. Olena had insisted that her other senses were more than capable of getting them back in one piece. But now, the guards looked panic-stricken.

'Your Highness, we're under strict orders from your father – you, *and* your companions,' Jonathan said, with a pointed look at Dash, 'are not to go in there.'

'I know, I know,' she muttered.

Dash felt a stab of pity for Olena. Her royal status put more restrictions on her than her blindness.

'Shall we go down to Heathton Falls, then?' Dash asked, suddenly longing to hear the sound of the crashing water.

'Sorry, stableboy, Her Highness is not to go beyond the gatehouse today.'

Olena sighed. 'You go, Dash. I'll just sit here, like the statue I'm meant to be.'

'No,' he said. He hated leaving Olena behind. Whenever he did, she would end up with a bunch of stuffy noblemen's daughters who spoke to her as though she were two years old.

They stayed in the gardens a while longer. Dash watched as the princess absentmindedly pulled little flowers from the soil and knotted them together in a floral string. Nearby, he could hear the clang of steel upon steel, and he knew that the squires were in the courtyard for training.

I wish I could join them, he thought. There was a loud shout of laughter and the sound of a sword clattering to the cobblestones – someone had been bested.

'Shall we go and observe?' Olena asked him, knowing full well where his attention had been. 'Obviously by "we" I mean you. I'll keep you company.' She was already on her feet, arm poised for Dash to loop his own through it. With her skirts swishing about her ankles, Olena let him lead her back through the gardens to the courtyard, where the young squires were parrying and blocking with blunted blades. The boys paused at the arrival of the princess and bowed, but she simply waved her hand.

'Carry on,' she said.

And they did. Dash watched in awe, his fingers itching to hold a sword, his feet tapping to the rhythm of the swordplay dance. He longed to be a squire with every fibre of his being. But he was a stableboy, nothing more.

'Did you know that Sir Caleb Swinton and Lady Yuliana will be coming to the castle in a week's time?' Olena said over the clashing of swords.

'Really?' Dash knew Olena didn't have much interest in the retired knight, but whenever she heard news she would always relay it to him.

'Yes. There's a feast and ball to honour the anniversary of his knighthood.'

'You mean I might get to see him?' Dash turned to face her fully, the parrying squires suddenly forgotten.

'You might.'

'Can you imagine?'

'Well, I've never *technically* seen him, but I've met him. He sounds old,' Olena said.

'He *is* old! The invasion was forty years ago!' Pa and Olena had told him the tale a million times, at his request of course. Sir Caleb had been the Commander of the King's Guard when mist dwellers had attacked Heathton. There had been a bloody battle outside the castle gatehouse. Young King Arden had been there, fighting alongside his men, when one of the mist dwellers had cornered him. According to the tale, mist had swept in all around the men, and no one could see what was happening – they could only hear the king's screams. But the young commander had charged in, his two battleaxes swinging – he'd cut the mist dweller in half, saving the king. The king had knighted him after that, and changed the royal sigil in his honour – to two crossed axes in a crown of fire.

Dash looked to the princess's guards. 'Were you there?'

'Do I look sixty years old to you, boy?' said Thomas, his face a mask of incredulousness.

Jonathan laughed and slapped his companion on the back. 'Ease up there, Thomas, it's an easy mistake with a face like that.'

'Shut it, Jon,' Thomas growled.

But Jonathan turned to Dash and the princess. 'My father was there. He told me once that they thought they were done for – they were surrounded by the creatures from the mist. They couldn't see, they couldn't breathe, and their swords felt heavier. That's when Sir Caleb charged. My father said he didn't just save the king that day, he saved them all. He saved Heathton. Maybe even the whole realm.'

Dash's eyes were wide as he looked at Olena. 'You never told me that!'

He wondered what it would be like to have a knight for a father instead of a stable master. Often at royal feasts and balls, Dash had to help his pa attend the horses of the noblemen and their young sons. Most were respectful to his father – he had held his position for many decades now, and had an esteemed reputation throughout the realm. But Dash didn't fail to notice the occasional snide remark, or worse, a command. He didn't fail to notice that no matter how polite a nobleman was to his father, he was a mere second in their day. Someone to be greeted, if at all, and forgotten.

Olena was lifting her face to the sky – and Dash felt the first few drops of rain hit the crown of his head.

'I knew I could smell rain,' she said, eyes closed.

'Your Highness,' Thomas said, 'we should get you inside before the downpour.'

'I like the rain.'

'Yes, but the king and queen won't be happy if you catch a chill.'

Olena sighed. 'Of course.'

The squires were packing up their equipment as it began to rain heavily. Olena elbowed Dash in the ribs, bunched up her layered skirts in her fists and broke into a run towards the castle. Dash burst out laughing and sprinted after her, gripping her hand in his when he caught up.

'Your Highness! Don't run!' Jonathan pleaded, jogging after them.

Dash was too quick for him, even as he pulled Olena along. Together they ran up the steps, into the entrance hall, and into the south gallery. Dash knew Olena loved to run too – but the guards would hardly let her. They were afraid she'd fall and that they'd get the blame for her scraped knees. Ladies, especially princesses, couldn't have scraped knees, Pa had told Dash. The grin was so wide on Olena's face that Dash didn't care about the talking-to he'd get after. Why shouldn't the princess have fun like all the other children? Her lack of sight made her no less able-bodied than the rest of them. They ran past the main gallery, hurtled through a group of courtiers in frills and fancy coats, and barrelled right into Commander Swinton.

A calm rage settled across the commander's sharp face as he bowed low to Olena. 'Your Highness,' he said.

'Commander,' she greeted him, trying to swipe the silly grin off her face.

Dash's heart nearly stopped. Commander Swinton – the son of Sir Caleb – was glaring daggers at him. His hair hung loose around his face, but it didn't hide the patchwork of yellow-and-purple bruising over one of his pointy cheekbones.

'May I escort you somewhere, Your Highness?' the commander asked Olena.

'No thank you, Commander. I can find my way,' she said, laughter still tugging at the corners of her mouth.

'Bye, Dash.' She patted his arm before floating off slowly in the direction of the music room.

Her guards caught up, panting behind Dash, but upon spotting the commander, they straightened themselves and steadied their breathing.

'Commander Swinton,' Jonathan said, bowing his

head.

'Shouldn't you be with your charge?' The commander's nostrils flared.

'Yes, sir.'

The guards made a show of leaving, heading towards the great hall.

'The music room,' the commander called out, irritated.

'Right, sir. Thank you, sir.'

They ran off in the opposite direction, and the commander sighed.

'I'm not a sir,' he muttered, and then froze, pursing his lips as he realised Dash still stood before him.

'You,' he snapped. 'The princess is not some lowly farm girl. She could get hurt running around like that. Stay out of the way.'

And with that, the commander strode towards the great hall, leaving Dash gaping in awe at the axes that gleamed across his back, and the silver hilt of the longsword at his hip.

Chapter Eight

Dimitri Swinton wished the stable master, Carlington, would keep his son under control. The boy was running amok around the castle again, and more and more frequently, the princess was getting caught up in his antics. It wasn't appropriate. Swinton was already having a bad day – a bad week, in fact. And now he had to give King Arden the news. That he'd not only lost the orphan girl to the Valians, but that they'd also left his men in tatters.

The great hall was empty and dark thanks to the grey skies outside. Usually during the day, the hall was bright, with over twenty massive arched windows allowing the sunlight to beam across the decadent table settings and the jewelled thrones on the dais. But today it was dim, the clouds casting long shadows across the room. Swinton nodded to the two guards at the heavy doors to the throne room, and bowing their heads, they stepped aside, allowing him through. Inside, the servants had lit hundreds of candles, so the room was bright and uncomfortably warm. Swinton resisted the urge to roll up his sleeves and undo the first few laces at the front of his shirt. King Arden spotted him from where he sat on his throne, chatting to the queen on the dais, the platform and its contents even more opulent than those in the great hall.

'Commander,' the king said with a smile, 'come, come forward.'

Swinton strode down the centre of the room and knelt before King Arden and Queen Vera. Arden was an impressive-looking man. Even sitting down he loomed over people. His build was that of a fighter, but though he'd once been a renowned swordsman, he now had the relaxed posture that came with decades of wealth and peace. He hadn't worn his sword in years; instead, he wore a jewelled dagger at his hip. He rested his hand on its hilt.

'Rise,' said King Arden, 'and tell me – what in the realm happened out there?'

The king didn't sound angry, but that was one of the things Swinton hated most about working closely with him – no one ever knew what the king was thinking, until it was too late. Several years ago, the previous commander had been involved in a scandal concerning a nobleman's wife and a brothel. At the time, the king had seemed calm, understanding even, much to the then commander's relief. It wasn't until some days later that the commander had been reprimanded, and publicly so. He now dwelled in the slums of the capital, doing anything he could to get his hands on opium and foreign wildflower. Swinton feared a day when he might be on the receiving end of that. Silently, he prayed to the goddess Yacinda that it wouldn't be today.

'Getting the girl was simple enough, Your Majesty,' he said. 'She had no solid connections to Angove – not since the old fisherman died. But when we reached the summit of the ranges the Valia kindred found us.'

'The Valians were all the way over that side of the crossing?'

'Yes, sire.'

'How many?'

'Five.'

'And you had ten men with you?'

'Yes, Your Majesty.'

'You're telling me that five *women* outfought my commander's hand-selected troops?'

'These were Valians, Majesty, not simple women.' Swinton didn't press the fact that Lennox had been the king's choice, not his.

The king nodded, and next to him, the queen looked elsewhere and rearranged her skirts.

'Details,' the king commanded.

'One of the men, Siv Lennox, was harassing the prisoner.'

'To what extent?'

Swinton glanced at the queen, not wanting to offend her.

'His intentions were not honourable, Your Majesty.'

'I see.'

'When we had retired for the night, he lay hands on her, and that's when the kindred showed up. I think they may have been watching us for longer than I'd care to admit.'

'Why didn't your scouts notice?'

'The Valia have other means of travelling through the ranges and forest, sire.'

The king nodded again. 'Yes, I've heard those stories, too, Commander. Which of the kindred? Anyone we've dealt with before?'

Swinton swallowed. 'It was what they call the Queen's Guard, sire.' Swinton bowed his head in apology to Queen Vera. She smiled grimly.

'Queen's Guard. There is no queen in Ellest but for the one who sits before you now,' the king said.

'Of course, sire. I was merely relaying their terminology to you. Of their matriarch guard, there was Athene, first-in-command, Tilly, Marvel and Petra. The usual suspects; we've dealt with them before.' Swinton took a deep breath. 'And Henri Valia.'

'What?'

'Henri Valia, Your Majesty, she was there.'

'Tell me, Commander. What is the Matriarch of Valia Forest doing attacking the king's men carrying out a royal summons?' The king gripped the arms of his throne.

'I'm not sure why they were there, sire. Though I do know they have different notions about what constitutes their territory. I believe they attacked due to Lennox's actions. To lay hands on a woman in what they deem their territory is a direct insult to the kindred and their ancestors.'

'The Hawthorne Ranges and Felder's Bay are *not* Valian territory.'

'No, sire.'

'And they interfered with your task regardless of the fact that they were on *my* land, attacking *my* men, and – where is the prisoner now?'

'They have her, sire.'

The king rested his head in his hand for a moment. 'Commander,' he said, 'this was supposed to be a simple mission – retrieve a commoner, a *girl*, from Angove. What other damages besides losing a prisoner of mine?'

Swinton took the verbal blow silently. He had let the king down; he'd failed to do his duty. The king could easily, and perhaps should, strip him of his title for this.

'Siv Lennox lost an eye, several of the other men have minor injuries – cracked ribs and the like – but no deaths. The Valians were careful about that.'

'Though they could have killed you, easily, by the sounds of it?' The king scanned Swinton's own bruised face.

The commander hesitated, before answering honestly, 'Yes, Your Majesty.'

'And Lennox's eye?'

'We were lucky we had Fiore Murphadias with us, Majesty. His grandmother was a healer in Battalon. He knew what herbs to pack the wound with. Lennox is in a lot of pain, but the wound hasn't festered. We think he'll live.'

The king nodded. 'I suppose his injury will be punishment enough for his careless actions. Though he will receive no pension.'

'I'll see to it, sire.'

The king pressed his fingers to his temples. 'And what of your private mission, Commander? Did you release the contents of the jars you were given?'

'Yes, Your Majesty. All but three. After we lost the girl, I thought it prudent to return to you as soon as possible.'

'Good. At least you made the right decision in that respect. Have you marked the coordinates you missed on the map?'

'Yes, sire.'

King Arden's jaw clenched and he tugged on his pale-gold beard. 'See to it that you get some salve for your own injuries, Commander.'

The queen's gaze fell to Swinton's swollen face, and he averted his own eyes, face flushing. The queen was always a quiet figure in his meetings with the king. She sat, often fidgeting with her skirts or jewellery, wordlessly absorbing everything that was said. He sometimes wondered how much the royal couple had to say to each other behind closed doors. But that was neither here nor there.

'Yes, sire.' Swinton nodded to the king.

'You know we can't let the Valians get away with this.'

Swinton remained silent.

'They've stolen a prisoner I've summoned, they've

attacked my guard, they're claiming territory that isn't theirs and they've named their matriarch "Queen"? Ever since the unfortunate death of Sahara Valia and all that business with the mist, I've turned a blind eye to their antics. However, it's been far too long, and they've done nothing but take advantage. And apparently preach treasonous notions.'

'What would you have us do, sire?'

The king stood, holding an arm out to the queen. Swinton saw concern flicker across her face, but it was gone as she got to her feet and took her husband's arm. The royal couple descended from the dais, and Swinton knelt again.

'Get up, Swinton. If we bothered with every formality in the book, we'd be here all day.'

Swinton stood, his head still bowed.

'Come to me in the morning,' the king said. 'I'll have a decision for you then.'

The king and queen left the throne room followed closely by their guard, and Swinton found himself alone in the magnificent space. He exhaled a long sigh of relief and loosened the ties at the front of his shirt. Though he had no idea what tomorrow would bring, it was over for now. His position, his ambitions were safe for the time being. Dabbing the perspiration from his hairline, he gathered himself and left the room.

On his way out, he glanced at the embroidered map that hung proudly beside the entrance to the throne room. All four kingdoms and their capitals had been plotted out meticulously – Ellest, with its farmlands, rivers and the Hawthorne Ranges, the mighty castle of Heathton to the west, the very castle in which Swinton now stood; there was Battalon to the north, with the palace beneath the celebrated shiprock stitched into the sandy cliffs; Havennesse, with the icy fortress of Wildenhaven at its centre; and Qatrola – the smallest of the kingdoms and the estate among the people of Tokarr.

Of the foreign lands, Swinton was the most familiar with Battalon. He had journeyed there twice. The first time had been as a foot soldier, as part of an escort to the esteemed Murphadias family from the capital – Fiore's. King Roswall of Battalon had exchanged a number of noble families with King Arden as a show of trust between the two rulers. Swinton had been in his final years of squireship. The second time he'd been to Battalon was as Commander of the King's Army, with Fiore as captain beside him, to aid the Belbarrow military in stamping out the Janhallow Desert rebellion.

It was not the fighting Swinton remembered vividly now, but the location itself. Its dry, sweltering heat, its endless dusty plains, and the rocky peaks that demanded climbing. He recalled the sweat stinging his eyes, his heavy boots sinking into the dunes, and the bushes of fountain grass that hid deadly snakes. His was a love–hate relationship with Battalon's desolate deserts and its firestorms. It was a continent that pulsed with the desire to be conquered, but to do so would bring any man close to death. Yet, it was addictive – pushing oneself to breaking point. As a Battalon native, Fiore rarely saw breaking point. The heat was nothing to him. His skin never blistered beneath the sun's punishment. His body never sagged with dehydration and fatigue. Swinton knew how lucky they had been to have Fiore with them that year. It had been his advice and tactics that had seen them through the battle, to claim victory against the Janhallow rebels.

He rubbed the scar on his chin as he took a final look at the embroidered map. He liked to study it whenever he had the chance, to remind himself of the other places he'd journey to when he was finally knighted. There was no more time for that now, though; he had to get himself cleaned up.

His chambers were as he'd left them. He'd instructed the servants not to disturb them in his absence. He hated the idea of people moving around his private quarters and tampering with his things, not that he had many. Swinton preferred the simple life. Closing the heavy oak door behind him, he rested against it and sighed. The past three weeks had thoroughly exhausted him. The travel alone was enough to render anyone a fatigued wreck, but the drama of the guard on the road – the bickering and sniping between the men on the way to Angove – had driven him to near madness. And then, the unacceptable behaviour on the return journey had nearly cost him. He hadn't, as the king claimed, handpicked the men. That had been Tannus, the weapons master, by the king's instructions. Swinton had only been able to insist on Fiore and Stefan. Though, he hadn't wanted to seem insolent by bringing this up to the king, especially when he was already on thin ice.

He walked across the room and sank into the soft armchair by the fireplace. As much as he longed to stay there, and perhaps indulge in a nap before dinner, he had things to do, the first of which was bathe. He had done his best to scrub the dirt from his face before he saw the king, but there had been no time for a proper bath. He bent down to unlace his boots. They were filthy; thick mud caked the soles, and they were looking on the shabby side. He sighed again, placing them by the fireplace. He couldn't afford a new pair just yet. Brushing away excess dirt from the ankles of his pants, he noticed new blisters and calluses on his hands from the riding. He'd have to wait to order a new pair of gloves, too.

He'd hoped he'd get the chance to go back down to the stables to see Xander, his horse, settled back in, but there wouldn't be time now. The rose-grey stallion had been his constant companion for almost ten years now, and Swinton hated it when anyone else tended to the beast.

There was a tentative knock at the door, and Swinton rose, barefoot, to answer it. It was Therese, the servant girl he'd asked to bring hot water. Her eyes darted to the patches of bruising on his face and flitted away just as quickly. Another girl came in behind her, and between them, they carried four heavy pails of steaming water.

'Here,' Swinton said, taking one from each of them.

'Thank you, sir,' Therese said, flushing pink.

'I'm not a sir,' he told her, making his way towards the bathing room.

Therese took the fourth pail from the other servant and followed Swinton. Placing the pails on the tiled floor, she wiped down the dusty tub. From the corner of his eye, Swinton watched her. She was a pretty young thing – probably no older than twenty. Strands of red hair fell over her eyes as she scrubbed at the inside of the tub. Swinton caught a glimpse of his reflection in the arched mirror above the basin. He grimaced. The left side of his face boasted myriad faded blues and yellowing greens, while his cheekbone was still puffy with swelling. He looked like hell, thanks to bloody Henri Valia. Irritation prickled as he cursed her arrogance, her nerve – what was she playing at, kidnapping the king's prisoner and assaulting his guards? The Henri he'd known had been smarter than that. He pushed his dark, matted hair from his brow and began undressing. Therese, who had finished cleaning, now put the plug in place, and began emptying the steaming water into the bath.

'Will that be all, Commander?' Therese said, not meeting his eyes, cheeks still pink.

He looked down at his toned bare chest, speckled with white scars. The coin of Yacinda rested against his sternum, and he realised he should have waited until she had left before removing his clothes. He wondered if she'd ever seen a naked man before. In that moment, he found her beautiful – her modesty and innocence tugging at something deep within him. But he snapped himself out of it.

'Yes, that's all. Thank you.'

She nodded and left the room, closing both the doors behind her. Swinton ran his fingers through his dirty hair again. He knew better than to dally with women beneath his station. He'd done it once before, and it had ended badly. He shook his head; he wouldn't think of it now. He pushed his pants down his aching legs, kicking them into the corner with his other soiled clothes, and stepped into the bath.

Gods, it's hot. Slowly, he lowered his body in, and let out a sigh of relief as he sank to the bottom. It was verging on scorching, but it was exactly what his sore muscles needed after weeks of riding. The scent of lavender hit his nostrils; Therese had added essential oils for his aches and pains. He leaned back and rested his head on the edge of the tub. He was in such a mess. Although the king hadn't said it outright, Swinton knew he was on thin ice, *very* thin. This blunder with the Valians and losing the girl, it would cost him. Every trifle like this made any possibility of knighthood seem decades away. And forget knighthood. This failed mission could have endangered his current position.

Who is the odd-eyed girl to the king anyway? Is her magic so powerful? Was she so important that the king would send some of his best men away from the castle, to journey for weeks to bring her to him? It was none of Swinton's business, of course; his business was to serve and nothing more. He dared not question the king, but the king hadn't mentioned magic at all, and so Swinton hadn't brought up Henri and her power either. It was stronger than he remembered. And sometimes, the Ashai were best left undiscussed.

Something about the girl had rubbed Swinton the wrong way. He wasn't sure if it was that despite her obvious vulnerabilities, she was stubborn – enough to defy him in front of a crowd of people. Or if it was the way she'd studied his men, somehow intuitive to their moods without actually knowing them. Or maybe he didn't like the way Fiore had sympathised with her. That was the last thing he needed in his guard.

The bathwater was already growing cloudy as he picked up the fresh cake of soap Therese had left, and began to lather up. 'Bleak' had been her name. Or what that young man had called her as they had dragged her out of Angove. One person. One person questioned why they were taking her. It looked like she'd lived on the streets for the past few years – her hair had been lank and knotted, with dirt caked on her face and limbs. It was also clear to Swinton that she was a drunk. He'd noted the way her eyes had often followed not only the men and their weapons, but the skins of wine tied to their saddlebags. Then she'd collapsed and had a fit. Her eyes had dulled and she'd dropped to the ground, her whole body seizing, spit foaming in the corners of her mouth. He'd seen that kind of episode before; it had been a soldier he used to know, a symptom of withdrawal from liquor.

What is this girl going to cost me and the kingdom? Especially now the Valia kindred are involved? If the king wanted to make a move on the Valians, he'd set into motion something that could not be undone. Swinton thought of the jars he'd carried through the mountains, and what he'd released among the old trees there, unknown to even his most trusted friend. He was playing a dangerous game.

The next morning, Swinton was summoned to the throne room.

'Commander Swinton,' King Arden greeted him, an elegant violet cloak pooled at his feet.

'Your Majesty.' Swinton knelt before the dais, noting that this time, the queen wasn't in attendance.

'I've made a decision regarding this unfortunate business with the Valians.'

Swinton waited.

'You and your best man will journey to Valia Forest and deliver a direct summons to Henrietta Valia and the orphan girl.'

'To Henri Valia, sire?'

'Yes. Their insolence cannot be overlooked. They know that to disobey a direct summons from the king is an act of treason. She will come. And you will make sure she does.'

'And if she doesn't, sire?'

'I'll hold you personally responsible.'

All Swinton could do was bow his head.

'Take whatever provisions you need. My best horses are yours to use, though I know Xander generally goes where you go.'

'You are generous, my king. When do we leave?'

'Tomorrow at dawn.'

'Yes, Majesty.'

'Go and make your preparations. You are dismissed.'

A flush of heat swept up Swinton's neck and rose high on his cheeks, a blush that gave away his shame. He had failed his king, failed himself.

'Thank you, sire,' he said.

With as much dignity as he could muster, Swinton left the throne room and headed straight to the armoury to tell Fiore the news.

Chapter Nine

In the early hours of the morning, Henri returned from her sentry shift. The whole forest had settled, and there were only the scurries of nocturnal beasts and the occasional bird call to contend with. Henri was very much at peace with the realm when she took watch. For those few hours, she could pretend she lived a simpler life. She stretched and swung herself back up onto the living bridge, where the others lay. Marvel groaned when Henri shook her shoulder. Bleary-eyed, the Valian grimaced and headed down to the lower platform to take over the watch. At the edge of the group, Henri found Athene. She was sitting with her back against a tree trunk, watching over Bleak, goosebumps raised across her bare arms.

'You should be sleeping,' Henri muttered, her knees cracking as she sat down beside her first-in-command.

'I know.'

Bleak was fast asleep wrapped in Athene's cloak, her breathing deep and steady.

'She's not Luka,' Henri warned Athene, nodding to Bleak.

Luka was Athene's teenage daughter. Athene had

Luka when she was no more than a teenager herself. She was a young mother, even by free-minded Valian standards, falling pregnant when she was barely fifteen. Luka was now in the midst of her kindred training, and Henri knew Athene missed the girl terribly.

'She's someone's daughter,' Athene said.

Henri rested her head against the tree and closed her eyes. 'Get some sleep.'

The dawn broke upon the living bridges before the world below, and so they were up and on the move well before the rest of the forest was awake. This journey was meant to have been a routine check of the bridges and to scope out if the mist had encroached further into their territory. According to the reports the king sent every year, the mist was advancing on all the territories of Ellest at the same rate. Henri suspected otherwise. In any case, the bridges and the mist were no longer her immediate problem. Now, all she could think of was the statement she'd made in rescuing Bleak from Commander Swinton, and how grave an insult it was to the king. She churned through the possible outcomes in her mind, not realising she was bending the trees alongside them to her will until Athene nudged her. Annoyed, she concentrated on the mossy path ahead and the trees whipped back into place. Her powers often seemed to have a mind of their own.

Her thoughts returned to the king. She'd met Arden on two occasions in her life. The first time had been as a young child, during the more prominent years of her mother Allehra's rule. At the time, the Valians had been in a bloody, three-year-long dispute with the royal family – a rebellion over how much they owed in terms of military resources. Allehra had eventually agreed to a peace treaty with the king: the first and last treaty to ever be made by the kindred. They would be indebted to no one. When it was settled, Allehra, Sahara, Henri and the most respected kindred met the royals and their entourage at Felder's Bay for a peace ceremony. Henri could remember the king and queen breaking bread with Allehra, and toasting to an enduring friendship between the Valia kindred and the royals. The famous knight, Sir Caleb Swinton, watched everything, every flicker of movement. At his side was his young son, mimicking his father's actions, wearing a grey tunic with his father's sigil embroidered proudly on the chest. Prince Jaxon and Princess Olena were yet to be born. Sahara and Henri were seated with the noblemen's children, who looked at them like they were giant serpents or teerah panthers – mythical beasts created by parents, used for scaring children.

The second and only other time Henri had come into contact with the royal family had been at Sahara's memorial. King Arden, Queen Vera, little Prince Jaxon and Princess Olena had all travelled from the capital to the Valia Forest to honour the memory of her sister. The funeral rites of one of the last remaining Valian descendants couldn't be missed by anyone, not even the king. It had been a blur to Henri, who had spent much of those days in a wildflower haze.

The king was nothing special, not from what Henri had judged. He possessed no unique gifts; he was no Ashai, that was for sure. He lacked the presence that born leaders had, and although he could command attention, it wasn't out of respect, or even fear. In Henri's mind, he was a bland, faceless man, who had somehow been fortunate enough to end up on the throne.

'You're worried,' Athene said quietly.

'I'm always worried.'

'Not like this. Something's different.'

'I shouldn't have interfered,' Henri allowed.

'You had no choice. It's the Valian Way.'

'The Valian Way ...' Henri shook her head. 'Be nice if it worked for the Valians every once in a while.'

'What do you mean?'

Henri sighed. 'Forget it.'

They continued walking, the sun bright and clear at its apex above, streaming golden rays across the bridges before them. Henri was quiet and turned right, moulding the trees with her power to steer those lagging behind in the right direction.

'What's the worst that can happen?' Athene asked.

'Don't be naive, Athene.' The trees bowed obediently at a casual flick of Henri's wrist.

'It's that bad?'

'Worse. We've always had a tense relationship with the royals. I've pushed it too far this time.'

'If it hadn't been this, it would have been something else, eventually.'

'True.'

'So, what's the plan?'

'Get back to the keep. Figure out who this girl is. Talk to Allehra. That's all I've got.'

'That's a start.'

'Ever the optimist.'

'Someone's gotta be.'

'If you say so.'

The others caught up with Henri and Athene, and the women kept their strides long, covering ground quickly and efficiently. Henri was just beginning to feel satisfied with their progress when a sharp whistle sounded behind her – Tilly's distress call. Henri whirled around, katars already clenched around her knuckles. But it wasn't an attack. Bleak was lying on her side, her body shuddering with convulsions, white foam bubbling at her mouth. Henri skidded across the moss on her knees, sheathing her katars.

'Hold her steady,' she commanded, shuffling to the edge of the bridge. She rummaged through the thick foliage overflowing onto the path, feeling her way along the leaves, until she felt a velvet-like texture between her fingertips.

'What happened?' she asked, plucking several leaves from the bush.

'We were walking and she just dropped.'

Bleak's whole body continued to jolt.

'Did she hit her head?'

'No – I caught her as she fell,' said Petra.

Henri nodded, putting the leaves to her mouth and chewing so the bitter-tasting sap ran. She moved back to Bleak's side and mushed the wet leaves into the girl's mouth, forcing them to the back of her tongue with her fingers. A second later, Bleak's body stopped convulsing.

'Is she going to be alright?' Athene asked.

'Should be.'

'What's wrong with her?'

'That's what I'd like to know.'

'I'll stay with her,' said Athene, 'you go ahead.'

'No. We need to get to the keep. Splash some water on her face and get her up. I won't wait.'

Bleak was proving to be more trouble than she was worth. Three days ago now, they'd been about to continue on to Angove River when she had *felt* the girl – her untamed magic had been like a beacon in the forest. Henri and her kindred had changed course, and watched as the girl was tugged along by a group of the King's Guard. They had watched as that vile man had eyed her greedily. Henri hadn't intended on interfering. To do so was to endanger their fragile relationship with the king. But the second the man had touched Bleak, all bets had been off. Valians never left a woman defenceless at the hands of a man, and they did everything within their power to quell that sense of entitlement. That was the Valian Way. Now, Henri watched as Bleak came to, her face dripping with water.

'Up you get,' said Petra, looping Bleak's limp arm around her shoulder.

'What happ—'

'You fainted, started having a fit. This happened before?' Henri asked.

'Once, that I know of. On the way up the Hawthornes from the bay.'

'Do you know why?'

Bleak shook her head.

'Keep an eye on her,' Henri told Petra. 'Let's move.'

Thanks to Bleak, the kindred moved at what felt like a glacial pace. Henri was restless, eager to start making plans and figuring out where all this left her and her people.

'What's happening?' she heard Bleak say weakly.

'There are consequences for what we've done,' Petra muttered, clearly aware of being within earshot of Henri.

'What do you mean? What consequences?'

'For meddling with the king's orders.'

'I don't understand. You're making it sound like a battle.'

'I'm not making it sound like anything other than what it is. Not all battles are shields and war hammers,' Petra said.

'I don't under—'

'You will. Now keep up.'

They moved at a brisk jog across the living bridges, which became narrower, with more forks in their paths, the verdant green stretching on and on out into the vast distance. Although Bleak's fitness was clearly not up to Valian standard, which was made apparent every time she had to dry-retch over the side of the bridge, she didn't complain as they pushed on. Her face was flushed pink, and her matted hair clung to her face with sweat, and still she said nothing.

Perhaps there is hope for the girl yet, Henri thought.

They passed over the rapids of Valia River. Henri could hear its current roar over the rocks, even from high above in the treetops. Had they more time, Henri would have permitted the kindred to stop and spear fresh fish for their dinner. But there wasn't a moment to spare. They needed to get back to the keep.

Finally, they arrived. A vibrant tunnel of arched trunks and branches greeted them, a passage that sang out to Henri with its ancient magic. Enchantments pulsed from within the official entrance to the outer Valian keep. Henri led the way through the passage, parting the hanging vines and greenery before her and stepping through. She had to stop herself from swaying to Valia's melody: breathings of a rich, magic-driven history etched in the trees, the murmurings of the breeze and the familiar sound of clanging steel from the training grounds. Nearby, young Valians were being shaped into warriors, honing their fighting skills with as much precision as dancers would learn their movements.

Henri heard Bleak's sharp intake of breath from behind her as the young Ashai took in the wonder of the forest and its inhabitants. The keep opened up into numerous timber platforms, built around the tree trunks, climbing up around them and into the sky. Dark vines clung to every surface, a strangling means of support for the structures, as though the forest itself was at one with whatever the Valians built into it. The keep was a kingdom unto itself in the canopy, with training grounds, private residences, communal areas and multi-level apartments sprawled outwards and upwards, as far as the eye could see. Henri nodded to the warriors stationed at the other end of the passage, her elite kindred only steps behind her. She took her first steps back into Valia, all manner of living greenery knotted and entwined to hold her kingdom, her home together. She allowed herself a single sigh, knowing that now she was home, the real work, the real struggle, would truly begin.

Chapter Ten

The sunset from Valia was breathtaking. The glowing orb of the sun dipped below the horizon of treetops, spilling its shimmering rays of rose pink, gold and lilac upon the forest below. Bleak surveyed the landscape from the entrance to the Valian keep, as though it could quench her insatiable thirst. She'd never seen a decent painting in all her life, but this ... She imagined it would look something like this. Athene pressed a grain bar into her hand.

'You must be hungry,' she said, following Bleak's gaze outward. 'It'll be a while yet till supper's on.'

Bleak bit into the bar, a combination of Valian grain, nuts and seeds, held together with sweet nectar. It was delicious and surprisingly filling for something so small.

'Let's go,' Henri's voice sounded from somewhere, and Bleak realised the whole group had been waiting for her, letting her admire the best view the realm had to offer. Brushing her hands off on the legs of her pants, she followed them, trying to shrink from the curious stares of the guards she passed. Almost immediately upon entering the keep, the living bridges on which they stood started to shoot out into more directions than

Bleak could count. They were like the twisting, turning alleyways of a city, and Henri navigated them without a glance at her compass. It was clear she knew the ins and outs of this place like Bleak knew the loops and pulls of Senior's fisherman's knots.

'Where do these all go?' she asked Tilly, craning her neck as they turned yet another corner and passed more guards.

'All over Valia; to people's homes, to the grounds, the armoury.'

'And they're all up here? Above ground?'

'Sure are. The kindred are people of the forest. We love it up here.'

Bleak nodded; she could see why. The canopies were brimming with life, with clean air, with freedom. She made sure to walk in the centre of the path. There were no railings should she lose her footing, which was likely, considering how much her head throbbed. She hadn't had a drink in three days – the longest she'd gone without since she'd discovered drinking. As she ducked her head to avoid yet another branch, she spotted movement on the forest floor. Through the canopy's thick foliage, she caught a glimpse of a group of women below, dressed in plain cotton tunics and pants.

'I thought you said all the kindred stay up here?' she asked Tilly.

Tilly looked down to where Bleak gestured. 'Oh, they're not kindred.'

'But I thought only Valians lived in Valia.'

'I didn't say they weren't Valians. I said they weren't kindred.'

Bleak squinted through the branches and leaves. The women below were going about daily life, weaving baskets, scrubbing linens on giant washboards, and stirring great wooden barrels of laundry.

'I don't understand,' she said, noting that the folk below peered up at the passing company, their faces awash with both fear and admiration.

It was Athene who answered this time. 'They're the Valians who didn't pass their training,' she allowed.

'What do you mean?'

'They didn't pass their training, and now they live in what we call the Sticks.'

'Why?'

'Many reasons.'

'They choose to live down there instead of up here?'

'Some choose, yes. But it's the Valian Way. To become one of the kindred, to live *this* life, as one of the elite warriors, you must pass the training.'

'And if they don't, they're *exiled*?'

'They're not *exiled*,' Athene snapped, her gaze flicking to Henri's back.

'They're forced to live *physically below you*. Sounds like exile to me. Worse, even.'

'Don't let me hear you say that again. They serve Valia better where they are. That is their purpose, as fighting is ours. It's the Valian Way.'

So the stories were true. No wonder the Valians

were thought to be so formidable if they banished their own people with such ease. Bleak's stomach churned. But she chastised herself – why was she surprised? She'd known from the moment she'd met them that the Valians were ruthless. She realised that the stares from below had settled on her – the foreigner in their midst. Suddenly, she could hear their thoughts: their curiosity and surprise almost shouting up at her.

'How often do you bring new people here?' she asked Athene.

'Never.'

'Never?'

'The last time we had guests was ten years ago. We haven't had anyone new here since then. Till now.'

They continued to follow Henri, who moved further into the keep. After passing through the outer structures and training grounds, the trees turned into loft apartments above, and clever watchtowers that were integrated seamlessly into their surroundings. Bleak was utterly disorientated. Women of all different ages and complexions went about their usual business in the structures around them. In the distance, Bleak could hear the clash of metal and instructions being shouted above it; as she now understood, the Valians were infamous for their brutal training. They trekked deeper into the territory, and began to pass what Bleak realised must be the majority of the private residences. Bright, pale timber homes worked around the natural structures of the trees; round windows gave Bleak a rare glimpse into the private lives of the Valians. From what she saw, everything inside was the same as out, everything made from the same honey-coloured wood: walls, floors, ceilings and furniture. Weapons hung from matching hooks inside, as though an art display, and in some apartments, thick grey furs carpeted the floors. The trunks of the supporting trees shot up through the private quarters and out through the roofs, all part of one seamless structure. As they passed the apartments, Bleak realised something was off-kilter. As someone who had spent her entire life surrounded by men, she now found that there wasn't a man in sight.

'Are there no men in Valia?' she mumbled to no one in particular.

In front of her, Tilly laughed. 'We have men here,' she said, 'but they're generally kept to the outskirts. They do the tasks that are conventionally women's roles.'

'Are they slaves?'

'Slaves? Gods, no. We don't keep slaves here.'

'Then where do they come from?'

'Some of them are seeking a better life from elsewhere, some are the sons of the kindred, some are the partners. There's nothing untoward about it, so you can wipe that look off your face before Henri sees.'

'But —'

'No buts. It's how we do things here. It's the Valian Way.'

There's that saying again. It seemed to be applied to everything here.

They walked through an inner circle of trees and bridges. This place was far more guarded than anywhere else. At its centre was an enormous trunk, so thick it would have taken ten of the long-limbed kindred holding hands to link around it. This tree was darker than the rest, with intricate carvings etched into its bark, flourishing patterns that meant nothing to Bleak. Henri ran her palm across it with a surprisingly gentle touch.

'Mother Matriarch, Allehra's quarters,' Tilly spared Bleak in a whisper.

The Mother Matriarch of Valia. This is where she sleeps. I'm at the Mother Matriarch's doorstep ...

'Leave us,' Henri said to the kindred, nodding towards Bleak.

Bleak glanced at Athene, who opened her mouth to protest. But Henri inclined her head ever so slightly to the side, and Athene bowed, following the others back the way they had come. Bleak blinked at Henri, amazed. When the kindred had retreated from their sight, Henri traced the carvings with her fingers, closing her eyes and muttering something inaudible. Bleak's heart jumped up into her throat.

Is this what I think it is?

As if in answer, the tree groaned, and to Bleak's disbelief, the whole carving crumbled, fine as sand, to reveal an archway into the tree.

'I thought ... I thought enchantments like that didn't work anymore?' Bleak asked.

'Things are different in Valia.'

134

'How?'

They stepped through the archway and into the massive trunk, which was surprisingly well-lit. A narrow staircase curled around its structure, and led up to a platform high above.

'How?' Bleak persisted.

'Verbal enchantments need a foundation of magic to draw from. It's not enough just to be an Ashai with a specific ability. In the past, because there were so many Ashai among the ordinary folk, there was always power thrumming nearby to draw from. Not anymore. The plague has left the realm's general foundation of magic depleted. As far as I know, only in Valia can these enchantments be performed.'

'But there aren't many Ashai here, are there?'

Henri shook her head and started up the stairs. 'No. But the immensity of our ancestors' power has left this place pulsing with a solid foundation of magic. We also grow and use special herbs to aid the magic.'

'What? How —'

'Just follow me.'

They climbed the stairs, which had the same carvings etched into them as the tree trunk.

'What is this place?' Bleak breathed, her eyes following the faint trail of lights disappearing up the stairs.

'This is where Allehra lives.'

Allehra. Not Mother, not Ma or Mama. Henri's face gave nothing away, and her thoughts, as always, were unreadable. Bleak wondered if the Valian enchantments had anything to do with that fact.

'We're going to meet Queen Allehra? Now?'

Henri didn't answer, just continued hauling herself up the steep steps.

'You'd make things a lot more pleasant if you'd just tell me,' Bleak muttered, scrambling after her.

Henri turned so fast Bleak almost stumbled back. The warrior queen's face was so close to hers, she could feel Henri's breath hot on her cheeks.

'I don't know you,' Henri said sharply. 'I don't know where you've come from, or where you want to go. You're untutored, undisciplined and just generally irritating. I've told you more than I should have already. And *if* I choose to tell you *anything more*, it will be on my terms.' She loosed a breath. 'We saved you. We saved you when we didn't have to. Quit your whining.'

Bleak swallowed. It was the most she'd heard Henri say in one go. The warrior queen's dark braid nearly whipped Bleak in the face as she turned and continued to stalk up the stairs. Bleak followed her, this time, in silence. When they reached the top of the staircase, they emerged onto a timber platform, and a thick, black door greeted them. Henri knocked loudly. They waited; no one came. Henri knocked again, this time banging her fist harder.

'Allehra,' she called. 'Allehra. I know you're in there.'

But there was no sound coming from within. Henri stepped back and put her palm to the door, closing her eyes. Bleak stepped back as well. Was she going to blast the door away?

'Damn,' Henri cursed under her breath.

Bleak knew better than to ask questions at this point, but Henri glanced her way.

'She's put an enchantment on the door,' she said, removing her hand from the black surface. 'Looks like we'll be doing this the old-fashioned way.'

Bleak watched as Henri studied the door for a moment, before striking out with her boot. The timber splintered down the middle but didn't cave in. Henri kicked it again, and again. On the third time it crumbled, as the carving had done below. Without waiting, Henri strode into the chambers.

'Henri,' a voice sighed from the far side of the room.

From the doorway, Bleak could see Queen Allehra sitting in a wingback armchair by an enormous window. She hadn't even turned to look at them. She was staring out into the distance, her midnight hair streaked with silver, catching in the breeze.

'Allehra,' Henri greeted her mother, perching herself on the desk near the window.

'I wish you wouldn't ruin my door every time you visited,' Queen Allehra said, her voice soft and tired.

'I wish you'd just open it when I knocked, but we don't always get what we want, do we.'

'Who's your friend?' Allehra hadn't yet turned around, and Bleak braced herself on the doorframe.

Like mother, like daughter, Allehra was unreadable.

'Remains to be seen,' Henri said, staring at her

mother.

Finally, Queen Allehra turned, looking not at her daughter, but straight at Bleak. And she truly looked. Bleak felt the woman's eyes not only sink into her own, but into *her*, into her whole being.

'Interesting choice of companion, Henri,' Queen Allehra said. 'It's not every day you bring a mist dweller into our keep.'

Mist dweller. Bleak's grip slipped on the splintered doorframe and Henri was blocking her escape within seconds.

Allehra watched them coolly. Bleak's fingers itched to snatch Fiore's dagger from where she'd tied it around her calf. She'd never be able to draw it in time to be a match for Henri. Even if she did, she wouldn't be able to best the warrior.

'Henri,' Allehra warned.

'What did you say she was?'

But Allehra was too busy considering Bleak to answer. She rose from her chair, her long skirts flowing about her bare feet. When she stood, Bleak saw how different mother and daughter were. Despite their blue-black hair and general beauty, Allehra was dainty, gentle in her movements and the way she spoke. Henri's beauty was hardened, intimidating, and she spoke with the sharp edge of authority. They were light and darkness, rock and water.

Allehra stood before Bleak, tilting her head as she took in her features.

'Who are you?' Henri demanded.

'I told you, my name's Bleak,' she said. 'I grew up in Angove, with Bleaker Senior, the fisherman, as my guardian.' She suppressed the urge to squirm away from the Mother Matriarch's intense stare.

Finally, Allehra stepped back and began pacing the room, her skirts trailing after her. Henri only took one step back, and still eyed Bleak suspiciously. Bleak had the distinct feeling that the young ruler regretted her moment of compassion in the mountains.

'Tell me, Henri,' said Allehra.

Bleak could have sworn she saw a flash of resentment in Henri's eyes. The young warrior queen went to the window, her gaze settling on the darkening sky outside.

'The kindred and I were doing our usual check of Felder's Bay and the mountains when I felt her.'

Queen Allehra nodded. 'I sensed her presence drawing nearer last night.'

Bleak looked between the two queens. What did they mean they could *sense* her? And *why* was her magic not working now, when she needed it most? And a *mist dweller*? She had so many questions, and yet she felt as though these women were only going to add to her confusion.

'King Arden summoned her,' Henri said.

'Why?'

Henri shrugged. 'Some nonsense about illegal magic use, treason of some form or another.'

Bleak baulked at Henri's casual tone – she was

speaking of *treason*. Treason could get them all killed, or worse.

'And you took her?'

'The King's Army were playing foul.'

'The King's Army?'

'Yes, Commander Swinton and all.'

'Swinton? Why would the king send his most valuable commander on an errand like this? Surely they didn't expect it to be difficult. And taking the King's Trail? It makes no sense. No one's used that trail for decades, not since Ellest started importing Battalonian ships.'

There was a map. Bleak bit back the words. From what she'd seen of Commander Swinton and his jumpiness, the expedition wasn't just about retrieving her. *Should I tell them?*

'I know,' Henri replied, 'and it's not the first time I've had reports of that lot lurking around the Hawthornes. Arden's up to something. More than his usual political horseshit. And I'll wager *she* has something to do with it.'

'That's enough,' Bleak said.

'What did you say?' Henri stepped forward.

'That's enough.' Bleak's voice was strong, although she could feel her knees trembling. 'I won't stand in silence any longer. I'm here. Stop speaking about me as though I'm not.'

Henri glowered, but Queen Allehra nodded slowly.

'My apologies,' she said. 'Your name is Bleak?'

'*Yes.* And I've never had anything to do with any

royal plans.'

'Doesn't mean you're not part of some scheme of his,' said Henri. She turned to Allehra. 'She's a mind whisperer.'

'I see,' Allehra said. 'Do you know how many of your kind of Ashai are left in the realm, Bleak?'

Bleak shook her head. 'How could I? How could anyone? Thanks to that damn decree all the Ashai have gone underground. Henri's the first open Ashai I've met in my whole life.'

'Try to imagine, though. Bleak, there aren't many Ashai like you left at all. Long ago, people saw your kind as the biggest threat. Mind whisperers were persecuted more so than any other Ashai folk. I'd say there are less than a handful like you left. And that the king wants to use you for something.'

'My powers aren't working,' Bleak found herself admitting.

Allehra smiled. 'They are, just not on a few select Valia kindred. We have wards against such things.'

'What?'

'Wards. Talismans. Herbs. Enchantments that protect us and our minds from your kind, and all Ashai, to a certain extent.'

Although Bleak had witnessed this type of ancient magic only moments ago, she still couldn't quell her disbelief. Ashai folk were one thing – swept under the rug, their importance and influence so vehemently denied that a whole realm of people overlooked their existence. But enchantments? That kind of magic was from folklore and myths.

'Bleak, you are powerful. Inexperienced, yes, but powerful. I can feel it,' said Allehra.

'I'll take your word for it.'

'Watch your tongue,' Henri murmured from the window.

Allehra dismissed this with a wave. 'The question is not whether you are powerful, but rather, what you want to do with that power.'

'What? I want to cure it. It's what I've been trying to do my whole life – get rid of it.'

'That's not possible.'

'So I've been told.'

'Then surely the next best thing is to have some measure of control?'

Bleak shrugged, feigning indifference. *What did these people want from her?*

'Training her is too dangerous,' Henri interjected, studying Bleak again from afar.

'Me? Dangerous?'

'You are dangerous in the wrong hands, if you're trained,' said Henri, before turning to Allehra, 'which is why we shouldn't do this.'

'The girl decides.' Allehra's eyes flashed with the same steeliness mirrored in her daughter's. 'Do you want to be in control of this?' she asked Bleak.

It seemed too good to be true. To be trained to control her magic by the Valians. It wasn't a cure, but it would give Bleak her life back.

'What's in it for you?' she asked. Senior had taught her enough of the world that she knew nothing in life came for free. When things seemed too good to be true, they usually were.

Allehra smiled again. 'When the time comes, and it will, you will accompany Henri to Heathton.'

'What?' Henri said, whirling around to face her mother.

'You don't see it yet, but you'll need her. The king will want you both, and you'll need to go together.'

Henri made an exasperated sound and folded her arms across her chest.

'This training will stop the voices?' Bleak asked.

'Not stop, it will control them, block them out when you need them to be, among other things.'

'Like what?'

'We won't know until we try.'

Bleak's chest was tight with anxiety. This might be the only chance she ever got to rid herself of this cursed ability. With their help, she might have a shot at a normal life.

'Not every Ashai gets the opportunity to train with the Mother Matriarch of Valia, in case you need more incentive,' Allehra said gently.

'I'd be training with you?'

Allehra nodded.

Bleak looked down at her hands to find Senior's rope weaving through her fingers. *How long had she been doing that?* Neither Valian had mentioned it.

'What about the king?' she asked. There'd be no point in leading a normal life if it was cut short by the monarch.

'We cannot know the future, Bleak, only what we can do today,' Allehra said.

'What's your decision, Angovian?' Henri pressed. 'I don't have all night for this.'

Bleak looked from one matriarch to the other. Was there really a choice to be made?

Chapter Eleven

Dash's heart felt as though it would burst from his chest as he tried to contain his excitement. He was helping his father prepare the horses for Commander Swinton and Captain Murphadias. His father had let him lead the commander's stallion, Xander, around the corral, warming up the mount's muscles before they rode out into the chilly dawn. Dash saddled the horse as well, using the little step construction Pa had made for him, and brushed the stallion's mane until it shone. He kept glancing to the courtyard, because at any moment the famous knight's son would stride out of the castle. Maybe this time, the commander wouldn't be cross with him; he *had* helped with the horses, after all.

But as he led Xander out of the holding stall, his father took the reins from him.

'Off you go now, Dash,' he said.

'But, Pa!'

'I said you could help with the horses, but you're not to be underfoot when the commander comes. He's a busy man.'

'Pa, please, he's —'

'I know very well who he is. And I don't want you in

the way.'

Dash's heart sank. He'd worked so hard all morning, before the sun was even up, just so he could hand Commander Swinton the reins.

His father's face softened and he squeezed Dash's shoulder. 'I can't have you in here,' he said, 'but perhaps you can watch from the rafters?'

A grin spread across Dash's face. 'Really?'

'You'll have to be as quiet as a mouse, you hear?'

'Yes, Pa. I'll be even quieter!'

'That's a good lad,' said his father, as he mussed up Dash's hair. 'They're due here very soon, so you best get up there now.'

With a boost from his father, Dash climbed into the towering bales of hay, and from there, up into the rafters. Someone had laid down planks of timber so the stable workers could store additional grain, hay and equipment. Dash spotted a small window at the other end and grinned to himself; he'd be able to watch them ride out of Heathton from here.

'Morning, Carlington,' a gruff voice sounded from down below. Commander Swinton and Captain Murphadias' armour clinked as they walked into the stables. Dash could make out the famous battleaxes strapped to the commander's back.

'Commander, Captain,' Dash's father greeted the men, dipping his head.

'Early enough for you?' That must be the captain.

'I'm always up in the wee hours,' Dash's father said.

'This way.'

Dash peered down through the rafters, watching his father lead the two heavily armed men to the stallions.

'Both warmed up.' His father stroked Xander's neck. 'Captain, this is Indigo.' He gestured to the other horse. 'One of the king's finest.'

'Would have preferred my own mare,' Murphadias said, taking the reins from the stable master.

'Darcy's stride doesn't match Xander's. It's a long journey,' Swinton said.

'Too right, Commander,' his father said.

'Everything I requested is in the saddlebags?' the commander asked.

'Yes, everything on the list.'

'Good. Let's go.'

'Very good, Commander,' his father said, standing back, allowing the men to lead the stallions from the entrance of the stables and out into the courtyard.

'Carlington,' the commander called as he mounted his horse. He flicked Dash's pa a gold coin. 'For your trouble.'

Whoa. Dash's eyes bulged. *He must be pleased with the horses.*

Dash's father caught it, looking up in surprise. 'Much obliged, Commander,' he said, tucking the gold piece into his breast pocket.

The commander nodded, then pressed his heels into the horse's sides.

Dash ran to the little window, and watched

Commander Swinton and Captain Murphadias canter out of the royal courtyard. The sun was peeking above the horizon now, washing the sky with pink and orange as they passed through the gatehouse and crossed the drawbridge. They looked like the knights in Dash's favourite picture book at home, sitting high up on their steeds, the commander's axes strapped across his back, glinting in the sun. The people at the markets outside the castle grounds parted and made a path for the two warriors, leaving for yet another adventure.

After Dash had finished helping his pa muck out the rest of the stalls, he set off to meet Olena at Heathton Falls. He didn't get far. Just past the gatehouse, the squires were training, and the weapons master, Tannus, was nowhere to be seen. Dash slowed his pace, studying the footwork of the more skilled boys, who parried in the shade of the looming maze hedges.

'What you gawking at, farm boy?' called one squire. Dash recognised him as Valter, son of the nobleman Xavier Wendley. Pa often tended to Lord Wendley's horses. Dash froze as Valter came towards him.

'Where's the blind fool you're always following?'

'What did you say?' Dash said, horrified.

'You heard me.'

'She's our princess. Take it back.'

'Make me,' sneered the older boy.

A wooden sword was thrown to him out of nowhere. *Fight?* He was expected to *fight* this boy? A squire, no less. Valter had been trained in swordplay. Dash only knew what he'd studied in books and practised in the privacy of his room, or the lofts above the stables. And now? Now he'd be fighting in front of all the royal squires. His palms were clammy. But what were knights for, if not to defend their princesses? He swallowed the panic rising in his throat and adjusted his stance. *I have to try.*

Valter lunged, a sloppy attack that showed he expected Dash to fall from the first strike. But Dash was quick. He stepped aside easily, leaving Valter to stumble forward where he'd imagined he'd collide with Dash. There was laughter from the boys who had gathered around them. Valter swore at them, and launched himself at Dash again, his sword aimed viciously for Dash's neck. Even with a wooden sparring sword, Valter's intense strikes could prove fatal. This time, Dash ducked, and struck Valter's legs from below with his wooden blade. Valter yelped and glared at Dash, seething. Dash took a steady breath. He'd angered the older boy now, and he attacked as Dash expected, with strong but unmeasured blows. The noise from the squires around them faded away, and it was as though it was just the two of them. Dash could hear his opponent's laboured breathing and the scrape of his shoes in the dirt. He was a heavy boy, bulky with muscle, and a belly that had perhaps enjoyed too many noblemen's desserts. Dash parried and ducked again, thinking of his footwork as much as the swing of his sword. Valter was sweating, his face already flushed, and Dash realised in that moment that there was a chance he could beat the brute. Dash feinted left and Valter fell for it, leaving Dash to make his final lunge. In the next moment, Valter was on his back in the dirt, his sword kicked away from his reach, with Dash holding his sword to his opponent's throat.

Suddenly, the world around him came back into being, and he realised that the squires were applauding him. Some approached him and clapped him on the back. Slowly, he let himself smile. He'd just beaten one of the *royal squires* at swordplay! He'd done it. He looked around at the grinning boys and pretended he was one of them. But then, someone pushed through the group. Valter's older brother, Adalrik Wendley. A senior squire.

'Valter's horseshit at fencing,' he said. 'Maybe we should get you up against one of the real men, if you think you're so damn good. See if the stable master's little son really can fight.'

'Come now, Adalrik,' said one of the other squires, 'he's just a boy – leave him be.'

Dash looked up at him. Adalrik was old enough to have wisps of soft hair growing from his chin and above his lip, and he towered over Dash. Without warning, he thrust his sword forward, sending Dash back in a defensive leap. Dash was tired from sparring with Valter, and he doubted he'd see the same favourable result with Adalrik. The wind picked up then, sending a shiver through the leaves along the maze's hedges and a wave of goosebumps across Dash's arms. A *true knight* would never back away from a rival, no matter how much bigger or stronger he was. Dash eyed his opponent, changed sword hands and stood with his feet apart. He *could* do this, he just needed to be smart about it.

Adalrik didn't wait; he struck out. Dash blocked, the impact of the blow singing through his wooden blade and up his arm. Dash used his slightness to his advantage, forcing his opponent to advance on him, leaving him to expose himself to Dash's lightning-fast blows. Dash struck Adalrik's side, and the older boy cursed, realising what Dash was doing. Adalrik changed his style of attack, forcing Dash backwards until he was almost at the entrance of the maze. Dash matched Adalrik strike for strike, but couldn't help glancing nervously behind him at the towering hedges and forking pathways.

'So you know a bit about swinging a stick,' Adalrik said, taking a step back. 'But I'll bet you three silver pieces you'd get lost in the maze and your peasant father would have to rescue you.'

Dash's heart sank, and he watched as the faces of the squires around them became eager, even the boy who had stood up for him. He looked down at his practice sword. He couldn't keep Adalrik's strength at bay for much longer, and now, a new challenge had been made. Could he retrieve the famous red flowers? His ma and pa had no silver to spare, let alone three pieces' worth. And Dash knew that the gold coin from Commander Swinton this morning was going straight to the smithy to pay Pa's debts. But if he walked away now, he'd never get another shot with the squires. *It's now or never*, he told himself, as he drove his sword tip into the soft earth at his feet.

Without a word, he turned and walked deep into the maze.

Inside, it was different. Smooth white pebbles crunched beneath his feet. But after a few minutes of walking, it was clear to Dash that only the first few metres into the maze were maintained for appearances. Beyond the first twisting pathways, the hedges became thick and overgrown, encroaching onto the footpath, and above him, they closed over, blocking out the sky in magnificent, unmanicured arches. Dash knew he should be marking his movements somehow for the way back, but he was already disorientated. The further into the maze he walked, the more he realised what a huge mistake he had made. *Three whole silvers.* He'd get a flogging for this, and the squires would tease him mercilessly, forever. As he worried, he turned left and then right, with no idea where he was going or what he was hoping to come across. On either side of him, the hedges quivered in the cool breeze, their dark leaves rustling. The maze was dark and chilly, despite it being near noon outside. Dash folded his arms across his chest, trying to keep his body heat in. He could no longer see the sky. The sunlight filtered in through the dense hedges in thin streams, leaving the pathways before Dash dim and daunting.

Will they ever find me in here? He felt the panic rising in his chest, and he had to fight to steady his breathing. He continued to put one foot in front of the other, slowly, cautiously. The paths before him were narrowing, and splitting off into more and more walkways. Soon, the hedges on either side of him were brushing against his shoulders as he ventured deeper still. The maze had well and truly swallowed him.

Dash didn't know how long he'd been walking, but his legs felt like lead, and unease had settled, a permanent stone in the pit of his stomach. A continuous, gentle wind blew through the passageways, sending loose, dead leaves rushing across the white pebble path, which split into two. Dash rubbed his eyes. All these forks in the path looked the same.

He stopped – he had heard something. A whisper. He scrambled, backing into the hedge, wishing he had brought the wooden practice sword with him. The whisper sounded again. One word.

What is it saying? Dash strained to hear, even though the voice seemed to sound as though it was coming from all around. It was in his ear, and far away at the same time.

Oremere.

Dash's breaths came fast and shallow, and his palms were clammy as he clamped them over his mouth, trying to smother the terrified noises escaping him.

'Who ... Who's there?' he managed.

Oremere. The voice sounded again. And this time, Dash felt movement by his boots. He jumped, shrinking further back into the hedge. He gasped. Green shoots rose up from in between the white pebbles, unfurling from themselves, heart-shaped leaves growing slowly from their sides. The dark buds at their apex flowered, and red velvety petals opened up to reveal a black centre that seemed to hold Dash's stare with one unblinking eye.

Magic? There wasn't supposed to be magic like this left in Ellest. He straightened himself, and the flowers continued to sprout and blossom, their growth spreading across the white pebbles and inching towards a fork in the path. Mesmerised, Dash found himself following. The flowers, as though they had a mind of their own, waited until he had caught up before they continued down the left passageway. Dash was no longer scared. He knew he was nearly at the heart of the maze; he could feel it somehow. The flowers bloomed faster, and Dash had to jog to keep up with the trail they were leaving him. The twists and turns were dizzying. He turned corner after corner, each hedge looking the same as the last, the wind still sending shivers across the stretches of deep green. The narrow path opened up abruptly. Thousands upon thousands of red blooms greeted Dash. They covered every surface at the heart of the maze. What once may have been stone garden furniture and statues, similar to those outside the maze, had been taken over by the vibrant blooms, with only glimpses of pale-grey stone to be seen beneath petals and greenery.

What is this place? Dash thought, utterly perplexed. He walked to the centre of the space. *A stone water fountain, that's what this once was*, he realised, taking in the height of the structure and the way its base, even covered in flowers, looked like a giant goblet. He ran his fingers along the ledge; the petals and stems were like silk against his skin, or at least what he imagined silk would feel like. But at his touch, the flowers shrank back. Dash frowned, and then plucked one from the mass before him.

Around him, the rest of the flowers vanished, leaving him in an old, empty water garden. The benches were similar to the ones on which he and Olena often sat in the gardens. The fountain was dry, but with the flowers gone, Dash could now see the statue of a woman at its centre. Her face was chiselled to perfection, with hundreds of freckles covering her smooth stone skin. Long, luxurious scarves covered her head and flowed down onto her gown, which in turn flowed into what would have once been the fountain's water. She was magnificent, probably one of the goddesses Dash had forgotten.

The flower in his hand pulsed gently, and somehow, he knew it was time to go. Something on the outside called to him. Dazed, he let himself be pulled along, the force he followed invisible. He wasn't cold on the way back, nor did the maze seem so daunting and untamed. He was calm.

I did it. He clutched the single red flower tightly.

When he emerged from the maze, the courtyard was quiet, and the wooden practice sword stood proudly in the soft earth, as though it had awaited his return.

Chapter Twelve

Soft, gold light filled Tilly's lodgings, and Bleak gaped at the jars filled with glowing beetles that lined the windowsills and shelves.

'Valo beetles,' Tilly said, dropping her pack by the door and rubbing her shoulder. Tilly had offered to share her apartments with Bleak while she adjusted to 'the Valian Way', whatever that meant. Bleak still had no idea how long she'd be here, and although she would have preferred to stay with Athene, Tilly seemed nice enough. Plus, Bleak was just happy to be off the road for a while. The seemingly endless travel in confined spaces had taken its toll on her; she was exhausted.

She marvelled at the space before her. The thick branch of a tree had grown through one window and out the other, and Tilly apparently used it as a place to hang her spare leathers and weapons. The apartment was striking in its simplicity, drawing inspiration in a practical sense from the nature that surrounded it. Tilly moved to the counter that lined one side of the room, and took two goblets from the shelf above.

'Feel free to look around,' she said. 'Probably the first time you've seen a place like this, right?'

Bleak nodded, and found herself walking to one of the doorways.

'Bedroom,' Tilly's voice followed her. Inside was a large mattress in the centre of the room, sitting on a frame that had been designed to look like it was floating just above the floor. A small set of drawers in the same style sat on either side of the bed, all made from the same timber as the entire apartment.

'I like it,' Bleak called back.

Tilly laughed from the doorframe and offered her a goblet. 'There's not much to it, and I don't spend a lot of time here, but it's still home.'

Bleak was hardly listening as her fingers closed around the stem of the goblet, the aroma of the wine inside it hitting her nostrils. Saliva filled her mouth as she brought the cup up to her lips. Gods, it had been forever since she'd had a real drink. The first sip, the moment the rich crimson liquid spilt across her tongue, was momentous. It took all her willpower not to guzzle the whole goblet then and there.

'This is ...' she started.

'Good, right? Valian wine is revered all around the realm – sweet but not overpowering.'

'Hmm.' Bleak took another gulp, closing her eyes. The flavour was incredible: smooth, rich and vibrant. She remembered herself. 'Thank you,' she said.

Tilly shrugged. 'There's plenty of it to go round.'

'No, not just for the wine – for letting me stay with you.'

'Oh, it's nothing. Don't mention it. I'll set the bedroll up in the spare room.'

'Thanks.'

Tilly led her to the other room. It was much the same as the bedroom but with a desk and bookshelf instead, though there weren't any books. On the shelves sat dozens of carved wooden creatures. Bleak took one in her hand. It was ... Well, she didn't know what it was – some kind of large, predatory cat, like in the children's bedtime tales.

'A teerah panther,' Tilly said, taking the figurine from Bleak and examining it herself. 'It's something of a hobby of mine, carving these mythical animals.' She reached for another piece, a serpent. 'When I want to forget about training and Valian politics, I make these for the children out in the Sticks.'

'They're good,' said Bleak, taking in the various forms on the shelves.

Tilly shrugged and placed the two she held back in their places. She gestured around the room.

'This was designed to be a study of sorts, but as you can no doubt tell, I'm not really one for academics. Anyway, the elite kindred all live in this section of apartments. You'll find a washroom and a number of privies down the end of the south-east path. Though, most of the kindred prefer to bathe down at the Stream of Rheyah, where the water's always fresh.'

She retrieved a bedroll from the cupboard and unhooked the tie around it; the mattress sprang free. It was the most luxurious bedroll Bleak had ever seen.

'Blankets are in here.' Tilly pointed to the cupboard. 'Help yourself to the wine and anything in the kitchen. You'll find we Valians have a very communal way of life. As for the lights, when you want them out, tap the top of each jar – the beetles respond to vibrations.'

'Thank you.'

Tilly nodded. 'First meal's at dawn.'

The warrior left Bleak standing before the shelf of wooden creatures, her goblet now empty. As soon as she heard Tilly's bedroom door close, she headed back out to the kitchen and filled her cup. After another full goblet, she conceded defeat and swiped the bottle from the counter, taking it back to her room. *There's plenty,* Tilly had said.

Bleak undressed, untying Fiore's dagger from her calf and placing it beside the bedroll. She rubbed the back of her neck and looked around the room. The past few days felt surreal. She still couldn't quite believe where she was and how she'd got here. Her knees cracked as she sat down on the bedroll, lifting the bottle to her lips and downing the wine. She thought about Bren. *Where is he? What's he doing?* She wished she'd stayed out on the wharf with him longer. If she had known it was their last night together, she might have done things differently.

Hours later, she was still thinking of him when she passed out, naked on the bedroll.

Bleak woke to the sun warming her face, and for a

moment, she thought she was back in Angove, waking up in the sand. Her head spun as she sat up and knocked over an empty bottle. At her feet were three more empty bottles, the goblet lying discarded on the other side of the room. Her face flushed in shame. Stifling a moan, she scooped up the bottles and hid them in the back of the cupboard behind the linens, hoping Tilly wouldn't notice the missing wine in the kitchen. She tugged on her clothes, her head feeling foggy, her stomach queasy. In that sense, life felt like it normally did, with a hangover keeping her company.

Tilly had already left. Bleak managed to find her way down to the camp below, and swiped a slice of toast from one of the buffets.

'Bleak,' Athene called, buckling her sword belt around her waist. 'I want you to meet my daughter, Luka.'

Athene pushed forward a young girl, around sixteen years of age, with the same fiery-red hair as her mother. In fact, Luka was the spitting image of Athene except for the height. Luka was short, and her arms and legs were corded with thick muscle, whereas her mother remained tall and lean. Perhaps Luka hadn't finished growing yet, or perhaps her father had been of smaller stature. The girl grinned and gripped Bleak's hand in an enthusiastic shake.

'Nice to meet you, Bleak, I've heard a bit about you.'

'Hi, nice to meet you, too.'

'My mother said you might want some showing around?'

'Uh, yeah, that'd be great, if you've got the time.'

'Sure. I've got training this afternoon, but I can spare an hour or so now?'

Bleak shrugged and bit into her second piece of toast. Athene and Luka embraced, looking more like sisters than mother and daughter to Bleak, before Athene left, looking as though she were going off to battle.

'Is everything okay?' Bleak asked Luka, watching Athene stride off, weapons swinging.

'Oh sure. The elite kindred just take their training very seriously.'

'She's just going off to train?'

'Yep, nothing to worry about. Come on. I'll give you the grand tour.'

Luka strode through the forest like she owned it, waving her hand casually towards the main residences and the training grounds of Valia, greeting everyone she passed by name. Clearly, being the daughter of the kindred's first-in-command had its perks. Bleak contained her shock as they took to the treetops and passed children as young as six wielding weapons against one another in the training circuits. Bleak tried to ignore the angry shouts of the instructors, but she couldn't help wincing at the slap of the hard blows finding their mark. There was no crying, no complaining. Those who were struck down either got back up, or they didn't.

'Luka,' Marvel called out from the ground below. 'Mother Matriarch wants to speak to the Angovian. You're due at her quarters in ten minutes.'

'Ten minutes,' Luka breathed, looking apprehensive. 'Hope you can run, Angovian.'

Bleak's chest burned as she tried to keep up with the young Valian darting through the trees. By the time they reached the Mother Matriarch's tree, Bleak needed to vomit.

Luka slapped her heartily on the back as she threw up into the dirt. 'Eight minutes. Not bad,' she said, grinning. 'Can't say you look fresh, though.'

Allehra was waiting for them at the foot of her tree. Bleak didn't trust herself to bow, so she nodded as best she could.

'She's a bit outta shape,' Luka explained as she bowed low.

'Thank you, Luka,' Allehra said. 'I believe you have training to get to?'

Luka bowed again and left them. Bleak tried to catch her breath before looking at Allehra.

'Are you alright?' Mother Matriarch asked.

Bleak nodded. 'Should be fine in a sec.'

'Take your time.' Allehra sat down on a moss-covered bench by the door of her quarters.

Bleak shifted from foot to foot, unsure of what was expected of her, oblivious to any protocols that needed to be followed when it came to a queen of Valia.

'Please,' said Allehra, 'sit.'

Bleak did as she was told, and took her place beside the Mother Matriarch.

'How do you like it here?' Allehra asked, smoothing

out the skirts of another flowing gown.

'It's nice.'

'Nice?'

'Yeah. Nice.'

Allehra looked amused. 'And you settled into Tilly's apartments well, then?'

'Yes, thanks.'

'Good, I'm glad to hear it. Now, I wanted to talk to you about your training.'

'What about it?'

'We should start today.'

'Today?' Bleak tried to tame her fidgeting hands.

'Yes. We are working with borrowed time. The sooner the better, I believe.'

'Alright. What sort of things will we be doing?'

'Leave it with me,' Allehra said.

Sweat stung Bleak's eyes as Queen Allehra circled her, training spear in hand. The two of them stood at ground level, in the centre of a mossy clearing, with Henri's elite kindred looking on from the outskirts, trying to appear disinterested.

'Use it, use your power. Pre-empt my strike,' the queen commanded.

Allehra had removed a leather pouch from around her neck before they started sparring. She had told Bleak that it contained powerful Valian herbs to protect her mind from being breached; Henri and her personal kindred wore them as well. They grew the herbs themselves in the forest, though where exactly seemed to be a secret kept tight-lipped.

'I'm *trying*.' Bleak ground her teeth. While the queen's mind was indeed open to her, her thoughts raced so quickly they were impossible to distinguish. It was as though there were a hundred voices buzzing from the Mother Matriarch.

'Not hard enough.' The queen's spear struck her legs out from underneath her, and Bleak landed hard on her backside.

'Again,' the queen said.

'Your mind,' Bleak panted, 'your mind is going too fast.' She adjusted her grip on her own spear, and blocked one and only one of the queen's blows. The queen, in her sixties at least, hadn't even broken a sweat.

'You have to find something to centre yourself, something to block out all the other noise, and *use your gift*. It's a natural instinct.'

'Not for me,' Bleak said, hitting away the queen's spear before it landed on her shoulder. A drink. A drink would make this so much more bearable, especially since even though she couldn't see Henri, Bleak could feel her watching. Always watching. She tried going on the attack, but the queen moved like water, dipping and arching effortlessly. Bleak went at her with all her strength and speed, jabbing the spear at Allehra, frustrated. The queen knocked the blows aside as though they were struck by a child brandishing a twig. Finally, Allehra's face softened and she lowered her spear. 'Perhaps we're going about this the wrong way.'

'You don't say.'

The kindred around the clearing tensed at her terse remark. It was rude of her. She shouldn't have said it, and with everything Allehra was trying to do for her …

The queen smiled, however, waving the kindred away and leaning both spears against a nearby tree.

'Come with me,' she said, beckoning Bleak to follow. 'Your services are not required,' she told the kindred guards.

Athene started after them. 'Allehra, Your Majesty, please. At least allow me —'

'Your services are not required,' the queen repeated, and pulled Bleak into the depths of the forest after her.

They walked downhill, Bleak slipping on loose rocks despite the leather boots she'd been given. After a time, they came upon a small creek and walked alongside it. The queen had put the leather pouch back around her neck, and so all was quiet but for the running water beside them. Bleak turned to the queen.

'You really trust me that much,' she asked, 'that you don't need your guards?'

The queen laughed. 'I have a guard, child.' She flicked her hand casually at the creek beside them, and Bleak frowned.

'Look closer.'

Bleak squinted at the water, ignoring her own grubby reflection. Above her, the sunlight streamed through the canopy. And then she saw her. Perched on a branch, amidst the leaves directly above them, was Henri.

'She would be on you before you could blink,' the queen said, not unkindly, 'but for what it's worth, I do trust you. There's something about you.'

'Is it because you think I'm ... a mist dweller?'

The queen shook her head. 'No,' and offered no more than that. Bleak was yet to have a chance to question the queen on that term. Every time she heard or said it to herself, a shiver of unease flooded through her. She tried to push it from her mind – now was not the time. As they continued to follow the stream through the forest, Bleak watched Henri's reflection in the water. Besides their hair, the way they moved was the first real similarity she'd seen between the two queens. Mother and daughter moved with a fluidity Bleak had never seen before. Perhaps all the kindred moved like that if they'd been training from such a young age.

'We need you to get a handle on your magic well before you go to the capital,' Allehra was saying.

'Just what do you think I'm going to be able to do to help Henri? She doesn't need me,' said Bleak, glancing back up at the canopy.

'No, but she will be summoned because of you. Do not disrespect the risk she took for you.'

Bleak nodded. 'I'm sorry.' The words felt strange in her mouth. It had been a long time since she had uttered them to someone.

'Don't be sorry, just try harder. You can do this.'

They came to a small pool at the end of the stream.

The water was so clear it looked like glass, and the flowers around it seemed even more vibrant than the rest of the forest. The queen sat down beside it, her flowing skirts billowing out beneath her.

'I knew someone who used to like coming here, to think,' she said.

Bleak sat down beside her. 'Who?'

The queen shook her head, and lifted the pouch from around her neck over her head. She placed it carefully on the emerald-green grass, and then ran her fingers through the water.

'Use your magic,' she said. 'The answers you want so desperately are all up here.' She tapped her temple with her wet fingers. 'Take your time.'

The buzzing voices started immediately; Bleak could only identify single words out of context. It was like a swarm of Allehra's thoughts circling her, disorientating her, making her head pound. She took a deep breath. If Bleak could get a handle on this, she could only imagine what she might discover. The most powerful ruler of Valia was opening her mind up to her, willingly, with no distractions. Bleak closed her eyes and focused. She realised that all the voices were Allehra's at different ages, from different points in her life, experiencing different moods, different emotions. Usually, Bleak could hone in on a core thought in the present, but not with Allehra. Bleak opened her eyes; Allehra was sitting incredibly still, staring into the pool before them. Wisps of silver-and-midnight hair danced in the breeze, but she made no move to brush them from her eyes. Bleak repositioned herself, crossing her legs underneath her and turning to face the queen front-on. She refocused. Her instincts were telling her to dig, no – *sift*. She needed to *sift* through the Mother Matriarch's thoughts; she needed to acknowledge each thought and go from there. She repeated this process. Each time, it was as though there was one less voice in the crammed space that was Allehra's mind. One by one, she sifted through what felt like decades' worth of thoughts, quieting the younger selves, brushing away the everyday observations until there was but one word shimmering before Bleak's eyes.

'Sahara,' she breathed.

The queen smiled sadly and turned to face her.

'That's enough,' Henri's sharp voice said as she landed softly on the ground beside them.

'Henr—'

'No. You've already said too much.'

Bleak hid her surprise as Queen Allehra bowed her head.

'Today's lessons are over,' Henri said, without looking at Bleak. Bleak waited for Allehra to object. She didn't. She looked from mother to daughter, neither saying a word. Bleak didn't need telling twice. She got to her feet and began to follow the creek back up towards the keep. Henri rounded on Queen Allehra well before Bleak was out of earshot.

'You think she'll have answers for you?' Henri yelled. 'Sahara is *dead*. And she died long before she walked out into that mist.'

Bleak quickened her pace. The last thing she needed was Henri catching her eavesdropping and throwing her out of Valia before her training had barely begun. Plus, she had a date with a flask or two of Valian wine. Mind whispering was thirsty work.

Later that night, Bleak sat with Luka by the fire as a wild boar roasted on the spit, and thought about her lessons with Allehra. *Sahara.* Who was she? Why did she have such a hold on both Valian matriarchs? Henri hadn't looked in Bleak's direction since. And Allehra. Allehra had locked herself in her tower. If Bleak continued to train with Allehra, she may get the full story yet. There were many secrets here, and Bleak was a naturally curious person, among other things. She was so busy analysing the events of the afternoon that she started when someone pressed a goblet into her hands. Wine. She could smell its fruity, smoky aroma, the same as the night before. She cupped the goblet like she would a new lover's face, greedy with anticipation. She tried to look casual as she raised it to her lips. She stifled a moan of pleasure, of relief. Tension drained from her whole body. She savoured the first mouthful, swirling it around with her tongue, but as soon as she had done that, she drained the goblet. She needed more.

'Thirsty?' Luka said, smiling.

Bleak shrugged. 'It's been a long couple of days.'

'I'll drink to that.' Luka raised her glass and threw

Bleak the wineskin.

Somewhere around her fourth goblet, the wild boar was carved and dished out generously. Bleak ate with her hands, having tasted nothing so good in years. Wine and wild boar went well together. It felt like it had been a long time since Bleak had had a belly full of food. She sloshed more wine into her goblet, filling it to the brim, slurping and then filling it once more. Gods, it was good. She was beginning to feel like herself again. So what if she was in the Valia Forest and the queens of Valia were at each other's throats because of her? No one *here* hated magic. She twirled the dagger she'd stolen from Captain Fiore between her fingers as she mulled over things. The last week of her life had felt so out of control. Horseback riding, attacks, training. She missed the sway of the sea, the waves spilling across the decks, the pull of the wheel beneath her hands. But she felt different here, like she finally had something to give, if only she could figure it out.

There was a shout, and a man's voice swore. Athene and Tilly emerged from the trees; Athene was holding a knife to a man's exposed throat, while Tilly steadied a white horse by its bridle.

'What is this?' Henri demanded from the other side of the fire.

'We found him wandering through the Sticks. Says he's trying to find you,' Tilly said, nodding to Bleak. Bleak focused on the person panting between the two women. Sun-streaked hair was swept back into a short ponytail;

a white shirt gaped half-open at the front, revealing a broad, tanned chest covered in fair hair. The man edged his throat away from the knife, and grunted as Athene dug her knee into his back, forcing him to the ground. Bleak stood slowly, her world spinning, dropping Fiore's dagger to the forest floor. She took two steps forward.

'Bren ...?'

Chapter Thirteen

Henri watched Athene bury her fist in the man's stomach in a sharp, upper-cut blow. He doubled over, wheezing. She gave Athene a nod, and her first-in-command hit him again, this time in the soft part just between his lower ribs. Across the fire, Bleak swayed as she spoke the man's name.

'Bren ...' She rushed forward to him. 'Don't hurt him!' she begged, gripping Athene's arm.

Athene looked to Henri.

'Take him to the pits,' Henri said, turning back to her plate. She'd had enough drama for one day. Whoever this man was, he could wait.

'No!' Bleak said, holding onto the man's arm.

'They're just underground holding cells,' Athene said, trying to peel Bleak's hands away.

Henri shot her a sharp look. She'd had enough of Athene's sympathies. Athene didn't meet her eye.

'Take her with him,' Henri said, thrusting her chin in Bleak's direction.

'What?'

'You heard me.'

Athene hesitated, and for a moment Henri longed

for the challenge. If she had to put Athene in her place, she would. It seemed like it'd been too long since her little sparring match with Commander Swinton and she could feel the restlessness building up in her muscles, along with the need to be slicing her katars. But Athene nodded to Marvel and Petra, and they took Bleak by the arms, albeit gently, and followed Tilly and Athene away from the fire, towards the pits.

'What are you doing?' Bleak yelled. 'We haven't done anything wrong! I'm supposed to be a *guest* here —'

Henri rolled her eyes, cursing the moment she'd decided to save the orphan girl. *Nothing but trouble.* And now she had to deal with another Angovian as well? *How did he find them?* It had been years since an outsider had breached their keep. Henri shook her head and called for ale. One of the younger kindred rushed to her side with an overflowing mug of amber liquid.

While Henri's elite kindred attended the Angovian youngsters, Henri watched the rest of her people. Athene's daughter, Luka, was surrounded by other trainees, waving her hands wildly as she told a tale. The others listened, utterly rapt in the story, loud bursts of laughter exploding from them. Henri envied them and their friendships. She'd never been able to have that; she had always needed to keep her distance, to draw the line somewhere. She was Matriarch of Valia first, friend second, which meant there was a limit to how deep her friendships could run. Luka caught her eye and smiled cautiously. Henri wanted to return it, but as always, something stopped her. She got to her feet and left them. She needed to be alone.

Henri took to the canopies again, slipping away from the crowd, and crossed the bridges to the outskirts of the forest, past the Sticks. Years ago, she'd had a training circuit built for only her and her finest elite kindred. Formal intensive Valian training was officially complete after the age of twenty, because most kindred had duties that kept them fit anyway, but Henri continued to train. She hated the idea of not being at her best, and relished putting her body to bed tired and aching.

Straw boxing dummies, weights and bars welcomed her as she stepped out onto the platform among the treetops. She unsheathed her katars and unstrapped her daggers and trinity stars, placing them on the bench beside the dummy. First, she did some breathing exercises. She inhaled deeply through her nose, feeling her lungs expand, and then exhaled through her mouth. She did this several times, attempting to calm the questions and objections that had hounded her mind during the day. Even though she was training alone, it was never wise to go into a fight with a heavy mind. She stretched, revelling in the pull of her muscles, in her own limberness. Then she turned to the dummy and unleashed hell upon it. Each blow had the precision of a knife, slicing through the air and finding its mark – clean and direct. She always made sure she was just as strong from her left as she was from her right, which meant putting her left side through several more sets.

She worked her legs, striking the dummy in the head time and time again. She didn't sweat – this wasn't an effort for her.

Mist dweller. Henri had only heard the term once or twice before. After Bleak had left her and Allehra earlier that day, Henri had demanded that Allehra explain it to her. As always, her mother had been infuriatingly cryptic, and Henri had walked away still not fully understanding the term. She recalled the stories of the invasion that had happened forty years ago – when mist dwellers had set foot in the capital somehow. There had been a supposed battle between them and the King's Army. It was the battle that had seen Caleb Swinton knighted for saving the king. The legend of Sir Caleb's knighthood claimed that the mist dwellers were vicious creatures, not people, covered in strange, dark markings. *Surely not?* Henri pictured the malnourished Angovian girl she'd just sent to the pits. What was the danger in her? She could hardly walk straight, let alone threaten anyone.

Henri had no doubt that these 'mist dwellers' existed, whatever they were. But how did they survive it? The mist was deadly, so what made these ... *people* immune to whatever toxins settled upon the skin? Though Allehra had stated the term calmly (not that Allehra was prone to panic), she had not explained herself. Surely the reigning Queen of Valia was owed an explanation when a mythical force was suddenly in her keep?

Henri put her legs through several more sets of drills

and pondered on the revelation further. Fine. Allehra could keep her secrets, as was her habit, so long as it didn't come back to bite them later. She bristled. So much for clearing her thoughts. The dummy was in shreds, its straw stuffing poking out at all angles and its base nearly unhinged from the spring.

Henri moved onto the weights, curling them up towards her body and then down again. As she worked her arms, she focused on her katars on the bench. The one thing she hadn't yet mastered was using her abilities without her hands. She knew it was possible, as Allehra and the matriarchs before her had been able to do so, but so far, she'd failed. She kept her hands busy, but focused on the weapons. All she wanted to do was lift one into the air and place it back down on the bench. Not a large task at all.

Nothing happened.

Henri heard the bridge groan behind her. Dropping her weights, she flung her hand towards the katar and sent it flying. There was a soft thud as it embedded itself into the tree, next to Athene's head. Athene didn't even flinch.

'One day, that'll find its way into someone you care about,' she said.

'What are you doing here?' she said.

Athene shrugged, setting herself under a set of weights. 'Same as you.'

'I doubt that,' said Henri.

But Athene was already on her back, lifting the

heavy weights. And so for a time, Henri pretended that she wasn't there. Henri came here to enjoy her own company, to absorb the rare silence. She focused on the other katar, willing it to lift into the air, just a fraction. Nothing. It didn't budge. Was she missing something? Had Allehra left out some key instruction? Henri felt Athene's eyes on her.

'Yes?' she said.

'I didn't say anything.'

'You know I hate that. You'll say it eventually. Don't run me ragged trying to get it out of you.'

Athene sighed. 'Why don't you like her?'

'Her?'

'Bleak.'

'I don't *not* like her.'

'You just sent her to the pits.'

'She was interfering with a prisoner.'

'He was obviously a friend of hers. Can you blame her?'

'I can blame *you*. Why are you questioning every command of mine?'

'Command?'

'Yes, Athene, *command*. You are the leader of my kindred, but you answer to me.'

Athene's shoulders dropped and she shook her head.

'What?' Henri said, perhaps a little too sharply.

'It's just ...'

Henri waited, despite her patience being at breaking point. They'd shirked this issue for far too long. Perhaps it was time everything bubbled to the surface. Athene got up from the weights bench and moved towards her, hands outstretched.

'Don't,' Henri said, taking a step back.

Athene took another step forward, and brushed a hand down the side of Henri's face.

'Henri,' she said, her voice softer.

'No.'

Athene took another step forward, resting her forehead against Henri's.

'You ask too much, Athene.'

'Henri, please, this is *me*. You ... You can trust me. You can let me in.'

Henri's stomach swooped. She could feel Athene's breath on her face, her mouth just inches away.

'I told you,' Henri said, stepping back, 'I can't do this.'

'*This?* You've already done *this*! What do you think will change?'

Henri glared at her. 'Everything,' she said. 'It's already changed.'

Bleak had made her see it. It was Bleak's arrival that had shown Athene's true colours. She would stand by Henri through anything, unless that something was part of her maternal instincts. She was loyal to Henri, but what had happened between them had shifted their dynamic, their roles and power. Henri couldn't have that. There was no room for questions, not in her kindred.

'I'm sorry.' Athene clasped Henri's hands in her own. 'I'm sorry, alright? It won't happen again.'

Athene held Henri's hands tight to her chest, and Henri could feel Athene's heart throbbing beneath them. But it wasn't enough.

'You're right,' she said, 'it won't.'

Athene baulked.

'Touch me again, Athene, and you'll regret it.'

'How can you say that?'

'Easily.'

'What ... What happened to you, Henri?'

Henri had had enough.

'We're done here.' She took her weapons from the bench, sheathed and strapped them into place, and strode away from the training area, leaving Athene blinking back tears.

Back in her apartments, Henri paced. It wasn't as though having relations with other women was forbidden. The kindred were famously open-minded. And even though her stomach dipped whenever she thought about her snatched moments with Athene, Henri wasn't sure what she wanted.

Unable to sleep, Henri made her way back down to the forest floor and soon found herself at the entrance to the pits. The guards stepped aside for her without a word, and she followed the dark, narrow stairs down into the underground. She took a torch from the wall and walked past a row of empty cells. For the most part, she was against prisoners. They required care and maintenance and they used up resources and supplies, all the while contributing nothing to the community. She also just hated the idea of people rotting away. But sometimes, exceptions were to be made. Even if they weren't long-term solutions.

'Henri!' Bleak's voice sounded from the end of the row, the bars of the iron cage rattling.

Henri took her time reaching the end of the cells, and when she got to Bleak's, she sat down on the bench opposite and unsheathed her katars, not even looking up.

'Henri, please – can you let us out of here? We'll be no trouble.'

Henri let out a cold laugh. 'You've been nothing but a pain in my side since we saved you.'

'I haven't meant to be,' Bleak said.

Henri busied herself by sharpening her katar on the guards' whetstone. 'Who is your friend?' she asked, still not looking up.

'His name is Bren Clayton. We worked the Heathton fishing route together.'

'Pleased to meet ya,' the man muttered.

Henri looked up, spotting him resting his tanned face against the bars of the cell, watching her.

'And what, exactly, is *Bren Clayton* doing in Valia Forest?'

'I was looking for Bleak,' he said. 'The king's men who took her, they didn't seem like, uh ... honourable sorts of fellows, ya see.'

'And you planned on taking them out yourself?'

'Hadn't planned anything, to be honest. Just knew I couldn't leave her out there with 'em.'

'She wasn't with them for long. You knew we had her.'

'Well, I heard the commotion from halfway down the mountain, but by the time I got there, I guess ya could say I stumbled upon a pretty sad bunch.'

'And?'

'One of the guards recognised me from Angove. Told me the Valia kindred had taken Bleak.'

'You followed us. How?'

'I just did.'

'I asked you *how*.'

'Horseback, across the forest floor. I knew enough to head south-west, and I barely rested. Every now and then I'd hear something that let me know I was on the right track. I dunno, really.'

'What did you hear?' It was impossible to track Valian kindred through the forest. The thought of this bumbling fisherman finding them made Henri uneasy.

Bren shrugged. 'I thought I could hear Bleak. Every time I started to doubt where I was going, I could have sworn I heard her.'

'What exactly?'

'Snippets of conversation, nothing of note.'

Henri clicked her tongue. What was going on? Even if it was possible that he'd heard them, which it wasn't, he'd been days behind them.

'You followed no map? No one led you here?'

'No. Just me and the horse. We rode hard. I followed what I thought was Bleak's voice.'

'Why?'

Bren looked at Bleak. 'I'm all she's got.'

'I didn't *need you* to *rescue* me,' Bleak snapped. 'Look where that's got us.'

Bren rested his face against the bars. 'Did I say ya needed me?'

Henri studied the man. Young. Definitely younger than her, but apparently patient.

'You've got training with Allehra at dawn,' Henri said to Bleak, getting to her feet.

'You're not going to let us out?'

'Why would I do that?'

'Because we haven't *done anything wrong*?' Bleak gripped the bars and was suddenly close enough that Henri could smell the stale wine on her breath.

'You got between my orders and my kindred. That's reason enough.'

Henri held her katars to the torchlight and inspected their edges, testing them with her fingertip. Yes, they were definitely sharp enough.

'Tomorrow, then,' she said, and took the stairs out of the pits, back out into the moonlight.

Chapter Fourteen

The muffled sounds of laughter and plates being scraped from above told Bleak it was morning. The pits had no windows and prevented prisoners from keeping track of time. The cells and passageways were as dim and dank as they had been the night before. Beside her, Bren was still sleeping soundly on his bed of straw. His shirt had risen up during the night, exposing the dark tattoo that ran down the length of his spine. Seven waves cresting, one for each of his brothers, two with additional markings signifying the passing of the two eldest, Willem and Tobias. Bren wore his grief with more grace than anyone she knew. She suppressed the urge to run her fingers down the markings, which all eight brothers had shared. A stab of pity jolted her. Bren ... The third son had taken on so much after Willem and Tobias. Five younger boys to help feed and raise, and Bleak had only added to that burden. She watched him sleep and tried to keep her guilt at bay. Senior had always said guilt was a wasted emotion. She took her length of rope from her pocket and began her ritual of knots.

It felt like an age since she'd been out at sea, and even longer still since she'd gone with Bren. He was the only Clayton who'd chosen the life of a fisherman; the rest preferred firm, dry land beneath their boots. Mrs Clayton preferred it that way, too. Bren shifted in his sleep, and Bleak returned to looping her rope between her fingers. He'd been good to her; he'd *always* been good to her.

The sound of footsteps on the stairs forced Bleak to her feet, and she peered through the bars of their cell. Tilly and Petra strode towards her, with Tilly cheerfully swinging a set of keys in her hand.

'You know, if you hated my apartment so much, you could have just said so,' she teased, unlocking the door. It swung open with a loud screech. Bren didn't move. Bleak hesitated.

'You've got an appointment,' Petra said, motioning Bleak forward.

She paused in the cell's doorway. 'What about him?' She nodded to Bren.

'Don't worry, we'll find something for him to do.'

'Like what?'

'Lots of things. Target practice comes to mind,' Petra said.

'Stud service, too.' Tilly winked.

Bleak unpinned her cloak from around her shoulders and quickly draped it over her friend. He'd be asleep for a good while longer anyway, and so without arguing with the kindred, she walked out into the blinding daylight and the fresh dawn air.

'How was your night in the pits?' said Queen Allehra, waiting for her by the unlit campfire.

'Fine. Athene was right – not as bad as it sounds.'

'Athene would know.'

'What do you mean?'

The queen shook her head and began to walk the same damp path as the day before. Bleak didn't press her. When they got to the clear pool, Luka was waiting for them. She bowed deeply to Queen Allehra and greeted Bleak with a grin.

'I thought it would be best if Luka assisted us today,' Allehra said.

Bleak wondered what else Henri had said to Allehra yesterday, and what she was so afraid of Bleak discovering.

'So,' Luka said, unsheathing two daggers at her sides, 'are we training?'

Allehra laughed. 'We had a different kind of training in mind.'

Luka's brows furrowed. 'Oh.'

Bleak held in a sigh of relief as the young warrior sheathed her daggers. There was no way in hell she'd do combat training, let alone with Luka.

'We're working on Bleak's control of her Ashai powers,' Allehra said.

'Right. I heard a rumour you were an Ashai.'

Bleak smiled grimly. Allehra took a step towards Luka and tugged a string tucked into the front of her leathers, revealing a small leather pouch at the end.

'Your mother armed you well,' Allehra said.

'It's hers. It's just a loan. She insisted I take it today.'

'A wise woman.'

Luka shrugged. 'She needs it more than me,' she said, lifting the necklace over her head, 'but I'm guessing you need me without this for the time being?'

Allehra smiled and took it from her. 'For the time being.' She motioned for them to sit and clasped her hands together.

Bleak and Luka sat opposite one another on the ground. Bleak could feel the damp seeping into the seat of her pants.

'Bleak, can you tell us about how your ability works?' said the Mother Matriarch.

Bleak bit her lip. She'd only ever explained her powers to one other person: Bleaker Senior. That had been a long time ago.

It's a gift, Half-Pint, an absolute gift, he'd said.

'Well,' she started, looking to Allehra, who nodded encouragingly. 'I hear people's thoughts. Sometimes I hear everything, sometimes nothing, and sometimes it's like I'm being crushed.'

'Can you control it?'

Bleak shrugged. 'Sometimes I can concentrate on one person and hear what they're thinking. But I can't always block it out if I don't want to hear it. It ... It's hard.'

She thought of Bren, whose thoughts she heard more loudly than anyone's, especially when he touched her, but she left this out. It was only with Bren, and none of

Allehra's business, she decided.

'I've never trained someone quite as old as you, Bleak,' Allehra said, 'but I've trained a few Ashai in my time, and I think we'll have to start with the very basics. Luka, I want you to think of an object, something simple. You'll need to picture it clearly, try to really focus on it.'

Luka nodded.

'Thought of something?'

Another nod.

'Good. Now, Bleak, close your eyes and concentrate on Luka's thoughts. Don't panic, don't let yourself be overwhelmed. You can do this. You proved that much yesterday. Try to find the item Luka's picturing. When you do, tell us what it is. Okay?'

'I'll try,' Bleak managed. She turned to face Luka fully, and took a deep breath. As soon as she closed her eyes, the buzzing began. A dozen or so of Luka's thoughts flew at her. She could hear the girl berating herself for getting distracted. For the first time, Bleak realised that she could hear both conscious and subconscious thoughts, or even needs that the mind was processing.

Focus, Bleak told herself, *an object. I'm searching for an object.*

Allehra had told Luka to *picture* it, so Bleak stopped listening to the words around her and instead focused on the shapes she could now see. They were blurry, a mere outline that could be anything really.

Don't let yourself be overwhelmed. Bleak repeated Allehra's words back to herself, and allowed the images to pull her towards them.

'A knife,' she said aloud, opening her eyes.

Opposite her, Luka frowned and looked to Allehra.

'Well?'

Luka shook her head, and Bleak sighed, unable to contain her look of disappointment. She'd been certain.

'Bleak, that was your first try – it's going to take more than that. Luka, what *were* you picturing?'

'An arrow, Majesty.'

Allehra's brows raised, surprised. 'Now that's interesting.'

'Why?'

The Mother Matriarch smiled. 'You got the general shape right and you got the type of object right – a weapon. If you'd mastered your patience, you may very well have succeeded the first time around. It's also shown us your weakness – a tendency to rush, to make assumptions.'

Bleak flushed. Did one exercise really reveal all that about her? She wanted to shrink away from them now. Being assessed so closely was no picnic.

'Let's try again,' said Allehra. 'Picture something else please, Luka.'

Luka bowed her head, and this time, when Bleak closed her eyes, she paced herself – *no assumptions*. Luka's thoughts rushed at her again, and Bleak heard each one before moving on to the next, trying not to dwell on how much this whole exercise breached Luka's privacy. A shape appeared, black and white, large and bulky. Its edges were soft, almost indistinguishable.

Take your time, Bleak chanted to herself as she studied the mass before her. Strangely, with a new calm settling over her, she found she could mentally step closer to the shape. She was now not just reading Luka's mind, she was *in* it. She moved closer still, and the image began to sharpen – a thick, vertical structure that opened out into – branches and leaves.

'A tree,' she said, the sound of her own voice dizzying as it wrenched her from Luka's mind and back to solid ground.

Luka nodded slowly. 'That's right.'

'Could you sense her?' Allehra asked.

'How do you mean?'

'Could you feel Bleak in your mind? Could you sense that something wasn't normal?'

Luka's brow furrowed. 'I don't think so? I mean, I wasn't really thinking about it.'

Allehra looked puzzled.

'Is that good or bad?' Bleak asked, looking from one Valian to the other, anxiety suddenly rising to the surface.

'It's unusual,' Allehra allowed. 'I've not trained a mind whisperer before, but from what I've read, your kind of Ashai have to work very hard to keep their presence hidden from whoever's mind they breach. And Luka, well – Luka was aware of what you were trying to do to begin with, so if anything, she should have been more alert to your presence.'

'What does that mean? Is something wrong with me?'

'No, child. I suspect that this skill is something you've honed without realising it since you were very young; a subconscious defence mechanism, perhaps.'

'Right.'

'Think about it. You've used your abilities to help yourself before, haven't you?'

'Help' is definitely a delicate way of putting it, Bleak thought, as she recalled the numerous times she'd used overheard thoughts to her advantage as the Fingersmith of Angove.

'Bleak?'

'Oh, I guess so.'

'And no one noticed then, correct?'

Bleak nodded but didn't elaborate. She didn't really want to discuss her pickpocketing habits with the Mother Matriarch of Valia. Allehra raised an eyebrow, though she didn't push the matter further.

'Luka, let's try some more complicated objects now. Be more specific,' she instructed.

It became easier, and for the first time, Bleak found herself enjoying her magic. For the first time, she wasn't stumbling blindly through someone's mind, nor were another's thoughts intruding loudly upon her own. She had some semblance of control. Despite the simplicity of the exercises, Bleak could already feel the benefit: her mind felt stronger, her magic was alive within her, not muted beneath the surface. She moved from object to object in Luka's mind, each time using less effort.

Allehra beamed.

'It's like a muscle that needs exercise. You seem to be in good shape, you just need to practise the right techniques.'

Next, they moved onto sentences, with Luka holding onto one particular phrase in her mind, and Bleak having to quieten the other thoughts, observations and memories swimming at the surface and locate it. This was more complicated. The images before had been easier to locate, but a string of words amidst all Luka's other thoughts proved far more difficult. It was like trying to untangle a frayed ball of yarn, unable to decide which piece was the end and which was the beginning, all the while trying to undo the knots.

Easy, she told herself. She wasn't meant to be rushing, she could take her time. She focused, catching a repeat of a phrase. That must be it. Inside Luka's mind, she followed it, as though she'd caught the end of the string, which now had a kite on the other end. She pulled it towards her … *Angovians smell like fish.*

Bleak's eyes flew open. Luka was smirking at her.

'Fish? Really?' she said.

'Really.'

'How many Angovians have you met, then?'

'Just the one.' Luka laughed.

Bleak rolled her eyes.

'I take it Bleak was successful?' Allehra asked, waiting for the girls to fill her in.

Luka wiped the grin off her face and bowed her head.

'Yes, Majesty.'

'Good. Again.'

Bleak and Luka practised all afternoon, with Luka attempting to make her phrases as obscure as possible, sometimes using song lyrics in the old Valian tongue and laughing at Bleak's pronunciations. Bleak was focusing so hard on catching the final phrase that she didn't realise how drained she felt until she stopped. Her torso slumped forward, and a dull ache throbbed quietly behind her eyes. She pinched the bridge of her nose, trying to ease the tension.

'Are you feeling alright?' Allehra asked, crouching down beside her and pressing the back of her hand to Bleak's forehead. 'You're warm,' she said.

'I'm fine.'

'We should have —'

'No, I'm fine.' Bleak had been searching for a cure for so long now, and this was as close as she was going to get to one. She wasn't about to give up when she was on the verge of discovery. This was the most hope she'd ever had. After all those journeys chasing after phantom healers in Heathton, the Valians had been the answer all along.

'You're sure?' said Allehra, her eyes clouded with concern.

'I can always come back tomorrow, I don't mind,' Luka added.

'Like I said, it's like any muscle,' said Allehra. 'It takes training to make it strong.'

Bleak shook her head. '*The huntress Rheyah gave us daughters of the realm,*' she said, 'that was the last phrase?'

Luka nodded. 'It's a quote from an old song, one of the few oral traditions still passed down to each generation of Valian kindred.'

'What's it about?' Bleak was stalling; she wasn't sure she could do any more.

'How Valians are demigods, descendants of the goddess Rheyah. It's a popular story around here.'

'I'll bet,' Bleak said, taking a deep breath.

Allehra was monitoring her carefully and placed a cool hand on Bleak's shoulder. 'That's enough for today. It's too soon to push further.'

Bleak didn't have the energy to argue. She nodded and accepted Luka's arm to heave her up.

Bren was sitting by the campfire with Tilly when Bleak got back to the keep. They had mugs of ale, and bread and cheese. And Bren's crooked smile was aimed at the Valian. Discomfort twisted in Bleak's gut, but she ignored it. Hunger hit her like a net full of fish on a deck, and she realised she hadn't eaten all day.

'When'd you get out?' she asked Bren, collapsing onto the bench beside him and taking a bite from the bread in his hand.

Bren looked to Tilly for confirmation. 'Couple of hours ago?'

Tilly nodded. 'Something like that. I felt sorry for the

poor bastard.'

'You let him out?'

'Sure did.'

'Thanks.' She went to take another bite of his bread, but he shoved her away and popped the rest of it in his mouth. He pointed to where the food was laid out on tables, only Bleak was too tired to get back up now.

'Where've yer been all day?' he asked her.

Bleak closed her eyes as she rested her head against the tree behind her.

'With Allehra and Luka.'

'Yer on a first-name basis with the Mother Matriarch of Valia?'

'Seems that way.'

'What'd ya do?'

Bleak shrugged. 'Does it matter?'

'Yeah.'

'They wouldn't want me to say,' she said.

'Since when do yer do anything that others want?'

Bleak's eyes flew open and heat rushed to her cheeks. 'What's that supposed to mean?'

Bren didn't reply, but the muscle in his jaw slid.

'If you're so hell-bent on knowing people's plans, you won't mind sharing yours, then,' she snapped.

'What do ya mean?'

'Well, you found me. I'm alright. Now what?'

'Can't ya just be grateful?'

'For what? Having me thrown in the pits with you?'

'For me giving a shit.'

'You didn't have to.'

Tilly shifted uncomfortably on the other side of Bren. 'I'll, uh ... leave you to it,' she said, and left before either could object.

'That's not the point,' Bren said quietly, staring after Tilly.

'Then tell me, what *is* the point?'

Bren tightened the tie around his hair and swept the loose strands away from his face. He sighed. 'We're ... Look, despite whatever's happened between us, we're family. B Senior was as close to a father as either of us had. He'd skin me alive if I didn't look out for ya.'

He nudged her with his elbow. Bleak didn't look at him; she didn't know if she could handle what she'd see in his eyes. Instead, she took the old length of rope from her pocket and began knotting. *King sling. Bimini twist. Spider hitch.* Looping and pulling, tightening and tying, before unravelling to start again.

Chapter Fifteen

Bleak was hungover. What little contents left in her stomach churned, threatening to come back up. Her head pounded as though her brain were swelling by the second, as though it were growing too big for her skull to contain.

Gods, what happened last night? She groaned and dragged herself from the bedroll in Tilly's spare room. The morning sun streaming in through the window burned her eyes and she groaned again.

'You don't look so good,' Tilly's voice sounded from the door.

'Really? But I feel so fresh,' Bleak quipped.

'Sure. Shouldn't you be at your training?'

'I don't know, you tell me.'

Tilly stepped forward and wrenched the covers back from Bleak.

'What —' Bleak cried out, scrambling to cover herself with her undershirt.

'Relax, I've seen a pair of legs before,' Tilly dismissed, her gaze falling upon Bleak's thigh, where much of her skin was marred by deep scarring.

'How in the realm did you get that?'

Bleak pulled the hem of her shirt down further.

'Do you mind?' she snapped. But Tilly continued to stare, where the scar still protruded from beneath the material.

'Who did that to you?' she breathed.

'No one. It's nothing.'

'Horseshit it's nothing.' Tilly leaned in and made to pull Bleak's hands away from the shirt.

'Stop – it's none of your fucking business!'

Tilly gaped at her, raising her hands in surrender. She took several steps back. 'Sorry.'

'Get out,' Bleak said, her pounding head forgotten, her heart racing.

Tilly nodded, hands still raised. She left Bleak on the bedroll, bare legs tucked carefully beneath her.

Bleak had already missed breakfast, and she was late, so late to her training. Trying to push Tilly's look of horror from her thoughts, she scurried down the ladder to the forest floor and bolted through the trees, trying to find the stream from the day before.

'Where ya going?' said Bren from behind her. Someone had given him a fresh shirt and pants, both of a far finer make than anything she'd seen him wear before. They didn't suit him, she decided.

'I'm late,' she said.

'That doesn't answer my question.'

'Where'd you sleep last night?' she heard herself ask.

'So ya don't remember anything, then?'

She shrugged, and continued to trek through the

undergrowth. 'What's there to remember?'

He sighed. 'Nothing.'

'Go back to the keep, Bren – I'm late to meet Allehra.'

'Since when do you have so much to say to the Mother Matriarch?'

'Since Henri saved me from being raped and probably murdered,' she snapped.

Bren stopped in his tracks. 'What?'

'Just go.'

'Bleak —'

'Go!' She found the stream and didn't turn back.

Allehra was furious. And Luka looked like she'd throttle Bleak with one nod from the queen. Bleak spluttered her apologies, but it was clear Valians made a habit of not needing to give them, and certainly not accepting them.

'I trust you know not to let that happen again?' said Allehra, arms folded over her chest.

'Yes. Sorry, again.'

Luka cleared her throat.

'Yes, *Majesty*,' Bleak added, feeling stupid.

Allehra was wearing another flowing gown, its billowing, light-blue skirts in stark contrast to Luka's dark, skin-tight leathers.

'Alright,' Allehra said, 'I want us to try some memories today.'

'Memories? I don't see how the past is going to help me in my current predicament.'

Luka shot Bleak a warning glance.

Don't forget who you're speaking to. The thought shot out to Bleak, clear as day, causing her to jump. If Allehra had thought the same, she didn't indicate it in any way. Instead, she squared her shoulders and said, 'The past has a way of showing us the right path. Inevitably, the same mistakes were made once before, and to know this is great power.'

Bleak dipped her head in acknowledgement and waited.

'Luka.' Allehra turned to the young warrior. 'I want you to think of something that occurred in your life recently. Something small – like a particular meal or conversation, something you saw, perhaps. It could be from yesterday, or last week at the latest. Bleak is going to attempt to identify it.'

Bleak looked at Luka. 'Are you okay with that?'

Luka shrugged. 'I lead a pretty simple life,' she said. 'Not much up here I wouldn't tell you anyway.' She tapped her head lightly. 'Do your worst.'

Taking a deep breath, Bleak focused on Luka's mind. She had grown accustomed to the buzzing of the surface-level thoughts, hearing Luka absent-mindedly spot a ripple in the pool, or observe some detail about Bleak's appearance: *She'd be much comelier if she didn't scrape her hair back in that messy knot...* And then the mental apology that followed: *Just in case you heard that.*

Finding Luka's musings and matching facial expressions distracting, Bleak closed her eyes. Exhaling through her nose, she concentrated. At first, it felt as though she were almost physically moving Luka's irrelevant thoughts aside. As though she were wading in the sea, pushing past the slimy weeds and debris. But then, just as sometimes the unexpected end of a sandbar catches one by surprise, she dropped.

Her stomach caught in her throat as she sank down, down into an entirely different level of Luka's mind. She was under the sea now, and it was dark. She seemed to glide forward into the shadowy passageway. This was more complex than before. Despite there being only one apparent passage, she felt disorientated and nauseous. Up ahead, lights shone out into the path before her – rooms? She came to the first one. Inside, she saw Athene – a younger, more hardened-looking Athene, speaking with a child. The child was Luka, perhaps ten or eleven years old. Bleak hovered in the doorway for a moment. The pair were in Valia, in the keep, surrounded by greenery, and yet beyond them were more doorways.

'Who your father is, is not important,' said Athene. 'What is important is Valia, and the Valian Way.'

Young Luka's face was puffy and wet with tears, her eyes betraying defeat.

'What *is* important?' Athene questioned.

Luka sniffed. 'The Valian Way.'

Bleak felt herself being pulled away from the door. She continued to glide further down the hall. She caught glimpses of the other rooms as she passed – Luka training with Tilly, Luka stitching a cut on her own knee, Luka in the kitchens with a young man – a cook. He was in a few of the rooms: Luka with her hands all over him, while he bore an expression of quiet, eager bewilderment. The next room contained an entire festival for the goddess Rheyah, where the kindred, dressed in warrior garb, drank and danced around the fire.

What am I meant to be looking for? Bleak paused. She couldn't remember why she was here. Where was here?

A shout of laughter startled her, and Bleak was pulled along to the next room. Henri was there, a younger Henri. She was there with Athene, at a training platform among the canopies. Luka looked on, hidden in the foliage, this time perhaps eight years old. The two women were sparring, but with big goofy grins on their faces – carefree smiles that Bleak hardly recognised. Athene tripped Henri and pinned her to the ground beneath her body.

'You let me,' Athene accused, her hair hanging loose, touching Henri's face.

Henri smirked. 'You'll never know.'

Bleak's heartbeat quickened. She shouldn't be watching this. She shouldn't be seeing Henri like this. The matriarch would surely find out and skin her alive; she hated Bleak enough already. As though some other force wanted to soothe her fears, Bleak was pulled gently from the doorway. The passage was endless. She squinted to try to locate the endpoint – *locate*. That was why she was here. To locate a specific memory, a *recent* memory. Bleak looked around. These were not recent memories; some were from years and years ago ...

'She won't mother a child.' A familiar voice broke the silence – another room.

Inside, Athene had teenage Luka by the shoulders. 'Not after everything she's been through.'

'So?' Luka said, frowning.

'She'll select an heir. And I can only imagine that will be you. Are you ready for that?'

'Me? Why in the realm would she choose me? There are dozens more talented.'

'We haven't spoken of others,' Athene said, drawing back from her daughter.

'But you've spoken of me?'

Athene said nothing more, busying herself on the other side of the room.

'You've spoken of me?' Luka said, louder.

The words echoed, suddenly booming inside Bleak's head. The room, the passageway, everything shot into the distance – she was dragged away.

'Bleak,' someone called, 'Bleak,' but they were so far away.

It took a few minutes before Bleak's blurry vision returned to normal. It was dark. Luka was no longer sitting before her. She was damp with sweat, and her whole body ached, as though she'd been on a massive journey.

'You're awake,' said Allehra's voice from beside her.

Pushing against the stiffness in her neck, Bleak turned to her. It was just the two of them. Concern rippled across the matriarch's face.

'What – what happened?'

'Are you hurt?'

Bleak looked down and examined herself. 'No, but ... I'm sore, all over,' she admitted. 'What happened?'

Allehra sighed and rolled her shoulders back. How long had they been here?

'You fell into a trance.'

'What?'

'A trance – some kind of deep meditation. Luka and I agreed it may be dangerous to wake you from it.'

'Is Luka okay? I didn't hurt her?'

'She's fine.'

Bleak looked at the darkened sky and heard the crackling fires in the distance.

'How long?' she asked.

'Difficult to say exactly.'

'How long?'

Allehra pursed her lips. 'My guess would be roughly eight hours, perhaps eight and a half.'

Bleak started. 'What?'

Allehra nodded, her mouth set in a grim smile. 'I know. I've never seen anything like it.'

A brief, cold sensation crept down Bleak's spine as she recalled the dark passageway and hundreds of rooms.

'Did I ... do anything? Say anything?'

Allehra shook her head. 'You sat there with your eyes closed. Sometimes you visibly tensed and I could see you sweating. But I had no idea what was going on. I had

Luka fetch one of our oldest healers, but she said there was nothing to be done. We had to wait.'

'So Luka left?'

'Yes.'

'And I was still inside her mind?'

'So it seems.'

Bleak exhaled shakily. The earlier enjoyment of her powers was gone, replaced now with a crippling fear. What if she'd got stuck in Luka's mind? What if she'd hurt Luka?

'What now?' she asked, swallowing hard.

'Well, I must ask – what did you see? Did you find Luka's memory?'

Bleak's pulse quickened. She didn't even understand what had happened yet. Did she truly have to tell Allehra?

'Bleak,' the older woman's voice warned.

'I didn't find the memory,' Bleak heard herself say.

Allehra opened her mouth to give another warning.

'But I found *other* memories.'

'What do you mean?'

Bleak squirmed under the queen's determined gaze.

'I – I must rest.'

'We need to know what happened.'

'Please.' The word came out more desperate than Bleak had intended. She was shivering, the cool night air like ice on her clammy, hot skin.

To her surprise, Allehra nodded. 'Very well. Tomorrow. You will explain this tomorrow.'

'Thank you.'

'Two sessions of training,' Allehra said in wonder, getting to her feet. 'I didn't think we would get so far so soon. But I've realised we need to train your powers alongside some physical abilities. You need them to be able to complement one another.'

Bleak sighed. 'Not sure if you've noticed, but I don't exactly have much to offer in that department. I'm not really built for fighting.'

'You need to learn that every flaw you think you have can be used to an advantage.'

'How?'

'People will underestimate you – that's a powerful thing.'

'Why me?' Bleak asked, searching Allehra's face. 'Why are you helping me?'

Sadness swept across the queen's face. 'I'm trying something new.'

Bleak insisted that Allehra go on ahead of her, and when she stood, her legs were weak, her muscles quavering with each step. She'd never thought it was possible to feel at once both a million years old and like a newborn calf finding its footing for the first time. But that was how she felt.

The heart of the keep was bustling when Bleak arrived, utterly spent from her training. She wanted nothing more than to swipe a bottle of wine and lock herself away in Tilly's apartments. But the thought of seeing Tilly so soon after this morning sent a hot flush of shame to her cheeks. Tilly had seen her scar, and the look of disgust on the Valian's face was now permanently etched into Bleak's mind. She couldn't bear the thought of facing Tilly after that, especially given how rude Bleak had been to her, kicking her out of her own home. Bleak turned her attention to the kindred feasting and laughing by the fire. Luka clapped her on the shoulder.

'Good to see you conscious again, Angovian.'

'Thanks.'

'You look like you could use a drink.'

'I could always use a drink.'

'Join me and the other trainees, then.'

Bleak opened her mouth to decline, when she spotted Bren. On the other side of the campsite, Bren was down on one knee, hammering a broken leg back into the underside of a table. His shirt was open, revealing his muscular torso, beads of sweat caught in his chest hair. Beside him, Tilly was laughing, handing him one nail at a time.

'Yeah,' Bleak said to Luka, 'why not.'

'We'll have to work on your enthusiasm,' Luka replied, handing her a flask of something, and tugging her through the throng of Valians. Soon, the night became a blur. The Valians Luka introduced her to didn't wear the same enchanted herbs as Henri's elite kindred, and despite Bleak's exhaustion, she found their thoughts open to her. The only escape was the drink. It was late when she staggered back into the camp. A number of hammocks had been hung around the dying fire, and when Bleak saw Bren's tanned arm dangling from one, she felt an odd sense of relief. She'd been too hard on him. He cared about her. He'd come here to protect her, and she'd been ... Well, she'd been her usual selfish self.

I can't help it, she told herself without conviction, as she slipped into an empty hammock nearby. With a full flask of ale under her arm, she felt herself finally drifting into unconsciousness, her fatigue tugging her down into its abyss.

The next morning, the keep was a hive of activity. The kindred were all dressed in their leathers, with their weapons strapped proudly to their bodies. Bleak rolled out of the hammock, her sore muscles still protesting at every movement.

'Luka,' she called to the stocky youth across the camp.

Luka dropped her armful of wooden training swords and jogged over. ''Bout time,' she said.

Bren appeared at Bleak's side, looking refreshed and holding a mug of steaming liquid; its sweet scent drifted towards Bleak.

'What's going on?' Bleak asked Luka.

'Oh, this?' Luka gestured to the chaos around them. 'Henri decided to inspect the training today, so everyone's trying to cram in some last-minute prac. Look, I gotta run – supposed to be at circuit one.'

'You're being inspected today?'

'Sure am.'

'Are you —'

'Nervous? Ha. Don't get nervous, my friend. Come watch if you want.'

Bleak glanced at Bren, who was holding his mug out to her.

'It'll help with the headache,' he said.

'Who said I had a headache?' Bleak grumbled, but she took the mug from him, cupping it in her palms and taking a long swig.

Bren shook his head and called out to Tilly, who was passing.

'Where's circuit one?' he asked, taking the heavy netted bag of water flasks from her and shouldering it.

Tilly grinned. 'Glad to see you're getting into the Valian spirit,' she said. 'Follow me. I'm heading there myself. I think Luka's up in the first round.'

Bleak downed the rest of the drink, savouring its smooth, sweet flavour. 'Round?'

'You'll see.' Tilly motioned for them to follow. She took off before Bleak had time to feel embarrassed – had the incident with her scar only happened the previous morning? She was losing track of time in Valia. Tilly led them through a series of twists and turns amidst the undergrowth, all the while chatting amicably with Bren about building new platforms in the canopy for the growing kindred population.

'Tilly showed me some plans for new wings of apartments last night,' he explained to Bleak.

'That's great,' she said. 'Guess that means training the younger kindred is going well?'

'It always goes well,' Tilly said, taking another turn.

'Well, except for those who fail and —'

Tilly shot her a warning look and Bleak shut up.

'The keep has a bunch of training circuits surrounding it,' Tilly told them. 'There are eight, I think – nine if you count Henri's private platform. But only the queen's elite kindred know where that is.'

'Have you seen it?'

'Sure have. I *am* one of her personal guard.'

'Pretty big honour, I guess.'

'You *guess*? There's no greater honour than to train and fight alongside a Valian queen.'

'That's what I meant,' Bleak added hastily.

Tilly shot her another glare. 'Careful, Bleak, there are some who are yet to make their minds up about you.'

Bren's eyes were boring into Bleak's back, and she did her utmost to ignore his panicked thoughts barrelling into her own mind. They heard the crowd long before they came across the clearing, a steady hum of chatter and laughter.

'Is this a formal event?' Bleak asked, scanning over the hundred or so Valian faces looking out eagerly onto the empty open space.

Tilly laughed. 'No, but when Henri says she's coming, everyone turns up. Ordinarily it's a dull affair.'

Bleak was only half listening to the answer. She'd noticed there was sawdust spread generously across the ground.

'What exactly happens here?'

Tilly followed her stare. 'Oh, relax,' she said, 'they fight. No permanent damage, mostly.'

'Mostly?'

'You a parrot now? It's a big opportunity to train before the queen,' she explained. 'The winners receive a private training session with the elite kindred, giving them an advantage over the rest for the next Choosing.'

'And the losers?'

'Depends on their performance. But most go to the Sticks.' Tilly rolled her eyes. 'Most of the folk in the Sticks lead happy lives, so you can wipe that look off your face.'

'Except they don't want to leave the keep?'

'Well, not at first. But they learn to love the Sticks. It's no less beautiful, and their responsibilities there are no less important.'

Bleak's stomach was churning, and she looked around uneasily. For a society that seemed to have so much right, this seemed very, very wrong.

There was a cheer from the crowd surrounding the clearing and Bleak saw Henri emerge from the other side. She looked as stern and fierce as ever, her trademark leathers clinging to her lithe frame, the same cold expression etched on her face. She took a seat on a carved wooden bench by Athene, down the other end of the makeshift arena. The kindred watched their leader, eyes shining with admiration, despite her dispassionate disposition. Allehra was nowhere in sight, but Bleak had learned to expect this. According to the other kindred, the Mother Matriarch had a reclusive tendency. And for this, Bleak was glad. It meant she could breathe easy for the morning, knowing she wouldn't have to explain the dark passages of Luka's mind.

Henri drew names from a cup, and two young Valians stepped forward from a group of trainees standing by Marvel and Petra. The girls faced Henri and bowed low. She nodded and told them to commence at their ready. The bloodthirsty thoughts of the crowd around Bleak were overpowering. She silently cursed Allehra – shouldn't she have learned how to *block out* thoughts first? Bleak rubbed her temples. She should have demanded that training. Not that she was in any sort of position to *demand* anything from the Mother Matriarch of Valia. Bleak got the distinct sense that Allehra was shaping the training sessions to suit her own agenda.

Bren nudged Bleak and nodded to the girls at the centre of the circuit. One girl, no older than fourteen, chose a blunted spear as her weapon, while her opponent shook her head at the selection and announced that she would win the challenge with her bare hands. Bleak's pulse quickened. These girls were friends, right? They wouldn't hurt each other for real, would they? The question was answered mere seconds later when the unarmed girl dodged the incoming spear and buried her fist in the other girl's stomach. Neither girl uttered a sound as they fought, their quiet stealth making them all the more impressive. After the first blow, strikes were matched with blocks and attacks, and the spear was snapped in half, now serving as two weapons. Time and time again, though, the fists won out, and the broken pieces of spear were eventually dropped and left forgotten in the sawdust. Blood leaked from one of the girls' noses, and Bleak could make out the red welts where the spear had struck. An empty space opened up beside Bleak; Bren had left, she realised. The fight continued, until finally, the girl who'd been originally unarmed took her opponent in a headlock, where she thrashed for a time before surrendering. The first victory was won, and to Bleak's surprise, the two girls embraced and clapped each other on the back. They turned back to Henri and bowed again, before Athene dismissed them. Neither was being sent to the Sticks.

'Wasn't so bad, was it?' Tilly said in Bleak's ear.

Bleak didn't respond. She was watching Luka enter the circuit. The redhead was grinning as she tightened her braid and shook her head, laughing at her group of friends, who whooped and clapped her on the back. Bleak turned her attention to Luka's opponent and her heart sank. The girl had none of Luka's muscle tone or confidence. She was slight, mousy even. Both girls selected a short sword and shield. Luka twirled her wooden blade effortlessly in preparation. It wasn't going to be a fair fight, and Bleak didn't want to see it. She turned away as the girls were bowing to Henri, trying to see a way through the crowd and back to the keep. With her back to the arena, she heard Luka's first strike find its mark, and a cry from her opponent. Bleak whirled around without thinking. This was wrong.

She shoved her way back to the front, but Tilly threw an arm out in front of her chest.

'What could you possibly do to help her? Leave it. She'll be fine. She's just being dramatic.'

But the pain in the poor girl's eyes said otherwise, and Luka knocked her attack attempts aside lazily. Bleak took a deep breath. How many times had it been her on the receiving end of an attack? How many times had she been knocked down by someone twice her size for the sake of entertainment?

Without realising what she was doing, she yelled out, 'Block right!'

Startled, the girl jumped but raised her shield just in time.

Luka shot Bleak an irritated look, but Bleak spoke again.

'Quick! Strike left!'

Luka swore and rubbed her shoulder as the girl landed her first blow.

Ignoring Tilly's protests, Bleak edged closer to the sideline as Luka raised her sword to attack.

Right feint, strike left, block, pivot, strike left, strike right.

Bleak called the movements out to the girl as they entered Luka's head, and with newfound confidence, the girl countered every move.

'This is horseshit,' Luka spat, throwing a glare in Bleak's direction.

Her opponent saw the opportunity and lunged – she had Luka at swordpoint. The girl's mouth was open, bewildered by her own success. Around her, though, angry calls broke out, and Bleak did her best to shrink back into the crowd. She was given a rough shove, and she stumbled out into the arena, everyone's eyes suddenly on her.

There was a flurry of movement as Henri stood and walked towards them.

'Neemah,' she addressed the smaller girl, 'an unexpected result.'

Neemah lowered her sword and bowed.

'And yet,' Henri said, 'however quick your reflexes seemed, they did not come naturally to you, despite your years of training.'

Neemah looked up at Henri, her eyes glazed over.

'What?' Bleak heard herself say.

Henri's kohl-lined eyes snapped to hers, narrowing. Bleak almost recoiled.

'If you have something to say, speak it plainly.'

'She ... She won. She beat Luka. Why isn't that enough?'

'Enough?' Henri's dark brows shot up and her grey stare turned icy. 'Are you intending on accompanying Neemah to battle? Where she will not only need to defend herself, but you as well? Considering you have no training or stamina to speak of?'

Bleak bit down on the inside of her cheek, her whole face burning at Henri's cold remarks.

Nostrils flaring, Henri turned back to Neemah. 'You are no longer permitted in the keep, unless requested by a high kindred. Alternative living quarters will be arranged for you in the Sticks.'

Neemah nodded, palming away her tears, and moved to return her sword and shield to the weapons table. She approached a severe-looking woman with grey streaks in her braid.

'I'm sorry,' she said, her voice fracturing.

The woman simply nodded and turned away.

Henri wasn't done. She turned to Luka.

'Interference or not, you should have won that fight. Your arrogance blinded you. Remember the difference between confidence and arrogance, Luka. One can shape victory at your feet; the other can get you killed. I don't want to see another display of the latter on my circuits again.'

A rare blush spread across Luka's face, and she nodded, bowing deeply. When Bleak returned her gaze to Henri's face, she found those piercing eyes glaring at her.

'You,' Henri said, her voice low, 'get out of my sight.'

Bleak spent the day shrinking away from angry glares and hostile thoughts. She found herself wandering through the dense forest, where moist, broad-leaved plants hung down before her face, dampening the shoulders of her shirt as she passed. The trunks, the branches, the damp and the greenery wrapped her in a blanket of shadow.

She didn't know where she was going, but she'd settle for anywhere away from that Valian hostility. In just a few days – *or had it been a week now?* – she'd forgotten what that felt like, the curse of the outsider. She hadn't realised until now, that she'd actually felt … comfortable here.

'Lady,' a soft voice said, 'can I help you with something?'

Bleak whirled around. A girl, not much younger than herself, smiled timidly at her. She wore a shapeless linen shift that was smudged with dirt, and a pair of sturdy black boots. She tucked a loose strand of hair behind her ear and adjusted the basket in her hands.

'Lady?'

'Who are you?' It came out harsher than Bleak had intended.

'Lyse,' she said, curtseying.

'I'm no lady, Lyse. Clearly,' Bleak said, gesturing to her own grubby shirt and pants.

'You are a guest of our queen, which makes you a lady.'

Bleak frowned. 'How do you know who I am?'

'Word travels fast in Valia, even out here in the Sticks.'

'This is the Sticks?'

Lyse nodded. She put her basket on the ground and crouched in the dirt. Bleak went to her and knelt beside her.

'What are you doing?'

Lyse's fingers combed the earth until she plucked

something from the ground, which she held up for Bleak to see. It was less than half the size of a grape, and beneath the dirt was a faded red colour.

'Maladoms,' said Lyse. 'We crush them and put them in poultices. They help soothe the kindred's aches and pains when they're not being too stubborn to use them.' The note of fondness in her voice surprised Bleak. Bleak palmed the dirt, mirroring Lyse's technique until she found a small bead protruding from the ground. She tugged and it sprang free. She showed Lyse, holding it between her thumb and forefinger. Lyse took it and blew the dirt away.

'Good,' she said, 'now we need about a hundred more.'

Bleak laughed, the sound shocking her. How long had it been since she had genuinely laughed? The question itself was sobering. She continued to scour the earth for maladoms alongside Lyse, revelling in the sense of being grounded, and taking pleasure in company for the sake of company, without the forced small talk. Lyse's thoughts were quiet and unobtrusive. She didn't sit there silently analysing Bleak like so many others did. For this, Bleak was extraordinarily grateful. Slowly, the basket began to fill, and Bleak realised how calm she felt, how the hostility of the morning had ebbed away. Smiling, she looked down at her hands. The lines of her palms were caked with dirt and her fingernails looked black. Lyse got to her feet, wiping her own dirty hands on her tunic.

'You must be hungry,' she said. 'Care to join us

groundlings for a meal?'

'Groundlings?'

Lyse laughed. 'It's what we non-kindred folk call ourselves, because we like having our feet planted firmly on the ground.' She offered Bleak an outstretched hand, and Bleak took it, hauling herself up. They walked through the forest. The platforms and living bridges Bleak had become accustomed to weren't visible from below, but here, at ground level, the forest became something that resembled a woodland village. As they moved further into the Sticks, Bleak noticed little cottages peeking through the trees, clearings with fences and crops climbing supporting stakes. Soon, they came upon other 'groundlings', as Lyse had called them. Men and women waved at them as they passed. Lyse led Bleak to an enormous tree. It had a doorway at its base, and a set of stairs leading down below the earth. Bleak raised a brow at her new friend.

'Come on,' said Lyse, resting the basket in the crook of her elbow and starting down the stairs. With apprehension written all over her face, Bleak followed. At the bottom of the stairs, the space opened up into a huge cavern – a hall – lined with long tables and benches, and jars filled with the same glowing beetles as in Tilly's apartments. And the food – a buffet table at the end of the hall was covered in serving dishes of roast vegetables and freshly baked bread.

'Help yourself,' Lyse said, 'I'll just take these to the apothecary.'

Bleak felt her anxiety surge as Lyse left her to her own devices and she found herself in yet another foreign place. Someone handed her a plate.

'Nice of you to try to help Neemah,' said the elderly woman holding the dish. Bleak accepted it with a nod of thanks.

'Was it?'

'A little naive, perhaps, but nice.'

'Right. I'm Bleak.' She offered her hand and then cringed at the dirt.

'A little dirt never killed anyone, girl.' The woman shook her hand firmly. 'And I know who you are. I'm Lindis, groundling elder.'

'Maman,' Lyse said, jumping the queue that had formed behind them, 'I see you've met the queen's guest.'

Bleak looked between Lyse and Lindis, confused. 'She's your daughter?'

Lindis barked a laugh. 'Gods, no, "Maman" is what all the foolish youngster groundlings call me.'

'You love it,' said Lyse, piling her plate high with roast pumpkin.

Lindis shook her head fondly. With her own plate brimming with food, Bleak sat herself down beside Lyse at one of the long tables, which soon filled. The other groundlings were all desperate to sit with Lyse, Bleak realised. The girl was popular, so much so that the groundlings paid Bleak barely any notice, leaving her to enjoy Lyse's stories with the rest of them. Lindis cleared her throat from opposite Lyse, and all the groundlings groaned, begrudgingly shuffling down the bench to allow space for their elder.

'Ungrateful wretches,' Lindis muttered, but her lips quirked with the hint of a smile.

She looked across the table at Bleak. 'You're bursting with questions, girl. Ask them. This lot loves to talk. The more questions the better.'

'We don't talk *that* much, Maman,' said a boy sitting further down the table.

'Rubbish. And not to mention your keen hearing, eh?'

The boy grinned, and then nodded to Bleak. 'She's right, though. Ask away, Angovian.'

'Uh ... I guess I was just wondering how this all works.'

'This?' said Lyse.

'With your people here, and, you know, the rest up there.' Bleak gestured above them.

'Ah, she feels badly for us,' said the boy.

Lyse smiled kindly. 'We like our lives, Bleak.'

'But you're forced to —'

'Live out here?'

Bleak nodded.

'Is out here not as beautiful as up in the trees?'

'I guess.'

'We have more freedom here than in the keep. We're not defined by violence and training. It's peaceful here. We all have our roles and responsibilities, but there is life to be had outside those, too.'

'Speak for yourself,' growled a voice from further

down the table.

Bleak's eyes snapped up from her food to the sharp-featured girl down the end, and then back to Lyse, who was glancing nervously at Lindis.

'Take your revolution-mongering somewhere else,' Lindis said, not even looking in the girl's direction.

'Someone *finally* asks what we think, and you're just going to —'

'Enough, Clara,' Lindis said. The kind, maternal smile from before was gone, replaced by a darker look. 'Bleak is our queen's guest, and your unhappy notions do not represent the majority out here in the Sticks.'

'But she's on our side, Lindis – she tried to help Neemah.' Clara jerked her thumb in Bleak's direction.

Bleak didn't hide her discomfort at being somehow caught in the middle of this.

'There are no *sides*, Clara. Now either stop this rubbish or leave. When this gets back to the queen, *and it will*, the rest of us do not want to be tarnished with the same brush.'

Clara shook her head furiously and shoved her plate back. With a final glare at Lindis, she left.

Lyse released a low whistle.

'Ignore her,' Lindis said, irritation etched on her face.

But the thoughts of those around Bleak began to seep into her own mind. They came at her, fleeting and furious ...

But Clara's right —

Wish she'd shut it around Lindis —

221

Clara's a damn fool —

There was nothing consistent about the thoughts around her, and to distract herself, Bleak turned back to Lyse, this time leaving her food untouched.

'What do you do here, then?' she asked.

'I'm a healer. Lindis is my mentor. She teaches about ten of us.'

'That's ... That's really great.' Bleak couldn't quell the uneasiness in her stomach, and she glanced around to see if she could see Clara.

Lindis passed Bleak a basket of bread. 'Any new place and its workings is a lot to take in.'

Bleak nodded.

'And no society is perfect, Bleak, no matter how much you want it to be.'

Bleak let the elder's words sink in, and took a thick slice of bread.

The keep was boisterous upon Bleak's return. The Valians were riled up after a day of training, with some of them even sporting split lips and black eyes, wearing them proudly. Bleak scanned the crowd, looking for Bren, and saw him tending to Tilly; he had her arm in his lap as he bandaged it. Bleak stopped in her tracks and watched as they chatted quietly.

What could he possibly have to say to a Valian? What do they have in common?

She had to acknowledge that Bren had never had any trouble getting along with people. It was in his nature to make conversation, to put people at ease. Bleak snatched up a bottle of wine from the refreshments table and slipped away from the keep once again. She lifted the bottle to her lips as she walked, and relaxed as soon as the delectable taste hit her tongue. Exhaling slowly, and feeling the stiff tension leave her shoulders, she found herself crossing a narrow bridge of tree roots. Beneath her, a stream rushed over mossy rocks, and small silver fish splashed in the clear water. Taking another swig from the bottle, Bleak eased herself down from the end of the bridge to the cool banks of the stream. Looking around, she decided to take advantage of the rare solitude. She was already tired of bathing in the kindred baths. The Valians would steal not-so-subtle glances at her naked, malnourished body, their pitying thoughts driving a flush of embarrassed heat across her face as she emerged from the water each time. And then there was her scar. The rippled, pale flesh took on the jagged shape of a mapped continent, covering a generous patch of skin from the side of her thigh to the top of her knee. The Valians loved gawking at it. It marked her in more ways than they knew.

She was nine when the second recorded plague had hit Ellest. It had infected young and old alike, struck them down with pus-filled sores and a core-shaking fever, and that had been only the beginning. Scared, she had hidden the ulcer on her leg that bubbled under her skin, but after a morning of trembling with a soaring temperature, Senior had found her out. He'd waited until dusk and then snuck her onto one of his ships and sailed out to sea. There, he'd knocked her unconscious, and with a surgeon's blade he'd borrowed from the Claytons, he'd cut out the rotting flesh on her leg and then some, to make sure he'd got it all. She'd awoken to the scent of burning flesh, and then pain like she'd never known, roaring through her. Senior had knocked her out again. They had stayed out at sea for days, though she couldn't recall any of it. Which was a mercy, because the size of her wound, and the grip the fever had had on her, were fierce.

Bleak shrugged away the memory. No matter her disfigurement or her slight, boy-like body, there was no shame at this deserted stream in Valia. Piece by piece, layer by layer, she peeled away her clothing. Naked, she took her first steps into the fresh water, its unexpected chill taking her breath away. The stream was only waist-deep, but it was more than enough. She let her body rock with the gentle current, keeping her feet planted firmly in the silt. The silver fish darted away from her, leaving her to duck her head under the surface, muting all the sounds of the forests and all the angry thoughts of the day. Water had always had a soothing effect on her. She came up for air, pushing the water back through her hair and away from her eyes with a sigh. She would stay down there forever if she could. She rubbed the dirt from her skin and did her best to clean beneath her nails. Ever since her first sea voyage with Senior, the easy pull of the water seemed to settle something within her. She floated on her back and gazed at the broken pieces of the night sky beyond the canopy. It was littered with bright, white stars, winking down at her.

'Bleak!' shouted a familiar male voice.

Bleak started, splashing wildly and swearing under her breath. She should have known Bren would find her. Dipping her torso below the water's surface, she looked up and saw his face looking down at her from the bridge. Her skin tingled; she was incredibly aware of her own nakedness. Goosebumps broke out across her skin.

'Don't —' she started to say, but Bren was already down the other side of the bridge.

She stayed where she was, careful to cover herself as best she could.

'Are yer alright? I was worried – no one had seen yer.'

'I'm fine,' she snapped. 'I'm *trying* to bathe, so if you don't mind?'

He spotted her pile of clothes and then took in her bare shoulders. He blushed.

'Sorry, I didn't think —'

'No. You didn't. Face the trees.'

Bleak saw him hesitate for a fraction of a second, before doing as she bid.

She made quick work of emerging from the stream and fumbled with her pants over her wet legs.

'Yer know,' he said, his voice cautious, 'I've seen yer undressed before.'

'Bren, not now,' she cautioned, pulling her tunic over her head.

He *had* seen her in various states of undress, when he was tending to wounds after a bar fight, and when she'd lived with his family and he'd walked in on her in the mudroom removing soiled clothes. But this was different.

Resigned to the fact that her now wet, clinging clothes left little to the imagination, she sat by the stream, hunched over the wine bottle.

'I'm done,' she told him.

Clearing his throat, he turned, his cheeks still pink, and sat down nearby. He watched her take a long swig from the wine.

'I didn't like it either,' he said.

Bleak looked at him blankly. 'Like what?'

'How they treated that girl. I couldn't handle it. I left.'

That's right, Bleak remembered. He hadn't seen her little outburst.

She shrugged. 'What can you do.'

'Leave.' He said it so simply.

The odd thing was, Bleak hadn't seriously considered it since she'd arrived in Valia. She couldn't leave, even if she wanted to.

'Come back to Angove,' Bren said.

She shook her head.

'You're just going to accept this?'

'What?'

'This life? These people?'

Bleak drank deeply before answering. She was only just coming to terms with it herself. What else did she have?

'They saved me, Bren. I'm in their debt.'

Bren ground his teeth and stared into the water ahead.

'I would have been killed, or raped, or both,' she told him, 'and they stepped in when they didn't have to. And now – well, now Henri's going to face consequences for that. And I need to be as strong as I can be for when that day comes.'

'Strong? What can *you* do that she can't?'

Bleak faltered. As far as Bren knew, she was just a scrappy orphan girl from Angove.

'Since when does Bleaker Junior care about debts?' he said.

'Since always.'

'Oh yeah? What about the debts you owe *me*? How many scrapes have I gotten yer out of? Only to face yer abuse the next morning?'

Bleak closed her eyes. 'I know,' she said quietly.

'Do yer?'

'Yes. Trust me, I know, Bren.'

Bren got up, dusting off the seat of his pants and staring down at her. Bleak's head began to throb as she tried to tune out Bren's lingering heated thoughts. He was right to be angry. She was selfish and ungrateful. He'd saved her so many times, mainly from herself. There he would be, peeling her away from her vomit in the gutter, tearing Maz's eager body off hers, cleaning her cuts and icing her bruises. Bren's mind dragged her through each memory, each one worse than the last, until she couldn't take it anymore. She got to her feet, clutching the bottle of wine, and walked away. He was better off without her.

She didn't care where she was going. Especially once she was more than half a bottle of wine in. Valian wine was *strong*. The lights of the keep became more distant, and she found it harder and harder to see through the forest. She stumbled over rocks and tree roots, all the while taking long swigs, trying to quench her unquenchable thirst. She didn't know why Bren cared. She didn't know why Bleaker Senior had taken her in. She didn't know what happened to her parents. She didn't know much at all, it seemed. Except that the wine helped. It helped her feel as though being alone didn't matter. That nothing mattered. It washed over the memories and thoughts that didn't belong to her, the ones from other people that insisted on crowding her mind.

Suddenly she slipped, lost her balance – she was falling, tumbling down a steep hill, ramming into trees and boulders, holding her hands before her face, trying to shield herself as she lost control. There was a thud as something blocked her way. She let out a moan of pain. With her head spinning and her whole body aching, she staggered to her feet.

She gasped.

Before her stood hundreds and hundreds of tree skeletons. Charred, naked trunks stretched up into the fog that surrounded them. It was a forest graveyard. Every tree within sight was dead, and not one natural sound came from within. Fog swirled around the trunks.

'We call it the Forest of Ghosts,' said a familiar voice from behind her.

Bleak nearly leapt out of her skin. 'Gods!' she cursed.

Henri ignored her and took in the forest for herself. 'It was over a decade ago now, but sometimes, I can still smell it burning.'

'What happened?'

'We always suspected the royals had something to do with it. It's where we used to grow these.' Henri tugged at the pouch of herbs around her neck.

Bleak swayed on the spot, and saw Henri glance at the bottle of wine at her feet.

'You're a drunk,' the warrior queen said quietly.

Bleak thought about arguing, about denying, but she was so damn bone-tired. 'I'm a lot of things.'

Henri nodded. 'We all are,' she said, and took the wine from Bleak without another word.

Chapter Sixteen

The raucous tavern in Grayside smelled like watery stew, sandalwood and ale. The trademark scent of travellers and drinkers from around these parts of Ellest. There wasn't an empty table in sight as villagers from all over the East Farmlands leaned against the dark timber beams and soaked their sleeves as they rested their elbows on the wet bar. Torches lit the walls, the warm light spilling across the laughing faces and heated card games. Swinton and Fiore looked on from their booth in the back corner, and dipped chunks of stale bread into the poor excuse for pork stew.

'I've had worse,' Fi said loudly.

'Me, too, I've tasted your version of palma pie,' Swinton replied, raising the heavy mug of ale to his lips.

Fiore laughed. 'What's wrong with how I cook my pie?'

'You mean what's *not* wrong with it?' Swinton said. He nodded to the barman, signalling for another round. He was in good spirits. They'd ridden hard for three days and covered decent ground. He and Fi always made great time when it was just the two of them riding.

'Commander,' the barman said, approaching with

a round jug of fresh ale. 'I trust everything is to your liking?'

'It's fine, Jasper,' said Swinton, giving a subtle shake of his head at Fi's look of disgust, 'thank you.'

'Anything you need, Commander. We're glad to see you back here.'

'Much appreciated.'

Jasper took his time filling each mug. 'Will you be attending the feast honouring Sir Caleb?'

'Unfortunately not, I have business to attend to for the king.'

'But of course, Commander. Still, it's a shame you cannot be there. You must be very proud. Your father —'

'I'm disappointed I won't be there to celebrate the anniversary of his glory,' Swinton cut him off.

Fiore choked on his ale. Swinton shot him a warning look.

'Of course,' Jasper said, bowing his head. 'I'm sure your father of all people understands – duty comes first.'

'Indeed.'

'Do let me know if there's anything else I can do for you, gentlemen.' Jasper scurried back to the bar.

'Gentlemen. He'll really say anything, won't he?' said Fi, brows raised after the eager barman.

'Leave him be, he's harmless.'

'Harmless, yes, among other things.'

Swinton laughed despite himself and poured more ale.

Fi raised his mug with a sly smile. 'To the glory of Sir

Caleb Swinton, then, your claim to fame.'

Swinton shook his head, but bumped his mug against Fi's and drank deeply.

'I don't know how you put up with it, eh?' said Fi.

'What?'

'Sir Caleb this, Sir Caleb that – drives me half-mad.'

Swinton shrugged. 'My father did this continent a great service when he saved His Majesty from the mist dwellers. He deserves the accolades and the feasts.'

'That must be equally tiresome.'

'What?'

'The mask of the proud son.'

'Mask? You don't think I'm proud of my father?'

'Even pride has its limits, my friend. Though I don't doubt you have it in cartloads.'

Fi was baiting him, Swinton knew it, but he was too sober to bite. He watched as his friend glanced around the tavern, not-so-discreetly trying to discern which women were accompanied by husbands and which were not. Swinton smiled.

'I believe she's a lady of the evening,' he quipped, following Fi's gaze to a woman in a deep-blue gown, cinched in tight at the waist.

Fiore didn't look away. 'So?'

'So nothing.'

'Exactly.' Fi grinned. 'We both know I don't need to pay for a lady's affections. I was considering her for you, old friend.'

'Me? I'm perfectly content where I am.'

Fiore snorted. 'Whatever you say, Dimitri. Just don't show her up to that pokey little room of yours, whatever you do.'

'What's wrong with my room?'

'*Room* is a generous term for that water closet.'

'We're on the road, Fi, I don't see the need for lavish accommodations.'

'Lavish? No, we wouldn't want that, would we.'

'Here we go.'

'Dimitri, you're Commander of the King's Army. You can afford to stay in a normal room every now and then, right? Unless it's what all the guards and squires suspect.'

'Which is?'

'You've got a gambling problem.'

'What?' Swinton laughed. He was well aware of the rumours. He'd developed a reputation for being short on silver over the years.

'You heard me. You're addicted to the gambling rush.'

'Am not.'

'I know. I practically live with you and I've never seen you roll a dice.'

'See?'

'So where's it go, then?'

'What?'

'Your salary? You've got a thing for Madame Joelle Marie's girls?'

'Don't be ridiculous. That's you.'

'Once upon a time, perhaps, and I'm not the one scraping my last silvers together every other day.'

Swinton's brow raised. 'You done?'

'Some of the men reckon you're hooked on wildflower.'

'I'd never get anything done were that the case,' Swinton said drily.

'Try telling them that.'

Swinton shrugged. 'We're out of ale,' he said pointedly.

'At once, Commander,' Fi said, standing up with a mock bow, 'at your service, Commander.'

Swinton held in a laugh as his friend sauntered off to the bar. It was in stolen moments like these that Swinton felt a rare glimpse of contentment. He loved being on the road with Fi. He even liked having someone challenge him. He'd grown up with squires, sons of noblemen who'd all feared him to some extent. His father's position was well-known, as was his to be next in line for the commander post. Those who didn't fear him sought his favour. It made friendships increasingly difficult. Until Fi came along. Fi was something else – personable, well-liked, many things Swinton feared he himself wasn't. And true to form, Fiore was at the bar, a small crowd gathered round him as he told some adventure tale, his hands waving expressively before him, the women surrounding him drinking in his tanned skin and Battalonian accent. Swinton drained the rest of his ale and relaxed back into the cushions of the booth. Years of drinking with Fi had taught him that once his attention had been stolen, there was no hope of gaining it back.

Someone slipped into the empty seat beside him. It was the woman Fi had spotted earlier. Her green eyes were lined with shimmering cosmetics, her breasts near bursting from her corset.

'I'm Georgette,' she said.

'Are you sure you're in the right place, Georgette?'

'You're Commander Swinton.'

'Yes.'

'And that's Fiore Murphadias.'

'You're very observant.'

She smiled and twisted to face him. She was striking, Swinton couldn't deny it. The cosmetics brought out the golden hues of her irises, and her mouth ...

'Excuse me,' he said, making to leave.

'Going so soon?'

'I'm afraid so.'

Her face flushed pink. 'Apologies, Commander, I ... I seem to have misread the situation.'

'There's no situation, and no need for apologies,' he told her as she shuffled from her seat to let him pass.

'Good evening, then, Commander.'

'Good evening, Georgette.'

He happened upon Fiore halfway up the stairs to the accommodations, pressing a young curvaceous beauty up against the wall. His friend's hands were tangled in the woman's hair, their breathing hitched as they kissed in a frenzy. Her fingers were at the laces of his jerkin. Swinton doubled back. He left the tavern and headed for the stables. His stallion, Xander, nuzzled his neck in greeting, as though he'd been expecting him.

'Hey there, comrade,' he said, stroking the beast's forehead before slipping on his bridle. Xander knew where they were about to go. Swinton could tell by the way his ears flicked and the direction in which he stood. Swinton finished saddling him and mounted.

'Ready for a quick visit home?' he said, brushing the flat of his palm down the horse's neck. Xander gave a soft snort and Swinton squeezed his sides. They galloped out of Grayside at a breakneck pace. Swinton had been waiting for the opportunity to get away all evening, and he didn't know when he'd get one again. He leaned in close to Xander's neck, urging the horse faster, relishing the cool night's air whipping the stallion's mane into his face. Together, they flew across the countryside, with the thundering beat of Xander's hooves pounding the earth. Willowdale was less than an hour's ride away. Swinton could ride there in his sleep, he'd done it so many times before. So could Xander. They kept to a steady gallop until they reached the outskirts of the village. He pulled gently on Xander's reins, and the pair came to a smooth stop.

Swinton's chest tightened as he took in the flickering lanterns in the windows of the townhouses and inn. Xander must have sensed his hesitation, as always, and the horse started forward again. They took the main road through the heart of the town at a slow trot. The thatched roofs, the windowsill herb gardens and the school building were all achingly familiar. But it wasn't until they passed the Willowdale Stables that his throat constricted. A lifetime ago, he'd spent much of his time there, with *her*. All royal squires spent a year training in Willowdale. Tannus, the royal weapons master, always said that the little rural town offered all four seasons in a day, and that the hard terrain was perfect for soldier life. That was the year he'd met her – *Eliza*. She had helped her father run the stables, where Swinton and some of the wealthier squires boarded their horses. Now, he took in the sturdy timber beams and locked gates, hearing the soft whinnies and neighs of the steeds within. He knew he would find no trace of her gentle nature and quiet passion left. Xander slowed and tossed his head in the direction of the stables.

'I know, comrade, I know,' Swinton said. He squeezed Xander's sides with his heels again, and they took off, this time to the burial ground. It was a little woodland clearing, not far from the corral where Eliza used to train the horses. Swinton dismounted and left Xander to graze. Hands in pockets, he wandered slowly towards Eliza's unmarked grave. She'd been buried beneath an ancient willow, her parents insisting that the tree was enough of a gravestone for their sweet girl. It had only been the three of them on that day, and Xander, who had only been a foal. Swinton and Eliza's father had dug the grave and placed her body, carefully wrapped in linen, down inside. The worst part had been shovelling the dirt back on top of her, his heart breaking anew each time the clumps thudded against her. How could just over a year with someone shape a person's entire future?

Swinton sat beside the base of the willow's trunk and lay a palm flat against the cool earth. Her bones lay beneath him. Grief clutched at his insides and he felt the pain bubble up within. He swallowed the lump in his throat. A long shadow cast along the bark of the tree. Xander stood solemnly beside him.

'We miss you,' he breathed, gripping a fistful of dirt and resting his head against the tree.

The next morning, Swinton was up at dawn. He saddled Xander and Indigo, having sent Jasper upstairs to wake the captain. Fiore was worse for wear when he emerged from the tavern.

'I know, I know,' Fiore said, rubbing his temples and taking the reins from Swinton's outstretched hand.

'I didn't say anything.'

'You didn't need to. Your look of disdain said more than enough.'

'There was no look.'

'There's always a look.'

The men mounted their horses and started down the road.

'Where'd you get to, anyway? I looked for you. Don't tell me the lovely Georgette had her way with you after all?' Fiore said, gnawing at a freshly baked roll.

Swinton laughed. 'Something like that.'

'Good lord, where's Dimitri and what have you done with him?'

'Enough, Fi. We've gotta get a move on, or we'll lose all that time we gained over the past few days.'

'Fine, fine. But I expect some level of detail over lunch.'

'There'll be no time for lunch.'

'Dinner, then.'

Swinton urged Xander into a canter. 'Dinner, then,' he called back, leaving Fiore in his dusty wake.

The scenery of the East Farmlands swallowed them whole. Swinton loved it out here, the plummeting, fertile hills, the grazing cattle, the sheer open space with the villagers and farmers few and far between. Most of all, he loved the straight, orderly rows of corn plants. Their leaves were such a vibrant green, reflecting the golden glow of the afternoon sun, and contrasting with the rich, dark soil at their roots. The cool breeze whipped his face as they rode. The air out here was fresh, unlike the stale scent of the capital and the rotting fish smell of the docks at Port Morlock. They rode at a gallop. Swinton wanted to gain as much ground as he could before another sunset. He figured they were about a day's ride from Valia River, and he wanted to get there before the following sundown.

'You're going to kill poor Indigo at this rate,' Fi shouted from behind him. 'Not every horse has had the same relentless training as your Xander.'

Swinton waved him off. There would be time for Fi's comments by the fire with a flask of wine, but for now, they needed to make haste. Swinton had chosen Indigo

239

for Fiore himself, with Carlington's help. He'd known they'd need a special horse to keep up, and Indigo had definitely been the best stallion for the job. They rode into the evening, well after the sun had dipped below the horizon, and it was only when Swinton felt Xander's energy flagging beneath him that he called for them to stop.

It was still warm enough in the season that they didn't need a tent. They could build a small fire and sleep beneath the stars. Swinton left Fi to cool and water the horses, while he scoured the nearby ground for firewood. When the fire was crackling, and both men had kicked off their boots, they rested against their packs and chewed on dried meat and hard cheese. Swinton's whole body was aching, and he longed for a hot bath to soothe his tired muscles. It would be a while yet before he could enjoy that luxury. He looked up to find Fiore watching him, concern wrinkling his brows.

'What?'

'You never told me what the king said about all the business in the Hawthornes.'

'Nothing of note,' said Swinton, 'just get the girl, get Henrietta Valia.'

'You weren't reprimanded?'

'Should I have been?'

'I don't know, Dimitri,' Fi said, suddenly serious. 'This whole situation makes me uneasy, like there's a lot more to it we don't understand.'

'It's not our job to understand.'

'No?'

'No. It's our job to do as the king commands.'

Fiore chewed thoughtfully. 'You know what my father used to say to me?'

'No doubt you'll tell me.'

'A good soldier does as he's commanded. A great soldier understands why first.'

'Typical Battalonian.'

'Why's that?'

'It's a dreamer's sentiment.'

'What's wrong with dreaming, old friend?'

Swinton took a swig from the flask, the harsh wine burning his throat as he swallowed. He passed the flask to Fi, silently hoping his friend wouldn't stay in his philosophical mood too long. His musings often led to heated arguments between the two men. Fiore took the flask and drank.

'I see you're in no mood for sparring today, Dimi?'

'I'd much rather hear about how you ended up in such a sorry state this morning, and why you slowed us down so much today.'

'Slowed us down? I was so far ahead you couldn't see me, old friend.'

'I must be going blind in my old age, then, Fi. It felt the other way round to me.'

Swinton sharpened his battleaxes by the fire as Fiore drank and talked. The Battalonian's voice was deep and melodic. There was something soothing about his tales, no matter how much debauchery they seemed to entail. Swinton listened as he ran the whetstone along each blade, testing the edge with the callused part of his thumb.

'What was Georgette like, then, eh?' said Fi, tossing Swinton the almost-empty wine flask.

'Fine,' he replied, shaking the flask at Fi, his brows raised.

'Talking makes me thirsty,' Fiore said with a grin.

'Everything makes you thirsty.'

'Life is thirsty work, old friend.'

'And you wonder why I have no silver left for fancy lodgings?'

Swinton finished the wine, and packed away his axes and the whetstone. He untied his bedroll from his pack and unravelled it.

Fiore opened his mouth, no doubt to inquire after Georgette again, but Swinton cut him off.

'Get some rest,' he told his friend, 'we ride hard tomorrow.'

'Makes a change,' Fi muttered from across the glowing embers.

Swinton lay down, feeling his spine crack and the muscles in his back protest. He was weary all of a sudden. There was still much of this journey to go, and he had a feeling that the easy days were behind them.

Chapter Seventeen

Dash heard the slap of leather before he felt the sharp burn of pain across the backs of his legs. He cried out and his body jerked, but Pa struck again, the belt breaking Dash's already welt-covered skin.

'How could you have been so stupid, Zachary?' Pa yelled, finally shoving Dash off his lap. Dash sobbed, unable to sit or walk. *Ten beltings. Ten beltings for sparring with the squires and going into the maze.*

'That's enough, Emmett. Master Dash knows he did wrong.' Ma was a reassuring blurry figure through his tears, but her soft hand on his shoulder only made him cry harder.

'He's got *no idea*, Dorothy. *None*. Do you know what could have happened to us?'

'All the same, Emmett. It's enough.'

Pa threw the belt to the floor and stormed out, the front door rattling on its hinges.

'Come now,' Ma said, helping Dash onto his bed to lie on his front. 'I already made a gypsyweed salve, wait here.'

Dash cried into his pillow. He didn't understand what he'd done wrong. He'd returned home from the maze with a handful of those rare red blooms and three silvers that he'd won fair and square from one of the squires. Ma bustled back into the room, a small wooden bowl clutched in her hands.

'Honestly, love,' she said, 'I don't know what got into you.'

'Why?' he sniffed. 'Why is Pa so mad?'

'Mad?'

'I thought I ... I thought the silver would make him *happy*.'

'Oh, Dash.' Ma sighed, applying the salve to the swelling welts. 'Your pa wasn't mad exactly. He was scared.'

'Scared?'

'Yes. There are a lot of things you don't understand yet.'

'Like what?' Dash sucked in his breath through his teeth as the salve stung his skin, but then pulled the heat from the wounds.

'Like how getting those silvers from the Wendley boy ... Well, it's insulting to a nobleman, Dash.'

'But I won them! It was fair.'

'I know, but those boys – you've embarrassed them in front of their friends, and, well, Pa works for their father, Lord Wendley.'

'So?'

'So, whose silver do you think that really is? Everything and everyone is connected, Dash. We each have our place in life, and yours is here with me and

Pa, not with the brutish Wendley boys, nor is it in that maze.'

'Ma, I saw —'

'Do *not* tell anyone what you saw, Zachary Carlington. You shouldn't have seen anything. You shouldn't have gone in there at all.'

'But, Ma, why —'

'Always with the *why*, Dash. *Why do I have to eat the green beans? Why can't I have more roast potato? Why do I have to help Pa at the stables?*'

'Well, why?'

'No, not this time, Dash. Or you'll get another ten beltings from your pa. There are some things in life that have no "why"; they just are. And this is one of those things.'

Dash sniffed again, his pillow wet against his hot cheek. He didn't understand. Beside him, Ma sighed and tweaked Bryson, Dash's favourite stuffed bear, on the nose.

'There are to be no more tears, Master Dash,' she said, 'and no more arguing with your pa. I won't hear any more of it.'

Dash nodded slowly. Mama took Bryson from his hands and examined him carefully, running her hands over the embroidered royal sigil on his front.

'I'd love to wash this filthy old thing, but I fear he'll fall apart.'

'I don't want you to wash him.'

'He's terribly old and dirty,' she said.

'I don't care.'

'No, I don't suppose you do. He belonged to your father, you know.'

'I *know* that,' Dash said, wiping his snotty nose on his sleeve.

Mama grimaced. 'Use a handkerchief, Dash, for the love of Connos. I'm the one who has to scrub those garments.'

'Sorry,' he mumbled.

Mama placed Bryson the bear next to him. 'I suppose we can start a new story before lights out, if you like.'

Bleary-eyed and clutching threadbare Bryson to his chest, Dash nodded. With the candles flickering, Ma stroked his hair and began an epic tale of the battle of the gods.

'Hundreds of years ago, all four continents had been one big mass of land. There had been many, many animals – big palma, famous for their incredibly warm fur, giant serpents, known for throwing entire ships off course and into the rocks, and teerah panthers, legendary cats bigger than horses that stalked the lands.'

Dash loved hearing about the mythical creatures, about how horses and teerah ran together in battle.

'Back then,' Ma said, 'the gods and goddesses lived alongside man in the heart of the realm. Rheyah, Enovius, Kuan, Yacinda, Connos, Liir, Vinyala, Lamaka. There was no conflict, no trouble. It was a peaceful time for all.'

'Until?'

'How do you know there's an "until"?'

'There's always an "until".'

Ma smiled. '*Until* one of our rulers, Doonan, an ancestor of King Arden, fell in love with Rheyah's youngest daughter, Liir.'

'Rheyah was the king of all the gods?'

'It depends who's telling the story.'

'You are.'

'Well, then, I was always with the Valians on this one – Rheyah the Huntress, the *queen* of all gods. There is no king. Though, don't go telling that to people.'

'Cross my heart.'

Ma looked at him sternly. 'Good,' she said. 'Now, after the mortal ruler fell in love with Liir —'

'Is this going to be a girl's story?'

'What?'

'A sappy kissy story?'

Ma frowned. 'Not even close,' she said. 'Are you going to let me continue? Without your silly interruptions?'

'Uh-huh.'

'Good. Now, as I was saying, the mortal ruler, Doonan, fell in love with Liir. It was not so surprising. Many mortals fell in love, or were at least infatuated with the gods. But to Rheyah's dismay, Liir returned his affections. It was the first and only union between mortal and immortal in our history. Not long after they wed, Doonan showed his true colours. Liir was with child, but sadly lost the baby. People say it was because her child was a mortal being carried in an immortal body. When she miscarried, Doonan blamed her. He said her body was poison to their child. One night, he had too much to drink and they argued about it, and he struck her.'

'He hit a girl?'

Ma nodded. 'But Liir fought back, and burned the man to cinders.'

'She *killed* him?'

'Yes, she killed him. She's the goddess of fire, after all. But when her mother, Rheyah, learned of what had happened, one death didn't avenge the pain and disrespect shown to her daughter. The mortals rallied against her, but she was god of all gods. And she had the serpents and the teerah at her bidding. They battled for weeks, and only because Rheyah allowed it so. Even after the battle, she wasn't done. She brought her wrath upon the land in one giant energy force that broke the continent into four pieces – the four kingdoms we know today.'

Dash let out a low breath. 'So the god queen won?'

'Yes, she did.'

'At fighting?'

'Yes – she's not the Huntress for nothing.'

He paused. 'But, Ma, girls can't fight.'

'Says who? Some girls can fight. Haven't I told you stories about the Valia kindred? Some say they are an all-women army. With the most skilled warriors in the land.'

As Dash was thinking, Ma pulled the blankets up to his chin and blew out the candle beside the bed. Ma was at the door, a stream of light filtering in from the kitchen.

'Ma?' Dash called.

'Mmm?'

'If Olena could see, do you think she would fight?'

Ma leaned on the doorjamb for a moment before she said, 'I think the princess is already fighting, love. In her own way.'

The next day, Dash's pants chafed painfully across the welts on the back of his legs as he mucked out the stalls.

'Don't you understand that everything we do, we do for *you*?' his father had yelled as he struck Dash with his belt.

No. Dash certainly did *not* understand. This had been his *chance*, his shot to become something other than the stable master's son. Dash shovelled the horse manure and soiled straw into the cart behind him. Pa had woken him up at the crack of dawn and was watching him like a hawk. There was no way Dash could sneak past him to get to the squires' training. After he'd emerged from the maze, he'd run straight to the squires' quarters, where he'd thrust the red blooms at the Wendley brothers. The other squires had erupted in applause, with one of them even lifting Dash up into the air. One of the kinder ones, Rainer, had told him to meet them for training the next day. This morning, Dash had tried to reason with Ma, but she'd sided with Pa, as always.

'Pa knows what's best for you, Dash. We both have to

trust him.'

Later, Pa only relieved him of his duties when Olena summoned him to the gardens.

'If you take one step towards that training ground,' his father said, as Dash hung up his shovel, 'that belting last night will look like kindness.'

'Yes, sir.' Dash didn't even look at Pa.

Dash hobbled through the rows of hedges and flowers, and spotted Olena at her usual place – the stone bench with the angel statues beside it. Her guards were stationed on either side of her.

'Hello, Dash,' she called.

'Are you still mad?' he asked, inhaling sharply against the pain as he lowered himself onto the bench. He hadn't shown up to meet her yesterday.

'Yes, but are you alright?'

'Uh-huh.'

'Really? I heard you got in trouble yesterday.'

Dash rolled his eyes. Olena may not be able to see, but she somehow had eyes and ears everywhere.

'It was nothing,' Dash said.

'Liar.'

Dash said nothing. He didn't want to tell her it had all started because of her. Perhaps she already knew.

'Do you know what's happening tomorrow?' Olena asked.

'Sir Caleb arrives,' Dash said.

'Yes, Sir Caleb arrives. I thought you might like to be my guest, to the feast.'

One of the guards looked at Dash, and then to the princess. 'Your Highness,' he said gently, 'I'm not sure Their Majesties would approve of your choice of guest.'

'I already asked my mother,' she said, without turning in the guard's direction. 'I told her you're my eyes, Dash. You help me to see.'

Dash wasn't allowing himself to hope. This wouldn't come to pass.

'I told her I'd sooner jump off the Heathton cliffs than be accompanied by one of those horrible noblemen's daughters. They barely speak to me, Dash.'

As thrilled as he was that the princess had rejected those stupid noble girls, he knew that there was no way he'd be allowed to attend the feast. He was the stable master's son. The royals and their courtiers may turn a blind eye to him keeping the princess company on an average day, and even when he attended her lessons with her sometimes, but not for a formal feast. Not for something as important as honouring Sir Caleb.

'My mother said we'll have to get you some formal attire, and perhaps say you are a distant cousin. I'm not seated at the main table anyway.'

'What?'

Olena raised her eyebrows. 'Why would they want a poor blind girl sapping the life out of the party? I'm – or rather, *we* – are to sit with our "friends", the noblemen's daughters and the squires.'

'I'm ... I'm really allowed?'

'*Yes.*'

Pa was furious again. But no matter how much he wanted to, he knew that to decline a royal invitation was considered treasonous. Dash could hardly sit still. This was happening. He was going to attend a royal feast. He was going to be in the same room as Sir Caleb Swinton. He was called to the castle first thing the next morning, where he and Olena took a lesson in formal dining etiquette. Dash never knew there was so much to learn about forks. For most of the lesson, Olena gazed towards the window, only half listening. She already knew all of this. This lesson was for his benefit. And so he listened, not wanting to embarrass his friend, or Pa for that matter, at the big event.

After the governess was satisfied with his table manners, Olena took his arm and led him upstairs. The hallways were lit brightly with candles and torches along the walls, illuminating portraits of past kings looking down on Dash. He wondered how Olena navigated the twists and turns of the hallways without sight. But she knew every step, every door. They stopped at a thick wooden door, Olena's hand reached for the handle and turned.

'Where are we going?' Dash asked, trying to keep the nerves from straining his voice.

'The royal seamstress,' said the princess. 'We can't have you attend the feast in your stable clothes.'

Inside the room, it was chaos. There were rolls of fabric lining every wall, and mannequins being shoved into formal attire, being pinned and prodded. All the while several harried-looking women bustled around, pins in their mouths, hair scraped messily off their faces and dress patterns clutched in their hands.

'Oh, Your Highness!' said one of the women as she nearly ran into Olena.

'Bertha,' Olena said with a smile, 'this is the cousin I was telling you about. Unfortunately, his trunk fell into the water as his guard was crossing the river and his best tunics were ruined.'

'But of course, of course. This way, Master ...'

'Zachary,' Olena said quickly. He shot her a look she'd never see. She knew he hated his first name. It was usually only used when he was in a tremendous amount of trouble.

'Master Zachary, this way. Let's get your measurements, then.'

From the way Bertha looked at him and fussed over him with her measuring tape, Dash realised that the seamstress knew exactly who he was. But for Olena, they would all pretend otherwise. Around them, the other women carried on with their work, sewing last-minute embellishments onto gowns and stitching house sigils onto tunics.

'Does Master Zachary have a favourite colour?' Bertha asked.

'Blue,' said Olena before Dash could answer. 'The deepest blue you have.'

'Very good, Your Highness.'

Bertha was careful not to prick him as she pinned

the fabric in place around him. The colour was indeed striking; even Dash thought so. A shade of blue like the clearest night sky, only better. And it felt expensive. More expensive than anything Dash had ever touched before. He'd have to be careful not to spill anything.

'What do you think, Your Highness?' Bertha said to Olena.

Dash gaped. That was *rude*! Didn't she know Olena couldn't see?

But Olena smiled and came over to them, running her fingers gently across the fabric. 'Feels like you've done a wonderful job,' she said.

Bertha beamed.

The distinguished guests began arriving well before nightfall, and the courtyard was brimming with carriages, big dresses and guards. Dash could see his pa directing the drivers towards the stables, while his stable hands took care of the lone riders. Dash had never seen such a display of wealth at close proximity. The biggest and best thoroughbreds in Ellest; ladies with glimmering brooches, jewels and glamorous feathered headpieces; and knights. So many knights dressed in their finest, with their house sigils embroidered proudly onto their breasts, and swords with elaborate pommels at their waists.

'That's why a lady must always dance on the man's left,' Ma had told him once. Not that Dash would be dancing. His education of nobility had started and ended at which fork to use.

Olena told him to wait with the other noblemen's children in the entrance hall. Despite not being seated at the royal table, she still had royal duties to perform and was swept away by the queen, who hadn't even glanced at Dash. He'd never seen the castle before during a grand event, and the building itself seemed to have come alive. Every candle was lit and waving in welcome as wealthy lords and ladies glided past. Every surface glistened, dusted at least forty times that day. It was a sight to be seen and Dash knew he'd never forget it. He'd never forget how, for once in his life, he was a part of the elite. No one looked at him, not because he was invisible, but because they saw him as one of them. With his messy dark hair cleaned, brushed and slicked back off his face, he blended right in with the highborn children of Ellest. He noted that his tunic and pants and shining black shoes were of an even finer make than those of his peers. He was, after all, the princess's foreign cousin. For tonight, he may as well be royalty.

And then, he arrived. Sir Caleb's carriage pulled into the courtyard. Dash could just make out the guards and the crossed axes on their sigils. Dash took a deep breath. He was really here. Dash was going to see his idol in the flesh. The royal family waited in the centre of the entrance hall, with all manner of dignitaries paying their respects and bestowing gifts. Sir Caleb and Lady Yuliana came through the doors. An awed quiet fell over the room, and King Arden strode towards the knight.

'Caleb,' the king greeted him warmly.

Sir Caleb dropped to one knee. 'Your Majesty. You do me yet another great honour.'

'Nonsense, get up, Caleb!'

Sir Caleb rose slowly, but kept his head bowed in respect. 'Your Majesty is too good to me.'

But the king swung an arm around the knight's shoulder and directed him to the rest of the royal family.

Sir Caleb took the queen's hand and pressed his lips to the back of it, bowing. 'Your Majesty. It is such a pleasure to see you again. Your beauty grows with every year. You remember my wife, Lady Yuliana?'

Behind the knight, Lady Yuliana curtsied, her heavy skirts rustling.

Sir Caleb moved along to Prince Jaxon. 'My prince,' he said, bowing again, 'you're becoming quite the swordsman, I hear?'

And finally, Sir Caleb got to Olena, who was smiling widely.

'Your Highness,' he said, kissing her hand, 'your beauty rivals that of even your mother.'

'I wouldn't know,' said Olena with a grin.

To Dash's surprise, the knight laughed. 'I trust they still can't keep up with you?'

'They try.'

Sir Caleb chuckled again.

'Sir Caleb,' said Olena, holding onto the knight's hand. 'Yes, Princess?'

'There's someone I would very much like you to

meet.'

'Any friend of yours, Highness, is a friend of mine.'

Dash's stomach swooped. She wouldn't. Olena wouldn't be so crazy, so foolish? But she was. She was leading the knight right towards Dash, and Dash could see the panic in the queen's eyes behind them. This wasn't part of their agreement. Olena was suddenly there, tugging Dash out of the crowd of nobles' children.

'This,' she said, pulling him forward, 'is my third cousin, Zachary.'

With his heart pounding wildly, Dash bowed his head, and to his astonishment, Sir Caleb offered a hand to shake.

'It's an – an honour to meet you, Sir Caleb,' Dash managed.

'Pleasure to meet you, Zachary.'

As Dash grasped the knight's rough, callused hand, a shock wave rolled over him, and the room before him disappeared.

Icy salt wind whipped his face, and he gripped the railing hard as the ship knocked against the choppy ocean. It was dark but for the moonlight. There was no one else out on the water, no one else on the ship, but for the girl steering. Her dirty, ash-blonde hair was pulled up in a messy knot above her head. She had a swollen, split lip, but fierceness fired her odd-coloured eyes as she steadied the big wheel before her. She tightened one of the ropes to her right, somehow unable to see Dash. Looking ahead, she took a deep breath, and Dash followed her gaze.

The mist billowed over the waves, tumbling in towards them in thick, ominous clouds. They were heading right for it. The ship shuddered as a massive, white wave broke upon the deck with a roar. Dash spun back around and stared at the girl in disbelief. Her mouth was set in a hard line, and she turned the wheel. She must be mad. Truly and utterly mad. Suddenly, the ship surged forward. The roiling mist swallowed them whole.

'You alright, son?' Sir Caleb was saying.

The entrance hall came back into focus, and Dash looked up, into the knight's concerned eyes, still gripping his hand. The mortification washed over him, flushing his cheeks and making him stumble over his words. Dash let go at once and mumbled his profuse apologies. But Sir Caleb didn't look irritated as Dash had expected; he didn't step back and move on. Instead, the knight's eyes lingered over him, puzzled at first, and then narrowing, as though committing his features to memory.

Chapter Eighteen

Swinton could feel the grit from the journey sticking to the sweat along his hairline. He tried to wipe it away on the back of his sleeve, but it only spread the dirt further across his face. Beside him, Fiore seemed perfectly comfortable, and Swinton silently cursed his friend's Battalonian tolerance for heat. They finally came upon the Valia River, the widest river in all of Ellest. Its waters raced across jagged rocks and foamed at its mouth like a rabid dog. Swinton dismounted and approached the old man who owned the barge docked at the river's edge. The man was hunch-backed, wrinkled and grey-haired. He'd been manning Valia River for as long as Swinton could remember.

'They ain't gonna be happy to see you,' he said by way of greeting, and nodded towards the towering trees on the other side.

'They never are,' said Swinton, pushing two silver coins into the man's dirt-lined palm.

'Any news from them, then?' Fi asked, jumping down from his horse as well.

'There'd sooner be news from a teerah panther.'

'Helpful, as always, old friend.'

'Don't "old friend" me, Battalonian. You're in Ellest now.'

Fiore shook his head and tried to lead the horses onto the rocking barge. 'A little help here, Dimitri,' he said, as the horses shifted nervously.

Swinton helped Fi get the horses positioned on the barge, and the old man stepped on after them, his fingers expertly threading through the ropes holding the boat in place. The barge lurched as it was set free from its tethers, and the horses whinnied. Swinton stroked Xander's nose.

'Easy there,' he muttered, bringing the horse's muzzle to his face.

The old man steered the barge through the currents with a long pole, navigating the deadly dips in the riverbed.

'What d'you want with the kindred?' he called out over the roar of the rapids.

'King's business,' Swinton said, holding Xander steady as the barge dropped suddenly, water sloshing over the side, wetting his boots.

'King's got a lot of business.'

Swinton ignored him and focused on the Valian side. There was no going back now. The barge dipped again. Finally, they crunched onto the sandy bank, and they led their horses back onto firm ground, while the old man roped the barge back to the timber posts.

'We'll be a few days,' Swinton told him. 'Will you be here when we return?'

'Might be. Lead a busy life, I do.'

'There are three more silvers in it for you if you are.'

The man considered this. 'I'll see what I can do,' he said, tying the final knot.

Swinton nodded and waved him away.

It had been nearly ten years since Swinton had visited Valia, and as the looming trees closed in around him, he remembered why he hadn't been back. He pushed the memories from his mind. If he went down that road, there was a chance he'd never find his way back.

On horseback once again, they moved deeper into the forest. Every rustle, every snap of a branch sent Swinton's hands to his battleaxes. The horses were also on edge, hesitating and stomping their hooves. The canopy thickened, and around them, the forest grew denser and darker.

'They sense magic, don't they?' said Fiore.

'Don't talk to me of magic.'

'You're not one for talking much these days, Dimitri. You make a poor riding companion.'

'Apologies the trip has been so unpleasant for you.'

'Oh, I wouldn't say entirely unpleasant,' Fiore said with a wink.

After a time, they stopped by a small creek to refill their canteens and water the horses.

'So, you pissed that you missed out on your father's feast?' Fiore asked, splashing his face with water.

'I'd rather be doing my duty than attending some fancy party.'

'I wouldn't,' said Fiore.

'I'm well aware of that. Sorry for spoiling the fun.'

'Not big on fun, are you?'

'Shut it. Let's get a move on.' Swinton shook his head, but couldn't keep the smile from tugging at the corner of his mouth again. Swinton had been batting away Fi's teasing for years. When Fiore's family had moved from Battalon to Ellest, there had been much gossip in the realm. Although the Murphadias family weren't royalty, they were nobles: incredibly wealthy and influential, owning several estates in Belbarrow. They journeyed to Ellest at the request of the king, and for a time, people speculated that Fiore was to be betrothed to any future princess. But Fiore had been placed in the King's Army, and more specifically, the gifted squire squadron. He had no formal training and had not even been in the royal guard of Battalon. This was all common knowledge, and so when the other squires discovered that a foreigner had been appointed to their squadron with little to no experience, there was trouble. The then-teenage squires plotted, pranked and rumour-mongered to the point where Fiore simply challenged them to combat. Although his style of combat lacked the traditional conventions, his undefeated record among the squires left them begrudgingly respectful of him. He advanced through the training with little effort, claiming that he felt as light as air without Battalon's pressing humidity.

The horses remained nervous, especially as they ventured further and further into the forest. Swinton's skin prickled, and he knew they were being watched, but they saw nothing, heard nothing. He glanced down at the scroll sticking out of his saddlebag, the purple royal seal glaring up at him. What were they about to walk into?

They weren't left wondering for long. Only an hour into the forest, something, *someone* dropped from the trees before them. Their horses reared. Swinton recognised the fiery-red braid of Athene. Fiore made to draw his sword, but Swinton held out a hand. No, they couldn't start off like that.

'You're later than we expected,' Athene said, raising an eyebrow at Fiore's attempt to mask his initial intentions. 'Leave your horses and your weapons.'

'We need the horses.'

'They'll be taken care of,' she said, nodding to the ten warriors who now surrounded them.

Fiore baulked, but Swinton slid off Xander and did as she asked. If he argued, Athene would realise just how much of a bargaining chip Xander was. Swinton tugged the scroll from the saddlebag before handing the reins over.

'Weapons, too. And *slowly.*'

Swinton began unstrapping his sword belt and the axes at his back, and removed the dagger from his boot. Fiore followed suit. Athene nodded to another kindred, who came up to them and patted them down roughly. They were groped and prodded with no mind for their dignity, but Swinton stood straight. He had done the same to others in his time. When it was thoroughly established that they were unarmed, the same woman blindfolded them. They were on the move. Swinton felt completely exposed, unable to see a thing, tripping and stumbling through the thick undergrowth of the forest. One of the kindred pulled him along at a pace that even he found difficult to match.

'How much further?' he asked.

No answer. Swinton couldn't detect anything unusual around him with his other senses. It smelled like flowering trees in the springtime, fresher than the farmlands they'd slept in only the night before. The only sounds he could hear were his own stumbling across the leaf litter and the branches above him rustling in the breeze. The kindred surrounding him didn't speak, and he couldn't even be certain how close they were to him. Every now and then he'd hear Fiore cursing not too far away, clearly battling with the tree roots and branches, but other than that the kindred and their forest remained a mystery. The terrain descended at one point, and Swinton felt his calves straining to keep him upright. After what felt like an age, Athene spoke.

'Your companion will wait here with the rest of the kindred. You – climb,' she said, placing his hands on what felt like a ladder before him.

You've got to be kidding.

'Can I at least remove the blindfold?'

'No.'

There was no arguing with her. Swinton took each

rung slowly, ensuring that the arch of his foot was firmly placed before heaving his weight up onto it. The ladder groaned, and he felt it give, just a fraction. Athene must be behind him. She was game. He had counted fifteen rungs so far, which meant he was well on his way to being *extremely* high up. He tried to force the churning in his stomach back down. Now was not the moment to lose it. As he reached for another rung, he found his hand creeping up the edge of a platform instead.

'Keep climbing,' Athene called from below him, 'pull yourself up onto it.'

'Easy for you to say,' Swinton muttered, hauling himself up onto what felt like a timber deck. Someone grabbed him under the arms and dragged him away from the edge.

'Didn't know you didn't like heights, Commander,' said Henri's smooth voice. She tugged the blindfold away from his face.

He blinked rapidly as his eyes adjusted to the dappled light, and the bright living quarters in which he now stood. Arched windows looked out onto the vast treetops of Valia Forest, it looked as though they went on forever, right to the horizon.

'Welcome to my humble abode,' Henri said, perching herself on one of the windowsills, arms folded across her chest. One of her eyebrows was ever so slightly raised, as though she found some cruel amusement in the situation.

Swinton felt naked without his weapons. Around

him, everything was made of pale timber. There was a lightness to this space that he'd never encountered in the capital, or anywhere. Crafted in the same grain of timber as the apartment itself were a matching table and chairs. Long benches stretched beneath both windows, and hooks housing weapons and garments lined the walls, leading off into other rooms. On one wall hung a dozen or so different katars – Henri's weapon of choice, as he well knew. Draped across the back of one of the chairs was a thick, grey palma fur. He looked back to the warrior queen, clad in dark leathers that hugged her frame, poised for violence. Even more unnerving was the hardness her face held. Perhaps once beautiful, now, her kohl-lined eyes shot suspicion wherever they looked, grey as stone, speckled with moss green.

The timber floor beneath him creaked softly as Athene swung herself up onto the platform.

'You're not needed,' Henri said, without even looking at her first-in-command.

Swinton hid his surprise. Henri wanted to talk to him completely alone? Athene didn't respond. She bowed her head and slid down a thick vine that hung outside.

'Sit,' Henri said, flicking a hand towards one of the chairs beside the desk.

Swinton sat.

'No doubt you have something for me?' she said.

'I do,' said Swinton, finding his voice hoarse. He pulled the now-crumpled scroll from his belt. At least the seal was still intact.

Henri took it and ripped it open. She scanned the parchment quickly, and then re-read it several times before looking up at Swinton.

'Have you read this?' She waved the scroll at him.

'I don't know its contents, no.'

Henri leaned back against the window frame and crossed her legs at the ankle. Swinton took in her lithe build and muscular limbs.

'What did you tell the king of our encounter in the Hawthornes?' she asked.

'The truth.'

'And what's that? Everyone has their own version.'

'That we had the girl, that one of our less honourable men made to assault her, and you and your kindred stepped in.'

'And?'

'And took the girl.'

'Ah, yes. The girl. Tell me truly, what does King Arden of Ellest want with an old fisherman's orphan? A drunk, dirty nobody? Why go to such lengths for one Ashai?'

Swinton rubbed the bridge of his nose. 'I don't know.'

'You don't know? *You* don't know? The Commander of the King's Army?'

'He doesn't answer to me.'

'Bleak has little to no control over her abilities. What's special about her?'

'Like I said, I don't know.'

'I find it strange that Arden does not entrust these matters to you. Don't you?'

'*King* Arden.'

Henri ignored this and moved to the table, where she rifled through some papers. 'I've heard he has a renewed interest in the Ashai people. There were rumours of a register.'

She slid a piece of parchment towards him. Swinton took a tentative step forward and gazed down at it. It was ripped at the top, where it had been torn from a noticeboard or shop window, but he recognised it. He'd seen many copies like it, had even ordered some of his men to hammer the flyers up in the village square. The king wanted as many Ashai as possible to come forward.

'Where'd you get this?' he said, running his fingers over the stamped lettering.

Register today for generous rewards, and the opportunity to serve your crown. Preserve your magical heritage. See Tannus Armenta at the castle gates for assistance.

Henri shrugged, pulling the flyer back towards her.

'Some friends I made in the capital know how much I enjoy the king's literature.'

Swinton ground his teeth. 'There is a register, yes.'

'I gathered. And what of you? Does the king know?'

Swinton's heart leapt into his throat. His eyes snapped up to Henri's. Her cold gaze bore into his. How much did she know? How much was just speculation?

'What?'

'You don't remember meeting me before.'

'We never met. Not officially. But I did see you at your sister's memorial. Ten years ago.'

Henri nodded, then proceeded to pick at her nails, looking bored. 'We "met officially" after the funeral rite, after we burned Sahara's belongings on the pyre.'

Familiarity stirred within Swinton, but he couldn't place it. That day, all those years ago. It held so much more than just Sahara Valia's memorial. Swinton swallowed the lump in his throat and forced himself to match Henri's stare.

'I don't remember,' he said flatly.

'There wasn't much conversation,' she said bluntly, and it was clear she didn't care whether or not he remembered their encounter, only that during it, she'd learned something about him, a weak spot in his armour that she was now about to exploit. He racked his memory. If he could figure it out, perhaps he had a shot at outwitting her, perhaps ...

The memorial came swimming back to him. The forest had filled with hundreds of nobles from around the whole realm, not just Ellest. They were all packed closely between the ancient trees, whispering among themselves. They couldn't see the ceremony taking place in what was now known as the Forest of Ghosts. Back then, it had been the most beautiful part of Valia, where rich green beds of herbs filled the air with a light, exotic fragrance. Everything was flourishing and nurturing the rest of the forest. But Swinton hadn't just been there to pay his respects. He'd been there with orders from the king, orders that he'd told no one of, not even Fiore. Henri *couldn't* know ...

'We "met" after,' Henri said. 'Hours later. There was drinking. Lots of it.'

'And?' Swinton forced himself to say. There were too many secrets he had been commanded to keep.

'I believe this,' she leaned forward and pulled at the chain around his neck, 'was removed.'

He jerked away from her, but her finger had looped around the chain peeking through his shirt and she pulled it towards her, revealing the coin of Yacinda soldered to the end.

'I imagine it contains some sort of gem or herb to stifle your own abilities. So when it was removed, it became obvious to me what you were.'

'You've known for all this time?'

Henri shrugged, leaning back against the desk.

'And you told no one?'

'Why would I tell someone that?'

Swinton forced himself to breathe steadily through his nose. 'The king doesn't know,' he found himself saying. His chest tightened as he cursed his own disloyalty. He shouldn't be telling Henri Valia a thing. Not a single, damn thing.

'I gathered as much,' she said. 'The coin grows weak, by the way.'

'What?'

'The herbs that were used to treat it, they've worn away. Its ability to shield you has started to falter, especially when your emotions run high. Didn't you wonder why I could use my abilities on you in the ranges?'

Gods, Swinton thought, the news hitting him like a blow. He took a deep breath and dug his nails into the arms of the chair. 'What ... What happened between us?'

Henri shook her head. 'Maybe you'll remember one day, maybe you won't. But it was clear I wasn't the only one who had lost someone in those days.'

Swinton got up from the chair. He would *not* have her take him back to that. *That* was none of her damned business. The warrior queen didn't move, she was as still as a stone, but she took in his movements, every step as he paced, every flicker of his eyes.

'So what now?'

'Now, we go to Heathton.'

Swinton stopped pacing. 'We do?'

'Thought you were going to have to fight me on it?'

'Do you blame me?'

'For many things, but not this.' Henri folded the parchment and slipped it into the front of her leathers. 'But we are going to do this my way.'

Just as he turned towards the exit, Henri looped the blindfold back around his face.

'Why stifle it?' she said in his ear.

'What?'

'Your magic. Why use the coin? Why give up that ability?'

Swinton's hand moved unconsciously to his chest,

where beneath his shirt lay the source of his control.

'What would you do, if you could see what's coming but could do nothing to stop it? What if, every time you needed your ability, it failed you?'

'That would never happen to me.'

'Then don't ask.'

She shrugged. 'One final thing, Commander.'

He turned back towards her voice.

'It takes a real bastard to hunt down his own kind, don't you think?'

Swinton was taken to the campsite. There, they removed the black cloth from his face and he blinked in his surroundings yet again. More trees, more greenery, apartments built into the trees, and, if he strained his eyes, he could see bridges above them, linking everything together. Around him, fearless warriors sharpened blades and eyed him suspiciously. Fiore was shoved down roughly beside him, his blindfold also removed.

'Did you tell her, then?'

'I gave her the summons, yes.'

'And?'

'And she took it better than I thought. Almost too well, really.'

'Oh?'

'Can't say more.'

'Right.'

The silence that hung between them was heavy. In the past, Swinton had always said more. Whatever he knew, Fiore knew. Now, the chasm of secrets between them was growing. It squeezed his insides, a relentless reminder of the inevitability of constant change. Swinton thought about the meeting with Henri. He didn't want to push the warrior queen, not yet. Not ever, if he could help it. She'd made it clear she wasn't someone who should be crossed. She'd made damn sure he knew that she was aware of his vulnerabilities. *No one* knew them. Despite his pride, he knew that if it came to it, he and Fiore didn't stand a chance against the kindred on their own turf. Not here. Athene was across the fire from him, analysing him. He wondered how many of her kindred Henri had revealed his secret to. Or was she telling the truth? Had she truly told no one? It was possible, if their previous encounter had been as intimate as she'd implied.

'What in hell is *he* doing here?' said a voice from behind him.

He whirled around, and there she was – the girl he'd failed to extract from Angove and bring to the king. She looked different since the last time he'd seen her – cleaner, fuller. She held a tattered piece of rope in her hands, which she dropped as her eyes latched onto his. In less than a second, she'd flung herself at him, and her small hands closed around his throat. Up close, the whites of her eyes were yellowed and there were deep purple shadows beneath them. Her thumb and index finger squeezed his trachea. He suppressed the urge to gag; he needed to feel the air in his throat once again. Swinton choked and shoved her away easily. She stumbled backwards, but rushed at him again as soon as she found her footing. None of the kindred stopped her; they looked on, more amused than anything else. A young man, who seemed vaguely familiar to Swinton, tried to grab the girl's arm, but she lashed out, swiping his hand away. He stared at her a moment and then shrugged. She lunged at Swinton again, this time aiming a kick at his groin. He blocked it, but the attack kept coming. It was Fiore who pulled her off him.

'Bleak,' Fiore said. 'Bleak, remember me?'

She turned to him, the wildness in her eyes fading to recognition.

'He …' she panted, glaring at Swinton, 'he would have let that creep have me.' She turned to Fiore, looking up into his face.

'No,' Fiore said, 'no, he wouldn't have.'

Fiore held the girl by the wrists gently. She wasn't pulling away, Swinton noticed. Fiore must have registered the silence around them, and dropped his hands.

'You're alright, Bleak,' he said, and took a step back. He nodded to the young man, who looked on from the outskirts of the group, eyes narrowed.

Swinton didn't say anything. He straightened himself and turned away. Clearly, his presence upset the girl. If he was honest with himself, he didn't blame her.

'You're here to take us to the king?' she asked Fiore.

'They are,' Henri said, stepping out into the clearing.

Swinton had to stop himself from turning around this

time. He hated having his back to the warrior queen, knowing how dearly she'd love to stab a knife in it.

'We'll leave five days from now,' she said.

This time, Swinton whirled around. 'We can't wait that long.'

Henri shrugged. 'I told you it would be my way.'

Swinton felt his jaw clench. He hated this. Hated being challenged in front of his men. Or man – the number was irrelevant. He was the Commander of the King's Guard, and the King's Army. Valian or not, who was she to argue with him?

'Those weren't the conditions,' he said.

'Conditions weren't stipulated, Commander.'

He paused. He hadn't seen the summons. He'd fought the temptation to rip that seal open every day, and he'd stayed true to his vows. He hadn't broken the royal seal. Though, perhaps a more sensible man would have.

'Let me see it, then,' he said, stretching out his hand.

'Fine.' She plucked it from the front of her leathers and tossed him the withered bit of parchment.

He caught it and took a few steps back, away from the centre of attention. He unfolded the soft paper and read. She was right. Nothing was, as she claimed, stipulated. All the parchment insisted was that the presence of Henrietta Valia and Bleaker Junior of Angove required in Heathton. They were to arrive within a fortnight from receiving the summons. Swinton racked his brain for more detailed instructions from the king. But they didn't come. The king had not provided him with further detail on how the two women were to be extracted from the forest. Was this a test? Would he be punished for some oversight later? He didn't return to the group immediately. He stared at the parchment, willing the terms and conditions to make themselves known. They didn't. He could decipher no hidden message or code, no matter how hard he stared at the inky page.

Slowly, he returned to Henri and extended the paper back out to the warrior queen.

'Fine,' he said.

Chapter Nineteen

Everyone knew about her drinking. It was obvious, or at least it was obvious now that she *wasn't* drinking. And Bleak had never wanted a drink more in her life. She stared at the back of Commander Swinton's head of coal-coloured hair. He looked completely out of place here. His armour, his tense stance and the way he spoke to Henri, all of it put her and the kindred on edge. Athene looked ready to slice him in half. Bleak looked away and swallowed, finding her throat dry. Wine, she needed wine. She scanned the tabletops.

'I had it taken away,' Henri said from beside her, toying with the king's summons between her long fingers.

'What?'

'The liquor. My kindred need all their wits about them with two King's Guard in our keep.' Without another word, Henri disappeared into the crowd of people. A lie. A lie of kindness, and Bleak didn't know if she was angry or grateful.

A familiar head of caramel hair was changing pots of stew over the fire.

'Lyse,' Bleak called out, and the girl's gaze snapped up to hers. Lyse gave her a broad smile, but continued to tend to her duties. Bleak faltered. Was she not allowed to speak to a groundling in the keep? Were there rules she didn't know about? Before she could approach Lyse, the girl had disappeared. A hush fell over the merry crowd, and Bleak strained her neck to pinpoint the cause. *Allehra*. Allehra padded through the camp, barefoot and wearing a gown the colour of sparkling wine. Each and every kindred bowed their head low as the Mother Matriarch passed. Bleak was shocked to see the commander and captain do the same. Everyone watched as Allehra walked towards *Bleak* and Bleak felt the burn of several eyes on her. Allehra took up a position beside her and gestured for all to continue with their business with a flick of her hand. The Valians went back to their food and conversations, though Swinton's eyes still lingered on them.

'Given the prompt arrival of our guests, we need to make the most of our time together. Where is Luka?' said Allehra.

'I ... I haven't seen her.'

Allehra looked sceptical. 'I heard of your little run-in at circuit one.'

Oh.

'Find her. Make amends. I expect to see you both within the hour. There is much work to do.'

Bleak heaved a sigh and pushed off from the tree she'd been leaning against. Would she never have a moment's peace again? She longed for an afternoon on the jetty, overlooking the water, a cold pint of ale in her hand and the coastal sun kissing her face.

I'll never take it for granted again, she promised herself as she moved into the throng of Valians to search for the stocky redhead. Bleak didn't know how she felt about helping Neemah. She didn't *think* she regretted it, but the trouble she'd caused Luka forced the guilt to tug from within. Luka had accepted her, included her, and offered up her mind for violation without a sniff of complaint. And Bleak had humiliated her. She did owe the young Valian an apology. She had to find her. But Luka was nowhere in sight.

Bleak squeezed between the kindred gathered around the fire and looked for Luka in her usual corners. She tried not to focus on the fact that she'd soon again be in the eerie confines of the warrior's mind, pushing her way through sixteen years of memories. She hadn't forgotten that she'd nearly lost herself there. Perhaps it was time she had an honest conversation with Allehra about it. Allehra could help her. Perhaps there was a way to anchor yourself to the present while delving into someone's past? Bleak was thinking so much about her training that she bumped into the commander, who was standing alert and tense at the edge of the keep. His burnt-umber eyes looked into hers, and she fought the urge to shrink away. She was *not* his prisoner. If anyone was in danger in Valia, it was *him*. She sidestepped around him, saying nothing. She should tell Henri about the map she'd seen him with when they were in the Hawthornes. She didn't know *what* exactly she'd seen, but his reaction had only made her more suspicious.

'I'm telling yer, the northern waters in high season are rough enough to turn any sailor's gut,' Bren was telling Tilly.

'Rubbish,' the Valian retorted. 'I've been all over the realm, and the East Seas around Moredon Tower are the worst. Even Henri was green for three days when we sailed from Felder's Bay to Havennesse. Bet you've never been —'

Bleak cleared her throat and both Bren and Tilly looked up, surprised.

'Have either of you seen Luka?' she asked, wringing her hands.

Bren shook his head.

'Try the outer keep. A bunch of the younger Valians have made one of the willows there their usual haunt,' said Tilly.

'Thanks.' Bleak ducked away from the pair, who launched right back into their debate. Bleak ignored the lurch in her stomach and continued to trudge through the undergrowth. The trainee kindred were gathered in the outer keep, throwing daggers at a board hanging from one of the trees.

'Bet you wouldn't be game to hold the target,' Luka said with a laugh as one of the young women threw a dagger and it landed at the very edge of the board, far from the star in the middle.

'Luka?' Bleak said, and the redhead turned around, her smile fading.

'What do you want?'

'To apologise.'

'Right.'

'No, really.'

The kindred around Luka were staring at Bleak with obvious dislike. They shifted impatiently, eager to get back to their game. Their thoughts buzzed almost in unison as Bleak took a step towards Luka.

'If you don't have a sense of loyalty in Valia, you don't have anything,' Luka said, picking up a dagger from the selection nearby and holding it by the tip, preparing to send it flying at the target.

Bleak knew what she had to do. She jumped in the line of fire and pulled the board from the tree.

'What the —'

Bleak positioned herself before Luka, lifting up the board, just above her own head.

'What do you think you're doing?'

'I'm sorry,' Bleak said, glancing up at the board. 'I truly am. And the way I see it, I trust you enough not to kill me with your next throw.'

'Yes, *you* trust *me*. I haven't done anything to make you feel otherwise. I haven't broken *your* trust. It's *your* loyalty in question, not mine.'

There was a murmur of agreement from the group.

'Three throws,' Bleak heard herself say, already feeling her palms growing clammy. 'You get three throws. If you feel like embedding a dagger in me at one point during those three throws, I won't hold it against you. Three throws, regardless of what target you find. But then we put the whole Neemah thing behind us.'

Luka considered the dagger she was holding, and then the board above Bleak's head.

'Done,' she said, and let the dagger fly. Bleak didn't even have time to flinch. There was a thud in the wood and she had to steady the board wobbling from the dagger's impact, a hair's breadth away from where her fingers were.

One.

A kindred passed Luka another dagger, and Luka adjusted her stance, side on, weapon raised. The wood thudded again. This time, the impact sang through Bleak's left hand. One of the women let out a low whistle through her teeth, enough to tell Bleak how close she'd just come to losing her fingers.

Two.

The third and final dagger was presented to Luka, and Bleak took a deep breath. She couldn't focus on Luka's thoughts with all the adrenaline pounding in her ears. Bleak looked straight at Luka, forcing herself to keep her eyes open and her breathing steady. The flick of Luka's wrist was a blur, and the dagger hurtled towards Bleak. *Impact.* Her heart stopped. Had it hit her? Was she in shock?

The kindred around her let out a cheer and hands clapped her on the shoulders. The board was taken from her. In it, the final dagger was buried dead centre in the target. Luka grinned at her and offered her hand. Bleak took it, still in shock as the Valian squeezed her fingers in a firm grip.

'How'd you know I wasn't going to hit you?'

'I didn't.'

Luka laughed and slung an arm around Bleak's neck. 'Best apology I've ever gotten,' she said.

Bleak wiped her sweaty hands on her pants. 'Allehra wants us to meet her.'

'Since when?'

''Bout a half hour ago.'

Luka was panic-stricken. 'Gods, Bleak – why didn't you say?'

'I wanted you to choose.'

'What?'

'I wanted you to choose to forgive me, not be forced.'

Luka stared at her.

'Well? Come on,' Bleak said finally. 'Lead the way.'

Luka yanked her daggers from the target, shaking her head in disbelief.

'What?' Bleak demanded.

Luka started back towards the keep, suddenly laughing. 'You're just not quite what we expected, Angovian.'

Chapter Twenty

The passages of Luka's mind were darker this time, made of black, glossy stone, as though the memories here had been solidified long ago, a permanent part of Luka's psyche. Even the ground beneath Bleak's boots was hard, shiny ore, and her footsteps echoed down the strange, eerie chambers. Once again, doorways lined each side of the passage, some leading off onto new passages of their own. Various versions of Luka filled these rooms, each pocket of memory heightened with tension and desperation that tugged at Bleak's own insides. She slowed at the door on her left.

Luka was in her early teen years, perhaps thirteen, but no older. She and Athene sat on the edge of a bed similar to the one Bleak had seen in Tilly's quarters. Athene had a comforting arm around her daughter's slumped shoulders, and Luka had her head in her hands, her wild, red hair unbound and spilling through her fingers.

'If I fight her, I'll win,' she ground out.

'Good. You're a skilled fighter, Luka,' said Athene.

'Ma, if I win, she'll go to the Sticks.'

'I know, but you have no choice. It's the Valian Way.'

'She's my *friend*, Ma. My *best* friend.'

'Luka, you *must* fight.'

'I can't —'

'You can, and you *will*.'

'I won't be responsible for banishing her.'

'You've helped banish dozens before her. Some of them were your friends, too.'

'And I hate myself for it. Every *damn* day.'

Athene's arm slid from Luka's shoulders. 'Do *not* use that tone with me.'

'Ma, can't you speak to Henri —'

'And bring attention to your weakness? Gods, Luka, have I taught you nothing?'

'She's my *friend*,' Luka pleaded as she got to her feet and started pacing the room.

'You think you are the only Valian to have lost a friend to the Sticks? She won't die, Luka.' Athene stood and stepped towards the young teen, her hands out, palms up, beseeching her daughter.

'She won't be a kindred anymore.'

'Neither will you if you refuse to fight her.'

'I'll fight anyone but her.'

'You know it doesn't work like that.'

'It doesn't work at all – these rules, they're —'

'*Don't*. Don't ever let me hear you turn your back on our people. I'm an elite kindred, first-in-command to Henrietta Valia.'

'I *know* who you are, Ma.'

'Do you? If you did, I don't think there would be a

choice here. I didn't think there was.'

'What?'

'Tomorrow, you lose a friend or a mother.'

'Ma —'

Bleak was tugged away, forcefully, like a rope had been tied around her chest and someone on the other end was reeling her in. These were long-term memories, she realised as she passed door after door, but they were also more than that. Rife with inner conflict and turmoil, these were all formative events in Luka's life, the choices that had made her who she now was.

'Go back to bed, Luka.' Athene's voice sounded from nearby. Six-year-old Luka's face peered out into the living quarters from the bedroom. Henri was sitting on the windowsill, her legs dangling over the other side, smoking a pipe.

'My side hurts,' said Luka, 'look.' She lifted her nightshirt to reveal a patchwork of blues and purples.

'You should have blocked faster,' Athene said. 'You'll learn.'

'Ma —'

'Back to bed, can't you see Her Majesty is here?'

Henri didn't turn around to greet Luka, but blew a cloud of smoke into the air above her head. Bleary-eyed, Luka simply stared at the matriarch's back.

'Luka, *now*.'

The small child disappeared into the bedroom, and suddenly, Bleak was beside her, looking out into the living quarters from a crack in the timber. Athene approached Henri and gently took the pipe from her.

'You're smoking too much of that,' she said, tipping the pipe upside down and tapping the bottom. Its dark contents fell, swept up into the breeze outside.

'You take liberties,' Henri said darkly.

'Someone has to.'

Henri was quiet, and her hand crept across the windowsill to reclaim the pipe from Athene. She took a pouch from her leathers and began packing the pipe with the same strange herbs as before.

'Your Majesty, it's been weeks since she died.'

'Died ... It makes it sound like it happened *to* her. She *chose* this, Athene.'

'You're angry with her. We can all understand that; she was your sister.'

Henri stood suddenly, and Bleak saw her clearly for the first time. The warrior's face was hollow and unusually pale. The kohl that lined her eyes had smudged, as though it hadn't been removed for days. Her braid was a mess, with wisps of her midnight hair framing her too-sharp jawline and highlighting the deep, purple circles below her bottom lashes. She looked crazed.

'My sister?' Henri snapped, her voice trembling with violence. Her hand lashed out, and a decanter of wine jerked from the benchtop and smashed loudly on the floorboards, making Bleak and young Luka jump. The wine pooled and crept across the timber, soaking into the grain like spilt blood.

'She wasn't just my sister,' Henri said, 'she was my

life force, my leader, *my queen.*'

'As you are now ours.' Athene reached out, hesitated, and then tucked a strand of hair behind Henri's ear.

Henri was very still, her fists clenched by her sides. 'I never wanted this.'

'I know.'

'I – I don't think I can do it.'

Athene stepped closer to her. 'Yes, you can.'

A muscle in Henri's jaw worked, and she shoved Athene up against the wall, their boots crunching atop the broken glass before their mouths crashed together. Henri's hands gripped the back of Athene's neck, bringing her closer, deepening their kiss. Henri's desperation and despair were palpable, and she clawed at the laces of Athene's leathers, which came undone beneath her frantic fingers. Athene's hands went to Henri's waist, bringing their bodies together.

Heart hammering, Bleak looked down at young Luka, who was still peering through the crack in the timber. She had seen it, seen it all. The invisible rope around Bleak's chest jerked her whole body, and she was out in the corridor again, her head spinning.

What am I looking for? The question was unnerving, reminding her just how easy it was to lose herself here. *A memory. A pivotal memory,* Allehra had instructed Luka. *Make it strong; the more emotion the memory holds, the more it will call out to Bleak.* At least, that was the theory. But something *was* calling to her. Her boots tapped steadily against the hard stone floor, and she followed the pulse of magic.

Dozens of kindred crowded around the training circuit, their eager bodies straining forward for the best view. Bleak looked on, somehow elevated above them, and immediately recognised the fiery-red braid whipping through the air as Luka twisted away from her advancing opponent. A sharp-featured girl struck out with her sword. Luka sidestepped easily but didn't take the opportunity to strike where the girl had left her abdomen exposed. *Clara*, Bleak realised with a jolt. She recognised her from the Sticks. She searched the crowd, and found Athene beside a younger Henri, standing feet apart on a platform with the other elite kindred. Athene's face was tight with tension, and her eyes hard with anger, as it became obvious that the blows from each girl were not destined to hit their supposed target.

'Quit playing with your food,' someone yelled from the sidelines.

The crowd's gaze shot to Henri, anticipating her reaction to the outburst. But her eyes merely slid from the source and back to the two trainees in the ring. Clara aimed another weak blow at Luka, and Luka let it strike her shoulder. Bleak could hear the intake of breath from Athene. The dance continued, the pair matching each other blow for blow, a performance, not a fight.

And then she heard what she knew no one else had.

'*Come with me*,' Clara whispered to Luka between her teeth.

The friends locked eyes for a moment, weapons

poised. Luka glanced up at her mother. Athene's expression was blank, but the knuckles gripping her elbows were bone-white. Luka turned back to Clara.

'I'm sorry,' she said simply, and lunged.

'You remind me of her,' Luka said, when Bleak came back to consciousness, her body aching and her breathing uneven.

'Who?' she managed, her eyes adjusting to the forest, trying to determine how much time had passed.

'Clara.'

Bleak nodded. 'That was the memory you chose?'

'Yes.'

'Why?'

Luka shrugged.

Bleak paused. 'You don't ever visit her?'

'What, out in the Sticks?'

'Why not?'

Luka shook her head. 'It's not the Valian Way.'

Bleak registered the cool sensation of the damp earth beneath her, and felt a hard grip on her shoulder. Allehra was still there.

'How long?' she asked, looking up. 'How long was I out?'

'Two hours,' Allehra said, helping her stand on unsteady feet. 'A huge improvement.'

The ridge between Bleak's breasts was slick with sweat, and her stomach churned. A pit of despair opened up inside her, a whirlpool threatening to suck her in.

The unhappiness was sudden.

'I don't understand,' she said, mopping her brow with the hem of her shirt, 'what use is this? I can't defend myself with this ability – worse. I become a liability. This magic, this so-called *power*, is no power at all, it's a weakness. I was right to seek a cure all this time.'

Allehra frowned. 'What happened in there? What did you see?'

Bleak told Allehra of the final memory and nothing more. That was what she'd been sent to retrieve and she'd done it. She owed Allehra no further detail, and Luka was her friend. Bleak would spare her from whatever humiliation and interrogation she could. She left the two Valians by the stream and started back to the keep, eager to escape the concerned looks and probing questions. She was so focused on putting distance between them that she bumped straight into Fiore.

'Sorry,' she mumbled, walking away.

'It's okay,' he said, and stepped to keep up with her. 'Care for a walk?'

She looked around dubiously at the dark forest. 'It's not exactly the royal gardens at this time.'

Fiore smiled. 'It's just a walk.'

Her head was throbbing and she desperately wanted a drink, but she looked at the man beside her; he was being kind to her. He had been kind to her from the beginning of this wretched ordeal.

'Right ... Uh, okay.'

'I'm overwhelmed by your enthusiasm,' he said, still

smiling broadly.

'You're not the first person to say that to me.'

He laughed. 'I'm kidding. Where do people go around here, anyway?'

She shrugged, but found herself wandering the only path that was familiar to her, this time following the creek upstream, towards the Sticks.

Fiore took a deep, appreciative breath. 'This is better,' he said.

Bleak said nothing, but looked to the canopy to see if Henri had at some point peeled away from the kindred to follow her. Though she didn't doubt the warrior queen could move above them undetected, Bleak got the feeling that they were alone.

'Do you like it here?' Fiore asked, catching her eye.

Bleak rubbed her aching temples, trying to distract herself from dipping into Fiore's thoughts as well. She wasn't sure she could handle another mind scrambling her own so soon after Luka's.

'I think so,' she said. 'I s'pose it's better than Angove.'

'You didn't like Angove?'

She shrugged. 'I like being on the water. But Angove, no. Not after Senior died.'

'Senior? The fisherman who took you in?'

She nodded. 'How'd you know about that?'

Fiore's brow furrowed in concentration. 'You know, I don't really know. Bleaker was pretty well-known at Port Morlock, and even in town, when he ventured inland. Guess it became common knowledge when he adopted a little beggar girl.'

'I wasn't a beggar.'

'No? Sorry, that's just what the rumours were.'

'Doesn't matter anyway.'

'Well, who were you, then?'

She bit down on the inside of her cheek and said nothing.

'We don't have to talk about it,' he said, touching her shoulder.

She ducked under his hand. 'Good.'

'So you're an Ashai. What kind of ability do you have?'

'You've got a lot of questions.'

'I seem to remember you having a lot of questions when we met.'

They reached the spot where only days before, she'd picked maladoms from the ground with Lyse. Nearby, the creek opened up to a small, clear-watered pool.

'They upgraded your shoes.' Fiore nodded to the black leather boots she was pushing off at the heel.

'Thank you,' she said, looking into his eyes for the first time. 'Thank you for ... for that. And everything, during that ride.'

His warm eyes were framed with dark, heavy lashes; they lingered over her. This time, he was the first to look away.

'I should have done more,' he said.

'You did more than you had to.'

On the balls of her feet, Bleak hopped across the

mossy rocks, and sat, lowering her sweaty feet into the cool water below. She stifled a moan of relief. Fiore sat down a rock away from her, leaving his boots on.

'I don't think we were ever formally introduced. My name's Fiore Murphadias, by the way. Everyone calls me Fi,' he said, holding out his hand as though this was the first time they were meeting.

'What a riveting tale,' she said, leaving her hands in her lap. She didn't need to get close to anyone. Closeness. It was overrated and generally brought her nothing but trouble.

Fiore didn't look hurt; he just shrugged and lowered his hand. Bleak ran her fingertips across the rocks crowding the creek. Some of them were as smooth as pebbles and dull in appearance, while others glistened with unknown minerals in the moonlight, their rough finish catching along the calluses of her palms. Just as she was about to turn back to Fiore, one of the rocks just beyond her reach caught her eye. She stood in the shallows of the pool, feeling the fresh water swell and swirl around her ankles. She moved towards it. Markings had been carved into the stone – letters spelling out a word she'd never heard or read. *Oremere.*

'What is it?' Fiore asked, craning his neck to see.

'I don't know,' she said, moving aside for him, 'just someone's scribble, I guess.'

'Probably an old Valian word, from centuries ago when they spoke their own language. I've not seen it before, though. They stopped teaching the old dialects where I'm from.'

'So you *are* from Battalon, right?' she asked.

Fiore laughed. 'Yes. Belbarrow, no less.'

'Were you in King Roswall's guard there?'

'Not quite.'

'What, then?'

'I was in private security.'

'Oh?'

'My father, cousin and I looked after the Battalon nobles.'

'Nobles looking after nobles? Sounds about right.'

This time, Fiore's smile was grim. 'We guarded them, trailed them ... Took care of their enemies.'

'Took care of?'

'Sometimes.'

Bleak nodded. It was none of her business. She didn't even know why she'd asked.

'What's it like up north?' she changed tact.

'Hot.'

'Hot? That's it? You really painted a picture for me there.'

He laughed again. 'My family and I lived in the jewellery quarter. Right in the heart of Belbarrow. From our balconies, you could see the entire shiprock that contains the palace. It's a formidable place. Beautiful, but formidable. There are firestorms every other week.'

'Firestorms?'

Fiore nodded. 'They start out as little wind funnels in the Janhallow Desert, but they move so fast they catch alight and barrel towards the capital.'

'Does everyone live underground, then?'

'No. Our ancestors created a fire-retardant coating. All our buildings are built with it; it's even in the paint.'

'Sounds very different to where I'm from.' Bleak kicked her feet in the pool. 'Most of my days have been spent out on the open water, with salt stinging my eyes and the wind whipping my face.'

'The desert and the sea. Very different.'

'I'll say. You grew up overlooking a palace. I came of age wiping fish guts from a deck.' Bleak stepped out of the pool and walked back along the stones to where she'd left her boots.

'In terms of differences, that's probably the least of it,' Fiore said.

There was the snap of a branch, and the two of them froze.

'Who's there?' Fiore called out.

The darkness before them was silent.

Fiore looked at Bleak. She shrugged and tugged her boots on over her wet feet.

'Athene or Tilly, no doubt,' she said.

'We were followed?'

She shrugged again. 'I guess I've gotten used to it.'

When they reached the outer keep, she bid Fiore goodnight and found her way back to the vine ladder she'd been using to get up onto the living bridges. As she pulled herself up, she realised she was getting stronger. On the first day, she'd struggled with all the climbing and travelling across the vast camp and canopy. Though she wasn't an athlete by any stretch of the word, her muscles were more resilient and her legs seemed to take longer strides. She marvelled at this development as she navigated the mossy bridges and numerous paths. She was eating better, and hadn't drunk in ... a day? Or was it more? Despite the utter despair she'd felt after her training with Allehra and Luka, she felt okay now. Good, even. She reached Tilly's apartments feeling lighter, and took off her boots at the door.

Inside, Tilly's bedroom door was ajar, a soft beam of light streaming into the living quarters. Bleak put her boots on the rack alongside Tilly's and went to say goodnight. She pushed the door open and took a step forward. Candlelight flickered across the tanned, broad back that faced her, casting shadows across the dark, cresting waves that ran down the spine, and the smooth, milky-skinned arm draped over it.

Chapter Twenty-one

Swinton watched the glowing embers of the Valian campfire, rolling his coin between his thumb and forefinger. The small, bronze circle was engraved with the face of a mouthless woman – Yacinda, the goddess of secrets. Lady Yuliana, Swinton's mother, had found it in the woods near their family's estate many years ago. She hadn't known about its power. But Swinton had felt it the moment he'd grasped it in his palm – as though a weight was suddenly lifted from his whole body. Until then, his visions had been crippling. He'd seen fire and mist swallow that sacred part of the Valia Forest, long before it ever happened. He'd said nothing. He'd seen Eliza, the woman he loved, die before death found her in the present. He hadn't been able to get there in time. He'd seen so many things he wished to unsee but couldn't. He had no idea who the coin had belonged to before him, but he suspected it had been treated with those rare Valian herbs, perhaps even had an enchantment cast on it. He'd soldered it to a metal chain himself, and hadn't taken it off in years. He was done with seeing the future. It only offered despair. But now, the protective herbs of the coin had grown weaker, according to Henri. His stomach churned. There was only one place he knew it could be restored to its former strength.

A clanging noise startled Swinton and he hastily tucked the coin back into his shirt. Bleak was scouring the benchtops and tables, shaking discarded flasks and peering into empty wine decanters. She looked exhausted. Her ash-blonde hair had escaped its tie and now fell into her harried face. She shoved it behind her ears as she continued her desperate search. She tipped containers upside down, tossed them aside and swore.

'Looking for something?' he said, resting his elbows on his knees.

She whirled around and regarded him with a cold glare. 'What's it to you?' she snapped, peering into another ceramic jug.

'Are you ... alright?'

'Like you care.'

He deserved that. He hadn't treated her well during their brief travels together. But now, they were both outsiders.

'We're not so different, you and I,' he found himself saying.

Bleak laughed sardonically. 'Yes, the Commander of the King's Army and the gutter rat from Angove have so much in common. We should share a meal together, get to know each other.' Her words were laced with bitterness.

Swinton wondered if perhaps the Valian matriarch was rubbing off on her too much. He got to his feet.

'Have you seen the captain?' he asked.

Bleak jerked her thumb in a vague direction behind her, and continued her scavenger hunt.

'Helpful,' he said, and left.

If he was honest, he found Valia Forest utterly disorientating. All the towering trees looked the same, there were no clear-cut paths through the undergrowth, and the thought of the kindred traipsing about above him in their treetop city made him uneasy.

'Lost?' Athene appeared from the darkness.

Swinton swore. He should have known she'd be lurking nearby. Henri was too cautious, too smart, to let members of the King's Army wander through her forests unchecked. Athene studied him, her eyes catching on the royal sigil embroidered on his chest. Her nose crinkled in distaste.

'What do you want?' he said.

'I was wondering where you were heading off to.'

'I'm looking for the captain.'

'Of course.' Athene looked bored, but didn't leave.

'You're truly going to follow my every step?'

'Would you expect anything less?'

'Do you wish to watch me bathe as well?'

Her gaze trailed leisurely down his body. 'You're not my type, Commander.'

'Don't test me,' he growled.

'I'd *love* to test you. See what *Sir Caleb's* son is really made of.'

Swinton knew better than to bite. 'If you see the

captain —'

'I'll give him a proper Valian welcome.'

Swinton suppressed the urge to throttle her. Valians were insufferable.

He found Fiore back at the campfire, stoking the orange embers back to life and nurturing the flames with carefully tended kindling. Bleak was nowhere in sight.

'You're popular around here,' Fiore said, prodding the fire.

'What?'

Fiore shrugged. Swinton took up his place on the bench and toyed with the chain around his neck as he watched his friend. Fiore hadn't said much since they'd arrived. It was strange, not to have the Battalonian's chatter filling the quiet.

'Spit it out,' he said.

'What?'

'Something's on your mind.'

Fiore met his gaze. 'What's going to happen to them?'

'To who?'

'Bleak and Henri.'

Swinton couldn't help the sigh that escaped him. 'I don't know.'

'Doesn't that bother you?'

'No.'

'The fact that we could be marching them to their deaths doesn't bother you?'

'No.'

'How can you be like that?'

'Like what? Loyal to the crown? Someone who does their duty?'

Fiore stood abruptly, frustration etched on his face. 'How —'

'You like her,' Swinton interjected.

'*What?*'

'The Angovian girl. Bleak. She's not one of your tavern girls, Fiore, she's been summoned by the king, you cannot —'

'I can't believe this.'

'It's not some trivial —'

'How dare you,' Fi said quietly. 'You have no right to question me.'

'I'm your commander.'

'I thought you were my *friend*, my *brother*.'

Swinton was increasingly aware that somewhere in the dark, Athene could hear every word. He ran his fingers through his hair, sweeping it back off his face. He couldn't win this.

'I am,' he said.

Fiore shook his head. 'You don't trust me.'

'What? That's absurd.'

'Is it? You don't tell me things anymore, Dimitri. You have too many secrets. And you're keeping them for the wrong people.'

'What do you mean by that?' Swinton stood and took a step towards Fiore.

'You're blinded by your loyalty to the king and your incessant need to match your father's greatness.'

Swinton sucked in a breath. 'Take a walk, Fi,' he managed.

Fiore nodded, and stepped back. Heat flushed Swinton's face as Fiore walked away. He stood there, shocked. There had always been things left unsaid between them, ever since Eliza, but he didn't know that was what Fi really thought of him. Swinton had never told anyone about Eliza. It was too painful, and she was a weakness he didn't want others to know he had. Back then, he knew Fiore had noticed the change in him, but had likely decided Swinton would come to him when he was ready, and he never had. It tended to bubble to the surface in other ways now, and Swinton knew Fiore's moral compass was the main catalyst.

He found the hammock he'd slept in the night before. He unlaced his boots and placed them neatly beside one another beneath one of the supporting trees. He peeled off his jerkin and folded it, leaving on the rest of his garb. He wouldn't be caught unawares by the kindred. Finally, he slipped into the hammock. Its material was soft and comforting, moulding to his shape and enveloping him in darkness. He wasn't tired; his mind was brimming with all manner of worries, but he had to try to get some rest while he could. He needed to be refreshed for the journey, and he needed to have his wits about him in a place like this.

The next morning, Swinton woke tangled in the hammock. Blinking, he looked around and saw the campsite through a pink-and-orange filter.

'You coming?' said a familiar voice from above. Fiore blocked out the sun.

'Coming where?' Swinton croaked. He felt queasy, and stumbled as he tried to swing himself out of the hammock. Fiore held the ropes firm and handed him his boots.

'Athene said they need help with a new training circuit.'

'What do you mean?' Swinton steadied himself against the nearby tree as he leaned down to pull on his boots.

'I don't know, Dimitri. They asked for help, so let's help.'

'We're not here to run chores for the Valians.'

Fiore threw his hands up defeat. 'Well that's where I'll be. May as well make myself useful.'

He left before Swinton had finished lacing his boots.

Bleak and Henri were nowhere in sight, and although none of the other kindred spoke to him, he knew they were monitoring his every move. He felt eyes boring into his back, even when he went to relieve himself. He found an unoccupied part of the keep, and ran through a series of exercises with his battleaxes, and stretched. He wouldn't allow himself to lose his edge just because they were out in the middle of nowhere. By noon, however, his discipline and patience were wearing thin. Frustrated, he realised that Fiore was right. They had nothing better to do than to make themselves useful here.

He found them working in the canopy, a fair distance from the heart of the keep. An impressive system of pulleys and levers brought planks of pale timber up onto the scaffolding above. He gripped the thick vine rungs of a long ladder that reached up into the trees.

Don't look down, don't look down, he chanted as he hauled himself up. The ladder swung as he climbed. It was clearly designed for far more lithe frames than his own.

'You came,' Fiore said, offering a hand when Swinton reached the top of the ladder. He grasped his friend's hand and heaved himself onto the platform, quickly stepping away from the edge. Swinton merely nodded, trying to focus on the framework of the construction site, rather than the height of it.

'This is Bren,' Fi said, gesturing to the Angovian, who was kneeling by the edge of the scaffolding, shirt off, with a mallet clutched in his big hands. Bren looked up and nodded to Swinton.

'Can't say it's nice to see you again, Commander,' he said, 'but we'll make do.'

Swinton could have sworn he saw Fi chuckle at that. But the Battalonian straightened his face and pointed to a stack of wooden planks.

'We're laying the flooring,' he said.

'I can see that.'

'You always did catch on quick.'

'Where do you want me to start?' The question was strange on Swinton's lips. It wasn't often he asked others for instruction.

Fi didn't hesitate. 'Start from that side there, and we'll meet in the middle.'

Swinton nodded, and balanced his way across the timber beams to the furthest side. A box of nails and a mallet awaited him there, and he knelt down to put the first plank in place. He lined it up meticulously with the existing flooring and hammered the first nail through it and into the support beam. There was something oddly comforting about the way the little piece of iron sank through the grain of the timber, disappearing but for the round head. It also felt good to hit something.

In the background, he could hear the warm banter between Fiore and Bren. The familiarity of their tones and the bursts of deep laughter drove him to focus solely on the work at hand. He hammered the pieces in place, working his way across the scaffolding, and occasionally looking back to admire the smooth floor he'd laid. He forgot about the dizzying height and concentrated on levelling each new plank with the rest. If he was going to do a job, he was going to do it right. From what he could see of Fi and Bren's side, they weren't as concerned about quality as he was. The physical work helped him take his mind off things, and his body relished the exertion. His shirt was damp with sweat, and it clung to his body as he raised the mallet.

'Dimitri,' Fi called out, waving a flask at him from across the platform, 'want a drink?'

Swinton shot him a look of annoyance. Fi knew

Swinton preferred to be addressed formally in front of strangers. But as usual, Fi ignored the look and simply threw him the flask. The water was warm on his parched tongue, but he drank it anyway.

'We should set you up with a sword or something,' Fi was saying to Bren.

Bren laughed. 'I've never been one for fighting.'

'You never know when it'd come in handy.'

'I wouldn't say no to some free tips, if that's what you're offering.'

'Sure, why not? You're built like a Battalonian, I could teach you a thing or two.'

'Built like a Battalonian?'

Fi flexed his bicep. 'You got bulk, old friend. Throw that weight around and you could do some damage.'

Another loud laugh came from Bren, and he nodded to Swinton. 'What about the commander, what's he built like?'

'A knight,' answered Fi, gesturing to Swinton's tall and limber frame.

Swinton went back to work. He could do without the horseshit men's bonding, especially when it was at his expense.

'Come on, Dimitri,' Fi said, mopping his brow.

'Let's just finish this.'

They worked well into the evening. Swinton didn't meet them in the middle; he laid flooring well over onto their side. His work was level and precise, theirs was mediocre at best. The two of them continued their jovial teasing and chatter.

Who cares, thought Swinton, *you won't see each other again.*

The days wore on, and Swinton hammered into place more than his fair share of timber planks. Fiore spoke less and less with him, and had taken to training the Angovian fisherman in the evenings after supper. At first, Swinton watched them swing their practice swords at each other, Fi teaching the young man a range of revered Battalonian techniques, ones that Fi had taught Swinton himself what felt like a lifetime ago. Except that Fiore and Bren laughed while they trained, something that Swinton had never allowed himself to do. He left them, and despite his dislike of heights, returned to the unfinished training circuit in the canopy. There he sat, looking up at the inky blanket of sky, tens of thousands of stars glinting down at him, as he wondered what tomorrow would bring.

Chapter Twenty-two

After the incident with Sir Caleb, Olena had looped her arm through Dash's and practically dragged him into the great hall.

'It'll be more suspicious if you're *not* here now,' she had hissed, plonking herself down at her seat and pointing sharply at the chair beside her. 'Everything's okay,' she said more kindly, patting his hand, 'you just got overexcited is all.'

'That's not —'

'Shhh, not here, Dash!'

Dash didn't say another word throughout the feast. And he didn't look at Sir Caleb as the king addressed the room in his honour. The food Dash had looked forward to so much all day tasted like parchment, and the expensive material beneath his armpits was wet and uncomfortable now. He needed to get out of there. But the feast had lasted for hours, as course after course was brought out and wine goblets were constantly refilled. The great hall was loud, filled with drunken, well-wishing nobles and their bratty children.

Who had that girl been? Why was she sailing into the mist? Or was Olena right? Perhaps he really *was* just overexcited at the prospect of meeting Sir Caleb. But somehow, deep down, he knew that wasn't true. It had been strange. More real than a dream. He had felt the spray of the ocean on his skin. Like he himself had been transported somewhere else.

That had been days ago. Now, Dash rushed to meet Olena in the gardens.

'Please don't be mad,' he begged, sitting down beside her and grabbing her hand. 'I know I was stupid. I'm really, really sorry.'

He hadn't seen Olena since the feast to explain what had happened. He still didn't understand what had happened himself when he'd shaken the knight's hand. Olena, whose posture was usually straight-backed and formal, was sitting with her shoulders caved inward, her cloudy eyes staring off in the direction of the cliffs. She took his hand from hers and placed it back in his lap.

'Please, Olena, I'm sorry. I hate it when you're mad,' he said.

'I'm not mad,' she said stiffly, rearranging her skirts. 'I'm engaged.'

Dash baulked. 'What?'

'Engaged to be married.'

'I know what engaged means. But that's silly, you're ... You're only fifteen.'

She nodded. 'The wedding won't happen until my seventeenth birthday, but Mother and Father wish to send me to Belbarrow, so I can get to know my betrothed.' Her voice was steady, but Dash saw her bottom lip tremble.

'Who is he?'

'King Roswall's son, Prince Nazuri, heir to the crown of Battalon.'

'But how? I don't —'

'They told me after the feast. I've been in detailed lessons about Battalon ever since.'

So *that's* why he hadn't seen her these past few days.

'But he's so ... *old*, Olena.'

'He's twenty-five.'

'That's old.'

She smiled sadly and took a steadying breath. 'It feels that way, doesn't it?'

'But ... You can't go, Olena.'

'I don't want to,' she managed, her voice cracking before the tears spilled over.

Dash moved to put his arm around her.

'Hands off the princess, boy,' said one of the guards.

'She's upset,' Dash argued.

'Don't touch her.'

'It's okay, Dash. Just leave it.'

But Olena couldn't go; she was his best friend. And to marry someone so old? What if the prince was mean to her? She would be a whole continent away.

'How do we stop this?' Dash whispered.

Olena shook her head. 'We don't,' she said. 'They have wanted this for a long time. I didn't realise. Only when Mother allowed you to come to the feast did I think something was going on. She was being so nice to me because she knew what was to come. They've created a brand-new wardrobe of gowns for me in the Battalon colours. An escort is on its way here now, ready to take me there in a few days. Nothing can be done, Dash.'

Olena didn't stay long with him in the gardens, and she didn't talk much. Dash didn't know what to say to her, didn't know how to make it better. He couldn't understand how a princess of the realm could have so little power over herself and her own fate. He thought the whole point of being a royal was that you could do what you wanted. And all this time, he'd thought she'd been mad at him about Sir Caleb.

Dash realised he was still sitting on the garden bench, long after Olena had taken her leave. He looked down at his boots and was startled. A single red flower, the same as those in the maze, blossomed in the grass by his feet. He swallowed and looked around, checking to make sure no one else could see it. Something wasn't right. Trying to keep calm, he stood. He needed to tell someone. Ma – Ma would know what to do. Dash took off from the gardens, finding no joy in the run this time. He went around the back of the castle, dodging a cart that was being unloaded into the kitchens. He came face to face with a pinched set of angry eyes.

'You,' said the castle cook, and lunged.

Dash tore away from the woman. He wouldn't survive another belting so soon after his most recent one, he was sure of it. But she'd left him no option but to take the entrance to the kitchens. He sprinted inside, slipping past a number of servants bringing in fresh food. He heard a crash behind him and winced, not daring to look back.

No, no, no – he wouldn't be caught. Not this time. He turned and leapt up the grand staircase to the second floor of the castle. He could hear the cook's, or maybe the guards' thundering steps behind him, but he bolted down an unfamiliar hallway.

Where can I go? He tried a door to his left – locked. And a door to the right – locked as well. He was running out of time. Whoever was chasing him was bound to round the corner soon, and he knew he was in so much more trouble now. A set of double doors appeared as he rounded another corner. Books were carved into the dark timber. *The old library* – this had to be the old library. Dash pushed the door. It creaked loudly, but he ducked inside. The room was filled with floor-to-ceiling shelves, lined with hundreds, maybe thousands of books. But Dash didn't have a second to spare. He raced down one of the aisles, eyeing a small, dark cupboard against the wall at the end.

Please don't be locked. He grasped one of the handles and heard the groan of the doors from the other end of the library. Without another moment, he flung himself into the cupboard, heart hammering, and gently pulled the doors closed after him. Darkness swallowed him as the latch clicked in place. Inside the cupboard, Dash tried to stop panting. He could feel his pulse throbbing in his throat as he attempted to push down his fear. If they found him now, who knew what they'd do. He breathed in the musty air that smelled faintly of paint, and adjusted his position slightly, feeling soft sheets beneath his hands. *This must be a linen closet ...*

The quiet click-clack of heels on the floorboards sounded. Two pairs, no urgency. Dash strained to hear over the pounding in his chest and through the muted effect of the cupboard doors. Voices drew nearer, murmuring softly. He pressed his head back into the side of the cupboard, trying to peer through the narrowest gap where the door hinges sat. Green skirts blocked the view. And then, the voices were nearly on top of him.

'— send her away?' It was the crisp voice of Queen Vera. 'She's only a young girl. She belongs with us, Arden.'

'I have worked tirelessly to ensure our daughter has a suitable match. This has always been our intention,' replied the king.

Dash squeezed his eyes shut. *Oh no, no* – he couldn't be here. If they found out ... He just *couldn't* be here. But he was trapped.

'I didn't think you meant for her to leave us so young. She will be with child before the time she's eighteen.'

'A child will give the girl purpose. What does she have now but her disability for company?'

'The girl is your *daughter*, Arden. She is more than a breeding vessel.'

'Of course she is,' snapped the king, 'but this is the way

of the realm. With this match, we're allied with Battalon for good, which makes us the strongest continent in the whole realm.'

'Your daughter's happiness truly means nought to you?'

'Not nought, but not enough to sway this decision. It is done, Vera. I suggest you stand behind me.'

There was a pause. 'I live to serve you, my king.'

'Good.'

'What of the Valian? I worry about inviting her into our home.'

'It wasn't an invitation. It was a summons. She has to answer for her crimes.'

'I fear for our children. Especially Olena. You know she is impressionable.'

'Impressionable as she may be, what can she possibly do? The girl is as blind as a bat.'

The queen was quiet at this, and the king sighed.

'It's the one thing those savage Valians do right – banish the weak.'

Dash swallowed.

'You don't mean that,' the queen said.

'It would have been a mercy to the girl.'

'Arden —'

The king sighed again and took the queen's hand in his. 'You shouldn't worry, Vera. You trust my judgement, yes?'

'Of course, you are my king.'

'Then do not worry yourself over such matters. All

will be well, I promise,' the king said, bringing her hand to his lips.

Dash heard the layers of skirts rustling once more, and the soft click of her heels as the queen left the old library. His legs were cramping up and he was worried he was going to run out of air in the tiny cupboard, but the king was still standing there. Still as anything, now leaning against one of the shelves.

'I was beginning to think you'd forgotten me,' King Arden said suddenly.

Dash almost jumped. There was no one else in the library – he hadn't heard any additional footsteps after the queen had left.

'I'm so glad to see you,' the king said, again to no one.

This time, a silken voice replied. 'I could never forget you.'

Dash couldn't see the woman, but her voice was as clear as day, even through the cupboard doors, almost as though it were in his head.

'How are you, Arden?' she said.

'Better, now that you are here.'

A quiet moan escaped the king's mouth, as though someone had touched him – but no one had. Dash still couldn't see the woman, no matter how he angled his head.

'We have much to discuss, Arden.'

'Yes,' the king breathed.

'Have you got the girl yet?'

'Not yet. I've sent two of my best men to retrieve her.'

'You did that over a fortnight ago.'

'Yes, but the Valia kindred interfered.'

'Which of the kindred?'

'Henri. I've summoned her along with the girl.'

'You impress me, Arden.'

'This is just the beginning. I can do more.'

'Have your mist trackers come back to you with their reports?'

'Most – the mist has gained another inch in the past few months; its pace has accelerated. I'm waiting on the return of one more tracker.'

'Good. And what of the jars you sent along with your commander?'

'All but three were released.'

'Truly?'

'Truly.'

'Our charges at Moredon Tower?'

'Secure and awaiting your inspection.'

'I want them well tended to. I'll have Langdon and Farlah there within the week.'

'Of course.' The king moaned quietly again, though Dash still couldn't see anyone with him.

'The beginning indeed,' the silken voice said. 'I like the sound of that.'

Dash stayed cramped in the linen closet, long after the bookshelves had stopped rattling, and the muffled sounds of the king's hitched breathing had ceased. The magnitude of this secret now gripped Dash, utter terror lacing around his heart.

There was no one he could tell.

Chapter Twenty-three

Henri honestly hadn't told anyone about Swinton and his abilities. She didn't know if she was waiting for the perfect moment to reveal his secret, or if deep, *deep* down, she had sensed his sorrow and had taken pity on him. She stood in the matriarch's grotto, far above the rest of Valia, waiting for Allehra. This place was sacred. No one other than previous matriarchs had stepped foot here, or even knew of its existence, hidden as it was in the highest branches of the tallest trees. It was simple – one large room with a vast balcony encircling it. It was where Henri had been sworn in as matriarch. She glanced inside. The table and chairs were exactly as she'd left them the last time she'd been here, an empty wine goblet still standing proudly on the tabletop.

This was a meeting place for the forest queens, a sanctuary, a secret. Anguish tugged in her chest. Sahara had never seen the grotto. It should have been her standing where Henri now stood. She looked down, over the edge of the balcony railing. From where she was, she could see Swinton, a lone figure not unlike herself, sitting on one of the incomplete training platforms, studying the night sky. She followed his gaze up to the millions of glittering stars. They winked at her, as though laughing at all her predicaments and the triviality of mortal life. Herself and Swinton and Bleak – all but mere specks in the face of the endless sky. Henri checked the time. Allehra was late, as usual. In fact, she made a point of it, as if to remind her that even though Henri was the Matriarch of Valia, the Mother Matriarch answered to no one. She heard footsteps on the spiral staircase below. Not one set, but two – Allehra was not alone.

Rage surged within Henri as Bleak's head appeared at the top of the stairs. When she stepped over into the grotto, she offered Allehra her hand, and the Mother Matriarch accepted it, allowing the young girl to help her onto the balcony.

'What is this?' Henri spat, not taking her glare off Bleak.

'I wanted Bleak to meet with us.'

'Then you should have arranged to meet somewhere else.'

'Come now, Henri.'

'Does this place mean so little to you?'

'Henri —'

'I asked you a question.' Henri's voice went quiet as she struggled to contain her anger and her magic, which was responding below her surface.

'This place means everything to me, you know that.'

'How can I, when you bring this gutter rat here?'

Bleak stood frozen dumbly to the spot, the same way she had the last time Henri had argued with Allehra.

Henri was utterly sick of this stranger being a part of her private conversations, her private relationships. This girl had no right to be anywhere near her, let alone in the matriarch's grotto.

'Bleak is no gutter rat. She is a mist dweller. And by the time this realm collapses into chaos, we're going to need her.'

'I very much doubt that.'

'Only time will tell, then.'

'You have insulted our ancestors by bringing her here. You have done a disservice to our kind.'

'Enough accusations. I know what it means to bring an outsider to the grotto. But if we do not work together, if we do not allow room for change, we may not have a kind to disrespect at the end of this.'

Henri folded her arms across her chest, glancing from Allehra to Bleak. What was it that they knew? Still fuming, she stalked inside and sat at her place at the table. The others followed. There were only two chairs, as there had never been any need to have more, which was the way it should be. Allehra gestured for Bleak to sit. Henri waited for Bleak to argue – the Mother Matriarch should be seated, the outsider should stand, at the very least. But Bleak merely nodded and took her place, as though she and Allehra didn't need to speak aloud. Henri took a deep breath. She needed to simmer, not boil over. Not before she knew what was going on.

Allehra turned to her and handed her a scroll, its seal broken. She recognised the seal – a mountain dog and a wolf's head bent close together, the seal of the Wildenhaven royals, capital of Havennesse, across the seas.

'We've had word from Eydis.'

'Since when does Eydis write notes?'

Allehra shrugged. 'Since always.'

'What?'

'Who's Eydis?' Bleak interjected.

'The Queen of Havennesse. We have an ongoing trade relationship.'

'Trading with Havennesse ceased years ago,' Henri snapped.

'*Legal* trading, yes. But we have maintained our relationship and our negotiations.'

'Under *whose* orders? I know nothing of this.'

'You never asked. You're too busy training and fighting and warmongering to consider what and who actually run this territory.'

Henri felt as though she had been slapped; heat crept up her neck and across her face. Who did Allehra think she was? No one spoke to the matriarch like this, not even her own damned mother. Especially not in front of some outsider. Bleak's discomfort was clear. She shifted in her chair, as though she were suppressing the impulse to leap from her seat and bolt away from yet another bitter mother–daughter feud.

'Watch yourself, Allehra,' Henri said, unfurling the scroll. Luscious, loopy handwriting scrawled across the length of the parchment in dark-green ink. Eydis always did have a way with penmanship.

Dearest Allehra,

I hope this letter finds you catching better tides than us here in Wildenhaven. I write to tell you of our mist tracker reports. Our most trusted trackers have returned with news of a three-inch increase in these past few months alone. It is spreading and encroaching at a faster rate than ever before, while trouble brews in the south. As many as ten known Ashai folk have vanished without a trace. We need someone in Heathton. We need someone to speak to King Arden, implore him to seek the truth, to see reason. I cannot say more for fear of this ending up in the wrong hands, but do not take this warning lightly. The mist is coming, and with it comes a power so hungry for magic, it threatens the whole realm.

Something must be done, Allehra, or in time, all will be lost.

Your beloved friend,

Eydis

Henri's eyes snapped up to Allehra's. Her mother's expression was grave, her graphite-and-green eyes dull.

'What is the meaning of this?' Henri said.

'Eydis is a seer, you know this.'

'And?'

'From what I understand, from what I've read between the lines of that letter, the king is mixed up in something terrible. Something to do with the mist, something to do with collecting Ashai folk.'

'But Eydis is not a fully fledged seer. How do we know these claims are accurate?'

'She would not have risked this letter if she were unsure.'

'What are you talking about?' Bleak asked quietly, sitting up straight-backed in her chair.

Henri regarded her coolly. 'You haven't read the letter?'

Bleak shook her head.

Henri slid the parchment across the table to the Angovian. Allehra had been wrong to bring her to the grotto, but if the girl was prepared to walk into Heathton, straight up to the king's gate, she had a right to know where things concerned her. Henri stood and began to pace the length of the room.

'We need to leave, then?' she said to Allehra, while Bleak read.

'Yes. Swinton would have sent word as to when they're expecting you. If you can gain the element of surprise, however little, I believe it will be to your advantage.'

'Do you have any idea what awaits us there?'

Allehra shook her head. 'Anything I have is mere speculation. My guess is he will want to keep Bleak. He seems too interested in her abilities to simply butcher her.'

Bleak looked up in alarm at this.

'But as for you,' Allehra continued, turning back to Henri, 'you know as well as I do we've had a long and complicated history with the Heathton royals. I don't know if he wants to kill you, keep you as a hostage or marry you off to his son.'

'What?' The former two options were no surprise to Henri, but the last – repulsive. The boy was barely seventeen from what she remembered. And was the offspring of Arden himself, no less. He could only be vile. And to become subservient to a male ... She'd rather be killed.

'Like I said, just speculation. A marriage would be one way of regaining control over Valia. Though, I'm not sure Arden would be willing to give up his only son's hand in marriage to a Valia kindred, even if it were the matriarch herself.'

Henri nodded, steeling herself for the worst. 'We leave tomorrow at first light, then.'

'Good,' said Allehra. 'And one more thing.'

'I should have guessed.'

'You will need to train with Bleak on the journey.'

'For a moment there I thought you said "train with Bleak".'

'I did. And you will.'

'Do you so often forget who the Matriarch of Valia is?'

'How could I, with you reminding me every two seconds? Regardless of how much power you have over me, Henri, you *will* train with Bleak. It is utterly vital that she remains in control of her abilities. She has been improving every single day; the learning curve has been enormous, but she has done magnificent work. We need her to be exercising that muscle every day, so she is at her strongest upon meeting Arden.'

'What good do you think she'll do? Mind read the king?'

'Perhaps. Perhaps not. Bleak can explain our progress over the course of your journey. There'll be plenty of time to talk then.'

'What do you make of the letter?' Henri said to Bleak. The parchment was unsteady in the girl's small hands.

'I want to know what's happening to the other Ashai. Where are they going?'

'You will find out soon enough,' said Allehra. 'I suggest you both retire for the night – you have the start of a long road ahead of you tomorrow.'

Bleak nodded and got to her feet, handing the parchment back to Henri.

'Thank you,' she said.

'For what?'

'For trusting me with that.'

'I don't trust you yet, Angovian. Not by a long shot.'

Bleak shrugged, suddenly looking exhausted. 'One day at a time, Valian.'

Henri almost laughed at the nerve of the girl. But she maintained her composure and watched Bleak's scrawny frame disappear down the stairs. Henri looked to Allehra.

'No sage words of wisdom? No final goodbye?' she said.

'You know we don't do that,' Allehra said, walking out onto the balcony.

'No, we don't.'

Allehra rested her elbows on the balcony railing and looked out into the night, the tops of Valian trees quivering in the gentle breeze.

'Well, until we meet again, Allehra,' said Henri, starting down the stairs.

Allehra didn't turn to watch her go.

'Until we meet again,' the Mother Matriarch replied.

Chapter Twenty-four

On her last night in Valia, Bleak found herself alone after mid-meal and headed to the stream. The quiet spot had become her sanctuary in the forest. She felt at ease here, where she was able to sit and gather her thoughts without intrusion. It was a welcome change from the chaotic heart of the keep. She sat on the flat rocks and ran her fingers through the cool water, realising how much she missed the sea – the pull of the current, the briny breeze tangling her hair. That life seemed a long time ago now, the life that was all about being on the open water with Senior and Bren. *Bren.* Her chest became tight at the thought of him.

She'd slept in one of the hammocks again, keeping to herself after seeing him in Tilly's bed. He hadn't mentioned it to her, and she hadn't brought it up. And why would he? He didn't owe her an explanation. He didn't owe her anything.

The bushes rustled behind her, and, as if summoned, there he was.

'Hey,' he said, settling down beside her. 'Haven't seen ya much.'

'I've been around.' It came out sharper than she had

meant it to.

He glanced at her, confused. 'We need to talk.'

'We *do* talk.'

His thoughts flew at her. *Is she pissed?*

'I'm not *pissed*,' she said before she could stop herself.

Bren stared at her. 'What? How did you ...?'

'It's nothing.'

'What just happened?'

She ground her teeth. Here it was – the conversation she'd been dreading forever.

'Bleak, what the *hell* is going on?'

'Nothing.'

'No,' he said. 'Don't ya dare tell me "nothing". I've been waiting for ya to talk to me in yer own time, to explain to me, yer *best friend*, yer only damned family, what's going on. Why the Commander of the King's Army showed up on *our* doorstep, why yer suddenly involved with the damned *Valia kindred*.'

'Bren, please ...'

'Yer an Ashai – I've figured that much out for myself. But ... Ya can't ... What kind of Ashai are ya?'

She can't be what I think she is. She just can't. She'd know —

'Bleak.' He gripped her upper arms.

'You know what I am,' she said.

His face fell. 'Ya can't be.'

She didn't say anything, just listened as it sank into Bren's mind and flinched at the anger that replaced his disbelief.

'Yer a mind whisperer?'

She just stared at him.

'How long?'

'What?'

'How long have you been this way?' Bren's wintry-blue eyes were full of hurt.

'Since Senior found me in Heathton. Probably since always.'

Bren shook his head. 'I can't believe you. After *everything* we've been through, you didn't trust me with this? I can't do this, Bleak. I can't —'

'Do what, Bren? You seem to be doing *just fine*.'

'What's *that* supposed to mean?' He got to his feet, and then it dawned on him. 'You know.'

Bleak stood and made to leave. This was not the conversation she wanted to be having. In fact, she didn't feel like talking at all.

'Bleak. *You* don't get to walk away from *me*. That's not fair.'

'None of it's *fair*,' she said, and left him there.

Bleak was awake well and truly before dawn. She sat with her legs dangling from the hammock, absentmindedly tying knots with Senior's rope. Despite not knowing what fate lay ahead, she was surprised to find herself eager to get on the road, to get moving. She was done hiding out in Valia. Perhaps in another lifetime, she would have loved it here, but it was not to be, not this time.

Henri appeared silently beside her, holding out a pack. 'We need to go to the armoury,' she said.

Bleak nodded and got to her feet. She shouldered the heavy weight and followed Henri through the keep.

'You told him?' Henri said, nodding to the fair hair poking out of the end of a hammock.

Bleak started. She thought Bren would be with Tilly.

'No,' she said.

'Good. He would only cause more trouble for us.'

Bleak nodded and continued after Henri. Perhaps it was good there would be no goodbyes between them. She wasn't sure what she would say or how she would say it. The memory of him in Tilly's bed made her stomach squirm; she pushed the image from her mind.

'The commander and captain are waiting for us by Valia River, I said we'd be quick.' The hushed, hurried voice Henri was using was new to Bleak, and if she didn't know any better, she'd guess that the Valian matriarch was nervous. She said nothing of the sort, however, and climbed up the vine ladder to the living bridges and armoury ahead. They moved in silence, jogging across a number of bridges above the camp. Henri had offered her custom-made Valian leathers, but Bleak had refused, insisting that her simple pants, shirt and boots were far more comfortable.

Bleak hadn't been to the armoury before, and let out a low, impressed whistle at the scope of weaponry before her. Swords, daggers, bows, spears, katars, throwing stars, axes and everything in between were displayed proudly on the shelves and hangers. Henri handed her a dagger.

Bleak pushed it away. 'I've already got one,' she said, lifting the right leg of her pants to reveal Fiore's dagger tucked into her boot.

Henri looked as though she might laugh for a moment, but she returned to the task at hand. Henri strapped all manner of blades to her body, her signature katars already at the sides of her thighs. She then took a hessian sack from one of the benches, its content clanging loudly.

'Let's go,' was all she said.

The two women re-shouldered heavy packs with rations and water for the journey, and made for the Sticks. Athene was waiting.

'I thought that had been too easy,' Henri said, not quite smiling.

'I'm just here to see you off, and to give you a few things from Allehra.'

'Oh? Farewell gifts?'

'Sort of. Not for you.' Athene turned to Bleak and opened a satchel she had at her side. 'Here,' she said, handing Bleak a forest-green leather wrist cuff.

'What is it?' Bleak said, turning it over in her hands.

Athene unbuckled it, looped it around Bleak's wrist and re-buckled it. 'It was made with our protective herbs,' she said. 'It should make managing your abilities easier. Perhaps soothe some of those headaches you get.'

'Hurry this up, Athene,' said Henri, irritated.

Without looking at her, Athene rummaged through the satchel again, this time extending two sheathed daggers to Bleak. 'There's a belt, too,' she said.

'I can't ... I can't accept these ...'

'You have to,' Henri snapped. 'No one rejects a gift from a Valian matriarch.'

Bleak took the daggers and belt and fastened the set around her waist. The weapons and their sheaths were beautifully crafted. Allehra must have ordered them made not long after Bleak's arrival.

'We need to go,' Henri said.

Athene nodded and closed the satchel. Bleak watched as the first-in-command met Henri's gaze, and for the briefest of moments opened her mouth as if she were about to say something. But Henri turned away before she could. They left Athene at the edge of the Sticks. Bleak thought of Lyse and how she hadn't had the chance to say goodbye to her or the other groundlings. Perhaps if she survived this, she'd come back and visit them.

'Let's pick up the pace,' Henri said, lengthening her strides across the mossy bridge path before her.

They'd been running the bridges for about three hours when Bleak heard the sound of running water. Her stomach dipped, remembering her fall at the crossing. She'd thought she was going to die. She felt nauseous just thinking about it. But it was not the King's River below, it was Valia River, and waiting by the water's edge were Commander Swinton and Fiore, holding the reins of four horses. When Bleak dropped down to the forest floor, she also saw that there was an old man with them, manning the ropes of a big barge.

Bleak and Henri strode out of the forest and the old man by the barge gasped. No doubt it was the first time he'd ever seen a Valian kindred.

'We'd like to cross with these men,' Henri said, not looking at either the commander or Fiore. Things were going to be ... tricky from now on, Bleak realised.

'Of course, of course,' said the man, tripping over his rope, 'no charge for you, m'lady.'

Henri simply nodded her head, as though this was to be expected.

'Ladies first,' said the old man.

Fiore handed Henri a set of reins and she led the restless beast onto the barge. Bleak followed with her own horse and watched the man untie the barge from its dock. He wasn't using the right knots at all. When all four travellers and their horses were onboard, she turned to him.

'What you really need is a mooring line fed through the centre of a cleat at the slip,' she heard herself say.

'What?' he said.

'To dock the barge properly. Your knots aren't secure. If there's a big surge in the current, like a flood or something, your barge'll be smashed to pieces on the rocks.'

'What do you know about barges, girl?'

'I know about knots. And ships. And how to dock them.'

She could feel the others watching her as they were pushed across the raging river. She had to steady herself on her horse's flank.

The old man considered her. 'What's this about a cleat, then, eh?'

When they docked on the other side of the river and disembarked, Bleak showed the old man how to tie his ropes more securely. By the end of it, Henri was tapping her foot and Swinton looked ready to strangle her, but the old man was happy. He slipped Swinton's silver into her palm.

'Where you're going, you're gonna need it, girl.'

She nodded in thanks and accepted his leg-up onto her horse. As soon as she was astride, Henri urged them all into a gallop, and they crossed over into the East Farmlands.

The East Farmlands was a massive territory in itself, housing several villages dotted around its crops and livestock. Bleak wasn't comfortable in the saddle at all. The extent of her experience on horseback amounted to those few days from Angove to the Hawthorne Ranges with the King's Army and Fiore for company. She was definitely not a natural rider.

'Not enjoying the ride?' Fiore said to her, laughing at her grimacing face.

'This wasn't my first preference for travel.'

'Shame you can't sail from Valia to Heathton, eh?'

'Well, if I had a say, I wouldn't be going to Heathton at all, would I now?'

They rode hard all day, and Bleak could tell that even stoic Henri was biting back her complaints. The sun was harsh, and her loose pants and shirt still made her feel as though she was swelling like dough in an oven. Henri must be suffering in her tight-fitting leathers, and even Swinton was mopping his brow. And then there was Fiore, who hadn't so much as broken a sweat, holding the reins in one hand and smiling absentmindedly.

'Aren't you hot?' Bleak couldn't help asking him.

'Call this hot?' Fiore said with a grin. 'Been to Battalon?'

'I have,' Henri offered from the lead.

'Then you realise this is practically winter for us. No true heat but for a summer on the fire continent. There's a reason we Battalonians pray to Liir.' He stretched out his arm from atop the horse to reveal the swirling black artwork of the almighty fire goddess. Bleak chanced a look at the patterns that crept up his forearm and disappeared under his rolled sleeve.

'Explains a lot,' Henri said, and turned back to the road before them.

They crossed fields of corn and wheat, and made their way through several paddocks of cattle and sheep. Yes, the East Farmlands were doing very well indeed. Of the farmers and villagers they saw, barely anyone spoke to them. Though Bleak was glad for it. Three unwanted companions were more than enough.

Her thoughts were never far from Bren. He would have woken up a long time ago now and realised she'd left him, yet again. It seemed somehow harsher than every time she'd left him beforehand. But he had Tilly there now; he'd be fine, she decided.

They came across a crop of sugarcane as night was falling, and it was agreed that they'd camp the rest of the night. When they dismounted, Bleak didn't let herself pause over the pain for a second. She watched Fiore and Swinton take great efforts to slowly stretch out their legs, groaning at the aches and raw spots. As Swinton unsaddled their horses, Henri started on the kindling for a fire, though she looked in no mood to be sitting around trading war stories.

Bleak wandered around collecting more fuel for the fire. *Mist dweller*, Allehra had called her, but who was she? Who was she *really*? She wasn't sure she was ready to go down that path yet, or if she ever would be.

They chewed on dried meat and bread from their packs. The chatter was light, with Swinton briefing them on where they'd be heading in the morning.

'I'll take first watch,' Henri said, cutting the conversation short.

Swinton's brow furrowed for a moment, before he nodded and turned his back to her. Bleak had felt her head drop half a dozen times already. If only there was some wine or ale to be had. She didn't dare bring it up, though. Henri got to her feet and moved to the edge of their campsite. Sucking on the end of a sugar cane, Bleak heard her sigh, and she felt yet another pang of guilt, this time for the Valian matriarch to whom she'd brought so much trouble. Bleak dreamed of the word she'd seen carved into the stone by the stream. It glimmered before her – *Oremere*. Was it a name? Who was he? Or she? Bleak would never know now.

The next day, Henri didn't look like herself. She had purple rings beneath her eyes, her face was smudged with dirt, and she moved with a stiffness Bleak hadn't seen before. The men were just as bad, if not worse. In contrast, Bleak felt fine, normal. She packed up her bedroll and stretched her limbs before the ride.

She gave Henri a grim smile as the warrior queen passed. 'Not my first time sleeping in the dirt,' she said.

Henri didn't reply, and simply tightened the straps of her katars around her thighs.

They took turns relieving themselves among the crops, and Bleak sincerely hoped the farmers gave the vegetables a thorough washing before they sold them at the markets. They started riding before the orange sun broke away from the horizon. The ground was still damp with the morning dew, and the paddocks full of crops around them were blooming with life. Some farmers were already out harvesting the wheat.

'Aren't half the people in the capital starving?' Bleak said as they surveyed the fertile land and the vast expanse of crops.

'Half the people in any capital are starving,' Swinton snapped. 'It's the choice they make for living in the capital.'

'Horseshit,' Henri said.

'Nobody asked you.'

'Tell me again why you think the capital is so amazing,' she said.

'I don't need to tell you anything,' Swinton snapped.

'That's what I thought.'

'Shut it,' Swinton hissed. 'Heathton keeps its people safe. King Arden is one of the few leaders in this realm doing something about the mist.'

'Oh? And what's that?'

'We have mist trackers sending reports every month. He even has it contained beyond the King's Forest.'

'And how did he manage that?'

'He erected a wall.'

Henri laughed, actually clutching her stomach as she did. It was a cruel sound. 'A wall, Commander? You think a *wall* is what's keeping out magical mist that's plagued this realm for decades? Your naivety amazes me.'

'Watch your tongue.'

'Watch who you threaten,' she countered.

Bleak sighed. This was going to be a long journey indeed.

The sun was high by the time they reached the King's Road. For a royal stretch of road, it was nothing more than a wide path of yellowed dirt.

'There's a town called Hoddinott an hour or so ride from here,' said Swinton. 'We'll rest there and get a hot meal.'

Bleak had to suck her stomach in to stop it from

growling. The bread and cheese they'd had to break their fast hadn't filled her in the slightest, not with all this travelling. She was dying for any kind of steaming roast meat.

'Commander,' Fiore called again, 'are we expecting visitors at the castle?'

'No. Why?'

'There's a company riding hard towards us.'

Bleak twisted in the saddle and looked back. Sure enough, there was a group of people on horseback – nearly just a speck in the distance, which seemed to be heading their way. Clouds of dust suggested they were moving at high speed.

'Be alert,' Swinton said, 'but maintain the current pace. I want to see who they are.'

They didn't have to wait long before the group was nearly upon them. They didn't stop, or even slow, but rode right past them.

'Blue and claret,' Fiore muttered, 'envoys from Battalon.'

'And you didn't know about them?' Henri jeered.

'That's not your concern,' said Swinton.

'You seem concerned enough for the both of us, anyway.'

When they got to the gates of Hoddinott, they dismounted.

'We don't want to seem imposing or threatening,' Swinton told the others. 'There's an inn just off the town square. We'll go there.'

The four travellers led the horses through the dusty streets. Bleak took in what she could, not that there was much to look at. A butcher with several pig carcasses hanging in the window, a baker, and oddly, an apothecary. The town in general was sleepy, with barely anyone out and about, though Bleak guessed many of them worked on the farms, or the cotton mill that she could see looming in the distance. Ahead, she watched Swinton and Fiore talk hurriedly. The commander had been restless since the Battalonian envoys had passed. If Bleak were to hazard a guess, she'd say that Swinton didn't like being kept out of the loop, or not having control.

At the end of the road was the inn he'd described. They tied the horses to the posts near the water troughs and walked up the creaking porch steps. Old and run-down, the Hodd's Nott looked as though it had been through the wars. However, despite appearances, inside was packed. Bleak had guessed wrong. The population of Hoddinott wasn't out working; they were in here, drinking. Drunks, whores, gamblers and all else in between chatted loudly within. It was as though they were all deaf. Perhaps everyone was, after spending so long in there.

'Commander Swinton,' a man called, making his way over to them.

Bleak had to grab Henri's arm to stop her from drawing her katars. The warrior queen was forgetting that they were in the king's territory now, where people were bound to recognise the Commander of the King's Guard. Maybe this was the kind of establishment the commander frequented.

'Leslie,' Swinton greeted the man stiffly.

'It's been too long, Commander, here – we've got a booth available for you and your —'

Leslie's mouth gaped as he spotted Henri. His eyes scanned her face, her long hair, and then trailed over the rest of her lithe body. Henri shrugged off Bleak's grip and drew one of her katars, slowly, making a point of putting it in front of her body. Bleak realised it must have been a long while since someone had dared to look at the Valian matriarch like that. The last person who had probably hadn't been able to look for very long.

'A booth would be great,' Swinton said quickly, gesturing for Leslie to show them the way.

Henri stalked after them, sheathing her katar, fury practically glowing from her. Bleak understood, she really did. Besides Valia, from what she'd experienced, the other territories had no respect for women. Women were objects, entertainment or servants, existing solely for the whims of men. Bleak didn't even blink at the leers aimed in her direction. When a hand reached out to grope her, she caught it before it touched her and simply flung it back to the offender. Bleak caught Henri staring at her.

'Spent a lot of time in taverns,' she said, raising her eyebrows at another man who called out to her.

Behind them, Fiore was visibly uncomfortable, but he

said nothing. Swinton was waiting for them at a booth towards the back of the inn.

'Ladies first,' he said, allowing Bleak and Henri to slide across the benches before he and Fiore slid in. The men now blocked the women from sight, and Henri took a deep breath.

'This was not the sort of establishment I had in mind,' she said, narrowing her eyes at Swinton.

'Me either. It never used to be this bad. When I last stopped by here, it was like any other pub. But it's changed. The clientele ... has changed.'

'You don't say.'

Leslie returned, and placed four steaming bowls of broth in front of them. He made to walk away, but Swinton grabbed his arm.

'You won't be joining us, Les?' he said, his grip still firm on the man's arm.

'Uh ... You honour me with your invitation, Commander, but I have clients to attend to.'

'Stay,' Swinton said, pulling Leslie down onto the bench. 'In fact, you're welcome to try a little of everyone's.'

'Oh, that won't be necessary, Commander.'

'Oh, but it is.' Swinton slid his own bowl towards the innkeeper. 'Drink.'

Bleak watched on, begrudgingly impressed as Swinton forced Leslie to sample each of their bowls. When Swinton was satisfied that none of them were about to be poisoned, he dismissed the whimpering innkeeper and pushed their broth back to them. Bleak brought the bowl to her lips and savoured the hot, salty liquid. It wasn't a roast boar, but it would do. She used the stale bread from her pack to mop up the dregs. She sat back, having almost forgotten about everyone else in the inn, and suppressed a sigh. A hot meal could always help lift damp spirits.

'I'm going to find the ... powder room,' she said. She slid past Fiore easily, and didn't give the group a second glance as she walked away. She let herself be swallowed by the crowd, and found an empty stool at the bar. She slid one of Swinton's silvers across the counter and ordered herself a jug of ale.

Chapter Twenty-five

Swinton wove through the throng of dirty bodies and spotted Bleak at the bar. She was drinking. He paused, watching her raise a mug of ale to her mouth and gulp down the liquid as though her life depended on it. If she got roaring drunk it wasn't his problem; he had his orders. He pulled up the hood of his cloak and continued through the crowd, sneaking out of the service entrance of the Hodd's Nott.

Outside, dusk had fallen, and there was a haziness to the town that hadn't been there before. Swinton untied Xander, checked his saddlebags and mounted. He urged the stallion into a gallop, and Xander's hooves thundered against the earth as they rode out of the town. He wished he didn't have to do this, he wished he could go back to Willowdale instead and visit Eliza again, but orders were orders, and only he could perform the task. He pushed on towards the King's River, where across the water, the West Farmlands lay. He had to complete this part of the mission, no matter the cost. He'd already let the king down. He wouldn't do it again, it was too dangerous. As he rode, he tried to push Fiore, Henri and Bleak from his mind. He wouldn't be gone long; he could make something up. Not that Henri would believe him, or Fiore for that matter. He wondered if they'd found Bleak at the bar yet. Henri would be furious. It hadn't escaped his notice that she'd ordered all the drink away from the keep as a means of keeping the Angovian sober. He clicked his tongue and leaned forward. They needed to go *faster*.

They passed more corn crops and the old cotton mill. Finally, after what seemed like an age, they arrived at the King's River. Just as Swinton had hoped, there was no one around after dark. There was a definite eeriness about the place with the tufts of cotton floating like ghosts across the dark sky, their reflections glinting along the surface of the river. Swinton dismounted and eased a sack from one of his saddle bags. Its contents clinked within, and he adjusted his grip to handle it with more care. What was inside couldn't be released this side of the river. He knelt down at the water's edge and reached into the sack. From inside it, he took a jar. The white contents within swirled and roiled. *Mist.*

Swinton studied it, feeling the familiar gut-twisting sensation of guilt grip him. There were five jars in total, some left over from when he'd been unable to release them in the Hawthornes. Deep shame rushed over him, and he remembered Henri's words. *It takes a real bastard to hunt down his own kind, don't you think?* It did, and he knew that. He knew there was no honour in his actions, not anymore. He didn't have a choice. He stood, grasping one of the jars in his hand. He looked across the water and wondered who lived there, what would become of them now, if they'd survive. He pitched the jar across the water and heard it smash loudly on the other side. *One.* He picked up another and threw it, the sound of glass shattering seemed to echo across the water's surface. *Two.* Another jar left his hand. *Three.* He could see the mist find its freedom, roiling over the ground to find its counterparts. *Four.* There was no going back now. He had been chosen for this and he had to finish it. *Five.*

He exhaled shakily and watched as the mist took hold of the land, quickly and confidently, as though it had a mind of its own. It was unsettling, and Xander whinnied nervously. He leaned against the beast and stroked his nose.

'Easy there, boy,' he said, trying to offer some reassurance to both of them, but there was none to be had. He wanted nothing more than to leave this all behind and ride to Willowdale, but he'd find no reprieve there either. Eliza was dead. And if she were alive, Swinton realised with a jolt, she wouldn't want to see him like this. There was no redemption for what he had done, no saving grace. He placed his boot in the stirrup and mounted Xander, taking one last look at the spreading mist. He wanted to be sorry, but he couldn't be. If this was what he had to do to protect his secrets, he would.

Chapter Twenty-six

Bleak pored over the map she'd stolen from Swinton earlier, the edges held down by her empty mugs of ale. It was the map she'd seen him with all those weeks ago in the Hawthornes. Small Xs in blood-red ink were marked across the trail they'd been on back then, and elsewhere, too – some in Valia, some in the West Farmlands. She didn't know the land well enough to identify exactly what these marks pinpointed, but she was intuitive enough to discern that something wasn't adding up. She smoothed out the crinkles in the parchment and took another sip of her ale. She considered the amber liquid – a minor slip-up on her behalf – but then again, who knew what would become of her? Wasn't she entitled to a final drink or two? She looked over her shoulder and peered through the crowd, to spot Henri.

Something wasn't right. The warrior queen was slouched down on the bench, her leather pouch of herbs on the table before her rather than around her neck, and that slime Leslie was beside her. Bleak folded up the map roughly, stuffing it down the front of her underclothes, and stumbled towards Henri. Where was Fiore?

She scanned the inn and found him lying unconscious at the foot of their table.

Leslie was advancing on Henri, and Henri wasn't moving to stop him – something was *very* wrong. There was no way Henri would let that letch within a yard of her with that look on his face. Bleak shoved people aside and reached Henri.

'What do you think you're doing?' she snapped at Leslie.

The greasy man looked up, surprised. 'The Valian asked me to keep her company while all her friends were otherwise occupied.'

Bleak stared at Henri. Only the warrior queen's graphite-and-green eyes were moving; the rest of her body was slumped down into the bench.

I can't move, the panicked voice rang out in Bleak's head. *He's poisoned me. Get out of here, you've got no chance.*

'Well, girl? Leave us be,' Leslie said, waving her away.

Run, Bleak, Henri said into her mind.

Bleak staggered into a stool, turning back to the rest of the inn.

'That's it, girl, go get yourself another round.' Leslie laughed.

Bleak steadied herself, taking the stool she'd bumped into. She whirled around and smashed it into the side of Leslie's leering face.

His head hit the table with a crunch; there was instant chaos. A man lunged for her, and Bleak slammed a metal mug of ale into his temple, picking up the stool again. Hers wasn't a delicate dance. There was no training, no discipline to her movements as more men from the inn advanced on her. She was scrappy, clawing and swinging, enduring as many blows as she herself dealt. But she kept getting up, flinging her arms and small fists wherever she could. This wasn't her first bar fight. Blood ran from her nose and from a cut above her eye. But it might be her last.

Henri was still slumped in the corner of their booth. Bleak heard her mind call out.

Use your magic.

Distracted, Bleak was hit over the head.

'Fuck!' she yelled, her fingers coming away from her hair bloody. She buried her boot in the attacker's groin and smacked him across the face with the legs of the barstool.

Use her magic? How in the realm could she do that? There were too many. This wasn't what she'd trained for. She had dipped into the memories of one person, one at a time, slowly, with all the time in the world. Here, she took hit after hit, thankful at least for the fact that the men were also brawling each other now.

She was tiring, though, staggering and supporting herself on the side of the bar as she swung at the men who kept coming. No, she could do this; she could do *something*. Allehra didn't send her across the realm with her only surviving daughter just to die on a dirty tavern floor. She had helped Neemah defeat Luka, hadn't she?

Bleak took another swing at her opponent to buy her a few precious moments of time. She closed her eyes and took a deep breath. Her eyes flew open again and her hands caught a post of timber about to hit the side of her face. She blocked another blow, and another. She parried clumsily around her attackers, hearing their thoughts before they struck. But Bleak needed Henri. Magic or not, she was only one fighter, and a small, untrained one at that. With Henri, she might have a chance. Without her, eventually their numbers and sheer strength would win out.

Bleak staggered again and looked around wildly, her eyes finding Henri, dribble running down her chin, and then Fiore still lying unconscious in the blood and ale on the inn floor. As another man made a dive for Bleak, she scrambled behind the bar. Someone wrenched her arms behind her back and a fist pounded her abdomen, knocking the wind from her lungs. She gasped for air. Whoever it was grabbed a fistful of her hair and yanked her head back. Her hands flew to her attacker's grip, clawing. Unable to get free, she gouged at his eyes. He released her, and she slammed her elbow into his face.

In that moment, something thrummed wildly within her, a buzzing reverberating through her whole core. She fell into herself, into a darkness she didn't know existed. The sounds of the brawling became distant; her ragged breathing stopped. There was a forceful push within her and then – the men started screaming.

Bleak came back into being to see the men clutching

their heads and falling to their knees. They begged, but she didn't stop, she didn't want to. She blasted their minds with her magic, until blood spilled from their ears, their noses and their eyes. Until there was no one but Bleak, Henri and Fiore left alive.

Chapter Twenty-seven

When Swinton returned to Hoddinott well after nightfall, he didn't know if Henri and Bleak would still be there. The gameswood drug he'd slipped the warrior queen would have worn off a while ago – he hadn't meant to take so long. He'd only spiked her broth to stop her from making a run for it with Bleak, or wreaking havoc on the inn. Despite appearances, there was generally no bite to follow the inn's bark, and with Fiore there, both women would have been more than safe. As he cantered up to the Hodd's Nott, he spotted their three horses still tied to the post, thank the gods. How would he have explained two missing charges *and* a prized stallion to King Arden?

Swinton walked up the creaking wooden steps, and even though the place was glowing with light, something was different. For an inn where, even during daylight hours, you had to shout to be heard, now it was silent. There was no yelling about the price of ale, no whores forcing laughter for their patrons, no voices coming from within at all ... Swinton drew his sword, and with one hand, pushed the heavy door open. He gasped.

Inside was a bloodbath.

There were bodies everywhere. Some were unrecognisable, their faces bashed in and mangled. Others looked untouched but for the trails of sticky blood running from their eyes and noses. Broken glass, broken stools and billiard sticks lay discarded on the floor. There was blood spattered on every surface.

Henri, Swinton thought. She'd clearly regained her senses earlier than he'd anticipated and had taken it out on the entire bar, like a wild animal, murdering these innocent people with her magic. He took a step inside and felt his body leave the ground.

He was slammed into the ceiling, his sword clattering to the floor and pain splintering his back. He was flung back to the ground and felt his cheekbone shatter.

Henri.

She wasn't done. She hurled him from wall to wall, through the broken glass and furniture. Pain lanced every inch of his body as he was bashed around mercilessly. Glass, timber and gods knew what else sliced open his skin, each impact rattling his bones and his mind. He still didn't know where she was. He couldn't see anything but blood and bodies, and his own undoing.

'Henri.' That was Bleak's voice. 'Henri, stop.'

'No.'

Blood from Swinton's head ran down his face and stung his eyes. He cried out as he hit the ceiling again. And again. Henri slammed him back into the wall, keeping him upright, and then she flew at him, her katars, their hidden blades springing free, pressed against his throat.

'Do you know what my kindred would do to you?' she ground out, her breath hot and stale on his face.

She knew it had been him.

'Do you know what the king will do to you?' he managed, his eyes flicking to the massacre around the inn.

'You think *I* did this?'

'Don't even,' he tried to swallow, but felt her blades pierce his skin, 'don't even try to deny it.'

Henri stared into his face, her nostrils flaring.

'She didn't do it,' Bleak said, emerging from one of the booths, looking badly beaten. 'I did.'

'You?' he croaked. 'How?'

Bleak didn't reply. Instead, Henri applied more pressure to the katars at his neck.

'You drugged me,' she hissed.

Swinton winced. She would kill him like this, little by little, slowly. He would choke on his own blood.

'You can't kill him,' Fiore said, walking out from the storage area at the back. He was holding a rag to his bleeding head.

'I can.'

'King Arden will see it as a direct attack on Ellest, killing the Commander of the King's Army. He'll burn Valia to the ground for it.'

Without looking away from Swinton's face, Henri addressed Fiore.

'You know what he did. That's an act of war on Valia.'

'I know what he did, and I don't agree with it,' Fiore said, 'but, we've got bigger problems.' He gestured around the inn.

Swinton and Henri followed his gaze to the carnage.

'We need to figure out what to do about this, or we're all dead,' he said.

Henri looked at Bleak, who was leaning against the bar, eyes glazed over.

Turning back to Swinton, Henri withdrew her katars from his throat. He exhaled the breath he'd been holding in, and touched his fingers to the small cuts near his Adam's apple; they came away bloody.

'There will come a time,' she told him, 'when you will die for what you have done here.' She sheathed her katars and walked over to Bleak.

Fiore rushed forward as Swinton collapsed, catching him under the arms. Throwing one of Swinton's limp arms around his neck, he dragged him to a nearby booth.

'Gods, you're a mess,' Fiore said under his breath.

Swinton watched as his friend went to the bar to find some alcohol to clean his wounds. This wasn't going to be pleasant ...

Swinton passed out from the pain multiple times. His whole body felt broken and on fire. It hurt even to breathe. Broken ribs, lacerations to the face and head, a dislocated shoulder, a broken cheekbone. Despite the extensive list of injuries, however, Swinton knew he'd got off lightly.

Fiore applied the alcohol to his wounds with the cold

precision of a castle doctor. Even amidst the haze of pain, Swinton knew Fiore was angry with him, and he didn't know what to say. He'd had no choice in leaving them. Perhaps the gameswood in Henri's broth had been a mistake, but they'd never know now. He'd followed the king's orders, only the others couldn't discover that. He stole a glance across the room and saw Henri trying to talk to Bleak. All Bleak was doing, though, was shaking her head. How in the realm had she done this? Had she known what she was doing?

'Did you find what you were looking for?' Fiore asked through his teeth. 'Don't insult me by telling me you've been in the privy the whole time.'

'Yes,' Swinton forced himself to say.

'But you won't tell me where you went?'

Swinton shook his head. 'I can't. Orders.'

Fiore narrowed his eyes. 'Then you deserve this. You should have been here.'

'And where were you? Why didn't you stop this?' Swinton countered.

'I was attacked.'

'So you failed just as I did.'

'Not just as you did, no.' Fiore was rougher with his wounds after that.

'We have to burn it,' Swinton croaked.

Fiore paused over stitching up one of his head wounds. 'What?'

'We have to burn this place to the ground.'

Chapter Twenty-eight

A dozen men were dead. Their minds had bled out of their noses, their eyes, their ears. They had been in so much agony, they hadn't been able to form words, only scream – a primitive, animal sound that made the hairs on Bleak's arms stand up. Their eyes had been wide, imploring someone, anyone, to make it end. She hadn't stopped. She'd given in to some baser instinct inside herself. She had *wanted* them dead. All of them. Bleak shuddered. She'd been right to want a cure, to put a stop to this 'power' of hers.

'They weren't innocent men,' Henri said beside her.

'Most of them weren't evil, either,' Bleak said, watching Fiore tend to Swinton's shocking wounds on the other side of the room.

'No,' Henri agreed, 'but these things ... They happen.'

'That's your advice?'

'I have no advice for you. Everyone deals with death in different ways, whether they caused it or not. You did what you thought you had to do to protect us. And for that, I owe you my thanks.'

Henri's gratitude hung thick in the air.

'I don't know how I did it ... Protected you, I mean ...

It could have just as easily been you lying here on the floor,' Bleak managed.

'That didn't happen, though.'

'No, but it could have.'

'You have more control than you think. I'm thankful for that.'

Bleak ignored the warrior's rare moment of humility. 'These men belonged to someone.'

'Someone they treated infinitely better than us. Or have you forgotten them attacking you? Have you forgotten the bastard who put his hands on me? None of them were going to stop.'

'We don't know that.'

'And if we did, would it make it easier?'

'I don't know.'

'Then there's nothing to be done,' Henri said, and started taking bottles of spirits from behind the bar.

Bleak could still feel her magic roiling within her. She wasn't tired as she usually was when she'd been in someone's mind. If anything, she felt stronger, the power within her hungrier. She didn't know what it meant, but along with her power pulsed horror like she'd never known. The kind of horror, she realised, that only comes with recognising the worst part of oneself, and having long-suppressed fears confirmed.

Bleak's thirst was at a record high. Despite the blood and tinge of death in the air, the most potent odour was the alcohol, and it made her mouth water. Henri poured the liquid out across the floor and over the bodies. The drunk within Bleak cried out in outrage – *Such waste! Such a horrible waste.* But when she realised that her thoughts were for the alcohol rather than for the men she'd killed, she too reached over the bar for the bottles and began sloshing the liquor across the floor. Together, they emptied the entire contents of the bar all over the inn and the bodies it now housed.

'How are we going to explain this?' Bleak heard Fiore ask the commander.

'I'm working on it,' he grunted, still not quite himself through the agony.

Bleak had watched Henri rip the commander apart. In theory, it looked exactly how Bleak imagined brutality to look. The relentlessness of it, adding pain to more pain, slowly and surely, as though there was all the time in the world for suffering. But despite the guilt she felt about her own actions, Henri's somehow seemed like … justice. All around Bleak, dead, red eyes looked up at her, shock still fixed on their marble-like faces. She spotted the bar stool she'd used as a weapon; clumps of hair and flesh stuck to it. She forced herself to swallow the bile that rose in her throat, and emptied the barrel of ale she'd been holding. She needed to get outside, to breathe in the fresh air and stop stepping over the mangled corpses she'd created. She needed to think of something else.

'I need to talk to you,' she muttered to Henri as she brushed past her. She headed out onto the porch, and Henri followed. Bleak grabbed a torch and motioned for the warrior to make her way around the side of the inn. There, she pulled Swinton's map from down the front of her undergarments, the parchment now stained with blotches of blood – whose, she didn't know.

'What's this?' Henri demanded, as Bleak passed her the torch.

Bleak smoothed the map out on the gravelly ground with her palms, placing a rock on each corner to hold it in place.

'I was hoping you could tell me,' she said, her voice still unsteady. 'I saw the commander with it before you rescued me in the Hawthornes. I didn't really think too much of it until his reaction. He didn't have it with him in Valia, probably because he knew he'd be searched, but I saw him with it again here, and when he snuck off … I took it.'

'You stole it?'

'That's hardly the most pressing crime of the evening.'

'Point taken,' said Henri.

'I thought you might know what these are.' Bleak pointed to the tiny red Xs.

Henri's brow furrowed as her eyes trailed over the map, down towards where Valia lay.

'That's the Forest of Ghosts,' she said, pointing to one mark. She moved on to the next. 'This is where we found you in the Hawthornes. The rest … They're not any particular landmarks that I know of, nothing special.'

Henri crouched and squinted at the map. 'It's not recent.'

'What do you mean?'

'This map and its markings are not recent. See how the ink is faded? And the map, it's still got the old borders of Valia.' She pointed to a section below Felder's Bay. 'This doesn't exist anymore.'

'So ...'

Henri shrugged. 'I don't know. Seems strange to be carrying around an outdated map – it's at least ten years old.'

Bleak stared at the map, taking in the markings yet again.

'Why didn't you tell me of this sooner?' said Henri.

'I only got it a few hours ago.'

'No, but you saw him with it weeks ago. You could have told me.'

Bleak shrugged. 'How was I supposed to know who I could trust?'

Henri nodded. 'But you trust me now?'

'These days, I make a point of not trusting anyone,' Bleak said, folding up the map and stuffing it back down her shirt.

'You saved my life today,' Henri said slowly. 'I am in your debt.'

'You saved my life in the Hawthornes. I'd say we're even.'

Henri studied her, failing to veil her surprise. 'Not many turn down a life debt from a Valian.'

'Would you rather I lord it over you?'

Henri grinned. 'No, I much prefer this attitude.'

Bleak nodded. 'Figured as much.'

Valian and Angovian made their way back to the front of the inn, and the reality of their situation hit Bleak anew. She glanced down at the leather cuff Allehra had given her, and twisted it around her wrist. Henri followed her gaze.

'That should have helped you,' she said, frowning.

'That's what I thought. Clearly, it's useless.'

Henri reached out and took Bleak's wrist, turning it over in her hand and studying the intricate markings carved into the leather.

'It makes no sense,' she said, tugging the small pouch out from the front of her leathers. 'These worked on you; you couldn't breach our minds. Why would the cuff not work to help you control your abilities?'

'Perhaps the herbs have weakened.'

'Perhaps ...' But Henri's knitted brow told Bleak the warrior thought otherwise.

Fiore emerged from the inn, Swinton's arm around his shoulder, and the two men clumsily made their way down the steps.

'We need to leave this place,' Swinton mumbled, his face already a patchwork of bruising.

No one spoke as they untied their horses from the posts and led them away from the building. Bleak swallowed the lump in her throat, trying not to picture the dozen bodies that lay within. Henri's expression was unreadable as she threw the torch she was holding into the inn. Flames roared to life, swallowing the fuel-covered furniture and corpses, engulfing the scene of Bleak's undoing. Black smoke billowed from the windows, escaping into the night's star-studded sky.

For the first time in a long time, Bleak felt the hot sting of tears in her eyes. But she wouldn't let those tears spill. Not here. She brushed the loose hair from her face and straightened, except something didn't feel right. The world around her blurred and slowed, a coppery taste spreading across her tongue ...

She was small and scared. Fear pounded in her chest, her little legs only able to stretch so far as she was dragged by her wrist through the thick smoke. But it wasn't smoke. It was mist. The mist. They had to find a way out, and fast – before they all perished.

'Faster, Alarise, we have to hurry,' her mother's voice said.

She was crying, the fat tears sluicing down her face, adrenaline throbbing between her ears, but she worked her legs harder, even though she couldn't see where she was going. Even though she stumbled over her own feet and whatever else lay beneath them. The mist had rolled into their open windows and seeped through the cracks under the doors of their home. Home. They would never go back there.

'Can we outrun it?' she heard her mother ask someone. They passed through a pair of elaborate iron gates. One was hanging from its hinges, blood dripping from its spikes. Her mother blocked her view with her body.

'We're only in the outskirts of it, so it hasn't taken hold of us yet,' her father answered. Though she couldn't see him, she knew he held her mother's other hand.

'Come now, keep up – we're going to be alright,' her mother said, trying to mask the panic in her voice.

The mist was making her dizzy, and she felt like she was going to be sick. But she swallowed and kept going. She didn't want to stay in the mist forever.

'Alarise,' her mother said, 'Alarise ...'

She felt someone holding her down, and tasted a bitter herb in her mouth. She jerked away, shoving the hands off her.

'Bleak, you're okay,' someone said, 'Bleak ...'

She came back to herself. *Alarise* ... She hadn't heard that name in well over a decade.

'Bleak,' Fiore said, staring into her face with concern etched all over his.

'What happened?' She felt the heat of the blazing inn on her skin.

'You had another fit.'

She gazed at the burning building. Explosions burst inside, and the alcohol-soaked foundations were groaning, on the verge of collapse. Smoke billowed from all crevasses, the thick grey-and-black clouds climbing up into the cool night air. Bleak watched it, trying not to think about the fact that they weren't only burning timber and furniture. This was a funeral pyre.

'What happened?' Fiore said.

Alarise. Mist dweller. Iron gates ...

Not too far away, Swinton was brooding by the horses but clearly listening, and for the first time, Bleak glanced sideways to Henri, seeking guidance. Henri looked from Swinton to Fiore and subtly shook her head at Bleak. The possibility for trust between the King's Guard and them was long gone now.

'I'm fine,' Bleak said, accepting Fiore's hand and getting to her feet.

They prepared the horses, adjusting their tack and saddle bags, but Bleak couldn't keep her gaze from the fire. Its flames licked the thatched roof, which creaked loudly as it caved in, sending sparks and embers flying.

'It won't always feel like this,' a rough voice mumbled next to her. Swinton.

'Won't always feel like this,' he said again, 'but you'll never go back.'

Bleak nodded silently. She'd guessed that much for herself, but hearing it from him was better than hearing the lies that no doubt Fiore, Bren and maybe even Henri would tell her.

'You've killed people,' she found herself saying.

'Many,' he said under his breath. 'It's easy enough to take a life. The hard part is living with it afterwards.'

So he'd done terrible things, too. He was staring at the blaze, his dark features not even slightly softened by the glowing light. Dark stubble shadowed his sharp jawline, and cuts and scrapes covered the rest of his face, making him all the more intimidating. Though his voice was gruff, there was a rare note of kindness in it when he spoke again.

'You'll remember this day for the rest of your life,' he said, 'but don't let it define you.'

His umber eyes locked onto hers for a moment, before he limped away towards the horses. Bleak turned back to the inferno; goosebumps raised on her arms despite the intense heat of the fire. She took Senior's length of rope from her pocket, a scrap that held so many memories and kept her sane.

It was no good to her now. Taking a deep breath, she threw it into the fire, the flames swallowing it whole.

Chapter Twenty-nine

Dash had always hated lessons, memorising history and facts he'd never use. He didn't understand why he wasn't being taught something useful, like how to nock an arrow to a bow, or how to start a fire. Now that Olena was leaving, however, he wouldn't be going to any more lessons, and that thought scared him. Ma always said the best thing to happen to him was an education. The icy bite to the air told Dash that the summer months were coming to an end, and now he would be spending his days mucking out stalls with his hands about to fall off from the cold.

Envoys had arrived from Battalon. Their claret-and-blue tunics stood out like blood on snow. Over the next few days, the castle was a continual flurry of movement. Fabrics, furniture, books and everything in between were being packed into royal carriages to be taken down to the docks and loaded onto the princess's ship.

Olena hadn't been herself. She hadn't asked Dash about the sky, about the colours in the gardens; she hadn't made fun of him getting into trouble with the cook again, or even probed him about what had happened with Sir Caleb at the feast. He hadn't told anyone about his vision. It seemed like a long time ago now, like a bad dream. He pushed it from his mind and thought of Olena again. She was quiet, withdrawn – as though she had accepted her fate and was in mourning.

One windy afternoon, a few days before she was due to start the journey to Battalon, Olena requested Dash's company at the cliffs. He wrapped his cloak around him tightly, bracing himself against the sharp gale, making sure he stayed away from the edges. With the thundering sound of Heathton Falls and the wind whipping his ears, he could hardly hear himself think. He spotted Olena. Her regular guards, Thomas and Jonathan, were gone, and instead she had four new guards with the Battalonian crest stitched onto the breast pocket of their uniforms.

'You're not going to jump, are you?' he said.

'Don't be stupid,' she said dryly, 'why do you think they're here?' She nodded to the men surrounding her.

Dash's heart sank. He'd never seen his friend so dark before, so hopeless. She closed her eyes and let the gust tangle her hair.

'What are we doing here? I thought you weren't allowed out of the keep?'

'There have been a few more allowances lately, since they broke the news.'

'Okay ...'

'I wanted to feel the breeze. The cold. I wanted to feel something. Apparently, Battalon is quite humid this time of year.'

Hot tears stung Dash's eyes, but he blinked them

back. Like hell he would cry in front of four royal guards and the princess.

'Why aren't you fighting?' he said quietly.

'What?'

'*Fight*. It's your life, isn't it?'

'My life?'

'Yes!'

'Oh, Dash, you don't understand.'

'Yes, I do.'

'No, you don't. I can't just do whatever I want – I'm a princess. A blind and unwanted one, yes, but a princess nonetheless.'

'You're not unwanted.'

Olena's bottom lip quivered. 'I know my father never had much love for me, but my mother ... I cannot believe she would allow him to do this. Am I such a burden?'

'The queen is fighting for you, Lena.'

'You can't know that.'

'But I do.' Dash took a deep breath. *Should I tell her? No. Not yet.* 'Princesses should be able to do what they want,' he said instead.

'Well, they can't.'

'Why?'

'It doesn't matter,' she said. It was the first time Olena spoke to Dash as though he were a child and she were a grown-up.

'It —'

'Let's not argue, Dash.'

'Can I come with you, then?' Dash blurted out. He

didn't know what it would mean to leave Ma and Pa behind, but Olena was his best friend. He was her eyes. She needed him.

She shook her head. 'It wouldn't be appropriate.'

'Why? We're best friends.'

'I can't bring the stable master's son with me to meet my prince.'

The comment stung. '*Your* prince?' Dash said.

'Well, that's what he is ...'

These weren't Olena's words. She was slipping away from him. He couldn't stand it.

'Olena,' he said.

'Mmm?'

'Do you want to know what happened to me the night I met Sir Caleb?' He kept his voice low, out of earshot of the guards standing nearby.

'I *knew* something happened!' she said, turning to him.

'You have to swear never to tell anyone.'

'Dash, don't you trust me by now?'

'Yes, but ... It could get me into a lot of trouble. Worse than the belting from Pa.'

'What is it? You can tell me.'

'I – I saw something.'

Olena's brow furrowed. 'Saw what?'

'Umm ...' Dash hesitated. He shouldn't be telling anyone this, let alone the Princess of Ellest, but ... Maybe if she knew, maybe she'd fight harder to stay, or take him with her.

'I was ... I was on a ship ... There was a girl —'

'What girl?'

'I don't know – I've never seen her before.' Dash glanced at the guards before continuing. 'I was on the ship with her, out in the middle of the sea. She didn't know I was there, and,' he took a breath, 'we sailed into the mist.'

'What?'

He nodded. 'It was really ...' Dash wanted to say scary, but a knight wouldn't be scared, and he certainly wouldn't tell a princess he was scared. 'It was weird,' he said, 'all in black and white.'

Olena's mouth fell open.

'What do you think?' he said after a time, unable to bear the silence.

Olena took a deep breath of the cold air. 'Have you told anyone else?'

'No.'

'Good.'

'Why? What's wrong?'

'Black and white, you said?'

'Yes.'

'And you were there, but the girl couldn't see you?'

'Yes,' he said again.

'I think that was a vision. A magic vision. I think ... I think you have magic, Dash. That you might be an Ashai.'

His face flushed. No. He couldn't have magic. Magic was bad. He'd never be able to be a knight if he had magic.

'I can't be ... *that.*'

'Why not?'

'Nobody in my family is.'

'Sometimes it skips a generation. Or more.'

'How do you know?'

It was Olena's turn to blush. 'I found some books,' she said.

'Books? But all the books on —'

'Not normal books,' she cut him off with a frown, 'books ... Books for people like me – for people who can't see. They were in the old library. Jaxon told me about them. He didn't know what they were about, of course. And there's no one in the castle who can read them ... except me.'

'What are they?'

'History books, mainly. But not like the ones Mrs Milner teaches us with. They're ... different.'

'How?'

'They tell a different story.'

'What?'

'I ... I don't think I can say any more.'

'You have to, Olena! What's wrong with me?'

'There is nothing wrong with you.'

'But there is! You just said so. I might have ... *magic.*' Dash said the last word as though it were the plague itself.

Olena moved closer to him, pity painted across her face. She smoothed out her blue-and-claret skirts, the colours of Battalon.

'I can't tell you everything, not now,' she said, 'but I'll tell you this – what we've been taught, it's a lie. There aren't just four continents. There are – or were – five.'

'Five?!'

'Shhh ... Yes, *five*.'

'Where is it?'

'It was south-east of Ellest. And it was swallowed by the mist. It used to be the biggest, the most powerful.'

'No ... That's not right, Olena.'

'People believe the mist has always been there, that it's unknown, uncharted land. Maybe that's ... less frightening than knowing there was once an entire continent there. That the mist can creep over onto our seas and islands and swallow us, too.'

'But – the mist hasn't come closer.'

'Hasn't it? That's the thing about lies, Dash – once there is one of them, you usually find more.'

'And what does this have to do with *magic*?'

'The mist *is* magic. The book I read said that the fifth continent wasn't like Ellest or the other continents where magic is rare and illegal. This place was full of magic; it celebrated magic. Ashai from all over the realm used to migrate there. They say the magic consumed it, and that's how the mist started. They say that the mist seeks out new magic to feed on.'

'I don't understand.'

'I don't either, not completely. I have many more volumes to get through.'

'There's more?'

'Of course,' she said, 'this is just the start.'

'Why can no one else read these books?'

'They're written in an old language for the blind – it's called quaveer. It originated in Qatrola.'

'How did you learn? Could I learn?'

'I don't think so, Dash. It took me a long time. I'll read the rest of the volumes for us, and when I'm done, I'll send for you from Battalon. I'll keep you safe, Dash.'

'I'm not scared,' he said.

'I am,' Olena countered. 'I'm scared of going to Battalon. I'm scared of having to marry Prince Nazuri, I'm scared he won't like me, and that he'll be mean to me. I'm scared of having no one to be my eyes, Dash. And I'm scared of leaving you here, to face your magic alone.'

It was the most Olena had said all at once in a long while. So much so that Dash sat there, stunned, for a time. She was scared of a lot of things. And he couldn't help her. He couldn't help his best friend. What kind of knight was he going to be if he couldn't help the Princess of Ellest?

'It's not magic,' he said. 'Are you taking all the quaveer books with you?'

'No.'

'Can you send one to me?'

'No, people will ask questions. I'll leave one for you, in the kitchen, under the old cupboard with the burnt soup pots.'

'Alright.'

'It's not easy, Dash, it's like learning another language.

You've got to learn a whole new alphabet.'

'That's okay, I can do it. And then I'll write you quaveer letters.'

Olena smiled and patted his arm, though Dash could tell she didn't believe him. He'd show her.

She stood to leave. 'I have to return to the castle.'

'So soon?'

She nodded. 'I have additional lessons with Mrs Milner on traditional Battalonian customs. Today's is on the Festival of Lamaka.'

'But I thought Battalon worshipped Liir?'

'They do. I suppose I'll find out this afternoon.'

Dash stood and looped his arm through hers, sadness latching onto him like a disease.

'When do you leave?' he asked.

'In three days' time.' She took her arm from his.

'Olena,' he said as she began to walk away.

She turned back towards him, her eyes full of tears.

He couldn't say what was in his heart then; it would only break them both, so instead, he took a step closer to her.

'What's it called?' he said, reaching out and squeezing her hand.

'What?'

'The fifth realm?'

She turned her head in the direction of her guards, who were still out of earshot, and squeezed his hand back. 'It was called Oremere.'

Chapter Thirty

An uncomfortable sense of unease settled in Henri's stomach as they started the final leg of their journey. They left the burning inn behind and crossed the King's River by ferry, moving further and further away from Valia and deeper into the king's lands. She would find no loyalty here, no respect. King Arden owned everything and everyone from here on. She stared at the gleaming battleaxes strapped across Swinton's back. He was at the head of their company and she preferred it that way. She didn't like having her back to the treacherous bastard. He was still badly injured thanks to her beating. Deservedly so. As they continued the journey, she enjoyed fleeting moments of satisfaction as she watched him wince when he mounted and dismounted his horse. She'd broken at least two ribs, though she wished she could have had him a little longer. The bruising around his face had blossomed into patches of murky purples and greens.

Good, she thought. *He's lucky he's not dead.*

They still hadn't received any answers as to why he'd left them defenceless at the Hodd's Nott. Though she'd bet her weight in Valian herbs that it had something to do with the map Bleak had stolen. The two of them had studied it again in their brief moments away from the men. Henri knew there was something strange about it, but she couldn't put her finger on what it was. She looked to her side to find Bleak staring blankly ahead, bumping along mindlessly in her saddle. She had been different the past few days. Her odd-coloured eyes were hollow and her words were laced with darkness. Henri had seen her throw her scrap of rope in the fire, the one that seemed to have meant so much to her before. Out of the corner of her eye, Henri sometimes saw the Angovian fiddle with her hands, as though she still had it.

Something had shifted between the two of them. Henri hadn't liked the girl at first – she was everything Henri found infuriating. And yet, by some miracle, the girl had saved them, and had given up a part of herself in the process. That meant something to Henri. She felt that she should talk to Bleak, provide her with some measure of comfort, reassurance. But she couldn't. To her, it was simple. The men who'd been in the Hodd's Nott were bad. Alcohol, opium or a terrible day in the fields were no excuse for laying hands on someone else. Henri suppressed a shudder as she recalled the way they had looked at her and made her skin crawl. Yes, they were bad men. No one deserved to feel unsafe in their own skin for someone else's pleasure. To Henri, the men deserved to die. Though from Bleak's face, and her reaction afterwards, Henri could tell it was not that simple to her. She knew the girl was questioning how far the men would have gone, whether or not they had families, whether they had deserved such a death, if death at all. Henri shook her head. Simple. It was very simple. But in that respect, Bleak reminded her very much of Sahara, considering things from all angles, analysing the consequences of their actions, even though these were brought on by the actions of others. Henri ground her teeth and spurred her horse into a canter.

The lands around them were beautiful, even Henri had to admit. She found herself marvelling at the expanse of open space. For someone who was usually so surrounded by trees and kindred in the forest, the East Farmlands were a different kind of paradise, if she could forget to whom they belonged. There was something liberating about the endless fields of grass and the casual nature of the farmers. For them, life wasn't complicated; it was a rhythm of planting and harvesting and transporting and then planting again, feeling at one with the realm. For a few brief moments, Henri allowed herself the luxury of envy. She would never know freedom like that.

After leaving Hoddinott, they travelled for two days, and for two days they saw no one of note on the road. They barely spoke between themselves. On the second evening, once they'd set up camp, Henri took Bleak aside, pulling her into the darkness by her elbow.

'I think it's time we tried your power again,' Henri said, recalling Allehra's request with a note of bitterness.

'Absolutely not,' Bleak replied.

'I was given an order.'

'Here I was thinking *you* gave the orders.'

Henri clicked her tongue, but ignored the barb. 'You're scared.'

'Damn right I'm scared. I could kill you.'

'I doubt it.'

'Forgive me for not taking the gamble.'

'Bleak, you *must* – training gives you back your control, doesn't it?'

Bleak scoffed. 'What control?' She waved the leather cuff on her wrist before Henri's face. 'This was supposed to help. It's done nothing! If anything —' Bleak cut herself short.

'If anything what?'

Bleak swallowed. 'If anything ... it's made me feel stronger, made my "power" surge with more ... vigour.'

Henri's heart nearly stopped. 'What?'

'Since leaving Valia, I've felt more powerful. I don't understand it. I thought maybe the magic in the trees, the history of your ancestors had something to do with it?'

'Perhaps,' Henri said. She took a step towards Bleak and held out her hand for the cuff.

Bleak unbuckled it and handed it over. The second the cuff dropped into Henri's palm, she felt the difference. The leather had been treated in one of the rarest Valian herbs, and the carvings, the carvings were *enchantments*. How had she not realised before? She ran her fingers over the markings and turned the cuff over in her hands. Her mother hadn't given Bleak herbs to help stifle her magic; she'd given her a means of unleashing its potential. Allehra had ensured that when the time came, Bleak would be able to protect her daughter, and she'd turned the girl into a walking weapon to do so. Who knew where the limits of Bleak's power ended?

'What is it?' Bleak asked, studying Henri.

Henri handed the cuff back to her. If she told the Angovian the truth, she'd toss the cuff. She was still so raw from what had happened in Hoddinott. But they may need that power yet.

'Nothing,' Henri said, ignoring the twist of guilt in her gut, 'nothing that I can tell anyway.'

Bleak gave her a long look, before shrugging and buckling the cuff back onto her wrist. Henri didn't hassle her about training again. Tomorrow; they could talk tomorrow.

They camped on the edge of a wheat crop, careful to ensure their fire was adequately contained. Amidst their quiet, she noticed the dynamic had changed between Swinton and Fiore. From what she gathered, Fiore hadn't agreed with Swinton's actions, and he now blamed the commander for what had happened with Bleak. He hadn't said so, of course; Swinton was his superior. But Henri could see it in his hesitations, in his sideways glances to Bleak, who now sat furthest from the fire, the reflection of the flames flickering in her odd eyes. Henri chewed her dried meat and stale bread with effort, and glanced at the others doing the same. Except Bleak. She held her bread where it had been ten minutes ago, untouched, in her lap.

'You have to eat,' Henri said.

The men looked up, following her gaze to Bleak.

'I'm not really hungry, you can have mine if you like.' She offered her roll to Henri.

Henri shook her head and pushed it back towards her. 'You're going to need all the strength you can get.'

'A bit of old bread isn't going to go very far,' she said.

'Eat it anyway.'

Bleak took a half-hearted bite and then tossed the rest to Henri. 'I'm done,' she said, getting up and walking over to where she'd set up her bedroll away from the group.

Fiore made to follow her.

'Leave her,' Henri commanded.

Fiore lowered himself back down. The three of them ate the rest of their bread in silence, and Henri was glad for it. The less they talked, the less they would argue.

Although she had become used to sleeping on the ground rather than in the trees, Henri still hadn't slept well since leaving Valia. The discomfort she could handle; she'd handled much worse in her training, but the vulnerability of it – she couldn't stand it. Knowing someone was taking watch wasn't enough. These men weren't her kindred, nor was Bleak, and they'd already proven how unpredictable they were. Henri rolled onto her other side with a frustrated sigh. She needed to be in her top form when she finally faced the king, and this wasn't the way to go about it.

It was almost a relief when morning came, but as soon as the sun rose and the pressure to sleep ceased, so did Henri's ability to keep her eyes open. Once she was up in the saddle and on the move again, she caught herself nodding off with the steady rhythm of the horse's steps.

She continued to let Swinton lead them. To keep herself awake, she studied the axes strapped across his shoulderblades – his father's signature weapons, she knew. From memory, his father's axes had remarkable carvings along the handles, beautiful scrollwork that managed to be understated and masculine. She remembered Swinton's father and his weapons from Sahara's memorial all those years ago. Sir Caleb and Lady Yuliana had stood close by King Arden and Queen Vera, just another set of faces in a sea of different nationalities, ages and ranks. Valia Forest had been overrun with people wanting to pay their respects to the dead heir. What Sahara had done was not made public knowledge. The mourners were told she had taken ill – an unlikely tale in Valia, but people didn't dare question the pyre they had burned without a body. Sahara *had* been sick; Henri had known it for a time. But it had been a sickness not of the body, but of the mind and of the heart.

Again she recalled the name her sister had carved into many a surface – *Oremere*. Who was Oremere? A friend? A lover? What had they done to bewitch Sahara so? Or was she simply lovestruck? As many of the hardest kindred had been at seventeen?

Oremere, Henri thought. *Where are you now?*

Henri took a deep breath and focused on Swinton's axes again. Even after all this time, she wasn't ready. She wasn't ready to face what her sister had done, what Henri herself had let her do.

Her horse slipped in some loose gravel on the road, and it wrenched Henri out of her memories and back to the present. She realised they'd reached Angove River, and in front of her, Swinton let out a frustrated huff.

'The river has to be at low tide for us to cross or it'll sweep us and the horses away for dead.'

'And you didn't think of this earlier?' Henri asked, glaring at him.

'It slipped my mind,' he said, voice low.

'Perhaps you've a brain haemorrhage.'

'Stop it,' Bleak said, 'haven't you inflicted enough damage on each other?'

'Not even close,' Henri retorted. 'It's enough when I say it's enough.' She raised her hand, feeling the energy in her palm surge. Bleak's hand reached across and pushed hers down gently; Henri acquiesced.

It would be hours until the tide changed, and so Henri and Bleak wandered downstream with their horses and planted themselves on the soft bank by the water's edge. For a time, they sat in companionable silence. Henri sharpened her katars and watched as Bleak knotted long reeds of grass together. While Bleak was immersed in her knots, Henri discreetly undid the string around her neck which held the protective herbs in place. She placed the pouch down beside her, and waited. She was as still as a huntress, doing her best to suppress her concerns. She'd never wanted to open her mind to this strange girl from Angove, or the mists, or wherever she was from. Her business was exactly that, *her* business. The thought of someone rifling around in her mind made her queasy. But despite Allehra's roundabout and secretive methods, Henri knew they meant Bleak had a role to play.

She allowed her thoughts to trail off, back to her sister, as they so often did. She never talked about Sahara, not to Athene, not to Allehra. In the days and weeks after Sahara's death, both women had wanted to talk to Henri about her sister, but Henri had refused. Her grief was too raw, and talking to them about it all didn't feel right, didn't do Sahara justice. They would never understand what it was to lose a twin, a part of oneself. And so she'd shut them down. Every time Sahara's name was mentioned she'd snap, or worse still, simply leave, until her sister's name was uttered less and less in her presence, and then not at all.

'She was sad,' Bleak said quietly. Henri saw her eye the discarded herbs in the grass, but the girl didn't object, and so Henri nodded.

'Why?' asked Bleak.

'She wasn't an Ashai, like me or Allehra,' Henri murmured. 'She didn't believe in the Valian Way. I don't know when she decided she'd had enough.' Henri sighed, resting her head in her hands. 'But she did. Ten years ago, she walked into the mist. I swear I felt the moment her heart stopped in there.'

Bleak reached out to her, and with a callused hand pressed Henri's leather pouch of herbs back into her palms.

'I'm sorry,' she said.

Henri swallowed. Was this part of the girl's power? To bring words tumbling from a warrior's mouth? Words Henri had never spoken aloud, words that she'd always thought would crack her in two? More than two. She put the leather pouch back around her neck, and then pointed to Bleak's cuff.

'That won't stifle your magic,' she admitted.

Bleak smiled grimly. 'I know.'

'You know?'

The girl nodded. 'It feels very different to the herbs you and your kindred carry. I knew it wasn't the same as soon as I put it on. It's ... dangerous, it ... It feeds a darker side of my power, if that makes sense. I was going to take it off after ... after what happened. But perhaps we need danger on our side in the capital?'

'I'd come to the same conclusion,' said Henri.

Bleak nodded and turned her attentions back to the river. 'What are we going to do?' she said, defeat lacing her words.

'I don't know,' Henri answered truthfully. The Angovian deserved that much.

'They'll split us up,' Bleak said.

'Yes.'

'We can't trust the commander.'

'We can't trust any of them.'

Bleak wrung the cuff around her wrist. 'Every woman for herself, then?'

Henri nodded slowly. 'If you can get away, do it. No matter what.'

Bleak offered her hand. 'Same goes for you. No point in the bastard having both of us.'

'Every woman for herself,' said Henri, taking Bleak's hand and shaking it firmly.

Behind them, the grass rustled as Fiore came to find them.

'Tide's going in,' he said. 'Commander says we should make a move.'

Dusk was falling yet again as they crossed the river on horseback. Henri took comfort in the sure-footedness of her mount as the current dragged around them. When they reached the other side of the river, the lights of the capital glimmered on the horizon. They'd be there in time for supper.

Chapter Thirty-one

Swinton could see the castle in the near distance, a view he'd had too often of late. In the warm dusk light, it loomed over the capital, like the king himself in his throne; the thick, stone-walled gatehouse, and beyond it, a fortress of sharp spires and turrets, keenly positioned arrow holes and sweeping marble steps. Swinton squeezed Xander's sides with his heels. Henri, Bleak and Fi followed closely behind. He could sense the Valian's wariness as they rode through the city of Heathton towards the castle, and once again guilt lapped at him like a foamy wave upon sand. He had no choice, though, or if he did, he'd made it long ago.

Townhouses lined the cobblestoned streets, and taverns on every corner were brimming with drunk, merry people who spilled out onto the sidewalks. He led the small company into the heart of the city, and commoners began to peer from their windows and gawk from their stoops. There was no hiding who rode beside him – *the Queen of Valia* – he could already hear the whispers. Henri sat straight-backed in her saddle, her tight braid, kohl-lined eyes and forest-green leathers screaming *outsider*. But the people were in awe of her, he realised. This foreign matriarch had earned their respect and fear through the legends told about her and her kind. He frowned. While Henri's presence was undeniable, he glanced at Bleak and saw that she had somehow faded into obscurity, had mastered the art of anonymity. The way she rode looked like she wasn't even part of the group, but merely had the unfortunate coincidence of riding behind them.

As they rode, Swinton tried to ignore the flyers, but the thick parchments with their sunny messages were nailed to nearly every shopfront, every fence post.

Register today for generous rewards, and the opportunity to serve your crown. Preserve your magical heritage.
See Tannus Armenta at the castle gates for assistance.

Swinton's skin crawled. *Magical heritage ...* No one in his family was an Ashai, not to his knowledge, and he'd never told *anyone* of his abilities. He'd come close to confessing to his father, once, in the throes of fresh grief after Eliza had died. But he'd stopped himself. His father was a knight; his loyalty was to the crown. Having an Ashai for a son would force him to choose, and it would have ruined him, one way or another. There was no one Swinton could ask about how abilities passed down through generations. Were there exceptions? Was an Ashai ever born of non-magic-wielding lineage? The only person he could ask now rode beside him, every glance in his direction filled with loathing.

The city centre was bustling. Merchants stocked their stalls and lit their lanterns – the moon market would open soon. They passed butchers, fabric shops and Swinton's favourite bakery. He watched as Henri and Bleak took in the sights: Henri assessing the dangers, Bleak fixated on a tavern she'd spotted. People moved from their path immediately; Swinton himself was easily recognisable with his dark features, battleaxes and Captain Murphadias at his side.

They came to an abrupt stop. Irritated, Swinton craned his neck to see what the hold-up was. A wagon was blocking their turnoff. A prison wagon, by the looks of the rusty iron bars and the filthy hands clutching them from within. He squinted and spotted a red 'M' painted on the wagon's side. He knew where it was going and who was within it. One glance at Bleak's pale face told him that she knew as well, or at least, she did now. She and Henri exchanged worried glances.

'Move,' Swinton said sharply to the guards blocking the street.

Alarmed, they obliged, and the wagon of doomed souls disappeared down the cobblestoned street.

When Swinton and the others reached the foot of the cliffs, they cantered up the narrow road to the castle. The sooner they saw the king, the better.

At the top of the hillside and the cliffs, where the castle overlooked the East Sea, the gates swung open, revealing the decadent courtyard within. The entrance steps were awash with sashes and blooms of claret and blue, and Swinton suddenly remembered the Battalonian envoys who'd passed them just days ago. He turned to Fiore with a frown, but his friend merely shrugged. The company dismounted before the steps, the guards nodding to Swinton and Fiore. Carlington, the stable master, greeted them.

'Good to have you back, Commander,' he said, taking Xander's reins.

'Good to be back, Carlington.'

Carlington turned towards the stables and whistled. Two young apprentices came running and proceeded to take their horses to be cared for.

'What's all this about?' he asked Carlington, gesturing towards the banners.

'You haven't heard, then? Princess Olena is betrothed to Prince Nazuri of Battalon. She's due to depart for Belbarrow in a few days.'

Swinton hid his surprise and ignored the incredulous look from Fi. He made for the stairs.

'Rest well, Commander,' Carlington called.

'And you.'

At the top of the stairs, a servant Swinton didn't recognise greeted them. He gave a respectful nod to Swinton and Fi.

'We are grateful for your safe return, Commander, Captain.' He turned to Henri and Bleak. 'Welcome to Heathton. His majesty has had rooms prepared for your stay. This way, please.'

Fiore gripped the servant's forearm. 'We didn't catch

your name.'

The servant was taken aback by the touch, and Swinton silently chastised Fi for not mastering his Battalonian upbringing better.

'Apologies, Captain. My name is Markuss.'

'When will we see the king?' Swinton interrupted.

'His Majesty has requested private audiences with each of you in the morning. A supper will be served for you and our ... guests in an hour, in the great hall.'

'Right,' Swinton said, turning to Henri. 'I'll see you there. Try to scrub up, will you?'

Henri glared at him and he shrugged. He didn't wait a moment longer before stalking off to his chambers, leaving Fiore and the others behind.

When he entered his rooms, he sighed with relief at the sight of his bed. He hadn't slept here for more than a night at a time in the last two months. It was good to be home.

The redheaded servant girl, Therese, brought in pails of hot water for his bath. He recalled the last time he'd seen her and how she'd flushed at the sight of him shirtless. This time, he left his clothes on as she poured the steaming water into the tub, and he turned away as her dress fell forward at the front and revealed the soft pale skin beneath. He could feel himself stirring and willed her to leave before he said or did something stupid.

She turned to him, biting her bottom lip. 'Will that be all, Commander?'

He couldn't help taking in her figure; his eyes lingered on her cinched waist and the curve of her hips, and those full breasts ...

He cleared his throat. 'Yes. That's all. Thank you.'

She left, and he loosed the breath he'd been holding.

Gods, it had been a long time since he'd felt a woman beneath him. He ached for that skin-on-skin heat, that momentary abandon of all that mattered. But every time he'd allowed himself that release, emptiness had rocked him to the core.

He struggled out of his filthy riding gear and let himself sink into the hot water, naked but for the coin around his neck, and sighed. What a nightmare the past few weeks had been. He'd have preferred the heat and exhaustion of fighting in Battalon to dealing with the antics of Bleak and Henri. They seemed intent on making his life difficult, and he knew that Henri wasn't done punishing him for the incident at the Hodd's Nott. He didn't regret it, despite his wounds. He'd done his duty, he'd remained loyal to the king, and his secrets were safe, for now.

He soaped up the washcloth and scrubbed the dirt from his skin, the filth clouding the water almost instantly. He went under, savouring the feeling of the heat wrapping around him and the world becoming muted. When his lungs strained for air, he reluctantly resurfaced, wiping the water from his eyes. He felt bone-weary, and yet he still had to muster the energy to face the king. With a final sigh, he hauled himself from the tub, the water sloshing from his body.

A towel slung low around his waist, he sank into the armchair in front of the crackling fire. Water dripped in steady, thick drops from his dark hair, and the coin of Yacinda swayed before his chest like a pendulum. He rubbed his aching temples before pulling his satchel bag onto his lap. He hadn't consulted the map since before Hoddinott – there'd been too many prying eyes around – but the king was bound to ask about it. He rifled through his bag, pulling out ink, a quill, scraps of parchment, a tin of pain-relief salve, a shaving blade ... He got down on his knees and turned the satchel upside down on the floor. Panic gripped him. He frantically sifted through the fallen contents without success. Dread hit him like one of Henri's blows, sharp and precise. The map was gone.

In the great hall, a dinner banquet had been laid out. The long tables were set with the usual glamorous gold plates, cutlery and goblets, and platters of roasted meats and vegetables ran down the centre. It smelled incredible, but Swinton's appetite was gone. Bleak – or worse, Henri – had the map, he was sure of it.

Fiore, Henri and Bleak were already seated at the end of the table closest to the dais. Henri had washed the grime from her face, but otherwise remained the same – her attire, her hair and her weapons, all a deliberate slight to the court. Bleak, however, looked like a stranger. She wore a pale-blue gown that pushed up her small bust and cinched in her already tiny waist. The servants had no doubt forced her into it, as well as pinned her wet hair to the top of her head, as was the current fashion. They wouldn't have dared attend Henri. Swinton expected Bleak to look uncomfortable, but with a full goblet of wine in her hand, the Angovian orphan's face was set in a bored, blank expression. Swinton took his place beside Fi and shot a look at the two women opposite, who were both lifting their drinks to their lips. He itched to confront them about the map, but now was not the time, and here was certainly not the place. There were eyes and ears all over the castle.

Despite his lack of appetite, Swinton cut into his food and sipped his ale, all too aware of the throbbing silence around them. The only sounds were the scraping of knives and forks, which made the quiet all the more prominent. The calm before the storm.

He noted Bleak pouring herself another goblet of wine. She was clearly treating this as her last supper. Henri, on the other hand, had barely touched her food, and was sitting with her shoulders back, eyes following every small burst of movement in the hall. A servant girl poured him another mug of cold ale. Bleak's eyes moved to his drink.

She raised her brows at him as if to say, *What?* and proceeded to take a long gulp from her cup.

Was it you? he wondered, still silently fuming over the loss of his map. His eyes cut to Henri. He didn't know whose hands it would be worse off in. He rubbed the scar on his chin and drank deeply from his mug.

Swinton made sure no one followed him after supper as he slipped away from the others and out of the castle towards the maze. He doubled back a few times, just to be sure. Only the silent guards and the king knew of this place. He didn't light a torch; a torch might attract attention. Instead, he stepped into the maze and into the darkness, knowing he could find his way without sight, for he only needed to follow the gentle tug of magic.

His skin crawled as he went further into the maze, the towering hedges closing in above him, blocking out the starlight. Although he couldn't see them, he heard the faint rustle of the red blooms blossoming at his feet. After all this time, he still didn't know how these flowers had come to be, or what magic fuelled them, but whatever it was, it wasn't good. Swinton's grip clenched around the pommel of his sword, his palms clammy. His weapons could do nothing for him now, but they grounded him all the same.

After a few more minutes, the narrow path he was on opened up and a carpet of red blooms lay before him. It didn't matter how many times he'd seen it before, the sight of the flowers rattled him in their aching beauty and terrifying sinisterness. At the heart of the garden was the stone water fountain. Swinton walked across the garden, readying himself, and placed a hand on the fountain's edge. There was a sound like a whisper before the flowers shrank back, receding until they revealed an expertly carved statue of an elegant woman, surrounded by layers of flowing scarves. Swinton had never asked the king who she was, but it was clear she wasn't the queen, nor was she a goddess of this realm.

He took a deep breath, trying to steady his heartbeat, but he couldn't stop the short gasps for air that escaped him. His hand found the coin of Yacinda beneath his shirt and he clutched it to his chest. What he needed to restore it was here, in abundance.

He could do this; he *had* to do this.

The air was suddenly colder around him as he stepped up onto the plinth and pressed a trembling hand to the statue's breast, over her stone heart. There was a loud groan as the entire statue began twisting at its base and sinking, taking Swinton deep below the earth.

What greeted Swinton beneath the maze was what his nightmares were made of. The stench hit him first – the overpowering, hot reek of human excrement and vomit. Swinton gagged and tried to breathe through the material covering the crook of his elbow. From the platform on which the statue had stopped, he could see the holding pen, the prison that left every other horror he'd witnessed behind in the dust. Crammed together were a hundred or more men, women and children from all over the continent, naked and filthy, their death sentences written all over their faces. Ashai. Each and every one of them a wielder of magic, an abomination, a means to a greater purpose. Like him. Hearing the statue crunch into place and seeing him above them, many cried out, in desperation, in anger, some trying to project their magic onto him. But the walls, the iron bars and the floors of the bunker had been coated long ago in powerful Valian herbs. Here, an Ashai's abilities were nullified. Swinton stood straight and made himself hear their screams, allowed his fear, his panic to rise up in him along with the bile now in his throat.

Someone cleared his throat beside him, and he had to stop himself from jumping.

Of course, he remembered, *the silent guard.*

'Soldier.' He forced his voice to neutrality, nodding to the man dressed head-to-toe in grey, the lower half of his face covered with a mask. 'You have what I requested?'

The guard nodded and took a dark vial from the folds of his uniform. It was a mixture, infused with the very essence of the same herbs that soaked the walls around them. It would recondition his coin, ensuring his protection once more. He tucked the vial into his pocket.

'And the report?' He held out his hand for the piece of parchment that was required with every shipment of Ashai.

The guard went to a small side stand and offered an envelope.

Swinton snatched it from him, so the guard wouldn't see his trembling hand.

One hundred and three. One hundred and three Ashai souls to be sent to Moredon Tower. It had been months since Swinton had come to collect the report himself, and he knew these were believed to be the last of the Ashai in Ellest. All rounded up like animals ready for slaughter. How long had they been rotting down here? How much longer would they suffer here before they were carted off, in groups of ten, to Moredon Tower?

Swinton could never return to the confines of his chambers immediately after a visit to the maze prison. Instead, he visited Xander in the stables and walked the long halls of the castle, checking up on the patrols and royal guards. It did nothing to quieten the raging fear that lived below the surface of his skin, but he did it anyway. As he turned a corner, he heard shouts coming from the south courtyard. He was instantly at the window, in time to see the guards tackle a fair-haired man to the ground. The man groaned as they pushed his face into the gravel and delivered hard, swift kicks to his abdomen. The Angovian fisherman. Bren.

Swinton's stomach plummeted. *What's he doing here?*

Swinton took off at a run, down to the courtyard where the guards were now hauling Bren to his feet. His lip was bleeding and his sun-streaked hair had escaped its tie, now hanging loose into his bright eyes. In his hand, he clutched a bloodied piece of parchment – the king's flyer.

'I'm an Ashai,' he was panting, 'stop – I'm an Ashai, I swear. I saw the —'

Swinton approached, stomach churning. *No, no, no* ... He knew for a fact that the young Angovian was no Ashai.

Bren spotted Swinton.

'He'll tell you,' he said, imploring Swinton, 'he knows me!'

The guards looked up and saw their commander. They stood to attention.

'What's the meaning of this?' Swinton demanded, steeling himself, looking to the highest-ranking guard, Stefan.

'Commander, we caught him trying to sneak into the grounds. He says he's an Ashai. We have to take him in, Commander.'

The boy was *daft*. If only he had waited. The situation was too precarious. Now he was here. And Swinton couldn't help him.

'Commander? He says you know him.'

Swinton wanted to knock some sense into the Angovian. What a fool he was. Swinton found himself nodding.

'He was in Angove. Do you not recognise him yourself, Stefan?'

Stefan studied Bren and nodded slowly. 'I think so, sir. He was with the girl, wasn't he? He was her friend.'

'Indeed,' he said, the word sinking in like an inked signature on a death warrant.

The men waited for his orders, expectantly. There was only one option here.

'Take him to the cells, there's a shipment due out to Moredon tomorrow. He needs to be on it.'

'Swinton! Where is she?' Bren started as the guards

began to drag him away. 'Are you taking me to her?' he yelled.

But Swinton had already walked away, leaving Bren to his struggles.

One hundred and three Ashai souls. And Bren.

Chapter Thirty-two

When Bleak returned to her rooms after supper, she found that someone had stoked her fire and lit the candles on either side of her bed. Her sheets were turned down and her pillows had been fluffed. She stood there for a moment, staring. So this was what it was like, living among the rich. She lifted the gown she was wearing over her head and hung it carefully back in its place. She looked down at the bodice that constricted her breathing and pressed her breasts together. Gods, how was she going to get herself out of it? She was twisting to see how it laced up in front of the mirror when there was a loud knock at the door. She walked towards it and pulled it open.

'Do you always answer the door like that?' Fiore said a little breathlessly, eyebrows raised at her undergarments.

She swiped a robe from the chair in the corner and wrapped it tightly around herself.

'What are you doing here?'

The Battalonian baulked at her sharp tone. 'I, uh ... It's about your friend, Bren.'

'What about him?'

'I thought you should know —'

A hand clapped Fiore on the shoulder. Swinton. The commander was out of breath, too, looking daggers at his friend, then at Bleak's undressed state.

'Captain,' he said, 'I've been looking for you everywhere. I must speak with you.' He glanced between Bleak and Fi. It looked bad, she realised.

'Fiore was just coming to me with news of Bren,' she said, still clutching the robe to her body.

'Who?'

'Bren.' She rolled her eyes. He knew very well who Bren was.

'I'll be there in a moment, Dimitri,' Fiore said.

'Not in a moment, *now*.'

Fiore turned back to her, urgency etched on his face, but the commander hadn't moved. It was clear he'd be escorting Fiore to their supposed meeting.

Fiore fumbled with his words. He shook his head. 'I just wanted to tell you, we received word from Angove. Bren has arrived safely and has returned to his family.'

Bleak's eyes narrowed as she looked from Swinton to Fiore. *Why the urgency?* She focused on Fi and attempted to sink into his thoughts, to find out the truth of the matter. She heard nothing. No contradictions. No lies. Her whole body sagged with relief. *Thank the gods.* No matter what happened to her, Bren was safe.

'Thank you,' she said, as Swinton released his grip on Fiore's shoulder and pulled him away from her door. She closed it and returned to the hearth, where she poured herself a wine. She had never known such relief. She hadn't even realised how much she'd been suppressing her concern for her friend until now, how much she'd pushed him from her thoughts altogether. She let herself picture his fair hair, broad chest and teasing grin. But as soon as she did, she remembered Tilly's arm splayed across him, the two of them in Tilly's bed. Her stomach turned and she reprimanded herself. Bren was safe. That was all that mattered.

Bleak didn't sleep well, despite the luxury of having a bed. She dreamed vividly of choppy seas and Bren calling her name. She woke well before dawn, hearing the servants already bustling about the halls, preparing the castle for the day ahead. When she got out of bed, the air was chilly, and the polished stone floor beneath her bare feet was like ice. Wrapping the quilt around herself, she moved to the little window on the far side of the room. Two storeys below was a group of squires training by torchlight in the fog. She watched as they artfully struck and dodged each other with wooden practice swords, the training master critiquing their footwork with harsh words. The boys' faces were scrunched up in concentration, their brows damp with perspiration.

Bleak wondered what it would have been like to have such structure to her childhood. Henri, Swinton and Fiore had all been trained and educated in the ways of their people. The extent of her education amounted to how to steer a fishing ship and what knots to use. She could tie a hundred different types of knots and gut a fish with her eyes closed, but she'd never have the discipline, the knowledge, the experience that they had. She wasn't ungrateful, though. She knew she'd had more advantage than a lot of other Angovian gutter rats. Senior had even taken it upon himself to teach her how to read, even if it had been with a pile of battered old trading contracts. She'd never liked it much, the reading; she'd always preferred a rope between her hands and the seas churning below the hull, but she understood why he'd taught her. She wondered what they might have read together, had they got their hands on a decent book.

She sighed and turned back to the room, considering the small bathtub in the corner. A bath might have helped the seedy feeling settling over her. She was hungover, she knew it, and she didn't care. She hadn't had a fit last night and her hands had stopped shaking, and for a while, even the tense royal dinner hadn't bothered her. If the king had dragged her all the way from Angove out here, by the gods, she'd at least drink the man's wine.

She decided it was too cold to bathe, and finding a servant to fetch hot water seemed like too much of an effort at this time of day, so she went to the wardrobe and rifled through the silken dresses.

Who did they belong to? She let her hands roam over the fabrics, quietly marvelling at the intricacy of the stitching and the creative detail of the cuts. If she focused, she could vaguely remember her mother in similar finery, and those layered skirts she'd clung to as a child. Perhaps if Bleak hadn't lost her parents, she might have grown up in gowns and petticoats rather than dirty tunics, pants and muddied boots. She'd never know. She glanced at her soiled clothes lying crumpled in the far corner of the room. She should have washed them in the basin last night and dried them before the fire, but by the time she'd celebrated Bren's safe return to Angove, she'd been in no state for domestic duties.

If I survive this, I'll quit, she thought. *I'll find some other way to manage myself.*

Bleak turned back to the dresses. Perhaps putting in the effort for the king would appease him. She snorted – *unlikely.* But yesterday's clothes stank of horse and smoke, so she squeezed herself into last night's bodice and attempted to mimic how the servants had laced her up. When her breathing was adequately restricted, she chose a silken lavender gown with silver thread embroidered down the front panel. She caught a glimpse of her reflection in the window. Her hair was wavy from being pinned wet the night before. It fell around her face now, highlighting her striking blue-and-hazel eyes. She stepped closer to her image, noticing the new freckles across her nose and the deep circles under her eyes. She swept her hair up into a careless topknot. The shorter strands at the front still escaped the tie and framed her thin face. She looked different; she couldn't deny it. Although the way she held herself was still that of a hot-tempered gutter rat, she somehow looked healthier. There was more muscle on her bones from all the exercise in Valia and on the road.

A knock at the door sounded. She shrugged and stepped away from the window, her dress swishing as she moved. She opened the door a fraction. Two uniformed guards greeted her.

'The king requests your presence,' one of them said.

'Now?'

'Yes. We'll escort you.'

Bleak's stomach churned uncomfortably. 'Is that necessary?'

'Wouldn't want you to get lost.'

'Umm ... Alright, I'll just get my coat.'

'Be prompt, if you will. The king has a busy day ahead of him.'

Bleak closed the door momentarily and looked around her rooms, panicked. Surely this was unprecedented? It was barely dawn – surely he didn't mean to have her killed so soon? Bleak twisted Allehra's cuff around her wrist nervously. The leather had faded in the sun, but the markings themselves were as bold as ever. It made her uneasy. Allehra had hidden its true nature from her, *and* Henri. What was so different about the cuff that not even the Matriarch of Valia could know of it? Bleak got the distinct feeling that she was being used. It didn't sit well with her. Another knock at the door sounded. She tugged down the sleeves of her dress, covering the cuff, took a fur from the wardrobe and wrapped it around her shoulders.

'Just a minute,' she said. She pulled on her Valian

boots and tucked Allehra's daggers into them. She lifted her skirts and tied the dagger she'd stolen from Fiore around her upper thigh with a sash from one of the dresses.

'Make haste, please, Miss,' called one of the guards.

She hurriedly rearranged her skirts, hiding where Fiore's dagger rested closely against her skin. She took a deep breath. Senior had always told her to trust her instincts – *when it feels like a wave's about to break, it probably will*. With one quick and final glance at her reflection in the mirror above the basin, she swung the door open and greeted the guards.

'Lead the way,' she said, with more confidence than she felt. She wondered if that's what everyone did in the capital: faked their assuredness until it became real. The guards' pace was rushed as they led her down the candlelit passages, shadows flickering across the portraits of kings and queens past. For all the bustling she'd heard outside her room earlier, there wasn't a servant in sight.

A large hand at the small of her back steered her around a sharp corner. Finally, they took her down a large staircase, through the great hall where they'd dined last night, and into the throne room. They planted her before yet another dais – before the king. He was a handsome man, she realised, tall and stately, even sitting down, with a sturdy, pale-gold beard, the whiskers of which he now tugged on as he considered her. Henri, Swinton and Fiore weren't there, and neither was the queen. Besides the two guards who'd escorted her, it was just Bleak and the king.

She curtseyed as best as she knew how. 'Your Majesty,' she said, her voice unsteady.

His gaze fell upon her.

'The cuff,' the king said suddenly, spotting the leather around her wrist. 'Remove it,' he barked at the guards.

Bleak started. The king missed nothing. A blustering guard approached and tore it from her. He threw the cuff into the fire, and backed away from her, face pale, returning to his position.

Bleak looked back to the king and fought the urge to step back. His smile transformed his face into something sinister, and there was more than that ...

The king nodded to the guards. 'Leave us,' he commanded.

Without a word, the men left, the huge doors clicking in place behind them. Now, they were well and truly alone. She could feel her heart hammering against her sternum.

'You're the one who calls herself "Bleak"?' he said, his voice as smooth as silk.

She nodded, clasping her hands together in front of her body.

'You've caused quite the stir in my household, *Bleak*,' he said.

'Your Highness?'

'Majesty,' he corrected her. '"Highness" is for princes and princesses. In any case, because of you, one of my men lost an eye and several others are currently off-duty thanks to injuries they received during your brief stay with them. I've had to postpone plans by weeks because of your unwillingness to submit to a royal summons.'

'I apologise, Your Majesty. I ... I didn't understand what was going on.'

'Do you now?'

Bleak looked up at him, her heart sinking. This wasn't going to end well for her.

'No, Your Majesty.'

Bleak focused; she was going to need her magic now. She needed to use it, to help herself, to help Henri, too. Letting the throne room fade around her, she concentrated on the king's mind.

A foreign power shot back at her. She had to steady herself after the invisible impact. She looked down at her naked wrist, feeling exposed.

The king clicked his tongue. 'You didn't truly think that would work, did you?'

Bleak kept her face blank. 'Your Majesty?'

'Don't insult me,' he said, his voice deepening. 'Trying to read the king's mind? How treasonous.'

'I —'

'Don't waste your breath on more lies.'

Bleak was silent. A strange sensation was spreading from where the cuff had rested against her skin, up her arm. Where was her magic?

Arden's nose crinkled with dislike as he gazed at her, tapping his long fingernails on the arm of his throne.

'So the rumours from the healers were true,' he said. 'A young mind whisperer amidst us. Seeking a cure, of all things.' His laugh was quiet but no less horrifying. 'I'd heard about an Ashai stupid enough to seek a cure in my city, but I had no idea it would be *you*. I'd recognise you from a mile away ...'

Bleak couldn't breathe.

King Arden leaned forward in his throne. 'You're a Thornton,' he said.

Her knees buckled. The sound of the name on his lips near stopped her heart.

'How?' was all she could manage. She needed to find that darkness within her, the one she'd found in Hoddinott, *now*. But what then? Kill the king? Could she kill him? Kill the royal household?

The king ignored her question.

'I find you guilty of *treason* and of using magic against the crown. I hereby sentence you to lifetime imprisonment at Moredon Tower, Alarise Thornton,' he said.

Bleak's breath caught in her throat. *Alarise. Alarise Thornton.*

The king rang a little gold bell at his side, and a different pair of guards stormed in, gripping her upper arms, their chainmail grazing her skin through the thin silk of her dress. The king nodded to the guards.

'Why?' She found her voice, broken and alone. 'Why do this? What have I ever done to you?'

'It's nothing personal,' the king shrugged, 'not for

me, anyway.'

'What —' she struggled against the iron grip of the guards, 'what are you doing to the other Ashai folk?'

'You'll find out soon enough.'

Vomit hit the back of Bleak's throat as adrenaline flooded her veins. She was going to die. She'd thought about death before, often even, after Senior had passed. She'd always imagined dying out at sea, with the waves crashing across the deck and the salt water filling her lungs. Not like this. This death would be slow, full of rot and anguish, on the whim of some crazed monarch, at the hands of some sadist who ran Moredon Tower. For the first time in her life, she turned to the gods, whose existence she'd never truly acknowledged before.

Help me, she pleaded silently, *I need help.* Help wouldn't come. Help had only ever come in one form in recent years, and she'd spurned it. *Bren.* Her chest heaved. She waited for her power to surge, as it had the last few times her emotions had bubbled over. Nothing happened. She clutched at whatever energy usually took hold of her from within, but it wasn't there.

'I said, take her,' the king snapped, and meaty hands closed around her painfully. She fought to stay calm. She would not give the bastard the satisfaction of tears or screams. Not now, no matter how terrified she was. She was dragged towards a different set of doors.

'Alarise,' his voice called, and the guards shuffled her to face him once more. His eyes bored into hers. 'Perhaps you'll find what you've been looking for all these years at Moredon.'

What did he mean?

She trembled as the guards pulled her along the halls of the castle. She paid no attention to where they were going; her mind was racing. *How did the king know?* Had she known him before her parents were taken? Did he know her as a child? What had happened all those years ago that had led them to this moment?

As they turned a corner, someone barrelled into her. Caught unawares, the guards loosened their grip, and she cried out in surprise, catching herself before she hit the hard floor. She found her footing, and met the dark eyes of a young boy – no older than ten. He was clutching a strange-looking book to his chest as he blurted out his apologies. For a second, he reminded her of someone – someone at the back of her mind, though she couldn't quite place who ... And then his thoughts slammed into her. *Oremere.* She staggered at the sound of the name. *Oremere.* It hit her again, and with it came a mess of dotted symbols, a language or code she didn't recognise. As Allehra had taught her, she focused, found her centre. The boy's mind was buzzing with the four continents, *Ellest, Battalon, Havennesse, Qatrola ... Oremere.*

Oremere ... *Where had she heard it? No, seen it.* The forest. Valia. A carving on a stone; a name or a phrase, from long ago.

The fifth continent, the boy's mind told her.

Suddenly, the image of a map filled her head. She recognised it as the one Bleaker Senior had used to navigate the seas. The masses of land were all spaced out across the waters, but below Qatrola was a continent she'd never seen. The boy looked at her with wide, fearful eyes – was it possible he knew what she was doing? Why did he look so afraid? The guards shouted at him angrily and shoved him from their path. She craned her neck to turn back to him, but he sprinted away.

It took Bleak a few moments to remember that the guards weren't taking her back to her rooms. They didn't go up the stairs, but down a spiral stone staircase she hadn't noticed before.

'Where are you taking me?' she demanded, as they led her through a maze of tunnels beneath the castle. She had a sinking feeling that she already knew where.

The dungeons were damp and cold. They were nothing like the pits in Valia. These were *real* dungeons. The men held in the cells they passed were practically animals, hissing and swearing at her as she was dragged along. The thoughts she heard from them were even worse. Some of them hadn't seen daylight in a long time, let alone a woman. She cursed herself for wearing a gown. She was freezing and exposed, her fur having fallen from her shoulders long before. The two guards were less than gentle when they threw her into a cell at the end of the lot. At least the straw she fell into was clean. They locked the cell door behind her and left her there.

Bleak looked at her miserable surroundings, ignoring the grunts from the cell beside hers. She'd slept in worse places.

She pushed all the straw into the back corner of the cell and tried to make herself a nest of warmth. Her skin was already covered in goosebumps and her teeth began to chatter. *Gods, it's cold down here.*

With a sigh, she settled down into the straw, trying not to think of what was to come. The boy came back into her head. *Oremere.* She mulled over the name. With her knees hugged tight to her chest, she pictured the map the boy had been thinking of. Ellest, Battalon, Havennesse, Qatrola ... and the *fifth* continent, *Oremere,* beyond the mist.

A cold, soggy meal was pushed through the narrow slot in the cell door for the fourth or fifth time. Bleak figured she'd been down in the dungeons for about two days or so, but with no windows, no sunlight, she couldn't say for sure. She could no longer feel her fingers, or her toes inside her boots, and her jaw ached from how much her teeth had been chattering. They'd given her a bucket to relieve herself in, but the prisoner in the cell next to hers made a point of staring whenever she needed to use it. The only thing that gave her comfort was the sharp press of Fiore's dagger against her leg, still hidden beneath her dirtied skirts. They'd taken the daggers Allehra had given her but hadn't thought to look for a third. She'd heard enough of their thoughts to know they saw her as no threat, just a pathetic scrap to be pushed around.

Perhaps before, she thought, feeling the blade again,

but not now. She would wait. She had always been good at waiting; for the perfect wave, the perfect burst of wind, the perfect storm. She hadn't seen any of the others, and understood that either they were trying to stay out of trouble themselves, or perhaps they were worse off than she was. She was glad that Bren wasn't here, wasn't caught up in all of this, whatever *this* was. She shovelled the cold gloop from the tray into her mouth, wishing she had a flask of wine to wash it down with.

Something else nagged at her. The little boy from the hall. He'd looked at her with recognition, and he seemed familiar to her as well. But that was impossible. She didn't know any children in Heathton. Then there was that word, or place: *Oremere.* If his thoughts had rung true, it would mean the history of an entire realm was a lie. The boy's frightened face filled her mind again, the way his tensed, slight frame and dark features had been etched with terror, as though he'd seen a ghost in her. Bleak shook her head. This wasn't helping her. She wasn't thinking straight. She was half-starved, she'd never wanted a drink more in her life, and she was surrounded by a dozen criminals who were in here for only gods knew what. The fifth continent could wait.

Time passed in waves down in the dungeons, and not for the first time, Bleak wished she hadn't thrown Senior's rope into the fire at Hoddinott. From her aching body, she knew she'd had another fit at some point, but time in darkness merged as one. One night, she even thought she'd heard Bren calling out her name. But she knew she was delusional for lack of food and sleep. She only heard him that once.

She had no idea how long the king intended to let her rot down here before sending her to Moredon Tower. Arden wanted to make her suffer, he wanted her humiliated and broken, though she didn't know why. Besides being born an Ashai, she didn't know what she'd done to offend him. She shuddered. Who knew what horrific fate awaited her there? Perhaps she deserved it after everything that had happened. Images of dead men filled her thoughts, the blood that had trickled from their eyes and noses, dried and cracked on their bluish skin. She wanted to shy away from them, but she didn't. She had done it. She had to acknowledge it.

'I heard they were keeping you down here.' Swinton gripped the bars of her cell.

From her corner in the hay, Bleak scanned over him. His clothes were clean, his sword was at his waist, and his skin was tanned from the sun. The bruises from Henri's beating were fading. She didn't spare a thought for the mess that she must look like.

'What's happened?' Bleak asked. 'Why am I down here?'

Swinton rested his head against the metal. 'You're here because you're an Ashai, and you'll be here until the king decides when he wants to put you on a ship to Moredon.'

'Figures,' she said grimly.

Swinton paced the stone path outside her cell for a

moment and then stopped.

'I'm sorry,' he said.

'For what?'

'For this. You shouldn't be here.'

Bleak shrugged. 'I was always going to end up here.'

'There was nothing I could do.'

'Didn't think there was.'

Swinton touched his hair again, this time tucking it behind his ear. He met her gaze. Guilt oozed from the man, and for a moment Bleak pitied him. Only for a moment, though. He was the first person she'd spoken to in days, but he was still cleanly clothed and fed on the other side of those bars.

'Alright, then,' he said.

'Thanks for coming.'

Swinton nodded. 'I won't see you again.'

'Here's hoping.'

There was a ghost of a smile. 'Good luck, Bleak.'

The impulse to suddenly blurt out her real name gripped her. What if she died with no one knowing her true identity but the king? She squashed the urge. There was no point now.

'You, too,' she said.

Chapter Thirty-three

Dash sprinted through the courtyard, past the stables and streaked through the woodlands, back to the cottage, gripping Olena's book hard under his arm. He rushed past Ma and slammed his bedroom door closed behind him. He collapsed on his bed, panting.

It was *her*. The odd-eyed girl from his vision. What was *she* doing in the castle? She looked different in a dress, but he'd recognise her anywhere. He'd never met her before in his life, and yet he knew her. And she ... she had stopped and stared at him – did she know him, too?

Ma opened the door and peered inside. 'Master Dash, what is the meaning of this? You race through the house, without wiping your boots I might add, and now you're slamming doors? You were not raised by —' She stopped when she caught sight of his pale face and the way he was clutching his knees to his chest. His heart was racing a million miles a minute and his hands were shaking. Ma approached and sat down on the edge of his bed.

'What is it, Dash?' She reached out and began to unlace his muddy boots. She pulled each one from his foot and set them down on the floor. Dash knew she wanted to scold him for traipsing mud through the cottage and for wearing his shoes on the bed. The normality of these facts helped him steady his breathing. He wiped his clammy palms on the legs of his trousers.

'Was it those squires again?' Ma asked, her brow furrowed with concern.

Dash shook his head. He couldn't explain this, that he'd seen the odd-eyed girl before he *really* saw her. They would send him away.

Before he and Olena had become friends, he had spent a lot of time with one of the handmaiden's sons. He was a funny little thing, with a talent for climbing trees – all the children liked him. But on his sixth birthday, his powers came through and the whole town discovered that he was an *Ashai*. Dash never saw him again after that. Everyone said that his family were ashamed, and had packed up their few belongings and moved out to the rural areas of Ellest. Some rumours even said they'd moved across the sea to Qatrola. Dash felt sick. What if that happened to him? What if he really *did* have magic? What if Mama and Pa had to leave Heathton because of him?

'Are you upset about the princess leaving?' Ma said, placing a gentle hand on the top of his head, her eyes full of sympathy.

Slowly, Dash nodded. It was true enough. He *was* upset about Olena, though upset was too small a word for the gaping hole he felt in his chest. She was his *best friend*, she was a part of him, and he was a part of her.

He was her eyes. Who would be her eyes in Battalon? He needed her help. Who else could he tell about the girl? About his ... magic? As if in answer, something stirred beneath his skin. Startled, he gripped Ma's hand. The hot sting of tears burned his eyes.

'Oh, Dash.' Ma pulled him close. She smelled of lavender soap and the herbs she'd been chopping. 'I know it hurts now, love, I know she's your special friend. But better she goes now, before ... Before you're both grown. She's a princess, love. You were never going to be able to be friends forever.'

Dash didn't know what Ma was talking about, but he spotted Olena's quaveer book on the floor. He'd dropped it when he'd thrown himself onto the bed. Ma couldn't see it. Olena had said no one knew about those books, that they were secret, and Dash had to keep that secret. He pushed off from Ma's embrace and wiped his nose on his sleeve. Ma threw her hands up in the air.

'Dash, how many times must I tell you not to do that? It's uncivilised! I'll get you a handkerchief.' She got to her feet and hurried out the door, failing to notice the thick foreign volume that had been just inches from her shoes. Dash shoved it under his bed and sat up as Ma rushed back into the room, thrusting a square of fabric at him.

'For the love of Connos, I can't understand why you and your father find manners so difficult.'

Dash blew his nose into the thin material and Ma wrinkled her own.

'Dry your eyes, too, Master Dash. We don't want your father seeing those tears, do we?'

Dash shook his head meekly and handed her the dirty handkerchief. With a sigh, Ma took it and gave him a sad look.

'It won't always hurt this much, love. I promise.' She closed the door behind her.

Dash slid onto the floor and ducked under the bed to find the book. He rested his back against the bedframe and hauled the heavy tome onto his lap. It fell open. The pages were thicker than other books, and were void of ink. Instead, patterns of perforated dots covered them. He closed his eyes and ran his fingers across them. He wasn't even that good at normal reading yet, let alone this strange language, but he was determined to learn what Olena knew. Especially if she was right, and he was an ... an *Ashai*. He turned his attentions back to the book, and pulled the notes Olena had given him from his pocket. She'd written the alphabet out for him. Each letter as he knew it was assigned a cell of six dots. Within the cell, the way the dots were emphasised told the reader which letter it was. Dash stared at Olena's precise handwriting, and ran both sets of fingers across the book as she had shown him. He was resolute in teaching himself this new language. If he could master it, he and Olena could write to each other in a code no one else could read! He ran his fingers over the bumps on the page again, willing himself to understand.

Dash stayed in his room all morning. He felt queasy

when he pictured the odd-eyed girl, the shock on her face, the guards dragging her away. He didn't *want* to think about magic, but his vision, the maze and the red flowers, and that strange silken voice talking to the king ... There was magic in Ellest, lots of it.

It was past noon when Markuss, one of the castle servants, appeared at the front door of the cottage. Dash had been summoned to see Princess Olena.

'Dash,' Ma called as he started to follow the servant. 'Goodbyes should be short and sweet, alright?'

He frowned and then continued after the servant. Ma and Pa had never liked his friendship with Olena, but he couldn't work out why. It made him special, having the Princess of Ellest as his best friend.

'People talk, Dash,' his father had said once.

But Dash still didn't know what that meant.

Olena was in the gardens, at her usual spot on the white stone bench. She had been strapped into a deep claret gown with flourishes of blue embroidery, and her buttermilk-gold hair was braided into a crown around her head with matching blue ribbons. Dash plonked himself down next to her, still staring at the foreign attire.

'Ten paces back, guards,' said Olena.

'Your Highness, we're supposed to stay close,' said one of them.

'That's an order,' she said, her voice sharp.

Dash stared at her. He'd never heard her sound like

that before. Commanding, confident – the voice of royalty. Perhaps that's what they were teaching her in her studies of Battalon. The guard bowed respectfully and nodded to the others. They all took ten paces back, giving Dash and the princess privacy for their last conversation. Olena sighed, as though she was tired before her journey had even begun.

'My escort and I leave tomorrow,' she told Dash, wringing her hands.

'We won't see each other again, will we?' he said.

Olena shook her head.

'You're sure I can't come with you?'

'I'm sure.'

'I wish I could.'

'I wish you could too. More than anything.'

Dash held her hand. Her fingers were smooth and soft, but freezing, so he cupped them between his palms to warm them.

'I've started reading those quaveer books,' he said.

'Oh?'

'It's really hard.'

'Told you so.'

'But I'm going to keep trying,' he said. 'We can write to each other in secret code.'

'No doubt someone else in the realm can read quaveer,' she said.

Dash tried to disguise his hurt, but he was never fast enough for Olena. She was always able to sense his feelings.

'I'm sure we can work it out,' she said, a sad smile at her lips.

'I'm going to study hard, Olena. I'll be able to tell you all about —'

'Shhhh … You can never speak of it aloud,' she hissed, her face panic-stricken.

'But to you —'

'To no one,' she said. 'You never know who might be listening.'

Dash's heart broke for her. Would she ever be free?

'You're really going.'

'Yes.'

'You'll be a queen.'

'Eventually.'

'Will you send for me, when you're queen?'

'You may not want to come by then. You may have made new friends.'

Dash shook his head. There would be no one else like Olena.

'Do you still want to be a knight?' she asked.

'A knight in the Queen's Guard.'

Olena smiled and handed him a small tin. Dash opened it and a sweet, buttery scent filled his nose. Sugar-oat biscuits.

'Stay out of trouble, Zachary.'

'Olena —'

'Your Highness,' a deep voice boomed from across the gardens. Dash nearly dropped the tin of biscuits. Commander Swinton strode towards them. His armour was freshly polished, and his hand rested on the pommel of his longsword as he spotted her guards standing ten paces away. A muscle worked in his jaw, and without a word from him, the guards hurried back to the princess's side. Dash's eyes bulged; the commander could command without even speaking.

'Your Highness, I must escort you back to the castle.'

'I have an escort, Commander.' Olena's voice was icy.

'The boy is also required at the stables, Highness.'

'His name is Dash, Commander, and he is required by my side until I say otherwise.'

The commander's expression didn't change. He was a stone wall. 'The king and queen wish to speak with you. Your time for goodbyes is at an end.'

Dash heard Olena take a deep, frustrated breath beside him, before she stood, pulling him to his feet as well and grasping his hands.

'Not appropriate, Highness.' Commander Swinton's firm voice cut in.

Dash could almost hear Olena screaming internally as she dropped his hands. She hadn't even left Ellest yet, and her prison sentence had already begun. Tears lined her eyes, but she didn't allow them to spill. She nodded once and turned away, back towards the castle. Despair gripped Dash's insides, and when she reached the marble steps, he couldn't help it; he called out one last time.

'*Olena.*' Her name already felt like a stranger's.

She paused mid-step, but it was Commander

Swinton who turned around, blocking Dash's view of the princess. The commander's eyes were dark, full of warning and dislike. He let Olena and her guard pass into the entrance hall and continued to stare at Dash.

Raw emotion stirred beneath Dash's skin, merging with what he knew now was his magic. Hatred and magic fused, and he focused those two elements solely on the gleaming battleaxes that now disappeared into the shadows within the castle.

Chapter Thirty-four

Henri was no prisoner. She was free to come and go as she pleased, for the time being at least, and she planned on making the most of that fact. She needed to see Heathton for herself. After supper, she peeled away from the others and headed out into the heaving capital, holding her hood in place to hide her telltale braid and kohl-lined eyes. The city was as filthy as she remembered it. Its alleyways were festering with grime, waste and patches of vomit. It smelled like urine and old sweat, and the locals loitering about were as charming as ever.

'How much for twenty minutes, mystery woman?' someone croaked nearby. Henri pulled her hood up further over her face and continued down the cobblestone road. It wasn't long before she found herself in the city's sordid underbelly. She had always thought that if you wanted to get to know a place, you should take to its slums, not its jewellery quarter. The slums of Heathton said a lot about Ellest. She turned down one of the many pleasure alleys, sidestepping a brawl that had broken out on the kerb.

Henri didn't linger. Instead, she moved at a brisk pace

along the cobblestones, ducking back onto the footpath whenever a carriage bell sounded from behind her. On this street, the taverns weren't like the regular inns up the other end of the city. The street looked right down into the well-lit bay windows of its establishments to reveal all manner of vices within, be it flesh, substance or information. Henri tore her eyes away from the dealings inside and found a yellowed poster, nailed to a hitching post up ahead.

Register today for generous rewards, and the opportunity to serve your crown. Preserve your magical heritage.
See Tannus Armenta at the castle gates for assistance.

It was the same as the one she'd confronted Swinton with back in her apartments in Valia. She'd seen many of these on their way into the capital as well. Her informant had been right. Arden was trying to round up every magic wielder in Ellest. *Why?* While Arden himself had never possessed any magical abilities, he'd always had a keen interest in those who did. Now, that interest had apparently morphed into an obsession. Did he merely like surrounding power with more power? Was he eliminating supposed threats? Henri had to know. If she managed to get back to Valia, she'd need all the information she could get.

'Can I interest you in something, lady?' said a smooth voice beside her.

Henri didn't turn towards whoever it was; she'd

known they were there.

'We've got something for everyone down in our little venue,' the man at her shoulder said.

'I've heard.'

The man stepped in front of her. Beneath the shadow of his hood, Henri could make out a strong jaw, and almond eyes with a heavy set of dark lashes. He was younger than she'd expected, and better-looking for a common street urchin.

He pulled the poster from the nail and held it out to her. 'I'm good at knowing what people like.'

'Is that so?'

'You'd like to know more about this,' he said, running his soot-stained fingers over the lettering.

'Your price?' Henri said.

He peered into her hood and ran his gaze brazenly down her cloaked body.

'The last person who looked at me like that died,' she said.

'I meant no offence, lady.' He smiled.

'Your information?' Henri crossed her arms over her chest and waited.

'Your offer of payment?'

'Your life, because I'm feeling generous.'

The man made to take a step back, but Henri had a katar to his ribs before his foot could touch the ground. She pressed him up against the stone wall of a nearby tavern and stared into his face. There was light in his eyes; he wasn't afraid.

'Who are you?' Henri demanded, applying pressure.

The corners of the man's mouth tugged, and he tried to manoeuvre away from her expertly placed blade. She pressed harder, and his breath whistled through his teeth.

'Who are you?' she asked again.

'They call me the Tailor of Heathton.'

Henri glanced down at his ragged attire. 'How have you earned a title like that with such poor presentation of your skills?'

A grin broke out on the man's face. 'As you can see, I know nought of fashion.'

'What do you tailor, then?' she ground out. She didn't have time for this.

'Stories. Truth. Gossip,' he said. 'I cut, sew and alter them, for a price.'

'You're a spy.'

'Of sorts.'

'*Who* do you spy for?'

'The highest bidder.'

Henri rolled her eyes. She knew she'd find no men of morals here. For a moment, she envied Bleak's talents. The Angovian could sift through the lies, and in Heathton, there was no shortage of lies. Henri took a step back from the Tailor and sheathed her katar. Spilling blood in the streets tonight would do her no favours, and this fool wasn't worth the hassle. She straightened her hood and turned to leave.

'A friend of mine works at Port Morlock,' he called

after her. 'The Ashai folk, the ones who come forward, they get loaded onto ships.'

Henri paused, only steps away.

'To where?' she asked without turning.

'The destination isn't for my friend to know.'

Henri made to leave again.

'But,' the Tailor continued, 'one would guess by the size of the vessel, and the supplies they're rationed ... They only go as far as Moredon Tower.'

'They couldn't fit more than a dozen at Moredon. It's just a lighthouse.'

'Is it?'

Henri lunged for him, but he was quicker than he looked. He flipped himself up onto the rooftop of the tavern. He looked down at her, grinning wickedly. One of his teeth was gold, she noticed.

'One more thing,' he said.

Henri waited.

'Valter and Adalrik Wendley. You'll need to remember those names.'

'What? Why —'

But the Tailor had already disappeared amidst the thatched roofs, leaving Henri to fume in the dark, alone.

Early the next morning, Henri dressed in her usual leathers, braided her hair and strapped her katars to her sides for her meeting with the king. She was Queen of Valia; like hell she'd dress as anything else when she met him. When she slipped past the guards stationed outside her rooms, she saw that the candles along the stone walls were still lit, their wax dripping and drying in thick clumps down the heavy bricks. Henri took her time. She wasn't due to see the king for another two hours, and this could well be the only opportunity she had to peek inside the old library. She'd made a note of it last night but knew she'd need the daylight; the heavy locks told her it was a forbidden place. Who knew what she would find there?

An elaborate carving of open books covered the doors. Henri traced the design with her fingers. It was easily the most beautiful thing she'd seen in this wretched castle so far. She suddenly felt energy pulse beneath her palm and jumped back. The sensation had vanished as quickly as it had occurred. She examined her hand. It hadn't been *her* energy. Usually, energy felt like a natural extension of whatever it was bound to, but in this case, there was something foreign about the pulse she'd felt. It didn't belong here.

Henri took her time examining the carving. It was a vast web of flourishing embellishments, wrapping themselves around the pages of the books. She touched the timber again. It was old, and its maker had taken great care to sand down the imperfections. *Valian oak*, she realised with a start. She pressed both hands flat against the doors and waited, but the energy from before didn't so much as flicker.

'You!' called a flustered guard from the end of the hallway. He jogged towards her, cheeks pink. 'We've been looking for you. You're due to meet with the king.'

'I'm not due to meet him for another hour.'

'The king has decided to push the meeting forward.'

'Of course he has,' muttered Henri. She should have known Arden would try to catch her unprepared. She gave the library doors a look of regret. She hated leaving something so beautiful, so inherently Valian, here to be forgotten amidst the rot of the castle. The guard motioned for her to follow, and he led her back down the passageways and staircases.

The king was waiting. A fur-lined violet cloak pooled at his boots, and his hand rested on the jewelled hilt of the dagger strapped to his waist. He was surrounded by a troop of heavily armed guards. There was no sign of the commander or the captain. Henri hadn't expected there to be. She dipped her head slightly when she reached the foot of the stairs.

'Your Majesty,' she greeted him stiffly.

King Arden looked amused. He picked an imaginary piece of dust from his turquoise tunic.

'Henrietta,' he said, eyeing her katars. 'How pleasant to see you after all this time.' He tilted his head to the side ever so slightly. 'I have something to show you this morning.'

She bit down on the questions and demands that threatened to bubble out of her. Questions would only give him more power. She fell into step beside him, realising that now he wasn't lording over her from the dais, they were the same height. He adjusted his gait ever so slightly, which told Henri that he'd just had an identical realisation.

She knew it was rumoured that Arden had once been a swordsman of epic reputation, though he wore no real weapon now. Such claims didn't faze Henri. She could take him in a fair fight, easily. The problem was, fairness was rarely a factor when it came to King Arden.

They walked down hallway after hallway, a complete guard in tow. Henri suspected they were taking such a route to disorientate her. She was ashamed to admit it had worked. Ordinarily, she had a keen sense of direction. It had been Sahara who always found herself lost amidst the living bridges. Henri would be charged with tracking her sister and bringing her back to the keep. But now, she had no idea where she was. The stone walls and torchlit passages all looked the same to Henri – cold and sapped of life. They were no longer in the main section of the castle; that much she knew from the lack of attendants and servants, and the too-quiet corridors. Wherever the king was taking her, it was off the map, so to speak.

The king's furs flapped about his ankles as he led the company down a winding set of stone stairs. The air became cool around her, adding to the prickling feeling already plaguing her skin. That same pulse of foreign energy throbbed around Henri again, and she fought to hide her shock. Her own magic flickered in her palms, as though the unknown energy called out to it, a siren trying to lure her to drown below the surface.

A door at the bottom of the stairs swung open and revealed the royal wine cellars. Huge barrels of ale from all four kingdoms were stacked high against one of the walls. Floor to ceiling with wine racks, dusty bottles filled every other space. Henri could only imagine how Bleak would feel seeing all of this.

'The finest meads and wines from all over the realm,' the king said, turning to her. 'Actually,' he moved to one of the far corners, his guards scrambling to cover him, 'this is my collection from Valia.'

Henri took a step forward and indeed recognised their seals and stamps on the barrels. How had the king acquired so much of their liquor?

'The lovely Allehra sends me numerous barrels and bottles every month,' he said.

Henri bit down her outrage.

The king turned to his guard. 'You're dismissed,' he said, 'except for Tannus.'

The guards bowed and proceeded to march back up the cellar stairs, leaving only one man by the king's side. He didn't look like a guard. He was a willowy man, with his receding hair shaved close to his head. Unlike the guards who'd shifted nervously in her presence, this man's stance was sturdy, confident, as though he'd love nothing more than to challenge her. Even beneath the warmth of her leathers, Henri's skin rose into goosebumps and her pulse quickened.

'This is Tannus, our royal weapons master,' the king said, flinging a careless hand in the man's direction.

'Tannus, if you could make sure Henrietta and I aren't disturbed.'

'Of course, Your Majesty,' said Tannus, bowing low.

From his bow alone, Henri could tell he was trained in martial arts. His long body was supple, flexible and completely in control.

Interesting, she thought, *he'd definitely last longer than the king.*

'This way, if you will,' the king said, leading her around another stack of barrels to face another wall of wine.

Her heart was pounding. The king lifted the hem of his tunic and reached for a large ring of keys. He removed a bottle from the crowded shelf, revealing a keyhole in the wall behind. After selecting a key and turning it in the lock, there was a click. The whole wine rack swung back with a loud groan, revealing a room behind it, double the size.

Henri exhaled shakily, realising she'd been holding her breath. There was nothing to do but to follow the king into the room. It was huge, lined with rows and rows of shelves. On the shelves were jars, hundreds of them. All different shapes and sizes.

The king reached up and took one, holding it out for Henri to see. She squinted, trying to see past the small, swirling cloud of fog inside it.

'Do you know what this is?' The king waited.

It wasn't fog, she realised. The king watched the horror settle on her face.

'I was fortunate enough to have an Ashai in my service, a long time ago now. We discovered many things together,' he said. 'As it happens, there are a number of Ashai folk who are immune to whatever toxins live within the mist. In fact, the mist has a rather peculiar effect on them. You see, it marks them. Patterns appear across their whole bodies, invisible to the naked eye, except on a full moon.'

Henri almost snorted. 'Here I was thinking the witching hour was just for children who stayed up past their bedtime.'

'Come now, Henri. We both know that's not true. My friend and I, and a few prisoners, we experimented with the mist. Studied who it killed, how it spread. Some Ashai are immune; ordinary people are not. Overexposure to the mist kills them. The longest a non-Ashai survived it was eight minutes.'

Henri looked up at the hundreds of jars that stretched to the ceiling. Why was he telling her all of this? And what was he doing harbouring a weapon that could wipe out his own kind? It made no sense.

'What are they for?' she asked.

'I have someone, in a high place, who likes things done a certain way.'

'You're king. You're the one in the high place.' Henri edged herself closer to one of the shelves. If what he said was true ...

'True, but don't be so narrow-minded,' the king tutted. 'A dear friend of mine has an interest in the Ashai folk; therefore I have an interest in them. So we use the mist to mark them, among other things, and send them on their way.'

'Send them where?'

'You already know the answer.'

'Moredon Tower.'

The king nodded, smiling up at his collection.

'Where's your friend?' said Henri, shifting her weight and inching a little further towards the shelf.

'Oremere,' the king replied, resting his hand on the hilt of his dagger.

Henri's knees buckled.

'Oremere? Your friend's name is Oremere?' she managed.

The king laughed. 'Amazing how ignorant you are. Oremere is not a *who*, but a *where*.'

'What?'

'Shocking, isn't it,' he said with a smirk. 'It lies beyond the mist, south of Havennesse and Qatrola, actually – I'm told it was once not so far from Valia. Can you imagine? All this time, it's been so close.'

'I don't believe you.'

'But you *do*. You've heard that name before, haven't you?'

Henri swallowed. 'Sahara ... Sahara knew something.'

'Perhaps that's what drove her to madness. Or was it – oh, that's right. *You* drove her to madness, you and your talent, and her with her ... nothing.'

Henri stood still, her mind racing. She had to *do*

something. She had to take the risk.

'I remember her funeral well,' the king continued. 'Poor Sahara Valia. She really was *nothing* compared to you – and everyone knew it. Allehra was a fool not to banish her to the outskirts along with the rest of the weak. Do you remember seeing me there? At the memorial? I spoke with your mother that night. We hadn't come to honour your sister – there's no honour in suicide. I summoned your mother and her best kindred to battle. We were having problems with Battalon – problems I wanted ended quickly. But she refused. As I suspected she would, really. You Valians have always been a thorn in my side.'

The king began to pace up and down the aisle of jars. 'It was a pretty little part of the forest, wasn't it? That part where you burned the pyre without the body? That part that held all your protective little herbs?'

The Forest of Ghosts.

'Well, myself and Commander Swinton had brought a couple of these,' he plucked a jar from the shelf and jiggled it at her, 'and we released the mist. I didn't know it at the time, but it wasn't the regular mist – it was fast-moving. It had engulfed a number of trees before we even had time to run. My dear commander saved my life that day. I probably should have knighted him for it, but it would have meant exposing what we'd done.'

'Swinton.'

'Yes, Swinton. He was young and eager. And I was his king. He didn't ask questions. He just did. But Allehra, she had followed us and brought fire down on the forest. She said she would rather see it burn than be taken over by dark magic.'

The king laughed. 'As if the mist or magic has its own agenda. I would have thought the great Allehra Valia knew better than that. So you see, it was *her* who created the Forest of Ghosts as you call it. Though from the look on your face, she never told you.'

'And why are you telling me?' Henri said, not daring to move a muscle.

'My high-placed friend has taken an interest in you.'

'Who is this friend?'

'She is everything.'

Henri swiped a jar from beside her and smashed it near the king. Shards of glass splintered across the stone floor, and the mist within rushed free, roiling at the king's feet, inching up his legs. Henri held her breath. Was she going to die? Was *he*? Arden was no Ashai. Tannus burst into the room and grabbed Henri in a death grip, pinning her arms behind her. She didn't fight. She could only watch as the King of Ellest looked up from the mist curling at his boots. He laughed.

'It kills ordinary people, Henrietta. I never said *I* was ordinary.'

The king crouched, putting his face level with the escaped mist. He pursed his lips and sucked the mist in. Power surged around Henri. Power that wasn't her own and wasn't the king's, although he somehow seemed to be channelling it. The king blew the mist from his mouth into an empty jar and screwed the lid shut. Henri stared at him. *Who was this man?* He wasn't the bland, simple man she'd met all those years ago. Something, or *someone*, had changed him.

'What do you want?' she said.

'I want you to meet her. As she wants to meet you. She has been waiting a long time.'

'She can't extend an invitation herself?'

'She can do whatever she pleases; she is the true queen.'

'As opposed to the false queen, your wife?'

'Vera is the Queen of Ellest, perhaps. But Ines ... Ines is the true queen of the entire realm, the monarchy as it was, centuries ago.'

He was delusional. There had never been a single monarchy. But Henri's eyes once again fell upon the jars of mist, the name of the supposed fifth continent still swirling in her mind. How much more was she ignorant of? Behind her, Tannus readjusted his grip. It was firm, but she could break it. To what end, though?

'Where am I to meet your queen?' she said.

The king smiled at this. He clearly liked the idea of this woman as his, though Henri could tell from the brazen manipulation playing behind the scenes that this woman would never be owned, would never be anything but her own master and the conqueror of others.

'You'll be our guest for a while longer. When Ines is ready, she will announce herself.'

Ines. Those four letters carried such immense weight.

'And then?'

'Then? Then the game begins.'

'And if I don't want to play?'

'Then Valia will. And Allehra will burn the whole forest to the ground before the mist takes hold. She spoils the fun like that. Tannus,' the king turned his gaze to the man who held Henri firm, 'take Henrietta back to her chambers for the time being. She doesn't look well.'

Henri didn't fight the grip around her arms. She let the man escort her back to her rooms, dragging her feet, a wave of shock crashing down on her. It was too much. It was all too much.

She was shoved into her empty quarters, the bed unmade as she'd left it, the fire down to its last glowing embers. When the door clicked closed behind her, and the quiet crunch of a key turned in the lock, Henrietta Valia sank to the floor and wept.

Chapter Thirty-five

Henri woke, body aching, on the plush rug in her quarters. She must have passed out from the exhaustion or despair, perhaps both. Glancing up at the window with a quiet moan, she could see that outside was grey, sheets of rain hammering down loudly. She had no idea what the time was, or how long she'd been asleep. Her magic must have reacted to her panic, and was now surging through her, unchecked, amplifying her devastation. She had doomed Valia. Doomed her mother and all of their people. If only Sahara could see her now.

Henri exhaled. She had to *do something*. She had allowed herself a brief moment of weakness. That was over now. She wouldn't wait in this place like an animal ready for slaughter. To act was to risk the horrors Arden and Ines had planned, but to do nothing ... That was not the Valian Way.

A key clicked in the lock, and Henri sprang from the floor, unsheathing her katars, ready to pounce. But it was only a redheaded servant girl with a tray of food. Arden liked playing the hospitable captor it seemed, at least with her. She shuddered to think of where Bleak was. The servant's eyes widened at the sight of Henri, and she placed the tray down with a clatter. The girl's fiery hair reminded her of Athene, and Henri felt a pang of yearning, of regret. She moved towards the girl to reassure her, but the servant ran from the room, the lock clicking into place behind her.

Henri approached the tray; mashed potatoes and pork. There was something else. Beneath the plate, a scrap of parchment stuck out.

Guard change at seventh hour.
Be prepared.
F.

Henri's eyes flew to the clock beside the wardrobe. Three hours.

She wolfed down the dinner and searched her rooms for anything and everything she could use. She grabbed two travel cases from the top of the wardrobe, and wrenched a multitude of ornate gowns and undergarments from the hangers and chest of drawers. Henri Valia wouldn't be leaving this castle, but a grey-eyed noblewoman might. Henri stripped and washed herself thoroughly at the basin in the washroom, making sure to wipe the kohl from her eyes. The water was freezing; still, she scrubbed until her skin was pink and raw. She fastened herself into a corset, opting to tie the laces at her front and then twist the contraption around to its correct position, growing clammy with the effort. She strapped her katars to her thighs, and made quick work of packing the dresses into the suitcases, also stuffing her riding leathers far down beneath them, along with her boots. The dainty slippers in the wardrobe were tiny, but Henri would have to make do – a noblewoman wouldn't be caught dead in old Valian boots.

Am I really doing this? She glanced at the note again. *Seventh hour.* She had to be ready. She couldn't hesitate. Taking Fiore's note, she held it over one of the many candles and watched the flames lick at the parchment until it was no more than ash. With the note destroyed, she returned to the washroom.

Still definitely a Valian, she thought, catching a glimpse of her hardened expression in the mirror.

She rummaged through the drawers until she found a woman's cosmetics bag, and wondered briefly whose room this had been. She tipped the contents of the bag into the basin. It'd been years since she'd seen anyone use this junk, but she'd noticed enough of Heathton's painted faces on the way in to hopefully mimic the current styles. First she undid her braid, letting her kinked tresses hang loose down to her waist. She tipped a handful of fine powder into it, rubbing it vigorously into the roots, lightening her hair's midnight colouring. She powdered her face, too, masking her tanned complexion with the pallid, pastel skin of someone who stayed indoors too much. She found an array of liquids and tools as she rifled through the cosmetics.

She rouged her cheeks and painstakingly painted her lips a vibrant red, as she had seen was the fashion in the streets yesterday. She looked *ridiculous*. Like a porcelain doll to be displayed on a shelf and never touched.

Two jewelled hair clasps gleamed from within the drawer beneath the basin. Henri twisted her hair on each side of her face and pinned it to her head. She shook her head at her reflection and returned to the bedroom. The dress she'd chosen was a navy-blue, long-sleeved gown, with embroidery of pale gold embellishing the panel down the chest to the cinched waist. Henri stepped into it, careful not to dislodge the katars strapped to her thighs. It would be a miracle if she was able to do the dress up alone. She managed it, though not without having to re-powder her hairline from the sweat. She packed the cosmetics back into their carry bag and stuffed it roughly into one of the bulging travel cases.

This is such *a flawed plan*, she thought. The travel cases would give her away instantly. A noblewoman would never carry *anything*. Henri sighed. One problem at a time.

In the full-length mirror, a pale noblewoman gaped back at Henri. She had to touch her face to confirm that this stranger was indeed her. The dress clung snugly to her waist and flowed out, masking the lumps where her katars were sheathed. She rummaged one last time through all the drawers. She only had a small amount of coin, and she would need everything she could to barter – if she got that far. To her surprise, she discovered a false bottom in one of the drawers, and pulled a jewellery box from the hidden compartment.

Yes.

Inside, more than a dozen opulent gems winked at her. With a surge of gratitude, she adorned herself with the heaviest necklace, thick with rubies, and tipped the rest into a velvet drawstring bag, which she tucked into her purse. That was it. Taking a deep breath, she sat on the edge of the bed, running through a thousand different outcomes of this plan in her head. Whether she stayed, escaped or died, Arden had declared war on her people. He had threatened their freedom, their livelihoods, and Henri would not stand for it.

She watched the time tick closer and closer towards the seventh hour, until she heard a key turn in the lock. No one entered. She had to leave. *Now.*

With her heart thumping against her corset, she opened the door. There was no one stationed there. She took the cases and placed them just outside her room, and closed the door behind her. She spotted a young servant boy down the end of the hall.

'You there!' she called out, clasping her hands together to stop them from trembling.

'M'lady?' he asked.

'I was expecting you twenty minutes ago. Take my bags. You've made me late.'

Confused and frightened, the boy picked up the travel cases and stood rooted to the spot.

'Well, don't just stand there,' Henri said sharply, 'let's

go. My carriage should be waiting.'

This was her plan? To walk out the front door? And what happened when there was no carriage waiting? Henri squashed her doubts and shot the boy a furious, superior look. He moved quickly down the hall, and Henri followed, her skirts swishing about her feet. They passed a number of guards, who glanced over her with appreciative eyes rather than suspicious ones. She exhaled the breath she'd been holding.

'Lady Wendley,' called a familiar voice.

Henri turned. Fiore was trailing after them. Gods, if anyone recognised her and saw them together ... He was taking a huge risk. He caught up, and if he was surprised by her appearance, he hid it well.

'Apologies for the interruption, Lady Wendley. The queen asked me to pass on her wishes for a safe and comfortable journey.'

Wendley ... The name sounded familiar. She sifted through her memories, it was on the tip of her – the Tailor. He'd mentioned that name. How had he – there was no time for that now. The guards at the entrance were respectfully averting their gazes, but it wouldn't last forever. She needed to get out of here, fast.

'Her Majesty is too kind,' Henri said stiffly.

'Peter,' Fiore said, turning to the boy holding Henri's cases, 'hail Lady Wendley a street carriage. Unfortunately, hers has a broken wheel axle.'

'What?' Henri snapped, crumpling her painted face into an expression of outrage. 'The carriage was in perfect condition when I arrived.'

'My sincerest apologies, m'lady,' Fiore said, waiting for the boy to step into the courtyard. He offered his arm to Henri, who took it and allowed him to lead her out of the guards' earshot.

'Where are you going?' he asked under his breath.

'Should I tell you?'

'I got you this far.'

Henri had no time to weigh up the consequences. 'Havennesse,' she said, 'if I can.'

'Not Valia?'

'I can do nothing from Valia.'

'What's in the winter continent?'

'Allies.'

'You think it'll come to that?'

'It already has.'

Fiore nodded. 'I had a feeling. Do you know any more?'

Henri wanted to tell him. He was going to be stuck here with the king, but she was out of time. 'I should go.'

'I know,' he said. 'Listen, go down to the docks. Look for a ship called *The Prince's Triumph*. It sets sail for Battalon within the hour. Ask for the quartermaster, Clarke. Say I sent you, that you need accommodation, and that you'll disembark at Port Whelton.'

'In Battalon?'

Fiore nodded impatiently. 'You'll be able to buy passage to Havennesse from there.'

Henri rearranged her skirts and glanced around.

'Anything else?'

'They have Bleak,' he told her. Henri let her mask slip. She had expected this news at some point, and yet it struck her like a fresh blow. She regained her composure and gave a curt nod, as though they were still discussing the state of her broken wheel axle.

'They have the boy, too.'

'Boy?'

'Bren. The Angovian. He claimed he was an Ashai, he tried to get to her.'

Henri's heart sank. 'Fool.'

Fiore was grave. 'They've already put him on a ship to Moredon. He was in a bad way. Most likely won't make the journey.'

'Gods,' Henri muttered under her breath.

'Go, before someone sees us,' Fiore said.

Every woman for herself.

'Thank you,' she managed.

Fiore offered a grim smile. 'Your carriage awaits, Lady Wendley,' he said, gesturing to the driver at the bottom of the castle steps.

'Until we meet again, Captain,' Henri said.

She accepted the footman's assistance up into the carriage, the bulky skirts hindering her movements.

'My lady,' an unfamiliar voice called. A messenger signalled for her driver to wait. Henri's stomach lurched, and on the side hidden from view, she lifted her skirts and gripped her katar.

'My lady,' the messenger said again, drawing closer to

her window. Henri saw the look of confusion cross his face. He didn't know the real noblewoman well enough to question her outright, but the suspicion was clearly there.

'Yes?' she said tersely.

'Your children, they await your arrival in the gardens. The showcase of their squire training is about to commence.'

Henri plastered a harried expression on her face and remembered the Tailor's words.

'Valter and Adalrik know perfectly well I have an appointment in town. Lord Wendley will be attending their showcase, as I told them earlier.'

Henri held her breath. Had she just given herself away? The Tailor had never mentioned a Lord Wendley.

The messenger visibly relaxed. 'Very good, m'lady.'

'Good. Now if you'd be so kind as to *move*. I cannot delay.'

The carriage bounced over the cobblestones and passed the smaller courtyard to the dungeons. Four burly guards flanked the locked gates to the prison below. Guilt clenched Henri's insides uncomfortably. Bleak was in there. She had saved the girl, only to bring her to her death. But she could do nothing now. *Every woman for herself.* She had to put her people first.

The carriage finally pulled away from the castle keep, and Henri forced her gaze forward. She and Bleak were even now. The girl had said so herself.

Henri couldn't, and wouldn't look back anymore.

451

Chapter Thirty-six

Trumpets sounded, and the crowd in the castle courtyard dropped into low bows. The princess and queen emerged first, and Swinton moved to shadow the younger royal as she made her descent. His handpicked guard fell into place alongside the rest of the royal family. Fiore guarded the king closely. Swinton, Fi and a select few had been chosen to escort the princess to Battalon. The entire royal household lined the courtyard to farewell Princess Olena, and to the girl's embarrassment, they applauded as she reached the last step with Queen Vera at her arm. King Arden and Prince Jaxon joined them, and the king took his daughter's hands in his.

'You'll make a fine bride,' he said.

'Thank you, Father,' she replied, blinking.

Prince Jaxon hugged her tightly. 'Write often, little sister. We'll arrange a visit as soon as you're settled. I've always wanted to see the great shiprock palace and the Belbarrow firestorms.'

The most powerful siblings in all of Ellest clung to each other with a helplessness that resonated deeply with Swinton. They knew there was nothing to be done, not yet. They were pawns in a much larger game, biding their time perhaps, until the day they sat in the players' seats.

'Queen of Battalon.' Princess Olena smiled grimly, her clouded eyes looking past her brother now.

'Queen of the Firestorms sounds better,' Prince Jaxon said with a forced laugh.

Swinton watched as brother and sister embraced for a final time. The princess then turned to the crowd she couldn't see, and with the grace of a woman beyond her years, nodded to the people once, before accepting a hand to help her into her waiting carriage.

Swinton couldn't help glancing around at the crowd. He spotted Carlington, the stable master, by the supplies cart, and his young son, Dash, watching the princess sadly. The boy would likely never see her again. Swinton forced his gaze elsewhere. He had to be alert. The Ellestian company was limited and he found himself having to direct an almost entirely foreign group. Fi looked comfortable enough; he always did. He chatted in the native Battalonian tongue to some of the envoys; he had them chuckling already. He gave his friend a pointed look – the king was under-guarded. Swinton didn't have time for this. He had a princess to protect and a ship full of people to get on the move. He called out his orders, checked their remaining cargo and triple-checked the secured fastenings of the princess's carriage.

'Relax, old friend,' said Fiore, who had been relieved of his guard duty and was mounting his horse beside Swinton. 'Everything is in order.'

'Can never be too careful, Fi.'

'You'd know. Been doing it your whole life, old friend.'

The barb stung, whether that was its intention or not, but Fiore had already urged his horse back to his Battalonian brothers. Swinton took a deep breath and pulled on his riding gloves. He tucked the coin of Yacinda back into his armour, grateful for its renewed power. He hadn't realised until he and Fi were at Bleak's door the other night just how strong it was now. With the touch of a hand on his friend's shoulder, he'd been able to project the coin's magic onto Fi, to protect him from Bleak's invasive gift at the right moment. Yet another secret between them. Swinton sighed. Exhaustion latched onto his soul, his whole body feeling heavy with it.

Slowly, their company moved into their places atop their horses and in their carriages. It was a short journey to Port Morlock, where they would board one of the royal ships. The crossing of the Northern Sea to Port Whelton at Battalon would take a week at least, depending on the winds, and then there was the journey from Port Whelton to Belbarrow. It would be a long time until Swinton felt at ease again.

Just as he went to mount Xander, the king approached him.

'Commander,' he said. 'Ride well.'

'I will, Your Majesty.'

'Are you looking forward to seeing Belbarrow again? As I understand it, you've always expressed a desire for travel.'

Swinton hid his surprise. 'Yes, Majesty. Very much so.'

Could it be that the king thought he was somehow rewarding Swinton by sending him on this journey? That he was trying to show Swinton more of the four continents as he'd so wished for in the past?

'Then I am glad,' said the king. 'You'll make a good companion for my daughter.'

'I'll do my best to keep her in high spirits, Your Majesty.'

'I'm happy to hear it.'

'We'll send word as soon as we reach each of our stops.'

'Good, good.'

'Will that be all, sire?'

'Yes, yes.'

Swinton bowed low and mounted his horse. Just as he was about to press his heels to the stallion's sides, the king pulled at his reins.

'You know, Commander,' he began.

Swinton looked down at his sovereign.

The king's eyes lingered on his threadbare gloves and tattered boots. 'I always found it odd that the leader of my army had such ... *well-worn* attire. I took an interest in where your salary seemed to disappear to.' The king looked out to the throng of people.

Swinton followed the king's gaze, which fell upon Dash, the stable master's boy in the crowd.

'Not much goes on in this realm that I don't know

about,' said the king, his mouth tugging upwards. 'Not much at all.'

Swinton's foot slipped in the stirrup. 'I see, Your Majesty.'

'I'm not sure you do, Dimitri. Not yet.'

He stared at the king.

'But you will.'

Swinton swallowed, his heart racing. He pressed his heels into Xander's sides. The horse lurched forward, and Swinton gripped the reins. King Arden *knew*.

Yes, Swinton thought, his terror, his guilt thick in his chest. He'd be whatever he had to be, to keep his secret safe. To keep Dash – to keep Zachary, safe.

Chapter Thirty-seven

Bleak festered in her cell for two more days before two guards came and escorted her from the dungeons. They clamped iron shackles around her wrists and led her past the other cells, answering none of her questions. The prisoners whistled and catcalled, but she didn't have the energy to snap back at them. She was still wearing the lavender gown from what must have been a week ago, which was grey with filth now. When they opened the door at the top of the stairs, the light blinded her, and she staggered out into the clean air. The guards didn't give her a moment to adjust; they continued to drag her through the back halls of the castle. When her eyes stopped burning, she saw they'd taken her into a small, bare room. The smaller of the two guards unlocked her shackles and pointed to two buckets of water and a small pile of clothes on a chair. 'You can clean yerself up. There's a tunic and pants for yer journey. Yer boots are well enough, eh?'

Bleak felt a deep pang in her chest; he had a southerner's accent like Bren. The larger guard folded his arms across his chest and made a point of eyeing her, but the smaller guard nudged him.

'C'mon, no need for us t'watch,' he said.

The larger guard grunted but turned and followed his colleague. Bleak approached the buckets and dipped her hand in. The water was freezing cold. She shuddered. Her bones were still chilled from the icy dungeons. But she stripped off her gown, leaving Fiore's dagger in place, and began to scrub her face and arms with the rag provided. The cloth got to her wrist and she stopped. Where Allehra's cuff had rested, the skin was no longer naked. The whorls and swirls that had been carved into the leather now marred her skin in deep blue, as though the design had somehow seeped through the leather and onto her flesh. She gaped at it – *how in the realm* —

As she looked at it, the tingling sensation she'd felt in the throne room with the king began to creep up her arm; there was a flutter of magic in her veins again. Someone cleared their throat outside, and she started. She washed herself as best she could, but left her bodice and undergarments on, knowing that at any moment the guards could stride back in unannounced. She felt weak, and she could tell from her feeble movements that she'd lost weight, but the faint hum of her returned power gave her comfort. The tunic they'd supplied was made for a man and swamped her small frame when she tugged it on over her head. She pulled the sleeve down over the markings on her wrist. She had the same problem with the pants she buckled at her waist, so she tucked the ankles into her Valian boots. For the first time in a week, she could finally feel her feet warming.

Finished, and unsure of what to do next, she sat on the chair and waited.

When the guards returned, they put the shackles back on her and took her to the throne room. The king was waiting.

'Apologies for leaving you unattended, Miss Thornton,' said the king. 'I've had a rather busy week.'

There it was again – *Thornton*. The name she'd long ago tried to leave behind, the name given to her by her parents, whom she'd also left behind. *How does he know?*

'You will be accompanied to Moredon by a special guard.' The king's eyes flicked to the rows of armoured men who lined the walls of the throne room.

Bleak hid her surprise. For all his intimidation tactics and threats, the king thought he'd need a dozen men to handle her? The quiet flurry of power beat beneath her skin. 'You will think of me often at Moredon, I'm sure,' the king said, tugging on his beard. 'Take her away,' he ordered.

Bleak was seized by the arms and hauled from the throne room. This time though, she wasn't taken down into the dungeons, but rather to the servery.

'Last meal,' one of the guards grunted, shoving her onto a wooden stool.

A large woman with a flushed face pushed a large bowl of broth down in front of her. The bread she was given was mouldy, but she picked the green splotches off and ate it anyway. She hadn't tasted anything this good since she'd been in Valia. The woman came back and sloshed some more broth into her empty bowl. As she did it, she looked at the guards and clenched her jaw, as though daring them to argue with her. They didn't. Bleak babbled her thanks profusely, but the woman – the castle cook, Bleak now realised – dismissed her with a flick of her hand.

The company of fifteen rode down to the docks of Port Morlock. Bleak was forced to share a horse with a guard by the name of Charlyn, whose thick arm around her middle kept her from falling. The *Arden's Fortune* bobbed quietly atop the water's surface, waiting for them. It was similar to the ships she and Bren had manned with Bleaker Senior, small, with a single mast and high sides, its unfortunate name painted in a flourish at the bow. Around them, the docks stank of rotten fish and waste. Bleak was taken back to the day Senior had found her hiding among the fish muck.

What am I going to do with this? he'd thought. It had been the day she had left Alarise Thornton behind. King Arden knew her then, perhaps even knew her parents. *How?* She had so many burning questions about everything – her parents, the king, the mist, the day at the docks nearly fifteen years ago ...

Bleak's hands were still tightly shackled before her, and so when they reached the pier, Charlyn had to help her dismount. A ring of keys jangled at his waist. For the first time all week, Bleak smiled. Climbing the ladder up the high side of the ship was no easy feat with limited movement of her hands, and even once her feet landed firmly on deck, she swayed and crashed into Charlyn, hard.

'Dammit, girl, can't you manage anything?' he cursed, pushing her off him.

Bleak let her face flush pink, and she shrank away from the heavy-set man. He tied her to one of the rails, shaking his head and muttering. There he left her and went to help the others cast off. She watched the fools make an absolute mess of the knots and the pulley systems. She could sail this thing in her sleep, but like hell she'd help them get *Arden's* fucking *Fortune* to Moredon Tower any sooner.

While they blundered about, Bleak looked around. The deck and the cabins below were basic, but she spotted a life raft positioned by the stern with a pair of oars. It looked light enough for her to tip over the side of the ship. Perhaps ... Perhaps she could make her escape on it. She also noted a discarded crossbow tucked away in one of the corners, by the netting. There were men everywhere, and she tried to shrink back into the timber of the railing, tried to make herself go unnoticed, invisible. She'd been in plenty of scrapes before, but here ... Here there was nowhere to run. Here, the enemy outnumbered her fifteen to one. She sat back, leaning into a bundle of nets, and adjusted Fi's dagger at her thigh. She was grateful for the slight edge she had. For she would need it. She knew that much.

Finally, the ship slid away from the wharf, and men let the sail down. Charlyn handed her a small tin. With some difficulty, she twisted it open and smeared the thick jelly inside over her already cracked lips. They were taking her to Moredon Tower, but gods forbid her lips get windburn. She nearly laughed aloud. The men went about their business, most of them grumbling that they'd been called to escort a gutter rat to Moredon on their night off. Clearly fed up, Charlyn snapped.

'What do you have to do that's more important than your duty to the crown?' he said, spit flying.

A stocky man with a dirty eyepatch whirled around. 'I don't know about these lads, but I had an appointment with Madame Joelle Marie.'

There was a burst of laughter from the group. Bleak started. She knew that face, that voice.

'You couldn't even afford the cleaner at Madame Joelle's, Lennox,' said Charlyn, wiping his grimy hands on a rag.

Bleak's whole body stiffened. It was him. Her skin crawled at the memory of his hands on her.

'What do you know about what I can and can't afford?' Lennox growled.

'Enough to know that a place like that is *well* out of your price range. Though I'd believe the fact that you've gotta pay for it.'

There was another burst of laughter.

'Piss off, Charlyn, no one asked you,' Lennox said, kicking a nearby pile of ropes from his path, his knuckles white as he clenched his fists.

Had Lennox seen her? How could he *not* have?

Charlyn merely shrugged, but his thoughts barrelled into Bleak.

Bloody bastard's never served at Moredon, that's for sure. King knows it's so bad he sends a batch of Joelle's girls over every two months. Not even those beauties can fix that place.

Bleak flinched at the image that flashed in her mind from Charlyn's – a corridor paved with thick, grimy black stones, and water pooling across the ground. Chains rattled along the walls.

She swallowed the lump in her throat and turned her gaze out to sea through a gap in the railing. She was trapped here with Lennox, before she'd rot to her death in the dungeons of Moredon. Her skin crawled.

Arden's Fortune picked up speed, and panic began to rise in Bleak. She'd travelled these waters often enough to know that the route to the island wasn't a long one. A few nights and she'd be back in a cell, or worse. She took a deep breath and ran her thumb over the blue marking on her wrist, trying to drown out the thoughts of the guards on deck. The mark felt no different to the rest of her skin, but its colour was deep and its pattern was the exact replica of the design on Allehra's cuff. It was truly as though the design had melted through the leather and onto her skin. Bleak sighed and closed her eyes. She lifted her face to the warm afternoon sun and gave herself permission to pretend, just for a little while. She pretended that the salt air was the southerly wind from Felder's Bay, and that the deep rumble of voices around her were those of Senior, Bren and the crew. That they'd let the nets loose soon, and play cards over some ale while they waited for the day's catch to tug.

Now, Port Morlock became a speck in the distance as *Arden's Fortune* sailed into the night and the early hours of the morning. Every time she was sure no one was watching, Bleak held her breath and moved meticulously so that she didn't rattle the bunch of keys she'd stolen. She tried key after key in the lock of her shackles. But there were still perhaps thirty or so to try. She was running out of time. She *had* to keep trying; there was no other choice.

Keys. Crossbow. Life raft. She knew it was a fool's hope, but it was all she had.

They kept to the coast of Ellest, and the sight of the continent kept Bleak calm, for a time. She watched as the jagged edges of the shoreline passed them, helping her measure the distance they'd covered. She looked out across the water, to the chalk-white rock face of the coastal cliffs. She would never see Angove again. She would never see Bren again.

There was a scream. Followed by another, and another. Bleak clapped her hands over her ears, heart pounding. Muted yet high-pitched wails laced with pain and terror rocked her. She looked around wildly as her head filled with the quiet screaming, with people begging for death. The crew were unchanged; they hadn't heard a thing.

Bleak stood up on unsteady legs and looked over the side of the railing. The screams were coming from beneath the water. She took a deep breath and tried to block them out, glancing down at the dark pattern that now marred her wrist. But whoever the screams belonged to, they demanded to be heard. Their torture was now the music of her journey.

The screaming came in waves, striking Bleak anew each time. Each time churning her stomach and forcing bile up her throat. It was in the very early hours of the third morning that Bleak's exhaustion finally dragged her under.

When she woke, it was still before dawn, and she was groggy and dry-mouthed. Her head felt clogged. She didn't know if she'd gone deaf from the screams, or if they had stopped. From where she lay, sore and hungry amidst the nets, she spotted a nearby guard.

'Excuse me,' she croaked, eyeing the flask at his hip. 'Could I —'

The man turned around, and she recoiled. Lennox.

'You,' he said, stepping towards her. 'What the *fuck* do *you* want?'

'Nothing,' Bleak said quickly, scuffling backwards.

'You wanted something, gutter rat.'

'No.'

'Go on, ask me. We're not done, you and I.'

He moved closer to her, and Bleak scrambled to her feet, her shackles rattling.

Where's the rest of the crew? She glanced around for Charlyn, but he was nowhere in sight, and the other men were all looking elsewhere, whether on purpose or not she didn't know.

'Don't be like that,' Lennox said, his breath sour on her face. 'Surely you want one last ride before you die.'

'Get the fuck away from me.' Bleak's temper surged up within her, taking over her fear.

Lennox's fist collided with her face. She felt her teeth ring and her lip split; blood filled her mouth and dribbled down her chin.

'Coward.' She spat blood onto the deck.

'You got a smart mouth for a little gutter rat.' He closed the gap between them.

She backed away towards the stern, where the discarded crossbow still lay.

Dammit, she thought, she hadn't managed to unlock herself, and now, now she was being cornered.

'Hey!' she yelled out, straining towards the other guards as Lennox grabbed the front of her tunic. The bunch of keys she'd tucked into her pocket fell to the deck with a loud clatter. Fiore's dagger was out of reach.

Fuck! Terror gripped her as Lennox lunged for her. This was it, *now*. She made a dive for the crossbow, landing on her back and swinging it round in front of her. She aimed, pointing it at Lennox's chest.

'I wouldn't come any closer if I were you,' she said, slowly getting to her feet, irons rubbing at her raw skin.

'How long you think this standoff's gonna last? Fifteen of us, one of you. You don't have the balls, anyway,' he said, nodding towards the crossbow.

'Try me.'

'What are you going to do?'

Suddenly, her mind was invaded by a hundred voices, crying, screaming, begging. She staggered. The remainder of the guards had noticed what was going on now, but she was so unfocused, they were mere blurs in her peripheral vision.

She kept the crossbow as steady as she could, pointing it straight at Lennox. She knew it was only a matter of seconds before someone tried to charge her.

Think, she ordered herself, but the screams inside her head were only getting louder. Her heart lurched. They were the people suffering at Moredon, she knew it, knew it in her bones. Charlyn rushed at her from the side, and she fired. Lennox keeled over, shrieking in agony, the arrow protruding from the soft part of his abdomen. Blood flowed freely from the wound, drenching his uniform in red. Charlyn's fingers closed around her arm. Everything went black, and with her heart lodged in her throat, Bleak gave into the darkness.

Her heart stopped. A sudden flash of light burst from her and shot right down through her. It exploded outwards, across the deck, a massive pulse of brightness that flattened the whole sea. She collapsed.

There was silence. It stretched out across the vast expanse of water, deafening. She didn't know how much time had passed when she opened her eyes. And when she did, she wished she hadn't.

Dead. They were all dead. Lines of blood streaked their faces, their mouths open in terror. A choked sob escaped Bleak. She had done this. Again. Their bodies lay slumped on the deck, smears of blood where they'd tried to escape the unknown horror. Charlyn's lifeless hand gripped her ankle. She shoved him away, horrified. This darkness, it lived *inside* her, Bleak realised. She felt it, even now, flicker within her, already just that little bit closer to the surface than before. The screams had stopped again.

Did I kill them, too?

Numb and shaking, she reached for the fallen set of keys by Lennox's body. She studied his frozen face, blood leaking from beneath his filthy eyepatch. She pushed aside the gut-wrenching anguish she felt at the sight of the other bodies, and focused on Lennox. She felt nothing when she looked at him. Except justice. He'd deserved to die. And she'd delivered.

Methodically, she tried key after key in her irons, feeling herself creep back into her own skin, and her anxiety, her guilt beginning to fester once again. The lock clicked and the irons sprang loose, dropping to the floor. Bleak rubbed her raw wrists and looked across the deck. She couldn't move them all, the bodies. They were big men, wearing heavy armour. She would have to sail with a crew of dead men. Her eyes fell on Lennox again.

It's better that they're dead, she told herself.

She made for the wheel, but something caught her eye. An offcut of rope was coiled by the folded spare sail on the deck. Crouching, she picked it up and threaded it through her callused hands. It was longer than the piece she had thrown into the fire at Hoddinott.

I can cut it to size ... Fumbling with her pants, she unstrapped Fiore's dagger from her thigh and unsheathed it, measuring the length of rope between her arm span. She cut it easily, and sheathed the dagger once more. Leaning back against the rail, she tipped her face to the fading sun, savouring the warmth it spread across her brow. Eyes closed, she let her fingers work the length of rope. *King sling. Bimini twist. Spider hitch.* Her hands stopped trembling. *Loop, pull, tighten.*

Once Bleak had checked the sails and the course, she wandered the ship. She found the smallest man and took his belt for herself, attaching Fiore's dagger to it. She raided the cabin below and stuffed food and supplies into a generous, waxed pack. Like hell she'd end up at Moredon, and like hell she'd go back to Ellest. She was on her own now. The dead captain's quarters were a mess, the desk littered with papers, maps and loose tobacco. Bleak rifled through everything, unsure of what she was even looking for.

Just something, anything *to tell me what I should do,* she thought, as her hands smoothed over yet another crumpled royal decree. And then she spotted a tall glass bottle of amber liquid. Whiskey. It was full and heavy as she brought it towards her. Saliva built up around her tongue as she unscrewed the lid and sniffed the contents. Just the smell of it made her head spin.

No, said a little voice in her head. *Not this time.*

With anxiety like a claw in her chest, Bleak slowly

placed the bottle down on the desk and backed away, shutting the cabin door behind her.

Another dusk fell, and the sweet scent of a storm brewing blew in from across the sea. Bleak eyed the flapping sail. She'd have to weather it – use the wind to her advantage. When the first drops of rain hit her face, she felt relief. Gods, she'd missed this.

Lightning cracked the sky in half. The storm hit. Rain hammered the deck in a hard, heavy sheet and the waves flung *Arden's Fortune* around like it was a child's toy. The bodies on deck slid from port to starboard, and as the seas became rougher, many were flung overboard, disappearing beneath the churning foam. Bleak shouldered her supply pack and tied a rope around her waist, securing herself to the mast. She fought with the wheel, steering against the current, the storm and everything else. Her wet hair whipped her face, and her teeth chattered with the cold. Wrenching the wheel to the left, she could feel the pull of the swell below, sucking at the base of the ship. She could barely see anything ahead, until the light of Moredon Tower, a steady cylinder, beamed out onto the black sea. Too close – she was too close to that horrific place.

Then, the energy around her changed. In the middle of a flash of lightning she jumped, heart near leaping from her chest. She could have sworn she'd just seen the dark-haired boy from the castle. His own expression of shock mirrored her own. And then he was gone.

She hauled the wheel right, veering the *Arden's Fortune* away from Moredon Tower. And there, just south of the tower, was not land, but mist.

Bleak straightened herself; she wasn't going to die for the king. She wasn't going to become a prisoner or experiment of his. She'd rather die with salt water in her lungs and mist in her heart. She was free. She had to try.

Steadying the wheel, the ship lurched forward. Bleak took a deep breath, and let the waves of mist rush in around her.

Acknowledgements

No novel is a solo effort, and from the moment I started writing, I've been lucky enough to have dozens of people supporting and encouraging me.

Firstly, I want to thank Kyra Thomsen and Claire Bradshaw. Two incredibly talented and generous writers, who also happen to be two of my closest friends. Ladies, I never want to write a book without you again. With you by my side, this has been the most rewarding experience thanks to your insights, as well as our daily chats and rants.

It was during the writing of this novel that I discovered the life-changing benefits of having beta readers. Kyra and Claire, as well as the beautiful Aleesha Paz and Kelly Blake, read the earliest versions of this book, and helped me shape it into something much stronger. Your kind and constructive feedback turned the bare bones of this story into something that thrummed with its own magic. I couldn't have done this without you.

Thank you to Dave Hickman, who was not only by my side throughout the creation of this story, but who completely supported my decision to go indie. Not many people understand an author turning down traditional options, but Dave did, and every time my confidence wavered, he was there to build it back up again. He also has my immense gratitude for helping me with the technological side of being an author – essentially helping me revamp my website, and brainstorming marketing ideas with me.

It's only been in recent years that I've really come to understand just how lucky I am to have had my education. In particular, I had the privilege of being taught by amazing English teachers throughout primary and high school, who encouraged reading past bedtime and didn't shoot down the idea that one day, their students could go on to do things like become authors.

The most important of these English teachers, however, is my mum, Bronwyn. From taking me to line up for the latest *Harry Potter* book at 7am on a Sunday, to understanding that a writer's work is actually *work*... You've played a major role in the writer I've become.

Long before I started this book, I started a little website called Writer's Edit (www.writersedit.com)... It was through this site that I came to be part of the most supportive literary community I've ever known. I'm so grateful for the support I've received, and the friends I've made. Special shout-outs to Kristin Prescott, Jenny Bravo, Zita Fogarty and Dan Murphy.

My gratitude also goes to two of my oldest and dearest friends, Lisy and Eva. You inspire me constantly with your creativity and selflessness. You're the first people I turn to in life for just about everything, and you've stood by me through every unpublished novel before this one.

To my sister Yasi, I honestly won the lottery when

you came into the Scheuerer clan. You're my biggest fan, my best friend and one of my favourite people in the world. I've never met anyone more generous or more understanding than you. You've helped me more than you know.

To Dad, Larn and Laura, you may not be big fantasy readers, but you're a hell of a lot of fun, and sometimes, that's just what a writer needs to pull her out of a slump.

To five-year-old Lilypad, when you're older, know that you helped me remember the joy in the simple things. Our backyard gymnastics and your general craziness brought much lightness to difficult days when I was working on this book.

To my publishing bestie, Ben Stevenson, thanks for the reassuring phone calls, the numerous beers and your impeccable voice of reason.

And on that note, thanks to all my glorious publishing friends. Special mentions to Aleesha (again!), Kat, Naomi, Hannah and Emily-May. I can always count on you for thoughtful insights, and hours of laughing.

While I wrote and rewrote this book, I was given the opportunity to work from a desk in the most wonderfully vibrant and creative space, along with some of the most generous people I know. Andrew Doenicke and the team, you've made life so much brighter.

I'd also like to thank my editor, Alexandra Nahlous, who helped me refine and polish this book into the best possible version of itself. Your kind words and thoughtful consideration of this story have helped in so many ways.

Thank you to Alissa Dinallo, who designed my stunning cover. I've worked with you for years now, Alissa, and your talent hasn't once ceased to amaze me.

Last but certainly not least, I want to thank YOU, my readers. Thank you for choosing this book, and supporting a new author. I hope you've enjoyed the characters and the action, and that you'll join us again when the adventure continues in *Book II*.

DID YOU ENJOY THIS BOOK?

You can make a difference.

Reviews are one of the most powerful tools for an author. They help bring books to the attention of new readers.

If you've enjoyed this book, the author would be incredibly grateful if you could spend a few minutes leaving a review on the Amazon page for *Heart of Mist*.

About the author

Helen Scheuerer is a YA fantasy author from Sydney, Australia. *Heart of Mist* is the first book in her high fantasy trilogy, *The Oremere Chronicles*.

After writing literary fiction for a number of years, Helen was inspired to return to her childhood love of fantasy by authors like Sabaa Tahir, V.E. Schwab, and Brandon Sanderson.

Helen is also the Founding Editor of Writer's Edit (www.writersedit.com), an online literary magazine and learning platform for emerging writers. Helen's love of writing and books led her to pursue a Bachelor of Creative Arts, majoring in Creative Writing, and a Master of Publishing.

She now works as a freelance writer and editor, while she works on the second book in *The Oremere Chronicles*.

www.helenscheuerer.com